3/22

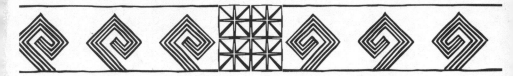

A PSALM OF STORMS AND SILENCE

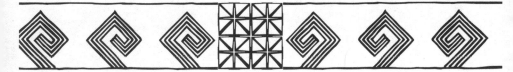

A PSALM OF STORMS AND SILENCE

ROSEANNE A. BROWN

BALZER + BRAY

An Imprint of HarperCollinsPublishers

To my sisters Rachel, Emma, and Mariah—I would
face down any demon for you.

And to all those still healing from pain they cannot talk about:
the journey isn't easy, but it's always worth it.

A Note from the Author

Please note this book depicts issues of self-harm, fantasy violence, emotional and physical abuse, anxiety and panic attacks, grooming, and suicidal ideation. I have done my best to approach these topics with sensitivity, but if you feel this kind of content may be triggering, please be aware.

SONANDE

Compass directions: N, W, E, S

EDRAFU SEA

SEA of DAKENDI

OBOURE

PREMSUA

OSODAE

KISSI-MOKOU

ESHRAN MOUNTAINS

FALANDA

TALAFRI

WASSIRA

ZIRAN

KALONGO

EASTWATER SAVANNA

DABUJA

THE SNOWLANDS

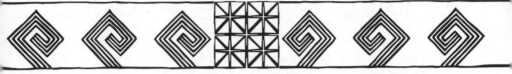

So you've returned for another story about the boy and the girl. The princess and the refugee, the zawenji and the ulraji—yes, I know the next part of their tale. We will return to their story in due time, I promise.

But before that, allow me to take you back to a night that had nothing to do with either, but everything to do with a different young boy hearing his adopted mother scream for the very first time . . .

The first contraction had hit the sultana of Ziran in the middle of a council meeting, and the viziers had been so deep in their debate about allocating grain for the upcoming stormy season that no one noticed the queen's distress until she was bent over the table, a blooming patch of water turning the bright scarlet of her gown bloodred.

By the second contraction, the palace midwives had the sultana secured in the birthing room. By the third, all seven of the High Priestesses had arrived at Ksar Alahari, sacred herbs and holy oils in hand to anoint the newest member of the royal family with blessings from the gods.

The fourth contraction was when the screaming began.

"Is having a baby supposed to sound like that?" whispered the queen's elder daughter as another of her mother's cries filled the air. As there was little an eight-year-old could do to aid the birthing process, Princess Hanane had been relegated to guarding the door, a task she took very seriously, and one that the soldiers actually protecting the birthing room allowed her to pretend she was doing. But now, several hours into the endeavor, her giddy excitement at the prospect of a new sibling had been overtaken by the harsh reality of what bringing a new life into the world actually entailed.

The princess shuddered as a series of low moans and frantic whispers slipped through the door. "She sounds like she's dying."

"That's not what a dying person sounds like," replied the princess's companion. Farid, the queen's ward who followed Hanane around like a second shadow, was prone to such ominous statements. He'd been this way since he'd arrived at Ksar Alahari almost a year prior, the sole survivor of the bandit attack that had massacred his diplomat parents, and even now he spoke in a soft voice almost devoid of emotion, eyes deeper and murkier than any ten-year-old's should be.

Farid's gaze shifted from Hanane's worried face to the sky beyond the balcony. Thick black clouds laced with white streaks of lightning roiled across the horizon, unusual for this time of year. "I would know."

Another scream rang through the air, and Hanane's eyes grew wide. After several agonizing minutes, the door finally opened. But instead of her silver-haired mother and a squealing infant, there was only the king.

"Baba!" Hanane scurried over to her father with Farid, as always, close behind. "Is it done? Is my baby brother here?"

"Not yet," sighed the king as he rubbed the bags lining his eyes. "And we don't know the baby's gender yet. You could have a sister."

"It's going to be a boy. I just know it," she declared, and at the sight of his daughter's childish bravado, the king laughed for the first time in days. However, the laugh died as the sultana's screaming began anew. Hanane's lip quivered, her eyes flitting between her father and the birthing-room door.

"T-They're both going to be fine, right?" she asked. The spirits of all the babies who had not survived seemed to hang in the air between them. If this one did not live, that would make four siblings who had never made it past the womb. Only Farid knew the secret names Hanane had given each one, for the subject was too painful for her parents to acknowledge.

"Of course they are," said the king, and he meant it, for what was left of his heart refused to consider otherwise. A bright flash of lightning rent the sky in two, followed by low peals of thunder that echoed like drumbeats. No doubt the acolytes at the Wind Temple were in an absolute panic trying to decipher what message Santrofie, He Born of Wind and patron deity of all Wind-Aligned, was trying to send.

The king glanced at the storm, muttered something too low for either child to hear, and lowered himself to the ground, ignoring the startled looks from the guards that he would do something so beneath his station. He opened his arms, and though they were nearing the age where such comfort seemed juvenile, both Farid and Hanane gratefully folded themselves within his embrace. "Your mother has faced far worse odds and survived. She is going to survive this too, and when she does, you'll have a new baby to play with."

Farid chimed in, "And even if you can't play with the baby, you'll always have me."

Hanane smiled at the boy. "That's true. I'll always have you."

A flutter of unease ran through the king at the way his ward brightened at those words, but he pushed it away. Farid had been more ghost than boy when he'd first come to Ksar Alahari, so withdrawn that one could be in the same room with him for hours and never know. The fact that Hanane had been able to pull him out of his shell was something to celebrate. And besides, wasn't that what every parent wanted, to have their children be as close as these two were?

The king began to speak again, but he was cut off by the midwives frantically calling his name. He jumped to his feet and sprinted into the room, and all the princess saw before the door slammed shut was a flurry of movement, her mother's sweat-slicked face, and several piles of bloodstained rags. Hanane began to shake, and when Farid reached out to comfort her, she shoved him away and clasped her hands together in prayer. She was Sun-Aligned, and so she prayed to her patron deity, Gyata the Lion, that her new sibling—ideally a brother—would be happy and whole and would always want to play with her, even when she did not feel like sharing her toys or sweets.

The priestesses had taught her that the gods rewarded those who gave offerings alongside their demands, and so she declared,

"I'll do anything you want, anything at all, if you just let them live."

The last word was barely out of her mouth when the loudest peal of thunder yet tore through the alabaster walls around them. The princess opened her eyes, and that was when she saw it: for a single instant, less time than it took a butterfly to take flight or a dead man to breathe his last, every drop of rain hung suspended in the air like a thousand tiny pearls. Hanane yelled for Farid to look, but as soon as he did, the rain was splattering to the ground once more.

Years later, this evening would become just another hazy blur among the stream of the young princess's childhood memories. But in that moment, she knew with a faith as strong as a mountain and as vast as the sea that she had spoken to the gods and they had spoken back—for not even a minute later, the unmistakable cry of an infant filled the palace, and all thoughts of promises and the deities who collected them left her mind as Hanane ran to go meet her sister.

1

Malik

In the center of a shining palace of alabaster and silver, on a crested hill deep in the heart of a golden desert, there was a boy. And in the center of this boy, there was a tree.

Of all the trees in the grove, this one was the most magnificent, its leaves reaching the highest and the lemons hanging from its branches the brightest yellow. Neither the tree nor the grove it stood in were real, but that was of little concern to Malik. For years he'd been convinced that his mind was a broken, barren place filled with nothing but the scars of his childhood; if it was capable of creating something this warm and full of life, then perhaps there was a chance he was not as broken as he'd been led to believe he was.

Yes, the lemon grove was perfect. Or it might have been, were it not for the snake.

"Foolish, stupid boy," the Faceless King roared in a voice formed of jagged skies and crashing waves, dark magic and darker obsession, as he thrashed against the binding that held him tight to the tree at the center of the grove. "You cannot keep me here forever."

Malik shuddered as the depths of the obosom's wrath radiated through the connection they shared. Long ago, the Faceless King had been worshipped throughout the Odjubai Desert as Ɔwɔ, the embodiment of the once-mighty Gonyama River. At the height of his power, he'd possessed the strength to drown empires and remake kingdoms.

Now he was here, stuck inside the mind of a simple human boy who barely understood what magic was, let alone how to use it. The indignity of the whole situation seemed to upset the spirit more than anything else.

The Faceless King twisted against his bindings once more, and the part of Malik's mind that the spirit occupied pushed sharply against his consciousness. It felt like being ripped in two from the inside out, and Malik fell to his hands and knees as he bit back a scream. This wasn't real. As soon as he woke, this would be over.

But Malik's hold over his mind was at its weakest when he was asleep, which was why the Faceless King had chosen now to make another escape attempt. As another wave of pain racked through his core, Malik reminded himself of all he had to lose if the obosom got free. The spirit also known as Idir, beloved of the ancient queen Bahia Alahari, held a vendetta against Ziran that only destruction could quell. If even a sliver of the obosom's immense power slipped through the binding, he would flatten the entire city and every person Malik loved without hesitation.

All this wrath in the name of a wrong that had occurred a thousand years before any of them had been born. A wrong that had only been committed in response to the tyranny of Malik's own ancestors, the Ulraji Tel-Ra.

Malik did not regret trapping the spirit inside his mind—but Great Mother help him, it hurt.

"You dare compare yourself to the ulraji of old?" asked Idir, and even though Malik had been sharing his mind with the spirit for nearly five days now, he still flinched at the sensation of Idir reading his thoughts. "Your powers are a mere fraction of theirs, and even they at their strongest would not have been able to hold me captive for long."

Another wave of the Faceless King's power pressed against Malik's skull, sharp as a scalding iron. Surely this should have been enough to wake him, but Malik remained locked in the struggle with no way to call for help. Would anyone looking at him see his body convulse with the strain of what was happening inside, or only his sleeping face? If Idir killed him and took over his body, would anyone even know?

"Trapping me in here was a clever trick, but you misjudged one thing," hissed Idir. "Just as all that I am has been revealed to you, so too has all that you are been laid bare before me—I know each twist and turn of your thoughts, all the dark corners of your mind that even you cannot face." Though Malik had bound the Faceless King in his emaciated human form, the obosom had retained the serpentine eyes of his true body, and it was those eyes that leered down at Malik with a hatred thousands of years deep. "And that is why I know you are not strong enough to keep me here forever."

Familiar tendrils of panic wormed their way into Malik's gut. What if Idir was right? After all, what was Malik's paltry understanding of ulraji magic against a spirit who had been revered as a god? Even with his storyweaving, what was he but painfully and ridiculously human? He couldn't do this, he never should have done this, he was only delaying the inevitable, he was—

No. *No.*

Malik knew that if he followed that spiraling thread of anxiety, it would lead to him begging for Idir's mercy like a coward. That was what the old him would have done.

However, the old him had died the moment he had plunged a dagger into his own heart on the last day of Solstasia. And the new Malik might not have been a god, but he was far from powerless.

"I don't have to be strong," said Malik, and even though every inch of his body screamed in protest, he forced himself to his feet. The words of his grandmother's old grounding mantra filled him, pushing back against the onslaught of pain and uncertainty.

Breathe. Stay present. Stay here.

Malik lifted his head to meet the Faceless King's challenging gaze with one of his own.

"I just have to be stronger than you."

If the spirit had been angry before, it was nothing compared to the surge of pure rage that Malik's words brought forth. The entire lemon grove reverberated with the Faceless King's indignation, and Malik tried to grab one of the trees as an anchor, only for his hands to blister from the heat of it. The ground turned to ash beneath his feet, and then Malik was falling deep into a recess of his mind from which there would be no escape. He pushed with all he had against the ever-growing void beneath him, but he still could not force his body to wake.

And then through the swirling chaos came a golden light—a single thread of nkra, the basic element from which all magic flowed. Though there was no way to know where it led, Malik grabbed on to it, for it was the only thing to grab on to. The warm scent of the earth after a spring rain flooded his senses.

Karina's scent.

The thought had barely crossed Malik's mind before he was falling again, away from the lemon grove and even the Faceless King, into a corner of his mind tucked away from all the rest.

The sensation stopped. Slowly Malik opened his eyes to a world filled with . . . green.

His surroundings were hazy in the way that places in dreams often were, but what stood out to Malik was the lush vegetation all around him, unlike anything that could be found in the Odjubai. The throaty calls of turacos and other birds, mixed with children's laughter, rang through the air, and the few squat mudbrick dwellings Malik could see had been painted in swirling geometric patterns from no culture that he recognized. He had never been here before, and yet somehow, deep in the core of everything Malik understood about himself, he knew this place.

The source of the laughter quickly made itself apparent as two girls ran past him, their faces blurred like paint running together on an artist's palette.

"Faster, Khenu! The elders will make us chop firewood if we're late again!" yelled the taller of the two girls, who ran by Malik with no indication that she'd seen him.

"I'm coming!" cried the smaller one—Khenu, apparently— and the quick, bird-like nature of her movements reminded Malik of his younger sister, Nadia. Khenu made it halfway across the path before she tripped over a tree root and went sprawling into the mud. She immediately burst into tears, and the bigger girl doubled back to help her with an exaggerated sigh.

"What kind of ulraji cries over a little fall?" teased the taller girl as she pulled her friend onto her back. Malik's eyes widened— this tiny child was an ulraji? This must be a memory of the past then, for only in ancient times could such information be shared so freely. But whose memory was this—the Faceless King's?

Malik took a step toward them, then froze as the scent of rain filled his nose once more. A buzz of energy that had nothing to do with his magic coursed through his veins as he glanced over his shoulder to see Karina standing beside him.

Her eyes remained on the two girls walking into the jungle, allowing Malik a moment to simply take her in. She seemed unharmed after her frantic, storm-fueled escape from Ziran several days before, her amber eyes bright and alert, her cloud of silver coils hidden beneath a green scarf wrapped around her head. Only when the girls were gone did the princess look his way, and though this was nothing more than a dream, the buzzing energy in Malik thrummed higher as her eyes swept over his face, lingering a moment too long on his lips and forcing him to recall the last time they had been alone together.

Five days since they had stood on the roof of the Sun Temple and shared the kiss that had undone him completely.

Five days since he had attempted to kill her to save his younger sister.

Five days since Karina had vanished from Ziran in a rush of wind and lightning as her older sister rose from the grave.

Such a short span of time, and yet the world as they knew it had rewritten itself completely. There was so much Malik wanted to say, explanations and apologies all crowding for space on his tongue. He took a step toward the princess, and then another when she did not move away.

"Karina," he began, and that was all he managed to say before her fist collided with his jaw.

"Malik? Malik!"

Malik's eyes snapped open in an explosion of pain as someone touched his shoulder. All at once, the instincts he'd honed over years of surviving his father kicked in. The ink-black wraith tattoo that normally swirled around his bicep scurried down to his palm, where it morphed into a dagger with a black blade and golden hilt. Malik grabbed the assailant by the front of their shirt with his free hand and pressed the knife against their throat with the other. The person balked, unable to pull away.

"Malik, it's just me! Put the spirit blade down!" they cried, and just as Malik realized it was his older sister, Leila, squirming in his grasp, he became aware of a second weapon pressed against the soft skin of his neck.

"Release her," said the Sentinel, and the only thing louder than the rapid beating of Malik's heart was the high-pitched keening in his ears from the warrior's proximity. He immediately let Leila go, and the Mark sank back into his skin as he placed his head in his hands, struggling to breathe. Where was he? What was going on?

Breathe. Stay present. Stay here.

He wasn't in the center of his mind fighting Idir for control over his own body or in a dream about Karina and the past. He wasn't a child cowering in a corner and praying to the gods that his father wouldn't find him, not this time.

He was in the infirmary of Ksar Alahari, where he'd been since the end of Solstasia. His sisters were safe. He was safe, though that might change if the Sentinel did not withdraw his weapon.

Leila took one look at Malik quivering in fright beneath the spear and snapped at the warrior, "Get that thing out of his face, you're scaring him!"

Back in their hometown of Oboure, an Eshran speaking in such a way to a member of the Zirani elite forces would have warranted a beating at best, death at worst. But it was a testament to how drastically their status had risen that the Sentinel simply looked Malik over, nodded once, and then withdrew to his post in the corner of the room. Leila clicked her tongue and muttered under her breath, though Malik did not miss the way she kept her hands placed defensively between them.

"I am so, so sorry," he choked out.

"Don't apologize, I'm the one who startled you awake." She uncurled her hands and wrapped her arms around herself. "It's all right. I'm not hurt."

But she could have been. That was why the Sentinel was here— not to protect Malik from the world, but to protect the world from Malik. He couldn't even blame Farid and the council for wanting to be prepared in case Idir escaped, but that didn't mean he enjoyed being under surveillance every moment of the day.

"Was it the Faceless King? Is he giving you trouble?" asked Leila. The Sentinel's fingers, tightening around the shaft of his spear, was the only sign that he was listening at all. Malik noted the red-and-silver sash slung over the man's chest; was that some sort of status symbol?

"A little bit—but I have him under control now!" Malik added at his older sister's look of alarm. Just to be sure, he reached deep inside himself and pushed against the binding that separated him from Idir. It held, the pain from his dream gone.

Unlike Malik, Leila was not an ulraji, so she did not fully understand what had occurred when Malik let the spirit into his body. In the days since the end of Solstasia, he had often caught her looking at him as if she expected a demon to burst from beneath his skin and kill them all.

Which, given what had just occurred, was not as unlikely as Malik wished it was.

But they would not have to worry about the spirit breaking free for long, as today was the day Malik was to begin his formal ulraji training with Farid. Under the former palace steward's tutelage, he would learn to control his powers and to fortify his mind so well that the Faceless King would never escape.

Malik's eyes fell to Nadia, who slumbered peacefully on the bed beside him, completely unperturbed by what had just happened. Good—this was the first night since returning from her time as a hostage in the spirit world that she had been able to sleep at all. She let out a gentle breath as he tucked the blanket under her chin.

Everything Malik had done, everything he had sacrificed, had been for that breath. Any pain he had to live through was worth seeing it again.

"He won't be able to hurt us anymore," Malik vowed, and a tremor ran through his mind.

Believe that as you will, little ulraji, Idir hissed. *Even the best-built wall has its weak points.*

An overwhelming urge to dig his nails into the flesh of his arms took hold of Malik, an old habit born from years of having no outlet for the magic burning inside him.

But instead he snapped at the woven rubber bracelet around his left wrist, the one his friend Tunde had given him during Solstasia. This was still his mind. He was still the strongest person here.

The discomfort must have shown on his face, for Leila gathered one of his hands with one of her own and used the other to touch the bruise purpling at the edge of his jaw. "Where did this come from?"

That was an excellent question. Malik wasn't sure how to explain the strange dream he'd had of Karina without mentioning how close the Faceless King had come to escaping right before it.

He had no right to dream about Karina anyway, not when the last time they'd been alone together he'd shoved a dagger into her heart. And though he didn't regret what he'd done, for Nadia's life had been on the line—or so he'd thought—the guilt was clearly affecting him more than he'd realized if he was conjuring up dreams of the missing princess attacking him.

And Karina's presence had felt so real too, as if he could have just reached out and touched her. Was there a chance that . . . no, what was he even thinking? His magic could create illusions, but no illusion could make a dream real.

"I bit my lip during the nightmare," he said. That must be it. He'd accidentally hurt himself in his sleep, and his fatigued mind had interpreted it as Karina punching him. That was all this was, nothing more.

The more Malik tried to unravel the meaning of Karina, the little ulraji girl, and the strangely familiar location he'd seen, the more tangled his thoughts became. Though he knew he should try to rest as much as he could before Farid came to fetch him, he simply sat there with Leila's hand wrapped around his own long after she had fallen asleep once more. The Faceless King's presence was easier to bear when he was awake, and Malik let himself focus on his sisters' breathing, the sharp scent of the herbs the healers had strung up through the infirmary to ward off the grim folk, the tickling sensation of the Mark scurrying across his back, anything except what his first day of ulraji training might entail.

It was in this exact position that Farid found Malik when he entered the infirmary just after sunrise.

"I didn't expect you to be awake so soon," said Malik's new mentor. The man was dressed as impeccably as ever, his dark hair combed neatly to the side and every thread in place on his blue kaftan, showing no fatigue despite the turmoil he and all of Ziran had been through since Solstasia's end. Farid didn't even glance at the Sentinel as he came to the bed, and Malik wondered what it must be like to not grow up in constant fear of the warriors. "Did you sleep well?"

"Yes," he lied. Leila bolted upright, her expression going from the soft confusion of sleep to hardened alertness the moment she laid eyes on Farid.

"Is today the day you finally stop treating him like a prisoner?" she demanded, and heat rushed to Malik's face. He loved his sister with all he had, but he wished she wouldn't be so sharp with someone who had been so generous to them.

"The man brought a girl back from the dead and staged a coup in the same day," she'd hissed when Malik had first told her of his plan to become Farid's apprentice. "We don't know what he's capable of."

But they did not know what Malik was capable of either, which was exactly why he needed Farid's training.

The older ulraji returned Leila's frosty glare with a gentle smile. "Indeed it is. In fact, I've arranged new lodgings for all three of you, and I'm certain you'll find them preferable to the infirmary. If all goes well today, we can have you settled by this evening."

Malik could hardly believe it. Permanent rooms for him and his sisters here in the palace. It was more than they could have ever imagined—but wait.

"What do you mean by 'if all goes well today'?" Malik forced himself to pull away from his sisters, wanting to appear strong and confident before his new teacher.

"I'll explain all that in due time. Come with me—just you, for now. Your sisters can join later," said Farid, and though Leila's frown deepened, Malik quickly moved to do as he was told. The lack of sleep caught up with him, but he fought the wave of nerves and fatigue down as he hurried to match his teacher's quick strides. "But first things first. You need to get changed, for you've been summoned by the princess."

2

Karina

Of all the backstabbing, silver-tongued, Great Mother-damned boys in the world, why did Karina have to dream about *him*?

"Look at that, the princess is finally awake," teased Dedele as Karina stormed across the sand barge the next morning. The still-rising sun had only begun to peek over the horizon in brilliant waves of pink and blue, so Karina had not even slept in that late, but her companions moved about the ship with an alertness that suggested they'd been up for hours. Dedele was on the lower deck cataloging their supplies, and after retying the knots that held down their calabashes, the former Fire Champion nodded at the bruises on Karina's left hand.

"Why do you look like you brawled a gorilla in your sleep?"

"Bad dream," Karina grumbled. That alone was not all that strange, as she'd been having nothing but nightmares since escaping Ziran. As soon as she fell asleep, she was back on that platform, acrid smoke filling her lungs as she watched Farid—her own family—turn against her and defy the Ancient Laws to raise her sister from the grave. Then her eyes would lock with the false Hanane's, and Karina would wake up with screams burning her throat, which was why she'd gotten barely half a night's sleep combined over the past five days.

But last night's dream had felt . . . different from the others. More *real*, like a memory she hadn't realized she'd forgotten, even though she had not recognized those girls or that village. Karina had only known one person there, and just remembering that expression on Malik's face, like he'd wanted to touch her, made her wish she had gotten more than one blow in.

"I saw Malik," Karina blurted out, only to silently curse herself for mentioning him. Talking about the boy implied she cared about him, which she most certainly did not—not after he had left her for dead. Even his name felt wrong on her tongue, as he'd been going by Adil during Solstasia. Who knew if his name was even really Malik?

However, neither of Karina's companions seemed as concerned about the dream as she was. Dedele simply let out a whistle as she tossed Karina a chewing stick. "Are you sure this was the kind of dream you should be discussing in front of a child?" she asked with a nod toward the third member of their small traveling party. Afua scoffed from where she sat cross-legged on the upper deck, purple light pooling from her palms into the worn wood of the barge.

"I'm not a child!" she protested, though the youthfulness of her voice betrayed otherwise. "I know all about kissing and those sorts of things!"

"It wasn't that kind of dream!" Karina snapped. She gnawed on her chewing stick with more force than necessary so she would not have to explain further.

She could normally handle good-natured teasing—in fact, she

was often the instigator of it—but then again, normally she was waking up in a palace with an army of servants at her beck and call, not on a tarp that smelled like what might happen if a pig carcass and a pile of vomit had a child. Normally she was not the most wanted fugitive in Sonande, and she did not have to check over her shoulder every second to see if any one of the dozens of threats that lurked the Odjubai Desert had come for her at last.

Malik was one of the people she had to thank for this new normal. Him, Farid, and every other traitor to the throne who had sent her running from her city—from her *home*—like a dog with its tail between its legs.

Karina absentmindedly grazed the thin line of puckered skin right over her heart. Though the wound Malik had given her had never brought physical pain, pulsing anger burned through her whenever she remembered how he had lured her onto the roof of the Sun Temple with an illusion of her dead sister all so he could kiss her with one breath and kill her with the next.

And Farid. Her guardian, her brother in all but blood, seeking her death as vengeance for a murder she hadn't even remembered she'd caused. Even now, she could still feel the bite of the chains he had clapped around her wrists and the searing heat of the flames he had used to create that monster wearing her sister's face. Karina's chest constricted as she recalled the moment that everything she had known about the world had flipped onto its head when she'd seen her dead sister breathe once more.

All at once, a powerful gust of wind slammed into the barge, and the ship tipped sideways. The three girls went sailing across the deck.

"Karina!" barked Dedele as Afua dug her hands into the wood, her magic trying to force the ship to remain upright.

"Sorry, accident!" Karina yelled back. Gritting her teeth, she reached deep inside for the thread of nkra that connected her to the air and willed it to calm. It whipped around them several more times before pulling back. Dedele muttered thanks to her patron deity, Ɔsebɔ the Leopard, before whirling on Karina.

"If you don't get those powers of yours under control, you're going to summon every Sentinel in a hundred-mile radius," she warned. "It's too early in the year for sandstorms, so any abnormal weather pattern will be traced back to you. You shouldn't even use your magic until we reach Arkwasi."

"I am well aware of that," Karina grumbled. It was easy enough for Dedele to tell her to stop using her magic when she wasn't the one trying to tame a storm beneath her skin. One wrong thought, one unguarded emotion, and Karina could freeze them all to death or accidentally trap them in a lightning storm, just as she'd done to her own father and sister all those years ago.

"You should practice those breathing exercises I taught you," suggested Afua, the slightest hint of fatigue in her voice from having had to expend so much magic so quickly. "The bedrock of all zawenji magic is emotional control, which starts with breathing."

Years of music training had taught Karina how to breathe, beautifully in fact, but she wasn't in a position to argue with Afua when the Life-Aligned girl was the only reason they hadn't died yet. Karina walked dutifully to the other side of the ship, far enough away from the other two that they wouldn't be knocked over by a stray gust if she lost focus, and settled into a meditation pose with her legs crossed and her hands folded in her lap. Whenever Afua meditated, she always began with a prayer to her patron deity, so Karina tried the same.

"I give praise to you, Santrofie, He Born of Wind, God of the Skies and All Born Under Your Protection. I give praise for the air that fills my lungs and for the wind that pushes lost sailors toward home. May I move through the world with the swiftness of a spring storm, and may your wisdom guide me through all the paths of life, from my first breath to my last."

This was where the faith was supposed to wash over her, where Karina was supposed to feel so in tune with her magic and the god who allegedly gave it to her that she would finally understand why people believed in the patron deities enough to dedicate life and limb to them.

It never came. She opened her eyes with nothing but that old twinge of disappointment where her connection to the divine should have been.

The golden dunes of the Odjubai Desert rolled past her in waves as vast as any sea—well, what Karina imagined a sea might look like. Like all members of the Alahari family since Bahia, she had been trapped behind the magic Barrier that protected Ziran, so she had never actually seen the sea herself. The destruction of the Barrier was perhaps the only good thing that had come from having fled Ziran as she had. No one in a thousand years of her family, not even her famed mother, had gotten as far from the city as Karina had.

Unfortunately, it was hard to enjoy the taste of freedom when she had to spend it running for her life.

Karina ran her thumb across the thin line where the sky met the earth, all thought of meditating forgotten. Somewhere past that line, was Farid sending more soldiers to drag her back to Ziran kicking and screaming? Or had they been given orders to strike her down wherever they found her? Was he scheming right now alongside the monster he had created from Hanane's corpse?

The wind stirred again as Karina tried to force down her memory of that creature's birth. The dead were the dead were the dead, just as the Ancient Laws always said. The true Hanane had died ten years ago, no matter what Farid believed. That thing that had crawled out of the fire was no more Karina's sister than Malik was Karina's ally.

She needed an army, one strong enough to rival the forces Farid had at his disposal. And the only other nation in Sonande with might to rival Ziran's was Arkwasi. That was what made these grueling days and hellish nights of travel worth it, the promise that at journey's end she'd find aid from the paramount chief in Osodae, their capital, and from the Conserve, the secret community of zawenji that had taught Afua all she knew.

And once she had the power of the Arkwasian nation at her back, she'd be that much closer to taking back what was rightfully hers.

But there was no point fantasizing about commanding her army if she buried the sand barge beneath a storm before then, so Karina turned back to the breathing exercises with renewed vigor. However, on her third failed attempt, she gave up and instead chose to watch the desert roll by. This far north of Ziran, all she could see was sand, rocks, dirt, more sand, a corpse, sand—wait.

Karina rubbed her eyes. The shape of a person's body remained, lacking the shimmering edge of a mirage.

"Dedele! Afua!" she called, her pulse quickening. "I think I see someone!"

In moments, the other girls were by Karina's side. Dedele unclipped her spyglass from the belt at her waist and peered through it. "Osebɔ's spots, is that a dead body?"

Karina snatched the spyglass from Dedele and squinted through it herself. They were too far from it to make out any identifying details, but it was impossible to miss the way the body convulsed against the sand. "They're still alive! We need to do something!"

Dedele stole her spyglass back with a scowl. "It could be a trap. A bandit pretending to be injured to lure in unsuspecting travelers and rob them."

Karina knew that, and yet . . . the memory of her mother's body falling to the ground flashed across her mind. "We have to at least check. Afua, hurry."

The Life-Aligned zawenji dutifully changed course. The second the ship was secured, Karina scrambled down its side and ran over to the person, an elderly woman old enough to have been her grandmother. Dark purple bruises bloomed over her wrinkled umber skin, and the thick red lines in the sand trailing behind her suggested she had clawed her way hundreds of feet until she had been unable to move another inch.

"Can you hear me, atti?" Karina asked, using the Zirani endearment for grandmother as Afua pressed a goatskin of water against the woman's lips. After a few scary moments of stillness, the woman began to drink from it greedily until she coughed and sputtered all over herself.

"M-m-my daughter," the woman croaked out once the coughing finally subsided. "Please help me, they took my daughter!"

"Who took your daughter, atti? What happened to you?" asked Dedele.

"They came last night, they grabbed e-e-everyone. Those who fought, they killed. I pretended to be dead, so they left me behind." The hands grasping the front of Karina's dress were so weak a fly might have batted them away. "Oh, my daughter! My only daughter! They took her! She's gone!"

The woman let out a howl like a wounded animal, and it was only Karina holding her up that stopped her from folding into her own despair. She did not specify who her assailants had been, but she did not have to; the horrors of the traffickers who roamed the Odjubai were well known. That this woman had survived one of their raids was either an act of luck or the gods, depending on what one believed.

As the woman continued her heaving sobs, Karina looked up at Dedele and Afua, her own anguish reflected on both their faces. "We need to do something."

"Do what, exactly?" replied Dedele. "Hunt down the traffickers and ask them politely to give back her daughter? Best case scenario, we end up dead. Worst case scenario, they realize who you are and—" Dedele cut off with a wary eye toward the elderly woman, but she was too deep in her own sorrow to realize what had almost been said. It was only because of the thick emerald scarf tied tight around Karina's silver hair that the woman hadn't been able to recognize her on sight, but it was a flimsy disguise at best.

Karina saw the sense in Dedele's argument. Both she and Afua had risked their lives to get Karina out of Ziran and were now risking them yet again to get her to Arkwasi. How could she put their sacrifices in jeopardy for a woman whose name she did not even know? Coming to her aid seemed even crueler than passing her by, for now they had given her hope only to wrench it away.

But it was more than compassion toward a stranger that kept Karina holding the woman close. Something Malik had said to her back in the necropolis underneath Ziran rang through her mind.

Do you not care about the hundreds of people who die crossing the desert each day or those lost to the unrest in Eshra?

His words filled her with as much shame now as they had then. For despite the fact that he was a traitor, that he had left her for dead, he'd been right. She hadn't cared about the refugees or the fallen, simply because she had never *had to* care. She had lived her life ignorantly tucked away in her alabaster tower, the suffering of those beneath her as distant as the suffering of characters in folktales.

Even now she was protected from the worst of the fallout of Farid's coup. When her people had needed her most, she had run. For all her magic and status, she had been completely and utterly powerless as the world had crumbled around her.

Just as she'd been the night she'd lost Baba and Hanane.

Just as she'd been the night she'd lost her mother.

Another breeze howled past their ears. How could she ever call herself a queen if she couldn't even save one old woman?

"If the traffickers don't come back to kill her, exposure surely will," she said softly, and even Dedele looked stricken at the thought of the woman rotting away in the sand. "If we can get her to the nearest town, she might stand a chance."

Karina regarded Dedele with the same steely gaze the Kestrel always used to use when she was facing down a particularly stubborn opponent.

Finally, the former Fire Champion let out a sigh.

"There's a small village called Tiru about an hour's ride from here," she said reluctantly. "I doubt the news of your escape has reached them yet, so it should be safe. But after that, no more stops until we reach Arkwasi."

Karina nodded along as she began to pull the old woman to her feet. Soon they would be back on the barge and the journey toward her revenge would begin anew.

But first, one small detour.

3

Malik

You've been summoned by the princess, Farid had said, as if this were simply a visit to the fishmonger. As if this wasn't the very same princess who a week ago had been nothing more than a pile of bones wrapped in a white funeral shroud.

Neither Malik nor his sisters had witnessed the resurrection, but it was all anyone had been talking about in the days since. The servants spoke of it even now as they prepared Malik for his meeting with her.

"I hear Mwale Farid keeps the princess locked away in the tallest tower, which can only be entered using a crystal key he wears on a chain around his neck," whispered one attendant to another as they scrubbed Malik down in the hammam.

"There are horns hidden beneath her hair, and her ears are pointed like a goat's," swore another as they dressed Malik in a black kaftan embroidered with gold, taking care not to agitate his still-healing wounds. "If you look into her eyes for too long, she'll steal your soul!"

It was the stuff of children's stories and fireside tales, which was how Malik's life had been feeling ever since he'd arrived in Ziran. But given that no one had actually seen Princess Hanane since the end of Solstasia, the rumors had taken on such life that the people might actually be disappointed if she did not have cloven feet or some other monstrous defect.

It was all Malik could do to keep one foot in front of the other as Farid led him deep into the heart of the palace. Due to the lingering threat of enemies from both within and without, Princess Hanane's whereabouts were being kept a secret even to those who resided there, and so Malik walked with a blindfold around his eyes and only Farid to guide his way.

He quickly lost track of the twists and turns on this convoluted path to wherever they were going. The fact that the Sentinel from the infirmary had come with them did nothing to calm his nerves. Every one of the man's echoing steps forced Malik to remember just how many of his people these warriors had slaughtered.

As if you couldn't do the same to them if you wished.

"Be quiet!" Malik hissed under his breath, and Farid's grip on his shoulder tightened.

"Is something the matter?"

"N-not at all!" Cursing himself internally for rising to the spirit's bait, Malik snapped his rubber bracelet until a small welt formed on the inside of his wrist. Great Mother help him, he hadn't even met the princess and he was falling apart.

The only good thing about the situation was that the grim folk, and by extension the wraiths, were nowhere to be found. He'd noticed it when he'd first come to the palace during Solstasia— something kept the creatures from crossing into Ksar Alahari. Malik made a mental note to ask Farid why as soon as they were done with whatever they were doing.

Left turn, right turn, then right again, then up a flight of stairs, another left turn until, finally, Farid ordered him to stop. Bile sloshed in Malik's stomach as someone announced, "Adil Asfour, Life Champion of Solstasia, has arrived, Your Highness."

Farid lifted the blindfold from Malik's face and dim torchlight flooded his vision. A cavernous arena built of stone that must have been ancient even when the palace was built lay before him. An array of swords, spears, shields, and other weapons lined one wall, while most of the room was taken up by a flat pit, the stone around which had been gouged with marks no human hands could have made. The sharp scent of recently doused fire hung in the air.

But the real sight to behold was Princess Hanane. Karina's elder sister sat on a raised platform overlooking the training hall, and pure terror froze Malik in place as she leveled her gaze on him with the weight of a ruler inspecting her newest conquest.

The rumors had been all wrong—there was no gray, rotting flesh here, no talons or claws where human hands should have been. The princess was beyond lovely, around Malik's own age with skin that shone like obsidian. The sharp tilt of her eyes was the same as Karina's, as was the soft curve of her jaw and the silver sheen of her hair. But the differences between them outweighed the similarities—where Karina had been full and soft, Hanane was willowy and thin. A smattering of constellation-like freckles dusted the bridge of her nose, and her silver hair cascaded down her back in rivers of locs instead of the free curls Karina wore. Even the soft pastel red of her gown was a far cry from the bold colors and patterns her younger sister preferred.

And she was barefoot. Somehow, this small detail disturbed

Malik more than anything else—if a person rose from the dead, they should have some kind of mark to show for it, but all Malik saw was a girl who wore her royalty like a second skin.

The council was also present, seated in half circles on either side of Princess Hanane, but she and Malik might have been the only two people in the world from the way she stared at him. She lifted a single finger and bid him to come closer.

"So you're the one who defeated the Faceless King." The princess's voice lacked the huskiness of her sister's but possessed the same commanding air that dared a person to try to defy her. Malik wondered if the constant comparisons between them had ever bothered Karina, before he remembered he was not supposed to care.

Inside his mind, the Faceless King shifted in discomfort.

Get away from the lich. The farther the better.

For once they were in agreement, but for all his nerves, Malik was not stupid enough to turn away from royalty.

"I am, Your Highness," he replied.

"Farid speaks most highly of you. You must be powerful indeed to keep such a creature contained."

Malik decided it best not to mention just how close the spirit had gotten to escaping the night before. "I am honored to hear that, Your Highness."

He did his best not to squirm as Princess Hanane's gaze swept over him. "They tell me you make illusions?"

Malik nodded. "Anything I can envision, I can speak into existence."

"Make something for me. Right now."

He mulled over it for a few seconds before he remembered how much the late queen had loved plants—perhaps her daughter did too.

A buzzing warmth ran through Malik's veins, not unlike the feeling of sitting before a fire after hours trapped in the cold. He could live a thousand lifetimes and never tire of this sensation—that moment when his words converted the invisible bonds of nkra all around him into pure magic.

"Which color flower do you like best? Red? Blue? Yellow with a pink center?" Hanane's eyes brightened as the flower materialized in the air between them, its petals shifting from the deepest red to cerulean blue to a warm sunlight yellow. The thrill of having an audience warmed Malik, making him feel more confident. More in control.

"I'm not limited to inanimate objects either. I can re-create living creatures as well, like—"

"Make a gorilla!" Hanane ordered. Malik had been thinking more along the lines of, say, a kitten, but he fulfilled the princess's request. She yelped in delight as the gorilla strolled up behind her and sniffed the back of her head, only for her smile to fall when her hand sank straight through the creature's head. "Your illusions can't be touched?"

Heat rushed to Malik's face. "Not yet."

Farid had moved from Malik's side to the princess's, and he now nodded at his new protégé. "It's said the storyweavers of old could create illusions so intricate they could starve a person for weeks, and they'd die convinced they had been eating a feast," he said. "In all my years of studying the mystic sciences, I have never heard of anyone retaining control of their body once a supernatural being had possessed it. You may not have mastered tangible illusions yet, but I'd guess it's from a lack of proper tutelage rather than skill."

The compliments were nice, truly, but none of that explained why they were gathered in some kind of fighting ring. More importantly, Malik couldn't shake the feeling of dread that came from being around a member of the undead. Just the fact that Princess Hanane was sitting there felt like someone had decided fire was no longer hot or north was now south. There was a fundamental wrongness in the air, one that kept the hair on the back of Malik's neck raised.

But Farid wasn't perturbed. He gazed at the princess with nothing but softness, and Malik supposed that if his mentor was not worried about her presence, he shouldn't be either.

"You're probably wondering why I've called you here," said Princess Hanane. "Today is the first Water Day of the new Water Era, and as is customary, a ceremony will be held at the corresponding temple for those under the Alignment of the current reigning deity. The duty of helping the High Priestess perform the ceremony usually belongs to the winner of Solstasia, but because the Water Champion Adetunde is still missing, the role falls to you as the runner-up."

"Tunde is missing?" Malik blurted out. How much had he missed in those five days in the infirmary?

Grand Vizier Jeneba spoke for the first time since he'd arrived. "Adetunde has not been seen since the last day of Solstasia. We believe he may have left the city with Karina."

The words should not have hit Malik as hard as they did. He'd already known that Tunde and Karina had shared a history before he'd ever arrived in Ziran. Tunde had loved her, and she must have felt some degree of affection back to have chosen him over Malik to win her hand in marriage.

Yet still the thought of the two running off together stung in a dark, ugly part of Malik that he hadn't realized existed until that moment.

Thick lines of worry creased between Farid's brows. "It is also possible that poor Adetunde was one of the many casualties of the storm Karina unleashed upon the city. But as long as his where-abouts remain unknown, you are the only one who can perform his duties, and we must make sure you are up to the task."

Malik followed Farid's gaze to the center of the pit, where the Sentinel who had come with them now stood shoulder to shoulder with two others. Understanding dawned on him. "This is a test."

"That is correct," replied Princess Hanane. "Today's Cleansing Ceremony is the first meeting of the court since my . . . since I returned. Though I myself will not be attending, it is of the utmost importance that the people see that the palace is still in control. They most certainly will not feel that way if the Faceless King bursts out of your body."

"But what about our training?" Malik asked Farid, hating how much panic slipped into his voice. "Isn't that exactly what you were going to teach me how to avoid?"

"Control is the cornerstone of all magic training, Malik," Farid said calmly. "Today's test is a lesson in and of itself. Pass it, and your education continues. But if you fail . . ."

The implication was clear: if Malik showed any sign of losing control over the Faceless King, they would kill him. Every struggle he had overcome would mean nothing if he could not convince these people that he had complete control over the magic within him.

Something he hadn't had even *before* he'd been sharing his body with a malevolent spirit.

The grand vizier chimed in, "The Faceless King is one of the most dangerous threats Ziran has ever known, which is why Bahia Alahari sealed him away in the first place. We must honor her wish to ensure this evil cannot plague our people once more."

A sharp spike of anger surged through Malik's gut. *Honor her wish?* roared Idir. *How dare they speak of her wishes when they did not even know her! Only one of us was a monster, and it was not me—*

Malik imagined slamming a lid down over the obosom somewhere dark and deep where he could not be seen or heard. The anger faded, but Malik could still feel it lurking beneath his skin. The terror must have shown on his face, for Farid strode over to him and placed his hands on his shoulders. "I'm sure you're frightened but don't forget that you have already bested the Faceless King once. I know you are strong enough to do it again."

If Malik could not have faith in himself, he should at least have faith in Farid's belief in him. Despite the fear curdling in his stomach, he nodded.

With one last encouraging squeeze to Malik's shoulder, Farid led him into the pit before returning to stand with the rest of the spectators. Once he was in position, Princess Hanane explained,

"When I give the order, you will be faced with a series of attacks from our Sentinels. Your task is to keep both your magic and the Faceless King restrained throughout." She pointed toward the ceiling, where Malik noticed for the first time a half-dozen archers perched in the windows overlooking the hall, each with an arrow aimed straight for his heart. "If you show the slightest hint of losing control, my guards have orders to strike you dead. Do you understand?"

The ground wobbled beneath Malik's feet, for even more frightening than what the princess was saying was everything she was not. Once he was dead, there was no way his sisters would be allowed to live, knowing what they knew. All three of their lives hinged on him succeeding.

"I understand," he whispered, the words feeling as if they were coming from somewhere far beyond his body.

The princess nodded. "Then you may begin, Commander."

The words were barely out of her mouth when the Sentinel with the red-and-silver sash charged toward Malik. He had only just registered that he had been in the presence of the commander of all Sentinels in Ziran when the first blow hit him in the side.

Pain tunneled through Malik's body. He managed to dodge the next two blows but was too slow to avoid a kick to the back from the second Sentinel. He crashed into the stone steps at the edge of the pit, and there he lay as the world swam in and out of focus, his magic flaring alongside the pain.

Really, Malik? Four blows and you're already down?

Malik let out a low moan in response. His magic burned at the back of his throat, ready to weave illusions that would subject these Sentinels to the very kinds of horrors he'd been forced to suffer his entire life.

But doing so would be a death sentence for him and his sisters. Malik folded the magic into itself until what had begun as a tsunami was nothing more than a thin stream. He had to hold it back, at least until this was over.

Malik had only just pushed himself to his feet when the commander barked something to the other two Sentinels. The subordinates fell back, and the commander leveled his gaze on Malik, his hand extended in front of him, palm upward. Bright orange sparks roared to life in the center of it, and they coalesced into a swirling fireball that he hurled straight for Malik's head. Malik barely managed to dodge the flames, his mind whirling to process what he'd just seen.

The Sentinels could harness nkra, just like him and Karina. The elite warriors of Ziran had *magic*.

But there was no time to reflect on this revelation as plumes of fire appeared throughout the pit, leaving Malik no choice but to run lest he be burned alive. He managed to weave between the walls of fire, only to crash into something hard—a slab of rock that jutted out from what seconds before had been smooth ground.

As the commander rained fire from above, the second Sentinel rumbled the ground beneath Malik's feet, making it impossible for him to find even footing. He hopped from fissure to fissure, twisting in and out of the plumes of fire. Through it all, he kept a tight hold on the binding in his head. It was all he could do to keep track of these threats when a jet of water crashed into his chest, courtesy of the third Sentinel.

Why are you putting up with this? whispered the Faceless King, his voice a sliver of calm compared to the nightmare raging around Malik. *Let go. Fight.*

The threads of magic that kept the obosom within him stretched as tight as they could go. Right now, there was no lemon grove to ground Malik and no thread on which to grab, just a swirling onslaught of earth, water, and fire with no end. The power to combat this was inches from his grasp. One illusion, and he could end this.

Malik's magic surged, and in his mind's eye, he saw the Faceless King tearing into the weakened binding, yes, that was it, so close, just a little more—

"No!" screamed Malik, and with the desperation of a cornered animal, he bit down on his arm. The metallic taste of blood exploded in his mouth, and with the pain came a sharp sense of clarity as he slammed back into control of his mind. Though the obosom howled with rage, Malik's grasp on the binding held, even as blood poured down his arm. An image of his sisters' faces flooded through his mind.

He could do this—for them, he could do this.

Time slowed into a swirl of fire and water and earth. Through it all, Malik kept his magic tamped down deep inside him. No thought filled his head except a steely determination that his sisters' blood would not be on his hands, no matter how much of his own he had to spill.

And then, after what felt like an eternity but could not have been more than an hour, Princess Hanane called out, "Enough."

The Sentinels snapped to attention like puppets pulled on

strings. Their elements vanished, leaving a muddy battlefield behind. Malik fell to his hands and knees, quickly reaching inside himself to check the binding.

It had held. He had passed.

He flinched as the Sentinels hauled him back to the platform, where Princess Hanane regarded him with a new respect in her eyes.

"That was quite impressive. You clearly—"

All emotion drained from the princess's face. She jumped to her feet and grabbed Malik's injured arm, ignoring the way he recoiled. "This bracelet," she said, her voice thick with an emotion he could not name. "Where did you get this?"

"It was Tunde's. He gave it to me during Solstasia," Malik replied.

The princess's eyes grew hazy and unfocused, and she clutched at her chest with the hand that was not in a death grip around Malik's wrist. "Tunde . . . the missing Champion, yes. Tunde, he . . . so familiar."

A tremor passed through Princess Hanane's body, and Malik almost thought he saw something moving behind her eyes when Farid placed a hand on her shoulder and pulled her back toward him.

"You need not concern yourself with Adetunde, Your Highness. It's handled," he said, and the tension seeped from the princess's body. To Malik, he said, "You have performed admirably today. I could not have chosen a better apprentice for myself. The Sentinels will take you to the infirmary so you can collect your sisters, and from there you will be taken to your new quarters to wait until I fetch you for the ceremony."

Farid's tone was not unkind, but something in Malik bristled at being dismissed so quickly after what he had just been put through. He had proved that he could subdue an entire spirit under the most strenuous of circumstances—surely that was more than admirable.

But his mentor's attention was on the princess now as he whispered soothing words into her ear, so there was nothing Malik could do but fall in step behind the Sentinels as they ushered him out of the room. He took one last look at Farid leading Hanane in the opposite direction, and the expression on the man's face was so soft it made Malik's heart ache.

No one had ever looked at him like that, as if his very presence made their world better.

He doubted anyone ever would.

4

Karina

There was something odd about the village of Tiru. Karina sensed it the moment its sleepy silhouette appeared on the horizon, and again the moment they stepped foot in the village proper.

It was just a little too neat—the dirt-packed streets between the buildings a little too clean and the smooth patterns drawn over the stone dwellings a little too new for what should have been a tiny trading town. Then again, perhaps she was being uncharitable; just because the rest of the world wasn't Ksar Alahari didn't mean it had to look ugly. Still, it seemed odd that a town that was little more than a caravanserai, a dusty souk, and a dozen or so houses could afford such niceties.

However, that was a mystery to be dealt with later. Right now, all that mattered was finding Fatima the care she needed.

"Oh, may the Great Mother bless you both," groaned the old woman as Karina and Dedele helped her maneuver through the streets. Thanks to the speed Afua's magic had granted them, they had arrived in the village before word of Karina's escape had. The soldiers searching for her had yet to flood the streets, and in fact, several of the buildings still wore their Solstasia decorations, which made Karina's heart twist.

"It's the least we can do, atti," replied Karina, shifting her body to take on more of the woman's weight and to make her walk faster. Even with her hair in neat cornrows beneath her scarf, and a cloth wrapped tight around the Wind-Aligned emblem on her left palm, Karina still felt dangerously exposed. These were the first people outside her own traveling party that she was seeing since the coup, and she found herself searching each face they passed for signs of treachery. Was that shepherd milking his sheep friend or foe? Was the spice merchant loyal to her or to Farid? Who here would come to her aid, and who would walk her to her own death if given the chance?

But as uncomfortable as this village made Karina, she refused to turn around until they'd had at least found a place for Fatima to sleep for the night. Karina's people had needed her and she had abandoned them—she would not do the same to this woman.

When they finally reached the caravanserai, Dedele said to Karina, "You stay with her while I see if I can haggle for a room. And for the love of the Great Mother, don't talk to anyone."

Dedele disappeared through the inn's wide wooden gates as Karina waited with Fatima beneath the shade of a thin palm tree. Afua had stayed behind to watch the ship. The sun was marching steadily toward midday, and Karina did her best to dab away the sheen of sweat glistening on the woman's brow. If she'd had better control of her powers, perhaps she might have been able to lower the temperature to one more manageable, but that was a risk she simply could not take.

"Just a little longer. We'll have a place for you to rest your head soon," she promised. Fatima looked up weakly.

"You remind me . . . so much of him . . ."

"Of who, atti?"

The woman moaned again. "But he's gone. And now my daughter, taken by those monsters. It should have been me! Oh, Kotoko, why wasn't it me?"

Fatima began to sob, and Karina quickly gathered her in her arms, more to muffle the sound than anything else. She had begun trying to comfort her when a deep voice cut her off.

"I'm telling the truth! The storm that passed through on the last day of Solstasia was caused by a witch!"

Ice ran through Karina's veins.

She forced down the rapid beating of her heart and scanned the street until she found the source of the claim—a rambling old man whose face was more beard than skin, and who already reeked of palm wine this early in the morning. His words slurred together, and he nearly knocked over several pieces on the game board in front of him with his frantic gesturing. "What else could cause a storm like that this time of year but a witch?"

Karina bit the inside of her cheek. If people were already beginning to suspect that the storm had been unnatural, then she was in more danger than she realized. Dedele was right—coming to Tiru had been a mistake. She had to get out of there, now, before a witch hunt ended her plans for revenge before they'd even truly begun.

However, raucous laughter from the drunk's opponent filled the air. He was a thickset man around Farid's age, though the jagged scars littering his hands and face suggested a life far from the plush halls of the Zirani royal court.

"If there are truly witches who can control the skies, then my great-aunt must be Princess Karina!" he wheezed. "You've had one too many pints of palm wine if you really believe something so preposterous."

"Mock the unseen world at your own peril, Caracal," warned the drunk man.

"On the contrary, I have nothing but respect for the unseen world, for certainly any world where I don't have to see your ugly face must be better than this one." He tapped a long finger against the game board. "Move your damn piece."

Karina immediately relaxed. Clearly this old man wasn't some agent sent by Farid if he couldn't even convince one mercenary of the truth. He didn't even know that the proper terms for magic users were zawenji and ulraji. But eventually news of what had occurred during the Closing Ceremony would reach even this sleepy corner of the desert, which meant the sooner they fled this place, the better.

The drunk was a better player than he was persuader, and in less than two moves his pieces had completely surrounded Caracal's. They were playing Four Friends, a strategy game named after a folktale about four mythical beings who had angered the Great Mother. Karina absentmindedly swatted a bug that landed on her shoulder and was considering going to check on Dedele when someone crashed into the drunk man.

"Oh, goodness, I'm so sorry, uncle!" the person cried as they knelt to help the man to his feet. Amid the commotion, no one noticed Caracal flick a single finger upward. Quick as a heartbeat, two of the pieces on the board lifted in the air and swapped places.

The game ended three turns later with Caracal's win. The old man muttered darkly to himself before passing the mercenary a handful of daira and storming off. Karina stared. Had that man just . . . had he just—

"Karina!"

Karina whirled around, hand flying to the hilt of the small dagger Dedele had lent her, but it was only Afua running for her with the hood of her djellaba low over her face.

"What did I tell you about using my real name—" Karina hissed, but Afua cut her off.

"I just spotted a squad of Zirani soldiers heading for Tiru, they're going to be here any moment!"

The normally unflappable Afua shook from head to toe as she delivered this message, and Karina could practically see the memories from the girl's time as a Zirani prisoner running through her mind. A long string of expletives came to Karina's tongue, but she swallowed them back as she gestured for Afua and Fatima to follow her into the caravanserai.

They pushed their way through a courtyard filled with merchants selling all manner of wares to travelers from every corner of Sonande. Dedele was at one such stall, haggling over a bag of papayas, and Karina did her best to keep calm as she sidled up to her friend.

"Afua spotted Zirani soldiers just outside the city. We have to leave now," she hissed through clenched teeth. To her credit, the former Fire Champion finished paying for the fruit without any hint that something was amiss. It was only when they had pulled away from the stall that her anger flared.

"I *told you* coming here was a bad idea—"

"I know, I know, you were right and I was wrong. Can we please focus on not getting captured so that you can live to gloat another day?"

"And what of Fatima?"

Karina's stomach twisted as the woman shook beside her. "We've done all we can, atti. I'm sorry, but we have to go."

The old woman gave a small nod. Disgusted at her own cowardice, Karina led her companions toward the exit. They had almost made it out when an explosion of red and silver pounded through the gate.

The colors of the Zirani royal army.

Dedele quickly shoved the group behind an empty stall, and from there they watched dozens of soldiers pour into the courtyard. No, no, this wasn't right—Karina knew for a fact there was no authorized concentration of soldiers this large anywhere near Tiru. Had Farid sent them after her?

But stranger even than the soldiers' presence was the group of mostly women and children they shepherded in. They were of varying ages and almost all dressed in tattered rags. Fatima took one look and let out a strangled grasp.

"They're here!" she said, the whites of her eyes shining stark with fear against her dark skin. "They're the ones who took my daughter from me!"

Dedele quickly clamped her hand over the woman's mouth to keep her from giving them away. But nothing about this made sense to Karina. If the Zirani army was out here trafficking women, her mother would have done something about it. Dedele gave her a pitying look.

"It's more common than you think. This must be how Tiru built its wealth, for there's no better way for a small town so far from the trading routes to gain riches than on the flesh market, and nobody to stop the army from participating in it."

The air around them crackled with energy as Karina's magic rose alongside her anger. "We need to do something!"

"They outnumber us five to one! At best they'll murder us for interfering with their operation. At worst they'll realize who we are and deliver us directly to Farid." Dedele's disgust mirrored Karina's own, but she did not move. "If you want to get out of here alive, the best thing to do is pretend you saw nothing."

Pretend she saw nothing? How was Karina supposed to do that when exploitation like this was exactly what her ancestors had given their lives to eradicate?

Doing nothing went against everything Karina had been taught to believe in. And yet . . . Dedele was right. If she died fighting these soldiers, there would be no one to rise against Farid. No one who would be in a position to one day stop wrongs like this from happening again.

Still, Bahia Alahari would have done something. Her mother would have done something.

But Karina was neither her famed ancestor nor her esteemed mother. She was just a princess with no realm, no throne, and no power to help anyone but herself. And so even though the guilt stabbed through her sharp as a knife, Karina stifled her magic and did the only thing she could do:

She waited.

5

Malik

"I can't believe they would do that to you!" The sharpness in Leila's voice was completely at odds with the gentleness with which she drew her fingers through Nadia's hair. "You could have died!"

Malik might have responded had he not been in the process of being stabbed. As it was, he was trying not to flinch as the seamstress finished pinning together his outfit for the Water Day ceremony. Silk-like layers of blue patterned fabric draped across his shoulders and chest, accentuating the frame that Malik usually kept hunched, and he had to admit that being pricked a few dozen times was a small price to pay considering just an inch of this garment could have fed every person back in Oboure for a year.

And it was all theirs—the jewel-lined clothes, the spacious suite of rooms, the servants waiting around to guess their every whim before they even had it. Malik could probably spend the rest of his life in the palace and never grow accustomed to this lifestyle.

When the seamstress was done with the final touch—a pendant of bright gold hanging from a string of beads tied around his waist—she took a step back and folded her hands demurely before her. "I have finished, Champion Adil. If anything is not to your liking, let me know, and I will fix it at once."

That was another thing Malik would never get used to, the deference with which people now spoke to him. Nobody would lower their eyes if they knew he was nothing more than a poor boy from Eshra. "It's wonderful. Thank you so much," he replied. Leila's expression made it clear she had much more to say, none of which could be said before the present company. "Would you give us a moment, please?"

The seamstress blinked at him in confusion, and it took a second for Malik to remember that nobility made demands, not requests, of servants. However, the woman quickly made the Zirani gesture of respect—three fingers pressed to her lips, then her heart—and hurried out of the room. As soon as she was gone, Malik lowered himself onto the divan across from where Leila braided Nadia's hair, and winced as his wounds from that morning screamed in protest.

"I don't think I was ever in any danger of dying. If they wanted to kill me, it would have been much easier to slit my throat when I was unconscious in the infirmary," he said.

Leila's scowl deepened as she ran the jeweled comb through one of Nadia's particularly stubborn tangles. "What type of teacher throws their student into the lion's den before they've even taught them anything? Besides, you said Farid's powers allowed him to stop your magic once before. If they're so concerned about yours spiraling out of control, why doesn't he just do that again until your training is complete?"

Leila had a point—as far as he knew, there was nothing stopping the man from cutting off Malik's access to nkra like he had back during the First Challenge, when Malik had tried to kill Karina on the Widow's Fingers. That certainly would have saved him several bruised ribs.

"What you can do, Malik, is a gift—no, not just a gift, a birthright," Farid had told him as he'd escorted Malik back to his quarters after the test. Malik had been in so much pain that the former steward had half dragged him there. "The powers of kings and gods, passed to you by your ancestors. Under my tutelage, your abilities will become a sight to behold."

Malik had never had a teacher who spoke about him as if he was someone worth putting his faith in. If he was going to be this man's apprentice, he had to believe that everything his mentor did was for a good reason, even when that reason wasn't always clear.

"The whole point was to see if I could control the Faceless King on my own. Farid doing it for me would defeat the purpose. And besides, he can't waste his energy on me every day when he has so many other responsibilities to take care of."

Leila's gaze fell to the thick bandage wrapped around the wound Malik had given himself during the trial. "I just wish you'd had some kind of warning. Perhaps then you wouldn't have had to . . . do that."

Malik truly appreciated how hard his sister was trying to understand his point of view, and the fact that the conversation hadn't devolved into her ordering him around was just one more thing that had changed for the better after Solstasia. But he didn't know how to explain to her without sparking her worry anew that, sometimes, pain was the only thing that made him feel in control of himself.

"What's done is done. All that's important now is that the council trusts me and that our place here in Ziran is finally secure."

Leila looked like she wanted to say something else, but shook her head and asked, "Tell me more about the princess. What was she like?"

Malik thought back to the girl seated before the pit, and how her steely facade had broken over Tunde's bracelet of all things. "She was normal," he admitted. "You wouldn't know what she really was just by looking at her."

Leila shuddered. "Well, let's pray to Patuo that your paths don't cross again. Illusions and evil spirits are bad enough. We don't need to add cavorting with the undead to our list of problems." She twisted the last ruby-topped pin into the elaborate crown of braids she'd woven into Nadia's curls. "And you're all done! Do you like it?"

Nadia stared at her reflection in silence, and her siblings exchanged a worried glance. Their younger sister had been a shadow of her former self ever since returning from the spirit world. She bore no physical marks from that time, but whatever she had seen on the other side had changed something deep within her that she either could not or would not speak about.

Willing the concern from his face, Malik knelt beside her. "Do you know what the color of your dress reminds me of? Our old hen, Fat Daisy."

The illusion of Fat Daisy sprang to life before them and began squawking across the room in a way that once would have made Nadia squeal with delight. But now she simply watched the chicken dance with that same blank expression on her face.

"I want to go home," she said, and the fake hen died as Malik pulled Nadia close to his chest, marveling not for the first time at how small she really was. Leila knelt to join them. "I want Mama and Nana."

Leila's face twisted, as close to tears as she would dare get around Nadia. Even though she was dressed in a fine cerulean robe that matched Nadia's own, she still wore the faded dark blue headscarf that she'd brought with her from Eshra. Leila never went anywhere without it, no matter how many more beautiful scarves she could now buy. Malik understood that need to hold on to any tiny scrap of the life they'd once had, even if it had been painful more often than not.

For all its finery and jewels, Ziran would never be the home or the family they had lost. That was why Malik couldn't allow himself to dwell on the past, for if he did it might pull him under completely. All he could do was move forward, and the only path forward for them was under Farid's protection.

"It's going to get better," he promised, and whether he was speaking to Nadia, Leila, or even himself, he did not know. All he knew was that this was one oath he absolutely would not break.

Their future would be better than their past had been.

Nadia nodded weakly into his chest, her eyes still focused on something only she could see. Leila was the first to pull away, and as she did so, she asked, "Are you sure you're ready for this ceremony?"

"I think so."

After all, it was only one event. It couldn't be that bad, right?

This was bad. This was very, very bad.

"We are so honored to have you performing the ceremony with us today, Champion Adil," said Water Priestess as she led Malik through the shell-lined walls of her Alignment's temple. "I'm sure Susono and all the gods are smiling upon us for your involvement."

Malik could only nod, for he did not trust himself to speak without throwing up. Farid had made today's ceremony sound like an intimate affair with maybe fifty people in attendance. But there were hundreds milling about the lower floor of the Water Temple, with dozens more streaming in by the second. Hundreds of eyes analyzing Malik's every move and judging him for not being Tunde.

Water Priestess went on to explain exactly what Malik's duties for the ceremony would be, but she may as well have been talking to a stone wall for all the information he retained. He felt his mouth moving to give some platitude about doing his best to usher in the new era, and then he was alone, and the walls were closing in on him.

I don't understand how your mind works, said Idir as black spots splattered across Malik's vision. *In the last week alone, you've faced down both monsters and gods, yet the mere thought of speaking before a crowd triggers your body's death response.*

Malik himself had no idea why his mind took things he knew were not threats and twisted them until the entire world felt like a battleground. He—he had to get out of here. This had been a mistake.

Farid had warned him to only use his magic in case of an emergency, but Malik quickly wove two illusions—a fake version of himself to wait until Water Priestess returned, and then a cover of invisibility over his body. Once the magic was in place, he slipped out of the room and past his guards. A cluster of strange bugs clinging to one of the banisters were the only ones who saw him go.

The scents of the Water Temple made Malik's head swim—a fragrant mixture of incense, water lilies, and sea salt, making him feel as if he had stepped beneath the ocean. He needed fresh air, and the only way to get it would be outside.

But there was no way to exit the temple without passing through the worshippers, and though they could not see him, their proximity made the knot of anxiety in Malik's stomach tighten. The majority of the people were gathered around short fountains, cleansing themselves before the prayers. Tension hummed through the air, and the attendees passed furtive glances from behind raised hands as they whispered about the state of Ziran in the wake of Solstasia.

"They say Adetunde ran off with Princess Karina . . ."

"The Life Champion is here today. How is he still alive after stabbing himself in the heart? Is he a sorcerer too?"

"I swear, Farid Sibari cares more about the girl than he does about actually running the city."

Malik felt each whisper like a needle to the skin. He wished Farid was here to help him navigate the court's web. But his mentor was back at the palace with Hanane, believing it would be best if he stayed out of the public eye for the time being.

Malik soon found himself in a room filled with reflecting pools hundreds of feet long. He crouched beside one with his head between his knees and tried to remember how to breathe. The

Water Temple lacked the wards that protected Ksar Alahari from the grim folk, and so the wraiths crowded around him, staring down at him with those bone-white eyes.

"Leave me alone," he groaned. "Please, just for one day, leave me be."

The wraiths ignored his pleas, as they always did, and crowded in closer. Malik counted to one hundred, and then backward from one hundred, and then up to it again. He filled his mind with every good memory he could think of—days spent walking their flocks of sheep through the fields back in Oboure and nights spent helping Nana with her cooking. Dancing with Karina, and how for the span of one song, they'd been able to pretend they were on the same side.

The panic slowly dissipated, leaving behind a dull ache. Malik sighed.

That girl has been staring at you for a while now.

Idir's voice snapped Malik out of his sulking. Just as the spirit claimed, a girl his own age stared at him from the entrance to the pool room. She glanced over her shoulder, and whatever she saw there made her bound the length of the room to Malik's side.

"I'm so sorry to impose," she asked breathlessly, "but would you mind pretending you've been completely and irrevocably charmed by me?"

Surprised, Malik nodded. An older woman appeared in the doorway, and the girl's grimace deepened. "Gods above, she's here! Quick, laugh like I just said something funny."

Malik did as she asked. When the woman looked at them, the girl put a hand on Malik's arm and leaned in close enough for him to see the red sheen to the braids wrapped in an updo around her head.

"Now look as if we are engrossed in a conversation so engaging, she wouldn't dare interrupt." The scent of leather and ink wafted off the girl, a comforting smell that reminded Malik of the few books his family had been able to afford. "If my mother sees me preoccupied with a handsome man, she'll surely leave me alone for the rest of the day."

Heat rushed to Malik's face; he'd never been called handsome before. The girl's mother looked at them with an approving gleam before sweeping out of the room. As soon as she was gone, the girl pulled away.

"My mother is like a shark in a blood frenzy at these gatherings. If I hadn't escaped her, she might have literally thrown me at the next eligible suitor who crossed her path."

"I'm glad I could help."

"I really can't thank you enough, if you hadn't—is that the Eye of Akhmen?"

The girl grabbed Malik's hand and peered intently at the lines of ink that made up the Mark, which he had forgotten to hide beneath his sleeve. "And the Torbek staff! I've never seen such accurate renditions of the Kennouan glyphs before. Where did you get this done?"

The girl's face flooded with horror at Malik's confused expression, and she quickly dropped his hand. "I am so, so sorry I just—I get so excited when I meet another student of Kennouan history. There are so few people left who have any interest in the ancient world."

Malik wouldn't exactly call his ties to Kennoua an "interest," but he wasn't about to explain his connection to the Ulraji Tel-Ra. "No need to apologize, but I don't believe I caught your name . . ."

"Oh, forgive my rudeness! My name is Yaema Anim. I'm a student at the university studying the histories and cultures of ancient Sonande. And you are?"

Malik's fake identity suddenly felt like a thousand-pound weight dragging him down. "My name is Adil Asfour. I'm here on behalf of the palace in place of the Water Champion."

Yaema's eyes looked like they might pop straight out of her head. "You . . . . you're the one who almost won Solstasia. Y-You're . . . that's you."

"I am." He wondered if this was how Karina had always felt, as if people were speaking to whatever image of her they'd constructed in their minds and not her real self. "But, please, no need for formality. I'm nobody special."

Malik could practically feel the embarrassment rolling off Yaema as she wrung her hands together. "You're the Life Champion, and here I was—it's just these events make me so nervous and I . . . I just wanted my mother to leave me alone for once, but if I'd known who you were I never would have—"

"You're fine, truly," Malik assured her, recognizing all too well the snare of anxiety. "Being around so many people you don't know can be so . . ."

". . . overwhelming," finished Yaema, and Malik nodded. The Earth-Aligned girl gave him a beaming smile that revealed a small dimple in her left cheek. "But still, I owe you for your help today.

If you ever find yourself sick of the trimmings and trappings of court, please come find me at the university at any time."

"It would be my pleasure."

And you say you don't know how to flirt.

Malik flinched backward. "I'm not!"

"You're not what?"

"I'm . . ." Suddenly Malik realized just how close this girl was, and he hadn't been flirting, he was just being nice, but oh gods, had *she* been flirting? And even if she had been flirting with him, he had completely ruined it by talking aloud to himself like some sort of madman and oh no she was still looking at him, what should he even say—

"I'm sorry, I think Water Priestess is calling me," he said, and then he bolted back to the waiting area with a speed that would have put a leopard to shame. Once there, he took the place of the illusion and mentally kicked himself. The Faceless King didn't say anything, but he didn't have to. Malik could feel the spirit's obvious amusement at the fact that a cute girl had tried to talk to him, and he had quite literally run from her.

But Malik only had so long to dwell on his own mortification, for less than a minute later, Water Priestess poked her head through the door and called his name.

It was time to begin.

The ceremony took place at the back of the temple, where a statue of Susono the Hippo rose from a small pool of water littered with sacred herbs and oils. Malik took his place beside Water Priestess as she addressed the crowd.

"My siblings, we are gathered here today in the wake of the most turbulent Solstasia our realm has ever seen. But even in the face of turmoil, the one thing that remains constant is the grace of the gods. It is by their mercy we exist at all, and it is the greatest honor of my humble life to guide you today as we usher in a new era ruled over by our patron deity, Susono."

Something about the cheer that rose up from the crowd made Malik's chest constrict.

It hurts because these cheers are meant for Tunde, but you truly won Solstasia. It hurts because they should be cheering for you, not him.

Malik gritted his teeth and strengthened his wall against the spirit. That wasn't it. Surely he wasn't so shallow as to be jealous of his missing friend.

Luckily, his role in the Cleansing Ceremony was a simple one. One by one the Water-Aligned of Ziran approached the pool, where Malik anointed them with holy oil before Water Priestess lowered them into the water and prayed over their bodies. He carefully spread the mixture over the first man's cheek and brows, then stepped back as the priestess submerged the man beneath the gentle waves.

"From water we all come and to water we all return—saints and sinners, prophets and fools alike." The priestess's voice magnified a thousandfold throughout the cavernous hall. "Let it embrace you, let it remake you, until all you are is all that was."

When the man finally broke the surface, he gasped for air with the fervent look of somebody who had brushed against divinity. Cheers and bamboo horns rang through the temple, and the next person in line eagerly walked up for her chance to merge with the sacred.

Malik and Water Priestess quickly fell into a comfortable rhythm of anointing and cleansing and anointing again. This was what he missed most about life before the discovery of his powers—the complete and utter faith that there was something more than him out there, and that it was so important that just being a part of it made him important too. He understood why the ulraji had sneered at the Zirani gods, but how could beings who had brought so much joy be completely bad?

Finally the last worshipper reached the front of the line. Malik's eyes fell to the all-too familiar red-and-black leather satchel hanging off the boy's thin shoulder.

His satchel, now in the possession of the child who had stolen it from him on Solstasia Eve.

The boy clearly recognized him from the way he shook with fear. Malik's irritation flared—if this boy hadn't stolen that bag, Nadia never would have been kidnapped by the Faceless King. So many people would still be alive.

But if this boy hadn't stolen that bag, Malik never would have befriended Tunde or become Farid's apprentice. He never would have recovered his magic. For every bad thing that had happened since that day, so much good had as well, which was why Malik gave the child a warm smile as he shuffled up to the pool.

"What is your name?" he asked.

The boy twisted his hands around the strap of the satchel as Malik himself had done countless times. "H-Hassan."

"Well, Hassan, would you like to know a secret?" Malik leaned in with a conspiratorial grin. "The bag looks a lot better on you than it ever did on me."

The boy let out a surprised laugh, and the tension melted from his body. As Malik anointed the oil over Hassan's brow and cheeks, he gave a silent prayer to the gods that the boy would live a long and prosperous life. Water Priestess gestured for the boy to come forward once Malik was done, but Hassan hung back.

"Are you scared?" Malik asked, and Hassan nodded. Malik turned to Water Priestess. "I'd like to hold him myself, if that is all right."

This was almost certainly against tradition, but the priestess nodded. Malik gently lowered Hassan into the water, cradling the back of his head like one might an infant. He saw himself reflected in the boy's large brown eyes, felt the way each of his muscles tensed as the water engulfed his small frame.

"It's all right. I won't let anything happen to you," he promised as Water Priestess began the prayer one last time.

". . . Let it embrace you, let it remake you, until all you are is all that was."

At the last word, Hassan's body jerked. The boy's limbs flailed, and Malik quickly pulled him free of the water and onto the tiled floor. A gurgling sound emerged from the boy's throat, but though Malik kept hitting him on the back, nothing came out. The boy continued to twist and scream until a voice that was not his rose from his body.

There can be no resurrection without renewal, ulraji. This was no longer the voice of a child but something fathomless, the words booming out like every wave in the world crashing together at once. *Our mother has been angered for the last time. Where mercy once reigned, now come pestilence and plagues. Where there was once goodness, now only storms and monsters. Thus is the price of resurrection without renewal. A ruler to resurrect, a ruler to renew. Only then will her anger be quelled.*

"Susono!" cried Water Priestess, but Malik could not marvel that a literal god was speaking to them when Hassan was dying before their eyes. His magic boiled to the surface, but there was no illusion strong enough to fight off whatever this was. The boy's eyes rolled into the back of his head as he repeated the divine words again.

A ruler to resurrect, a ruler to renew. A ruler to resurrect, a ruler to renew. A ruler to resurrect, a ruler to renew.

And there Malik knelt, completely powerless, as the boy drowned to death in his arms.

6

Karina

Karina wasn't sure she could take another second of this.

One hundred and fifty daira for someone's grandfather. Three hundred for someone's daughter. Four hundred and fifty each for a pair of teenage girls, eight hundred if bought together. The soldiers rattled off their wares with sickening efficiency to the patrons of the caravanserai, and the exchanges occurred with a fervor akin to a cattle market. Karina silently pleaded for someone to intervene, but of course no one did, as the only people with the power to end this were the very ones conducting it.

But the soldiers could not stay forever. Once their grisly business was done, they would be on their way, and so would Karina and her entourage. This would be over soon, she told herself even as shame at her own uselessness burned within her.

Great Mother above, let this be over soon.

One of the soldiers barked for the next woman to step forward There came a sound of scuffling, and then a sharp cry. Fatima's face went slack with recognition, and none of them were fast enough to stifle the scream that tore out of her.

"My baby! Oh please, not her!"

Dedele quickly covered the woman's mouth again, but it was

too late. Several sets of heavy footsteps pounded toward their hiding place, and Karina only had a few seconds to curse under her breath before jumping to her feet, her face twisted into the most gracious smile.

"Is something the matter over here?" asked the taller of the two soldiers, the tip of his spear glinting in the sunlight. Karina fought the urge to spit in the man's face.

"I appreciate your concern, good soldier, but my family and I are fine. What you heard just now was my grandmother. She has a weak constitution, but with a bit of rest and a good meal, she'll be feeling well in no time."

The head soldier narrowed his eyes as his gaze moved between Karina and Fatima, no doubt noting their lack of physical resemblance. "Where is your family from?"

"A tiny village not far from Kissi-Mokou. We were on our way home after Solstasia and stopped here to replenish our supplies."

A bead of sweat dripped down Karina's back. The strain from folding her magic away deep inside herself caused a blooming ache behind her temple, which she continued to grin through even as tears burned at the back of her eyes. She felt Afua quivering beside her, unable to hold back her fear of these soldiers and her time as their captive.

The head soldier muttered something to his companion, too low for her to hear. His hand tightened around his spear.

"The four of you come with us," he ordered, and Karina did the first thing that came to mind—she grabbed the sack of papayas and swung it at his face. The man staggered backward with an angry cry, blood and fruit flying everywhere.

"Run!" Karina screamed.

Her friends scattered, leaving Karina to grapple with the second soldier. Though she'd had the element of surprise, he was both larger and stronger than her, and he quickly pinned her arms above her head and lifted her off her feet. Karina kicked in his grasp, her powers pounding for release.

"Arrest seems far too lenient a punishment for this one, don't you think?" The soldier with the broken nose sneered through the rivers of blood running down his face. "You're going to regret laying a hand on me, girl."

The man's fist swung into her gut. Pain exploded through Karina's body, and any semblance of control she'd had shattered into bits. A guttural scream tore from her lips, and the wind rose to meet it, swirling around them in a raging cyclone. The man's eyes bugged from his head.

"Witch!" he roared, and another wave of power from Karina lifted them both into the air. The soldier's body twisted within the gale, until his face suddenly slackened, and a voice deeper than his own spilled from his mouth.

Our mother has been angered for the last time. Where mercy once reigned, now come pestilence and plagues. Where there was once goodness, now only storms and monsters. Thus is the price of resurrection without renewal.

Karina's heart thudded in her ears—the last time she had heard this voice, it had been coming from Afua when she'd petitioned the gods for information about the Rite of Resurrection.

This was the voice of Santrofie, He Born of Wind. Karina's patron deity.

But how? Why?

As quickly as the divine voice had come, it was gone, and the swirling cyclone of wind dropped them both onto the sand. There was an audible crack as the soldier's neck hit the ground at the wrong angle. Karina tried to push to her feet, but her legs were shaking too much for her to stand.

For whatever reason, Santrofie had taken control of this man's body to pass a message along to her, and now he was dead.

And she would be too if she didn't get out of here.

Karina was finally on her feet when a sense of wrongness filled the air, like a discordant note rising above an otherwise perfect melody. A thick black cloud shifted over the sun, blanketing all of Tiru in shadow.

No, not a cloud—no cloud clicked and hissed like that. People all around the village stopped to point and stare, too awed to remember to be scared.

Until the swarm descended, and all hell broke loose.

The locusts dropped onto the village with the ferocity of a lion pouncing on its prey—not one or two bugs like had been fluttering around all day, but hundreds of thousands in a cloud so thick that day became night. There was nowhere to run from them, and their screeches were unnervingly human as they bit through flesh and clothes alike.

Just as Santrofie had warned.

"Dedele! Afua!" Karina cried. She dove to the ground, trying to keep the insects out of her mouth. The Zirani soldiers had scattered, their weapons no use against such a small yet mighty foe.

The villagers were even worse off without armor to protect themselves, and Karina watched in horror as one by one they fell to the ground, their bodies covered in blankets of the creatures.

Forget the soldiers. Forget even Fatima. The only thing that mattered now was returning to the sand barge and getting as far away from this hell as possible. With a burst of adrenaline, Karina pushed herself to her feet and quickly grabbed a sword off a fallen soldier. With one hand she held the top of her dress over her mouth, and with the other she swung wildly, attempting to clear a path out of the caravanserai.

She had almost made it when she saw that, despite the chaos, a few of the soldiers were trying to haul the trafficked women back into their wagon, choosing their investment over their own lives. Fatima had gone to her daughter and was screaming as one of the soldiers tried to pull them apart.

Karina took one look at the open gate to the caravanserai, toward freedom and the chance for revenge that awaited her in Arkwasi.

And then she turned and barreled straight for the soldiers.

"Let them go!"

Without thinking, she thrust her free hand forward, and her magic burst forth. The wind sliced through the air and tossed the men against one of the inn's stone walls. The last soldier standing ducked Karina's clumsy swing easily, but he couldn't avoid the handful of sand Karina threw in his face. He stumbled back with a sharp cry, and she took advantage of his confusion to stick her sword deep into his gut. His body fell to the ground with a wet thud, and Karina brought her shaking hands to her mouth.

She'd killed before, but never intentionally. It had been so . . . easy.

But there was no time to despair, for the fury of the swarm was only growing. Karina ran over to the panicked refugees.

"You're free!" she shouted. She wouldn't think about the blood staining her hands or the viscera beneath her fingernails. She couldn't. "Go now!"

The women shrank away from her in fear, and Karina bit back a scream of frustration; why had she risked everything to give these women a chance to escape if they weren't going to take it?

But then a crack loud as thunder filled the air. The cyclone Karina had created had expanded, and locusts now swirled through its depths as it ripped a palm tree clean from the ground. The tree flew toward the souk, where people were still running in every direction trying to escape the swarm.

"No!" screamed Karina, and she threw another gust of wind to spin the tree off course. It crashed against a wall with a thunderous boom, but the cyclone continued to rage.

"Go somewhere far away from here!" she called to the refugees, and it only then occurred to her that they might not speak Zirani.

Fatima's daughter—actually a middle-aged woman, not a baby at all—stood protectively in front of her mother. There was something familiar about her that Karina could not quite place. An understanding passed between them, and Fatima's daughter nodded at Karina before shouting orders to the rest of the group in what sounded like Darajat. The refugees scattered for cover, leaving Karina alone to deal with the devastating combination of her own magic and the wrath of the gods.

Karina tried once more to calm the winds, but the more she pulled on the threads of nkra, the more intense the storm grew. Gritting her teeth, she decided to switch tactics. Perhaps if she called a second cyclone that ran counter to this one, the two would push each other to a stalemate.

The locusts' screeching intensified as Karina frantically whirled the second cyclone into being. But instead of pure wind, bright flickers of lightning lanced through the swirling mass. Even though she had intentionally summoned the twister, fear froze her in place as a bolt of lightning escaped the second cyclone and crashed into the stand where she and her friends had hidden just a few minutes earlier.

Flames devoured the wood in seconds. Cold sweat broke out over Karina's body as, for the second time in her life, she watched a fire of her own creation spiral out of control.

Karina tried to push her energy into calming the chaos she had unleashed, but she had control over the sky, not fire. No choice left but to run, she plunged blindly into the crush of locusts and fire and smoke, sprinting with all her might in the direction of the sand barge. Sounds of terror echoed all around her, and Karina hoped that Dedele and Afua had not gotten caught up in this disaster she had worsened.

But then up ahead—salvation. The outline of the sand barge loomed through the blur, and Karina could just make out Afua and Dedele waving frantically at her from the deck. A flicker of hope bloomed in her chest.

With a last surge of energy, Karina charged for the ship, her arms swinging wildly to blow away flames and locusts at every turn. Her fingers finally closed around the ladder that would hoist her up onto the ship—only for a strong hand to wrench her backward. She tried to summon the wind to pull her attacker off, but it refused her commands, as if someone had ripped the threads of power from her hands.

Her captor yanked her head back, and Karina was forced to look up at Caracal, the mercenary from the caravanserai. The cold kiss of his blade bit against her throat.

"Look at that. Seems as though I've caught myself a zawenji."

Malik

The arrival of the locusts was later described to Malik as something from a nightmare—one moment there had been a bright afternoon sky, the next a cloud of pestilence from which there was no escape. The locusts had torn into rich and poor alike, their piercing cries so human-like that soon every street in Ziran was filled with wailing.

Luckily, Malik had already returned to the palace by the time the attack began, and Ksar Alahari was so well fortified that those within its stone walls were under no direct threat from the creatures. But Eshra was no stranger to locusts, and he had lived through enough pestilence-induced famines to know that the terror had only just begun. The nobility hiding behind their stone walls and barred windows would be fine, but the common folk— those who had no choice but to brave the pests, for there were still fields that needed tilling and mouths that needed feeding—would suffer the most.

However, as terrifying as the locusts were, they were nothing compared to the horror of Hassan's death.

Malik replayed those last moments of the ceremony over and over in his mind, searching desperately for any action he could have taken to save the poor boy. Would Susono still have used Hassan to deliver her message if Water Priestess had been holding him? Would the boy be alive now if Tunde had been there instead of Malik?

So many ifs, yet none that could change the reality that Hassan was dead and Malik was to blame, for he was the one Susono had meant the message for. The boy had been so small too, barely older than Nadia, and the last memory of his too-short life had been of Malik's frightened face. The fact that he hadn't provided the boy any comfort in his final moments tore into Malik far worse than the locusts ever could. His mind was still trapped there, reliving the moment Hassan had breathed his last, when someone loudly called his name.

Malik snapped to attention as Farid's face swam into focus. "Are you all right? I've been trying to speak to you for a while now," his mentor asked, and there weren't enough words in all the languages in the world to express how not all right Malik felt.

"I'm sorry, I just . . . I can't stop thinking about him. About Hassan." The incessant screeching of the locusts against the shuttered window wasn't helping to calm him either. "I should have done something—"

"There was nothing you could have done." Farid ran a hand through his hair, his face drawn tight. "Can you repeat again exactly what the boy said before he passed?"

A shudder passed down Malik's spine as Hassan's terrified face swam through his mind, but he dutifully recited Susono's message once more:

Our mother has been angered for the last time. Where mercy once reigned, now come pestilence and plagues. Where there was once goodness, now only storms and monsters. Thus is the price of resurrection without renewal. A ruler to resurrect, a ruler to renew. Only then will her anger be quelled.

Farid began to pace, not that there was much room to do so. They were currently in the former steward's personal workshop, and the room was far messier than Malik would have expected from the man who had kept Ksar Alahari running for years. Parchment and scrolls occupied every open surface, and Malik was currently balancing on a precarious pile of books, which in turn was balanced on a statue of a jackal.

"What I do not understand is why Susono told you the locusts were coming at all. Her dominion covers water, not insects. Why would she deliver a warning of something she did not cause?"

"She repeated the words *resurrection* and *renewal* several times. Could that be a reference to the resurrection of Princess Hanane?"

Malik had simply been thinking aloud, but from the way Farid's face tightened, he knew he'd said the wrong thing.

"Hanane has nothing to do with this," his mentor snapped. "Though her mother and sister were both zawenji, Hanane has never displayed any magic ability. And even if she'd been able to summon the locusts, Hanane is far too good-hearted to ever hurt anyone."

Malik suddenly felt like a child again, trying to figure out exactly what he had said to trigger one of his father's volatile moods. "You're right, I'm sorry, it was a stupid idea," he said hurriedly.

Farid's scowl deepened as he began flipping through one of the books on his desk. "Hanane causing this, how absurd . . . but if not her, who? Kotoko, perhaps? None of my records show anything like this, and I just don't understand—gah!"

With a frustrated cry Farid tossed the book, and it crashed against the wall several inches from Malik's head. The Moon-Aligned ulraji panted heavily, but his anger quickly melted into regret.

"Oh, Malik, I'm so sorry, I didn't mean to scare you. Put down the dagger, it's all right."

Malik looked down. Without realizing it, he had summoned his spirit blade and now held it defensively in front of his chest. He sheepishly ordered it back into tattoo form. He needed to calm down. Farid wasn't his father. Just because he was upset didn't make him a threat.

"I'm sorry, I just . . . I'm sorry."

Farid knelt beside him, grabbing one of Malik's hands in his, and Malik had to force himself not to flinch. "Breathe, Malik. You're all right."

Hassan's death and Driss's death blurred together in Malik's mind until it was Hassan falling over that railing in the Azure Garden, Driss drowning in his arms.

He was a murderer twice over now.

"Malik, look at me."

He did so. Farid's gaze was filled with nothing but compassion as his eyes roved over the tears streaming down Malik's face.

"You've been through so much today. Of course you're panicked. But this isn't your fault. The only ones to blame are those vile creatures who deign to call themselves gods—Susono, the Great Mother, and all the rest. They were the ones who chose to murder an innocent boy for the sake of whatever twisted game they're playing. I don't know what they have planned, but we are going to figure it out, little brother."

Malik had been called little brother before by Leila, of course, but the endearment was different when Farid said it. They shared the kind of connection that only two people who understood both the wonders and horrors of magic could share.

"Let's think about this logically. 'A ruler to resurrect, a ruler to renew.' If the first part of that line does refer to the Rite of Resurrection, then the second part must refer to another ritual—a Rite of Renewal."

Farid began sorting through the mountain of parchment on his desk, sending a cloud of dust into the air in his haste. "Rite of Renewal, Rite of Renewal . . . I have never heard of such a thing. Perhaps if Karina hadn't thrown *The Tome of the Dearly Departed* down a gorge, we'd be able to find information about it in there." Farid turned to Malik. "Do you recall any other strange occurrences today?"

Malik was about to say no before he remembered the dream. He summarized it for his mentor as quickly as he could, though he left out Karina's presence. Things were already chaotic enough without mentioning his silly attachment to the princess.

When he was finished, Farid's eyes gleamed with excitement.

"Why didn't you say something earlier? This can only mean one thing—you saw a glimpse into the Faceless King's memories."

Malik could practically see the wheels turning inside his mentor's mind as he examined this new piece of information. "The Faceless King has existed since the dawn of time; if there is any creature alive who would know about this Rite of Renewal, it's him. Do you think you could look inside his memories once again?"

Idir had been silent this entire time, but at Farid's suggestion, the obosom balked. *Touch my memories, and it'll be the last thing you ever do,* he warned, sending a sudden spasm of pain through Malik's body.

"But I thought the council didn't want me using the Faceless King's powers?" Wasn't that why he had let the Sentinels beat him to a pulp that very morning, to prove that he would not do exactly what Farid was asking him to do?

"That was before a blanket of pestilence fell over the city and a god killed a child in your arms. Circumstances change, Malik. This isn't an ideal solution, but if there is any chance at all that the answer to our problems is lurking right in our midst, we need to take it."

Farid's argument made sense, but Malik was still uneasy. His mentor knelt beside him once more. "You know I wouldn't ask this of you if we had any other choice, little brother. If you absolutely can't do it, I understand. But remember what is at risk if we don't at least try."

Farid was right. Malik didn't know if he could access the Faceless King's memories without weakening the binding, but he had a duty to try, if nothing else.

The wound Malik had given himself during the test throbbed as he nodded. "I'll try."

Farid beamed at him. "Oh, thank you so much. And don't

worry, I'll be by your side the entire time—"

Someone knocked on the door to the workshop before barging straight in.

"I need to talk to you, Farid," Princess Hanane demanded. Her regal outfit from that morning was gone, replaced by a thin nightdress with a thick orange-and-blue patterned shawl over her shoulders.

Her presence seemed to shift something in Farid, and even his voice sounded years younger when he said, "I thought I told you to stay in your rooms."

"I don't need to stay in my rooms, I should be out there!" she exclaimed. Malik pressed back against the wall, trying hard not to stare at this girl who shouldn't be. "My people are suffering, and I'm hiding in my rooms like a coward—"

"You are biding your time and gathering information before you act, as a good queen should. Your mother never made any move before she knew everything there was to know about the opponent she was facing."

Princess Hanane began to shake. A sour taste filled the air, and Malik tensed as a feeling like someone scratching their nails over his bones filled his body. "No, you don't understand . . . being here again, it's . . . I can't stay here any longer, I can't *be* here."

The princess had died during a fire that had torn through this very palace ten years prior. Malik couldn't imagine what it must be like to walk the halls of the place where you'd passed. No wonder she looked so distressed.

Farid placed his hands on the princess's shoulders and pressed his forehead against hers. "Do you trust me?" he murmured.

The dark thing that had clouded Princess Hanane's eyes passed. She took a deep, shuddering breath. "More than anyone else in the world."

"Then trust that everything I have ever done, and ever will do, is in your best interest. There are forces at work here whose goal we do not comprehend. The best thing you can do right now to help your people is to stay here where you're safe until we know what is going on." Farid cupped Hanane's cheek with his hand. "I am always on your side. So much has changed in the last decade, but that never will."

Malik didn't know why his own chest was drawn so tight, or why he got the sense that he was watching something he was not supposed to see. All he knew was that when Farid looked his way again, it was clear that their meeting was done. Doing his best not to draw attention to himself, he slipped out of the workshop, trying to shake the feeling of Princess Hanane's undead eyes on him all the way back to his quarters.

8

Karina

When Karina was four years old and Hanane twelve, the Kestrel had sat them down in her private garden on a beautiful summer's day and told them what to do if they were ever abducted.

"There are going to be people who wish to harm you because of who you are and what you represent," their mother had said. "No matter how they threaten, no matter how they follow through on those threats, there is more at stake than just your life. We hold the fate of every person in Ziran in our hands, and that means we have to be willing to die before we divulge anything that may put them in danger."

Though Karina had not understood the implications of torture at the time, Hanane had. "Have you ever been captured?" she'd whispered.

The sultana's gaze fell to the thin scar running the length of her forearm. "Only once."

"What happened?"

The queen lifted her head, and that was the first time Karina saw not the mother who had raised her, but the famed Kestrel of Ziran, the warrior who had clawed her way to her own reign through battles and blood and loss.

"I made them regret it."

This was the memory that looped through Karina's mind as her captor forced a gag into her mouth, a sack over her head, and ivory shackles onto her wrists. The latter were the most frightening, for the second they touched her skin, her magic died within her. No matter how deeply she called for her powers, nothing called back.

Karina had received extensive training against torture in the years since that conversation. It did not matter what these people said or did to her, she wouldn't tell them anything. And when she got free, she would make this Caracal regret ever laying a hand on her.

After a short march, the mercenary ordered her to kneel. She did so and felt a second person tying a thick rope around her waist to what felt like a wooden beam. Horrific images of all kinds of brutal interrogation tactics flashed before Karina's eyes as the sack was lifted from her face and dim light flooded her vision.

She was in a thinly furnished room containing two pallets, two stools, and the table she was currently tied to. Caracal was leaning so far back on one of the stools that it was a miracle he hadn't toppled over. His hand flipped a short dagger into the air, deftly catching it from tip to handle to tip again with every toss.

"Good evening, Your Highness. You caused quite the storm down there," he said sweetly, and Karina was gripped with a sudden wave of panic.

This man knew who she was.

Her first instinct was to scream for help, but her mother's advice cut through the terror. *Don't panic. Analyze your surroundings. Act only when you have a plan.*

Karina swallowed down her fear and took stock of the situation. Caracal knew her true identity, which was less than ideal. But Afua and Dedele weren't here, which meant they were likely safe. And if the mercenary had simply wanted to kill her, he would have done so already. As long as she was alive, she had a chance.

She tried once again to summon her magic—nothing. When that did not work, Karina drew herself up as much as her bindings would allow and spat, "Let me go."

"Only a fool with sheep's wool for brains would let you free after your little display."

A voice behind her chimed in, "I saw a goat turning in your cyclone. It was terrifying. I couldn't look away."

The speaker was the lithe teenager who had bumped into Caracal's opponent during the game of Four Friends. A slanted scar on their right cheek with two small circular scars beneath it marked them as dulyo, one of the divine genders exalted among the people of the Eastwater savanna. They now sat cross-legged on the floor twisting their hair into thick knots, the day's winnings sorted neatly on the ground before them. Seeing the two together made the pieces click together in Karina's mind.

"The game earlier today—you cheated! The two of you worked together to trick that man!"

"*Cheating* is such an ugly word," drawled Caracal. "I prefer to think of it as Ife using their charms to provide me an undisclosed advantage."

The teenager waved. "I'm Ife."

As far as Karina could tell, she was dealing with a pair of petty thieves rather than master torturers. If she was careful about this, perhaps she could make it back on the road to Arkwasi unharmed.

"Clearly you know who I am, so I won't insult you with a lie," Karina said in the sweet voice she'd learned from years of playing the court's mind games. "My name is Karina Zeinab Alahari, and I am most pleased to make your acquaintance."

If there was one thing Karina knew about thieves, it was that they'd do anything for even the chance of coin. Perhaps she could buy both her freedom and their silence. After all, the odds were low that they knew she currently had no more access to her family's riches than the average street urchin did.

She continued, "If your plan is to ransom me back to the palace, I regret to say they will rip you to shreds once they learn what you've done. However, if you let me go unharmed, I guarantee you will be paid a fair sum for your trouble. Surely five hundred daira should be enough to change both your lives for the better?"

Caracal's lips twisted upward. "As if we'd take five hundred measly daira over the thousands tied to your head. I have no idea what you did to upset the council, but the amount they're offering for your return would keep me and Ife comfortable a thousand lifetimes over."

Of course Farid had offered a bounty for her capture; Karina would have done the same were their positions reversed. Yet imagining the man who had raised her reducing her worth to cold numbers and zeroes hit her harder than she'd expected.

"How do you know about that?" she asked, because if she didn't keep speaking she might start crying, and she would personally hand herself over to Farid before she did that. "There is no way that news could have reached Tiru so soon."

"We saw you summon that storm on the last day of Solstasia, and I have my ways of moving fast when I need to. When it happened again here, it wasn't difficult to put the pieces together." Caracal balanced the knife on the tip of his finger. "I'd hand you over to the soldiers downstairs right now if I wasn't worried they'd steal the reward for themselves. No, come morning we're marching you straight back to Ksar Alahari, princess."

Hope slipped through Karina's fingers like yolk through a broken eggshell. If she couldn't lie her way out of this, then there was just one path left: the truth.

"The council is full of traitors who murdered their own queen in a violent bid to grab power for themselves," she began, and it felt so good to let her anger rise after days of suppressing it. "That's why they're hunting me down; they want me out of the way as the rightful ruler. But I have allies waiting for me in Arkwasi who would see me back on my throne. If you release me so that I may go to them, you will be rewarded most handsomely once I've reclaimed what is mine."

"But what about Princess Hanane?" asked Ife. "The line of succession goes elder daughter to younger. She's the rightful ruler, not you."

Ife said this with no malice, yet the words still hit Karina like a smack to the face. They were right—by the laws of Ziran, Hanane *was* ahead of Karina in the line of succession. There had been no doubt about this before . . .

Before her death. Before Karina had burned her alive in an inferno of her own making. She had seen the burn-riddled corpse afterward, which was why she absolutely refused to consider . . .

that *thing* Farid had summoned as her sister.

"The dead are the dead are the dead," Karina said softly. "That monster my steward created has no more right to the throne of Ziran than either of you. The royal family of Arkwasi has been allied with mine for generations, and I know they will take up my cause. You can too. If you help me reclaim my birthright, you will receive something worth more than all the gold in the world—a queen in your debt."

The only sound for a long time was the scratch of the locusts batting against the thin doors. The noise had lessened since the initial attack that morning, but Karina had no doubt that the creatures would return in waves until the gods' anger was sated.

Without warning, Caracal hurled the dagger Karina's way. She flinched back as it landed hilt-up before her, the point dug several inches into the ground.

"If you truly believe the Arkwasians are going to hand you an army the moment you step foot on their lands, then you're a damn fool. What makes you so sure they haven't allied themselves with your enemies already? You have a better chance of finding the lost city of the zawenji than you do amassing an army."

Karina looked at the still-quivering dagger, then up at Caracal, then back to the dagger. Her thoughts returned to the game piece that had moved without anybody touching it. "How do you know that word . . . *zawenji*?" she asked slowly. Suddenly it made perfect sense how the man had been able to catch her so easily, and why he hadn't shown any surprise that she could do magic.

"You know the word *zawenji* because you are one," she said breathlessly. "You're Wind-Aligned, just like me. But all the zawenji in Ziran become Sentinels . . . you were one once, weren't you?"

The pained expression on Caracal's face was all the confirmation Karina needed. Despite their situation, she couldn't help
but feel curious about the man. She'd never met another zawenji
besides Afua and Commander Hamidou . . . well, technically, her
mother had also been one, but Karina had not known that until
after she'd passed.

Coupled with the curiosity was a twinge of sympathy. The Sentinels only existed because her family had been stealing the zawenji
children of Ziran for generations and enchanting them to follow
their masters' every command, no matter how gruesome. She had
seen firsthand how Commander Hamidou had struggled to fight
against the enchantment, and in that moment, Karina missed the
wise old woman so much it was hard to breathe.

However, her sympathy was not enough for her not to use this
new knowledge to her advantage.

"The penalty for deserting the Sentinels is death," she said, and
this time she filled her voice not with the honey of a con artist,
but with the steel of a queen. "Take me back to Ziran, and I will
expose the truth about you. You'll be dead within the hour, and
all this will have been for nothing. But if you choose to keep my
secret . . . you could teach me how to be a proper Wind-Aligned
zawenji, so what happened today doesn't happen ever again."

Karina had expected refusal, or even anger, at her proposition.
What she had not expected was for Caracal to burst into hysterical
laughter.

"Me! Teach you how to use your powers!" he barked between
heaving laughs. "Imagine me as a teacher, holding some brat's hand

like a nursemaid! Ife, tell her just how ridiculous she sounds!"

"Caracal lacks the basic compassion, patience, temperament, and all-around disposition needed to be an effective teacher," Ife replied.

"Blunt, but precise." Caracal wiped a tear from the corner of his eye. "Trust me, princess, you wouldn't want me teaching you how to wipe your own ass, much less how to use magic."

Shoving that crude image aside, Karina snapped, "Then kill me right now, because I will die if you take me back to Ziran, and you will too once I reveal you for the deserter you are."

Karina refused to look away from the glare Caracal threw her. She had no doubt that this man could kill her as easily as he could snap a twig in half—and would feel even less remorse for doing so. But she was also certain that his desire to save his own skin was far stronger than his desire to make a quick profit.

Ife looked at the silent war happening between Caracal and Karina, their brow furrowing in confusion. "What's happening? Is something happening? It feels like something is happening."

Caracal was the first to break the stare. "Mangy, pus-infested wart on Hyena's backside—the only thing that's happening is you and I are going to bed. We can decide what to do with our guest in the morning." He muttered under his breath as he dug in his robe's pocket. "All this zawenji bullshit is such a pain in the ass. I'd be much happier if my powers went away for good."

The man pulled out a pipe and proceeded to stuff a brightly colored substance inside it, light it, and smoke. A heady, fruity smell filled the air as Ife twisted the last of their knots into place before covering their head with a silk scarf for bed. Sensing that all talk was done for the night, Karina settled into the most comfortable position the ropes would allow and silently listened to the locusts buzzing outside. Hopefully, wherever Dedele and Afua were, they were protected from the swarm.

And hopefully Farid and every other person who had ruined her life had been eaten alive by it.

Thinking about the swarm brought Karina's mind back to the message she'd received in the seconds before it had descended. *Where mercy once reigned, now come pestilence. Thus is the price of resurrection without renewal. A ruler to resurrect, a ruler to renew.* Santrofie had warned her of the coming locusts, but why? And what did the second part of that mean?

Karina leaned back and closed her eyes with a frustrated sigh. She'd had enough of gods and riddles to last her for a lifetime. Let her focus on escaping Caracal and Ife first, then she could figure out what her patron deity wanted her to know.

One more night. She had already survived this long. All she had to do was survive one more night.

Another rule of being abducted was that you should never sleep in front of your captors. That was the surest way to end up with a knife between your ribs or worse.

But Karina was so tired, and so much had happened since she'd found Fatima just that morning, that it was a miracle she had stayed awake as long as she had.

So at some point after midnight but before dawn, Caracal's gentle puffs of smoke and Ife's surprisingly loud snores blurred together until Karina was blissfully, foolishly asleep.

At first there was nothing. And then there were trees.

She was in an orchard of some kind, branches of lemon trees waving gently above her. It took her several moments to realize she was dreaming—there was no sign of her captors or her ropes. Yet it felt so real, as if she could pluck any one of the fruits and taste the tart juice on her tongue.

Two voices broke through the silence. The first was low and mocking with a well-honed edge, reminding her of a crocodile pretending to lounge in the mud when really it was waiting for the right moment to strike.

"You can keep this up as long as you like, boy, but surely you realize you are going to tire long before I do."

The second voice was much smaller, but Karina felt the timbre of it beneath her skin.

"That may be true, but even after I tire, you'll still be trapped here."

Malik.

She quickly hid behind one of the trees, torn between curiosity at what was happening and anger that for the second night in a row, she was dreaming of him. At the very least, this time there weren't any strange little girls around.

Curiosity won out, and Karina peeked out from behind the tree trunk at the scene unfolding before her. Malik stood in a clearing, in the center of which was the largest tree she'd seen yet. Tied to it was an enormous black snake whose body was almost as thick as the trunk it was tied to. Her stomach clenched; this had to be the Faceless King.

"I've said it several times now, but I'll say it again: I have no information about the Rite of Renewal to share with you," said the creature, and Karina could hardly believe this writhing black mass had once been Bahia Alahari's husband. Of all the things she'd learned at the end of Solstasia, this was the hardest to wrap her mind around. She'd never felt less than human, but if this thing was her ancestor, what did that make her?

"You were the one who first told Farid about the Rite of Resurrection," replied Malik. "I know you know about the Rite of Renewal. Tell me about it."

The last time Karina had seen Malik in person, he'd been stabbing himself in the heart after offering his body to the very creature he was arguing with. When he'd appeared in her dream last night, she'd struck him so quickly that there hadn't been time to actually look at him.

But now Karina drank him in, her eyes roving over the determined furrow between his brows, the golden undertone of his skin. He seemed different somehow, this boy who had both comforted and betrayed her in equal measure, as if someone had whittled away the excess of him to reveal the essence beneath. Though his hands shook, he stood up to the Faceless King with a bold defiance that made something in Karina's stomach turn over.

Then again, this was all a dream. Her mind was just conjuring what she wanted to see, nothing more.

The Faceless King leered down at Malik, row after row of razor-sharp fangs breaking through his smile.

"Threaten me all you want, but there is no hell you could put me through worse than the one I've already survived. But you may try. And thanks to you, little ulraji, I have nowhere to be but here."

9

Malik

After leaving Farid's workshop, Malik had spent several hours in that bleary half state between meditation and sleep, trying to enter the lemon grove. He had been about to give up when he had opened his eyes to the yellow and green, and the black monster leering at him through it all.

He should have taken that as a sign this was going to go horribly wrong, for the Faceless King's strength was slowly returning if he could now switch from his human form back to his snake one. Malik's control over his mind felt parchment thin, but he could still access the spirit's emotions. Not his thoughts, and certainly not his powers, but this connection was how he knew deep in his bones that the Faceless King was lying about not knowing the Rite of Renewal.

However, Idir knew with just as much certainty that Malik had no way to take this information from him without jeopardizing the binding. So now they were at a stalemate, neither willing to budge until the other did first.

Malik wished that confronting the Faceless King had been a last resort, but Farid had given him this task—his very first as an ulraji apprentice. He couldn't let his mentor down, not when the

Rite of Renewal might be their only chance of avoiding another disaster like the locusts.

"Surely there's something you must want in exchange for information about the ritual?" Malik asked.

"Are you truly offering to make another bargain with me after the last one ended so disastrously for everyone involved?" Idir snorted. "Fine, there is one thing I desire: freedom. Let me out of this wretched prison so I never have to sit through your inane thoughts ever again, and I'll tell you all you wish to know about the Rite of Renewal."

"If I let you go, do you promise not to harm any more humans?"

"I'm not sure you wish to know what the price for that request would be."

"Then, no."

The Faceless King shrugged as much as a snake spirit tied to a giant tree could shrug. "Then watch every person you've ever loved die a gruesome and ultimately preventable death."

Malik took a deep breath and reminded himself that this was how conversing with the grim folk always went in the old stories. It was in their very nature to be as unhelpful as possible, twisting a person's words into so many knots that you'd often leave a conversation with them more confused than when you began. Idir's eyes kept flitting over to the trees behind Malik, but he wasn't stupid enough to turn his back on the spirit. This was just another one of the creature's distraction tactics.

"While you're here, I have a series of demands that will make this body more habitable for the both of us," said Idir. "First of all, you need to sleep more. I hate feeling exhausted all the time.

And why are you so sweaty? I don't think it's healthy for a person to be this moist—"

"I don't want to take the information from you by force, but I will if I have to," Malik warned, and for a second, it looked as if the Faceless King might try to lunge at him, binding be damned. But then his face grew eerily calm.

"You are doing all this to impress that simpering fool you call a mentor, aren't you? Tell me, how much of that bond you feel with him is genuine, and how much of it is you craving the paternal affection your own father never gave you?"

A seed of doubt tugged at Malik, but Idir was not done. "Or perhaps this is motivated by guilt? Do you truly care what happens to Ziran, or are you simply doing this to assuage your conscience over your role in Driss's death?"

Driss's lifeless body flashed before Malik's eyes. "It was an accident," he said, the words sounding hollow to his own ears.

"You might not have pushed him over the edge, but is it still an accident if you did not save him when you could have?"

Malik's memories of Driss's death, so resolute just moments ago, now wavered. That day on the stairs of the Azure Garden, he had reached his hand out to Driss, but the Sun Champion had refused to take it. There was nothing more Malik could have done to save him . . . right?

Leaves began to fall from the lemon trees as Malik's hold on the binding began to slip. He hadn't intentionally killed Driss. He knew he hadn't. That had to be true because the alternative was—no.

The Faceless King's sneer grew, and Malik knew that his own growing panic was exactly what the creature wanted. He felt his grip on the binding loosening, and from the depths of his anger and fear poured the one thing he could think to say that might disarm the spirit.

"You accuse me of acting out of guilt, but yours is heavier than mine could ever be," said Malik. "I'm not the one who had a thousand years to avenge my son and failed."

Even as the words left his mouth, a part of Malik screamed to stop—monster or not, no parent deserved to have their child's death thrown in their face.

But he was *sick* of being tossed around like some kind of plaything. Now all Malik wanted was to make the obosom feel the same helplessness that he felt every day.

He pressed on. "Do you think your son is watching now from wherever his soul resides? Does he see what you have become? How sad it is that not only could his father not protect him in life, he has abandoned him in death as well."

The Faceless King let out a roar that shook the entire grove, and control of the binding came back to Malik as the obosom's thoughts spiraled with rage. The spirit's memories burst to the surface of his consciousness, and without thinking about what he had done or what he was about to do, Malik grabbed the edge of them and pulled.

Trickle stream river trickle stream river trickle stream river flood in flood out every day fish seaweed reef shore trickle stream river trickle stream river flood in flood out trickle stream river again and again and again and again motion and tides in and out never changing never breaking never ending.

He was a single raindrop falling onto Mount Mirazzat. He was a stream bending clear through a canyon pass. He was the Gonyama River roaring to life in an endless cycle of motion and tides and shores and his thoughts were not thoughts because thoughts were for simple creatures like humans, what need did he have for thoughts when he was eons of existence swelling and breaking like the tide, pure motion and power given life, he was endless, he was infinite, he was—

No. *No.* He, Malik, was none of those things because these were the memories of a being tied so deeply to his river that they were one and the same. Malik was still himself, but he did not know how much longer that would be true as the line between where his mind ended and the Faceless King's began eroded.

Trickle stream river trickle stream river movement tides dawn dusk dawn dusk dawn dusk—no, Malik had to pull out of this— trickle stream river motion movement tide in tide out fish and boats and nets and reefs and trickle stream river and through the blur images sprang to life only to dissipate quick as bubbles bursting in the shallows.

An endless prison beneath a cracked, broken sky. A young man with dark eyes and even darker heartbreak.

"Tell me how to revive the dead," Farid asked, and then the bubble burst.

A palace now—no, not just a palace. The silver pillars of Ksar Alahari, but a different time, a different queen. A child ripped from the world by his mother's hand, and a scream ripped from Malik's throat as he—not him, Idir watched his only son die. A war ended, a legacy secured, and a hatred cemented for a thousand years.

Another bubble, another memory. A queen surrounded by high rock walls before a towering statue littered with fluttering white creatures, the air alive with divine power. The dream shifted again, and he was sitting at the bottom of his river, the tendrils of seaweed swaying against him as he stared upward toward the world of humans, craving what could never be. A face peering curiously down into his domain—the same queen from earlier but younger, less broken, less scarred.

What do you wish for? Malik asked, not in the language of words but in the language of breaking tides and swirling eddies, the language of magic. Bahia's eyes crinkling in laughter, his heart swelling with longing and confusion, for what was there to long for when he was already infinite? *Do you wish to see Kennoua fall?*

I don't wish to see Kennoua fall, she sang back, and what he wouldn't have given to lie by her side beneath the desert sun, to feel the touch of her cheek against his skin. *I wish to see Kennoua burn.*

But the doomed romance between Idir and Bahia Alahari was nothing Malik did not already know. Was there any way to steer this flood of memories toward the Rite of Renewal?

However, no mind enjoyed being intruded on, and Idir's had now sensed Malik's unwelcome presence. A pain like a thousand needles pressed into his skin, and it was a terrifying thing, to be in one's own body yet unable to command it. His own mind battled against Idir's, trying and failing to grasp on anything that could help him wrest back control.

He thought of his sisters, and his control grew. He thought of

Farid, of how good it felt to have someone who truly believed in him, but it still wasn't enough. His mind cycled through a million jumbled thoughts that went nowhere.

Until it landed on Karina.

His memories of her were a golden anchor in the onslaught, and Malik latched on to them to keep from being swept away. The soothing calm of her voice when she'd saved him during the raid. Her body flush against his, first when they'd danced the zafuo, then in the necropolis, and then again on the roof of the Sun Temple. The moment he'd tried to kill her and felt their magic connect on a deep, intimate level.

He had few memories of Karina, but it was the intensity of them, the looming realization that whatever was between them still lay unfinished, that allowed Malik to push back to full control. As he did, he saw her so clearly, as if she was right there beside him, battling through the onslaught of Idir's mind same as he was. Against his better judgment, he reached for her, and she grabbed hold of his hand as another burst of memory overwhelmed them.

To complete the Rite of Resurrection, four things you will need . . .

They were the Gonyama River, and the river was watching a group of hooded figures standing around a corpse. Malik didn't recognize their faces, but he recognized the dark tattoos slithering across their skin—the Ulraji Tel-Ra. Karina stiffened beside him.

. . . first, the petals of the blood moon flower, freshly crushed . . .

A low chanting filled the air as the ulraji sprinkled a dark red substance into a fire, just as Farid had on the last night of Solstasia.

. . . the heart of a king, freshly warm . . .

The chanting grew as one of the ulraji threw a glistening, still-beating human heart into the flames as well.

. . . the body of the lost . . .

Together, they lifted the corpse and tossed it into the fire.

. . . complete control of your nkra.

The flames roared a pure, blistering white, and then a hulking figure crawled out of them to cheers of adulation, before the memory shifted to a city under siege. Swarms of locusts tore into flesh as earthquakes rent the ground to bits. The stench of plague filled the air, so thick that even across the centuries Malik felt as if he was drowning in it. An earsplitting roar bellowed in the distance, the sound unlike any creature Malik had ever heard.

Four items to resurrect. Four items to renew.

The Ulraji Tel-Ra hurried forward, a struggling captive in tow.

. . . the scepter to form the altar touched by gods . . .

The leader of the Ulraji Tel-Ra brandished a green scepter with a jackal's head carved into the top, and with it he drew a series of symbols into the ground. From the symbols rose a crystalline structure that shone despite the black-red sky overhead.

. . . a song half-forgotten played on the flute lost to time . . .

A haunting melody filled the air as another one of the ulraji played an ornate flute inlaid with gold. Bile rose up in Malik's throat, but he was powerless to stop the ulraji as they hauled their captive to the edge of a vast lake.

. . . a psalm prayed near water that connects this world and the next . . .

Another roar from the unseen beast as the ulraji said their prayer, the water of the lake sloshing with a variety of colors unnatural to their world.

   . . . and the soul of a queen, to bind it all together.

They removed the sack from their captive's head, revealing an old woman with long tattooed marks down her face and an elegant jeweled tiara across her forehead. Before she could even scream for help, the ulraji shoved her into the water, her body sinking silent as a stone beneath the waves. The tremors and the pestilence and the storm mounted and the hellish creature screamed again, barreling toward the lake—

And stopped.

The destruction calmed, the world shifted into peace once again, the monster vanished into thin air. The ulraji celebrated among themselves, imminent destruction narrowly averted. But there was no joy in Malik, for the full weight of what they had just seen and the meaning of Susono's warning slammed into him.

To perform the Rite of Renewal, they were going to have to sacrifice a queen.

If they didn't, the world as they knew it would be gone forever.

10

Karina

Karina knew this was just a dream. She *knew* it. But after the locusts, and her own powers spiraling out of control, and being captured by Caracal, watching the Ulraji Tel-Ra—the very people who had enslaved her ancestors—sacrifice an innocent person was too much. A scream poured from her mouth, and though he looked just as frightened as she was, Malik dropped to his knees beside her, his hand on her back the only thing keeping her from collapsing into the dirt.

"Get away from me!" she screamed, pulling away from his soft touch, and she was still screaming when she slammed awake in the caravanserai. Her captors stared down at her, eyes blurry with sleep. The only other sound besides Karina's frantic breathing was a gentle tapping at the shutters.

"What's the matter with you?" demanded Caracal.

"Nothing, it's just—a nightmare. I had a nightmare," she forced out. The man muttered something about princesses ruining his damn sleep before rolling back onto his pallet. Ife eventually succumbed to slumber too, leaving Karina to puzzle out what she had just seen.

The last thing she remembered was desperately fighting off

sleep here in the caravanserai. Then the next thing she knew, she'd been dreaming of Malik arguing with the Faceless King, and that had turned into some kind of vision? A vision of ancient Kennoua, the Rite of Renewal, and . . .

. . . and the end of the world.

It sounded silly to think in such absolute terms, but there was no other way to describe the complete desolation she'd witnessed.

Here was what Karina knew for sure—first, the Rite of Resurrection had only been one half of a greater whole meant to be done in tandem with the Rite of Renewal.

Second, after the Ulraji Tel-Ra had performed the Rite of Resurrection, disaster after disaster had torn Sonande apart, starting with locusts like the ones that had descended this morning. It was only after they had performed the Rite of Renewal that the destruction had ended.

Third, while the Rite of Resurrection had required the beating heart of a king, the Rite of Renewal required the soul of a queen.

And last, she was the only queen in Sonande for a thousand miles.

Terror, thick and cold, crawled through Karina's chest, and she suddenly felt like a child again, wishing for her parents' comfort after a bad dream. But there were no parents for her now, no sister. Just herself, and the chilling reality that her death might be the only thing that could save their world.

Ife's comment from earlier ran through her head. *But what about Princess Hanane? She's the rightful ruler, not you.*

As much as Karina loathed admitting it, a solid argument could be made that the resurrected monster had a claim to the throne. If Karina passed the title of sultana to the lich, perhaps it could be sacrificed for the ritual instead . . . were it not for Farid. After all he'd gone through to perform the Rite of Resurrection, Farid would murder every person in Sonande before he let anyone lay a finger on the lich's head. The Eshrans had no monarch, and the queen mother of the Arkwasi, the Arkwasi-hema, was too well guarded deep in the jungle for anyone to get to her.

Which meant that the only queen available for the Rite of Renewal was Karina herself.

The first hints of a migraine pulsed at the back of Karina's head, the aura that preceded it muddling her thoughts. A cruel voice in her mind not unlike her mother's whispered, *Tunde gave his life for the first ritual. It's only fair you should give yours for the second.*

Tears burned Karina's eyes as the small voice grew louder. There had to be a way to save Sonande without sacrificing herself. If only that incessant tapping would cease, maybe she'd be able to get her thoughts in order.

Tap. Tap. Tap.

At first Karina had assumed it was just the locusts, but it was now far too loud for that. She glimpsed the quickest flash of movement through the thick wooden beams Caracal had nailed over the windows to keep out the insects before someone screamed far below.

"The stables! Somebody's let the animals loose from the stables!"

The screeching of animals mixed with the confused cries of the inn's guests jerking awake filled the air. It wasn't hard for Karina to imagine the absolute chaos happening in the courtyard right now as dozens of horses, camels, and beasts of every type rushed madly for freedom.

Caracal's Sentinel training must have kicked in, for he was up in seconds with a warrior's precision and no sign of fatigue. He swore loudly, yelled at Ife to keep watch over Karina, and ran to check the status of their animals. Karina and Ife stared at one another.

"I don't suppose you know any good jokes?" they asked, and before Karina could respond, someone crashed through the shutters and shoved a dagger against Ife's throat.

"Don't scream or I'll cut you open," warned Dedele.

Ife shrugged the shoulder that wasn't pressed against Dedele's side. "Honestly, I was expecting someone to come for her sooner. Someone always comes for the captured princess."

"Karina! We're here!" Afua hauled herself through the window with far less grace than Dedele had and ran over to Karina's side. Warmth spread through Karina's body as Afua's magic untied the knots binding her to the table. Karina jumped to her feet, wobbly after so many hours trapped in the same position, as Ife watched it all unfold with active excitement.

"If you're going to tie me up, make sure you get my legs too," they suggested. "Oh, oh, and you should blindfold me so I can't tell anyone how you got out." At Afua's and Dedele's confused glances, Ife shrugged again. "It's a staple of every good story that at some point someone ties you up and leaves you for dead. I don't know when this will happen again, so I need to take advantage of the opportunity while I can."

Karina and her companions did just that. Once they were sure Ife was secure, Karina covered herself with the cloak her friends had brought her, and they raced out of the caravanserai.

The courtyard of the inn was in complete disarray, for not only had Dedele and Afua released all the animals, they had also destroyed most of the merchandise. Now merchants were yelling at merchants, soldiers were yelling at soldiers, and one particularly ecstatic donkey was galloping off into the moonlit night. Coupled with the damage from earlier, Tiru was in such chaos that no one noticed the trio slipping out of the village toward Dedele's ship.

"Three times I've saved your ass now, princess!" Dedele barked as they hauled themselves over the sand barge's railing.

"Luckily for you, it's quite the ass to save!" Karina screamed back.

They quickly settled into their usual spots, and Dedele began to raise the sail. "Back on course to Osodae?"

Karina's mind still reeled from all she'd learned. As much as she hated to admit it, Caracal's argument that the Arkwasians would not help her had merit. Setting aside the fact that Farid might already be in contact with them, who was to say that once they learned of the Rite of Renewal, they wouldn't choose to sacrifice her in order to protect their own queen mother? If Karina were in their position, she wasn't sure she'd side with an outsider over one of her own.

"No, not Osodae," she said.

Dedele balked. "I thought the plan was to get you to Osodae so you could meet with the Arkwasi-hene and those zawenji Afua knows? If we're not going there, where are we going?"

"Give me a second!" Karina crouched on the ship's deck and placed her pounding head between her knees.

Going to Arkwasi was too risky, and returning to Ziran was out of the question. The Eshrans were powerless to help her, and her family's relationship with the various tribes of the Eastwater savanna had always been tenuous at best. All of Sonande was a viper pit, and Karina was the hapless hare desperately trying to navigate her way through it.

And then there were the omens, each one worse than the last until there would be no corner of Sonande left to destroy. Even if she somehow found someone willing to ally with her to defeat Farid, the win would be worthless if the world ended.

There had to be a solution that could solve both her problems—revenge against Farid and quelling the gods' wrath without having to sacrifice herself. Karina parsed through the dream once more until her thoughts landed on the glimpse she'd seen of Bahia Alahari in a cavern surrounded by all seven patron deities.

Karina's head snapped up. To Afua, she asked, "Have you heard of the lost city of the zawenji?"

Afua bit her lip. "I have. My teachers called it Doro Lekke— the Sanctum. They said it was the center of zawenji magic in the old world, before it was almost destroyed during the Pharaoh's War."

"Where is it?"

"No one knows. The people of Doro Lekke put an enchantment over it so that it's always moving. The knowledge of the city's changing whereabouts and the key to it were entrusted to a single immortal guardian."

Dedele looked between Afua and Karina as if they had both lost their minds. "Enchanted cities? Immortal guardians? We don't have time for this right now, we have to leave!"

The explanation lay on the tip of Karina's tongue, but something stopped her from sharing it. In the wrong hands, the truth about the Rite of Renewal could mean her death. But who could she trust if not these girls who had given up everything to save her? She never would have made it this far without them, and she'd need their help if this fledgling plan of hers was ever going to bloom.

Heart in her throat, Karina quickly summarized the destruction she had seen in the vision, how the Rite of Renewal had been the only thing to end it, and what must be sacrificed to perform it.

"Do you remember the story of how the gods personally granted Bahia Alahari the power that allowed her to defeat the pharaoh once and for all? Back in the caravanserai, I saw a vision of the moment they blessed her with all seven zawenji powers. It happened inside Doro Lekke. If we can find the city, we can take the power for ourselves and defeat Farid before he can perform the Rite of Renewal."

By the time she was done, the other girls were staring at her, their expressions unreadable. "So if no one performs the Rite of Renewal before the last omen, the Great Mother is going to destroy Sonande?" Afua squeaked out, for once sounding like the child she truly was. "E-Everybody is going to die?"

"That's why we need to change course," Karina argued. "I know Farid, and I have no doubt that once he hears of the ritual, he's going to double his efforts to capture me. But if we get to the Sanctum first and obtain the power hidden there, we can stop him. And we might be able to appease the gods to stop this attack on Sonande before it gets any worse."

There was a chance that Farid would never learn of the Rite of Renewal, but it was slim. As for Malik . . . had that actually been him in the dream? Karina had no idea who he truly was, or whose side he was on. She didn't even know exactly how his magic worked. But whoever he was, he couldn't be trusted.

Afua began to nod slowly, but Dedele's grimace had only deepened. "But killing Farid won't change the fact that a queen needs to be sacrificed to stop the omens from striking Sonande."

Dedele's demeanor shifted ever so slightly, and a warning bell rang through Karina's mind. She unconsciously took a step away from her friend. "Magic like this always has a loophole. Once we obtain the power of the gods, we can exploit it."

"The Rite of Resurrection had no loophole," said Dedele, and Karina's stomach turned over at the memory of Tunde's desecrated body. "If that ritual required a royal sacrifice, I don't see how you can avoid one now."

Dedele had always had a rather sharp demeanor, but this side of her was something new entirely. Karina took another step back. She bumped against the barge's railing, nowhere to go.

"Exactly what do you want me to do? Am I supposed to just walk back to Ziran and surrender myself to Farid?"

"You said yourself the swarm was only the first omen, and that each one would be worse than the last. If what happened to Tiru is happening all over Sonande, that's millions of people who would be saved if you—" Dedele stopped abruptly, and Karina wondered just how many people in her life were going to turn their backs on her when she needed them most.

"Say it," Karina spat, the wind around them dangerously still.

"I know you don't want to sacrifice yourself," said Dedele, her fingers flexing like she was itching to grab something. "I don't want you to *have* to sacrifice yourself. But if the choice is to give up one life or lose millions of others . . . the answer is obvious, isn't it?"

When put so plainly, the answer *was* obvious. No one life could ever be worth more than millions. But when that life was *her* life . . . perhaps Karina truly was the selfish monster everyone seemed to think she was, because she knew then, with a gut-wrenching certainty that she did not want to die, even if it meant every other person in Sonande could live.

The realization must have dawned on her face, for in an instant, Dedele's expression shifted into that of the fierce fighter Karina had first met during wakama. She unsheathed the dagger strapped to her waist and flipped it around so that the point aimed straight toward Karina's chest. Dedele lunged for her, and it was pure luck that Karina dove out of the way before the blade caught her in the shoulder.

"You promised you would protect me!" Karina screamed. The wind batted weakly at them, agitated at Karina's distress.

"That was before we knew how angry the gods are!" Dedele cried, and the anguish Karina heard there hurt almost as much as the betrayal did. "I'm not going to sit by and watch the world end if all it takes is one sacrifice to save it!"

Karina had one leg over the railing of the ship before Dedele hooked an arm around her neck and yanked her backward. Even though the former Fire Champion only meant to subdue her, Dedele did not pull back any of her blows. Afua's head whipped back and forth between them, unsure of who to help as they went rolling across the deck.

For all her magic, Karina's physical strength was nothing compared to Dedele's, and stars danced in her eyes as she kicked and clawed uselessly against the bigger girl. Great Mother be damned, had she really come so far and lost so much just to be handed over to Farid by one of the few friends she'd thought she had left?

No. *No.*

With a strangled cry, Karina channeled her power into Dedele and pulled. The air in the other girl's lungs whooshed out of her body, and Dedele's eyes bulged from her sockets as she let Karina go. Gasping like a fish dropped on land, the former Fire Champion's hands scrabbled at her neck, as if that might somehow pull the air back into them. Her last expression was one of complete condemnation before she fell to the deck, her body deathly still. Only then did Karina snap the thread of power free.

She was barely aware of her own body as she rose to her feet, her head ringing like a bell. Afua crawled over to their friend—even after what had just happened, Karina couldn't think of Dedele as anything but—and pressed two fingers to her neck.

"She's still breathing," Afua declared, and Karina let out a sound of relief. She hadn't killed her.

But she could have. It would have been so easy to do too, and that was what frightened her most.

"What . . . what are we going to do now?" asked Afua, her voice laced with fear. Karina's mind whirled, trying to sort through the ever-shrinking list of paths open to them. They could technically move the ship using Afua's power alone, but neither of them had Dedele's expertise in avoiding the dangers that stalked the desert. Trying to find Doro Lekke on their own was akin to suicide.

What they needed was someone who knew their way around the desert, who could help Karina reach the lost city quickly and safely. Someone who had more to gain from the success of her mission than from her failure, and who already knew the truth about magic.

Someone like Caracal.

Karina turned to Afua, taking in the wideness of her friend's eyes, the sweat sheening her brow from all the magic she's been expending. Afua should have been running around without a care in the world like other children, not embarking on a dangerous quest to who knew where.

"I think I know someone who can help us find Doro Lekke." Honestly, Caracal was just as likely to run a sword through her gut as to help her, but the risk seemed worth taking compared to certain death. "I know this isn't what was promised when we fled Ziran. If you would like to return to your family instead, I understand."

Letting Afua go free when she knew as much as she did went against everything Karina's mother had taught her about protecting herself, but Karina didn't care. No matter how desperate or hopeless things may seem, she would never harm Afua.

Never.

The Life-Aligned girl was quiet for a long time as she looked down at Dedele's unconscious form. When she raised her head, determination filled her eyes. "I promised you I would see you to safety, so that's what I'm going to do," she declared. "Besides, us zawenji need to stick together. My family has one another—you have me."

A lump of affection rose in Karina's throat, and she awkwardly passed it off as a cough. She gave one last look at Dedele and found only sadness where her anger should have been.

"Let's go," she said to Afua, already beginning to scramble down the side of the ship.

Whatever happened next, they needed to be far away from Dedele when she woke up . . . whenever that might be.

"You do realize that when most people escape from someone who's held them hostage, they don't go back, right?"

Karina bit back an irritated response, not wanting to anger her last chance at help. Sneaking back into the caravanserai had been easier than sneaking out of it had been, so now she and Afua stood in the doorway while an incredulous Caracal stared down at them, half looking as if he might tie her up again simply for annoying him.

"I have a proposition for you. A better one this time," she said quickly. Ife peeked over the man's shoulder and waved—good, someone had untied them.

Caracal raised an eyebrow, and though he didn't move from the door to let them in, he didn't reach for his blades either. "Luckily for you, the stampede earlier has me wide awake. Let's hear it."

"Remember the lost city of zawenji you mentioned earlier? It's real. I've seen it, and I think if we work together, we can find it. Once there, I'm going to follow in the footsteps of my ancestor Bahia Alahari to obtain the blessing of the gods in order to take back Ziran."

Caracal's incredulous look didn't waver, so she added, "Think about what reaching Doro Lekke would mean for you too. You said you wanted to get rid of your magic? This is your best chance. The power at Doro Lekke is strong enough to strip it from even the most powerful of zawenji. By the time you get out, you'll be an entirely different person. One with no ties left to the Sentinel life you left behind."

Karina did not believe in destiny. She detested chance. But she knew opportunity when she saw it, and one stretched before her now, tinged with blades and battle scars. After all, when Bahia Alahari had made this journey, she had changed the world. If it had worked for her ancestor, surely it would work for her too.

Karina held her breath as she watched Caracal weigh the chance to be rid of his powers against the risk of being caught aiding Sonande's most wanted fugitive.

"We'll need supplies," Caracal said slowly, and Karina bit back a rather undignified squeal of glee. "And if we don't find this secret magic city, I reserve the right to hand you over to the soldiers and become ridiculously wealthy at any time."

"Understood. And after we find this secret magic city, my promise from before stands. Once I am sultana again, I will pardon your desertion from the Sentinels and you will be free—from both your magic and your past."

Fire blazed in Caracal's eyes, and Karina knew then that no magic or god would be able to stand between the man and the one thing he craved most of all—freedom. No doubt he'd cut her down the first chance he got if that might help him achieve it.

Karina could work with ruthlessness. You couldn't be betrayed by someone you didn't trust.

She stretched out her hand. "Do we have a deal?"

He clasped her hand with one of his own. Karina wasn't sure if she imagined the wind vibrating around them in anticipation of this union between two zawenji of the same Alignment.

Caracal gave her a smile befitting the wildcat he was named after. "We do, Your Highness."

11

Malik

Farid took the knowledge that they were all about to die far better than Malik had expected him to.

"Of course. The heart of a king for resurrection. The soul of a queen for renewal. Two rituals. Two sacrifices."

Malik nodded along with his mentor, too preoccupied with the pain radiating up his arm to join in his enthusiasm. After plunging into Idir's memories, Malik had only regained control of his body when he'd cut along the inside of his right forearm. Just like during his test, the bright bloom of pain had helped, but now both his arms were bleeding and sore.

Farid had yet to acknowledge either bandage as he paced animatedly around his workshop. "When I first visited the Faceless King years ago, he made no mention that the Rite of Resurrection was only the first of two rituals."

That blathering excuse for a monkey's refuse didn't ask.

Malik decided it was best not to share the spirit's commentary. And he shouldn't be disappointed that Farid hadn't noticed his wound either. They had far more important things to worry about than him.

"All this feels so familiar," Malik mused. "Pestilence, followed by quakes, followed by plague, followed by monsters. I know I've heard this before, somewhere."

Farid mulled over his words for several minutes, then his eyes lit up. He dug through the piles upon piles of documents on his desk until he pulled out an ancient bundle of loose parchment held together by fraying thread. On it was an image of griot sitting on a log in front of a roaring fire, a gaggle of children in a half-moon around him—a book of children's folktales.

"'The Tale of the Four Friends,'" Farid said triumphantly, and after flipping to the desired page, he began to read aloud.

In the olden days of traveling and suffering, four friends—a monarch, a fool, a prophet, and a beast—gathered together to enjoy each other's company as old friends do. At first the food and conversation flowed well, until the monarch declared that he alone in all Sonande had power to rival that of the Great Mother.

"This must be so, for why I else would I have so many lands filled with so many sweet fruits to eat?" he claimed.

Now, this was during the time when the gods were closer to our world than they are now. Upon hearing the monarch's boasting, the Great Mother kissed her teeth and said, "If this is what you believe, then I shall send a swarm to devour all your sweet fruits, until your lands grow bare and your children go hungry. Then you shall know there is none who rivals me."

"Does this not resemble what happened to us yesterday?" Farid pointed to the illustration on the next page, which depicted a cloud of insects hovering over a field of wheat as frightened people ran for cover.

But though the locusts ate until the fields were bare, the four friends did not heed the warning. The next day they met again, and this time it was the prophet who claimed, "Surely I must be the only one with power to rival the Great Mother, for why else would the skies always clear so beautifully whenever I give my orations?"

Upon hearing the prophet's boasting, the Great Mother kissed her teeth and said, "If this is what you believe, then I shall shake the earth from its core, until there is nowhere to stand for people to hear you speak. Then you shall know there is none who rivals me."

The next illustration showed an earthquake tearing a small village into bits. This continued for the next two friends—when the fool and the beast also boasted of their prowess, the Great Mother called down first a sickness and then a massive nightmare creature to tear across Sonande and humble their egos.

It was the latter that made Malik pause. Because the tale did not specify what the Great Mother's monster looked like, the artist had drawn a mishmash of every creature imaginable, with horns and claws and scales all along its body. It was a thousand times more frightening than the bushwalkers Nana had used to scare him with, and he shuddered to think what would happen if he ever came face-to-face with such a thing.

Only one creature realized what was happening— Osansa, the gray kestrel. Mourning the arrogance that had destroyed the world, she took her scepter to create an altar on the water, and she played on her flute a tune so beautiful it drew the Great Mother's attention to her. Then she prayed with her heart laid bare before the god above all gods, and because it was beautiful, and pure, and true, the Great Mother took her life as payment to spare Sonande, and all was well once more.

Malik could not tear his eyes away from the image of Osansa bleeding away on the altar as the people of Sonande rejoiced thanks to her sacrifice. It was a gruesome story, but all the best children's tales were.

"Did this actually happen?" he asked, and Farid shook his head.

"All stories contain a thread of truth; that's what makes them worth telling. I doubt the events happened literally as depicted, but I believe it refers to the Rite of Renewal all the same. Sometime far in the past, someone performed the Rite of Resurrection without doing the Rite of Renewal, and the gods retaliated. Then the tale became relegated to children's myth to pass the lesson along that the rituals should never be separated."

Farid tossed the book haphazardly back onto the pile and gave Malik a warm smile.

"Now that we have a plan, I will share it with the council so that we can mobilize our forces and capture Karina as quickly as possible."

"You're going to kill Karina?" Malik wasn't sure why he was so surprised. Of course Karina was the most logical sacrifice for the ritual. It wasn't like they could just pluck a queen off the streets and be on their way.

But there was something about the nonchalance with which Farid discussed murdering the princess that unsettled him. The two had grown up together; Farid and Karina even shared the same age gap that Malik and Nadia did, meaning he had likely helped raise her. Yet Farid spoke of her death so . . . easily.

Farid peered at him. "Does the thought of sacrificing her bother you?"

"It's just I've been . . . seeing her, recently. In my dreams, that is. Not those kinds of dreams!" he added quickly as his mentor raised an eyebrow. "It's more like, whatever I see, she's seeing too. At first I thought it was just in my head, but when I had the vision tonight, she was there. I don't know how that's possible, but if it's true, that means she knows about the Rite of Renewal as well."

Farid's smirk flattened into a thin line. "And why didn't you mention this before?"

"I—I didn't think it was actually her at first. I don't understand how this is even happening."

His mentor ran a hand down his face and slowly blew out. "It was your power and hers combined that destroyed the Barrier surrounding Ziran. It's possible that in that moment the amount of nkra you shared was so great, you each left a spark of your power inside the other. Not enough for you to use her magic or for her to use yours, but perhaps enough to let her access your mind in moments of vulnerability, such as when you're asleep."

"So Karina and I are connected now?" Malik's heart twisted in on itself as he scrambled to think of anything incriminating about him Karina might have glimpsed. "She can just see inside my head whenever she wants?"

"If my theory is correct, then yes, though probably not with any sort of precision. However, this also means you should be able to see inside hers."

This had to be some kind of mistake. Exactly how many people were inside Malik's head, and what did he have to do to get them all out?

Farid continued, "You must do everything in your power to guard your mind from Karina. We can't risk her learning of our plans through you. If she appears before you again, let me know immediately."

Malik bit his lip and looked down, a swirl of emotion he could not name filling his chest.

"Are you sure killing her is the only way to complete the ritual?" He wasn't sure why he'd asked that. Now that he no longer needed Karina to die so that Nadia could live, what happened to her wasn't his concern. And yet he couldn't stomach the thought of her lying on some altar with her head cracked open like the kestrel in the story. "Maybe we could go after the Arkwasi-hema or some other, smaller regional queen—"

"Malik, are you in love with Karina?" Farid asked, and Malik wished that the earth would swallow him whole.

"No!" Of course he wasn't. He didn't even know Karina, not truly. Besides, she'd made it very clear what she thought about him when she'd chosen to be with Tunde over him after the Third Challenge.

And yet there were moments when she'd look at him, and Malik would wonder if maybe . . . just possibly . . .

"Oh, Malik." Farid sighed in the tone of a parent delivering an uncomfortable truth their child was not ready to hear. "Anyone can see that you and Karina forged a connection during Solstasia. I know well how heady that feeling can be—that someone you desire might desire you back. But it was a lie. I've seen Karina do the same to others just like you time and time again—promise them the world only to cut out their heart and throw it at their feet when she got bored.

"I mean, what do you have to offer her, truly? Karina has had suitors from every corner of Sonande vying for her hand since before she was born. Princes and wise men, people with more wealth than you could possibly imagine. Compared to that, what about you—a farm boy from a tiny town in Eshra—would appeal to her? You, a descendant of the very people her family has spent centuries trying to eradicate? At best Karina considers you a threat to be dealt with. And at worst? You are nothing."

Farid put a hand under Malik's chin, so he could look nowhere but at him.

"But when *I* look at you, Malik, I see a boy with the potential to become one of the most powerful men this world has ever seen. But you'll never get the chance to be all that you can be if we don't complete the Rite of Renewal, and to do that, we're going to have to sacrifice Karina."

Farid wasn't saying anything Malik hadn't already known. Of course he and Karina existed on opposite ends of the social structure. Of course compared to the suitors she'd had in the past, compared to *Tunde*, he was nothing. But hearing it from another person—realizing that every one of the flaws he'd spent so long picking apart were so obvious to everyone around him—pushed him to a new level of humiliation. If someone were to cut him open right then, surely they'd find nothing but air where his heart should have been.

"Don't let Karina waste any more of your time than she already has," said Farid. "Let me focus on finding her. You focus on locating the scepter and the flute for the ritual. Of course, if you feel you're not up to this task, I completely understand. I will never make you do something you're not comfortable with."

A thousand emotions warred within Malik, but one floated to the surface—a primal, burning need to prove that he was more than the stupid farm boy from the backwater corner of the world nobody cared about. More than a plaything for a princess to spit on and throw away.

He didn't want to be nothing anymore. Farid was offering him the key out of that life—if only he was brave enough to take it.

"I'll do it," he said softly. "I'll help you complete the ritual."

Malik had agreed to Farid's plan, but he did not have final say on whether to execute it.

Princess Hanane did.

That was why, a few hours later, Malik found himself standing beside his mentor in the throne room as he explained what Malik had discovered about the Rite of Renewal to the princess, the council, and the highest-ranking courtiers. The locusts still raged outside, but this deep inside the palace, they were a terrifying but ultimately survivable menace.

There were nearly fifty people in attendance, the majority being the highest-ranking scholars, merchants, nobles, and other upper echelons of the Zirani elite who had a stake in the coup. The combined wealth of all the people in this hall was enough to buy Oboure several times over, and every time Malik remembered this, he felt like a child dressed in a grown man's clothes—amusing, but grossly out of place.

But even more surprising than the people who were in attendance were the people who weren't. Driss's family, for one—no one had seen them since his untimely death right before the Third Challenge. A glaring absence, considering the Rhozalis were one of the most powerful families in Ziran.

A death you caused. You're the reason he's not here, and you know it, whispered the Faceless King, and Malik forced away the memory of Driss's mangled, twisted body lying at the bottom of the Azure Garden stairs.

The other glaring absence was Tunde. Their last full conversation had been an argument, and it pained Malik that things between them had ended on such a tense note. He prayed that the rumor his friend had run off with Karina wasn't true, though whether this was because he did not want to imagine the Water Champion as his enemy, or because he did not want to imagine the two together, he didn't know.

But though Tunde was not present, his family was. They sat huddled close together, cocooned in a thick nervousness that kept the other members of the court from bothering them. However, all eyes were on Princess Hanane and her reaction as Farid explained that the only way to avert the disaster coming for them all was to capture her sister. Just like Malik, none of them knew what to make of the undead princess, and they all watched each tilt of her hand and twitch of her jaw for any sign of the unnatural.

The princess kept her expression impassive, and only when Farid was finished did she ask, "You are certain that the only way to appease the Great Mother's anger is through this ritual?"

Farid nodded. "All things in this world demand equilibrium; magic is no different. When that equilibrium is disturbed, chaos reigns, as we are seeing now with the locusts."

A flutter of unease rippled through the room. Though Farid had revealed the existence of magic to the people during Solstasia, few trusted it.

"And how much of this is connected to my . . . return?"

"The power I used to resurrect you contributed to this shift in the balance, yes." Farid had warned Malik beforehand that he would only be giving the court bits and pieces of the truth, for he did not trust them with all of it. "But you yourself contain no magic."

Princess Hanane turned her attention to Malik, and his entire body stiffened under the weight of her gaze. "And what about him? How do we know this isn't his doing, or the Faceless King's through him?"

Fifty pairs of eyes snapped Malik's way. He snapped at Tunde's rubber bracelet to quell the bolt of fear that lurched through him.

"I did some research into him after he was named Life Champion," added Grand Vizier Jeneba from where she stood behind the throne with the other council members. "The records for Adil Asfour only go back a few years. Isn't it suspicious that all this turmoil only began when this boy arrived in our city?"

Malik could practically feel the suspicion rolling through the crowd. The penalty for illegally entering Ziran was torture, but what was the punishment for lying to the entire court in order to participate in one of Ziran's most sacred traditions? And if they were this angry about his false identity, how much angrier would they be when they discovered he was an ulraji? What would they do to him? To Leila and Nadia?

The answer was simple: nothing, because he wouldn't let them. He was more powerful than every person in this room. With a single illusion he could trap them here until they forgot everything they thought they knew about him and his family. They'd be completely at his mercy—

No! Malik dug his nails into his thigh, hissing as the sudden pain brought him back to himself. Why was he even thinking this? Ulraji or no, he would never be someone who used magic solely to get his way. That was the Faceless King talking, not him.

And thank the Great Mother that Malik did not have to defend himself, for Farid cut in, "You are correct that this boy is not really Adil Asfour. His real name is Malik, and from the start, he had his suspicions about Karina. When he brought them to me, I had him conceal his identity so that he could investigate her in secret. He is a hero, and should be treated as such."

Farid turned to him. "Thank you for all you've done for Ziran, Malik," he said, and it was the strangest feeling, hearing his true name finally spoken at court—but not an unpleasant one.

Malik might have been the storyweaver, but Farid was the one who truly worked words into magic. With just a few lies, the court's suspicion had melted into appreciation. Only Princess Hanane still regarded him with that cold gaze, and though a part of Malik wanted to curl up and hide, he lifted his head defiantly to stare back at her. He might not belong here, but neither did she, and it didn't seem fair to let her cow him like this.

"Malik isn't the threat, Hanane," Farid said softly. "Karina is."

The timbre of his voice shifted, as if this was a private conversation between the two of them. "The final choice of what we do with her rests in your hands. But before you make your decision, you should know the girl you once loved is gone; the one who replaced her is a threat to both you and your people. Don't allow sweet memories of the past to cloud your judgment of the present."

Hanane remained still save for the slightest curl of her hands around the arms of the throne. What Farid was asking her to do— to sanction the hunt and eventual execution of her own sister . . . Malik didn't know how a person could do such a thing and come out of it with their soul intact.

But perhaps the princess had lost her soul on the way back to this life, for she gave the slightest of nods. "Do what you must to protect Ziran."

Some of the tension in the room dissipated then, and the conversation shifted to the logistics of mobilizing the Zirani army and strategies to poison the locusts and protect the city. The grand vizier had begun to call the meeting to a close when Tunde rose to his feet.

Wait—no, this wasn't Tunde. Just a boy who looked alarmingly like him. One of his younger brothers, most likely.

"Thank you for providing us with information after the chaos of Solstasia." The angry glint in the boy's eye belied his polite tone. "But I have one question for you: Where is my brother?"

The council exchanged uncomfortable looks as Farid's gaze swept over the boy. "What is your name?" he asked gently.

"Adewale. My older brother was Adetunde, the winner of Solstasia."

A thud rang through the air as Hanane bolted out of her seat, her hand clutching her chest. "Adetunde's brother," she whispered. "You're Adetunde's . . . my—"

"Let me handle this, Your Highness," Farid said sharply. Hanane blinked out of her daze before sinking sheepishly back into her seat. Her eyes remained trained on the young man, as if he might disappear if she looked away for even a second.

Farid turned back to Adewale, his court-practiced smile back in place. "As to your question, Adewale, I'd be happy to discuss this further in private—"

"None of us has seen nor heard from my brother since the prayers at the Sun Temple," interrupted the boy, and irritation flickered across Farid's face. "He would not have left the city without telling us. So where is he? I want to see him right now."

Murmurs of unease rippled through the crowd, and Farid's eyes narrowed. Slowly, his mouth slipped into a sad smile. "I was hoping to wait until after the meeting to approach your family in private, but if you truly want to know here and now . . ." He turned to the nearest Sentinel. "Please fetch Adetunde."

After what felt like far too long, the Sentinel returned, a large white bundle in his hands. Fear muted his senses to a dull roar. There was no way—that couldn't be—

"It seems that after the Sun Temple, Adetunde discovered what Karina had been plotting, and he went to confront her," Farid said quietly. "When he did, she did this."

The Sentinel uncovered the cloth from Tunde's corpse, and the scream that his mother let out at the sight of the bloody, gaping hole where her son's heart should have been would haunt Malik for the rest of his days.

Malik's vision tunneled to a single pinprick. He knew death. He'd seen it linger for years over a person, slowly ruining them bit by bit until they were practically a corpse on their feet. He'd seen it steal an infant straight from its mother's arms, and he'd seen it parade through a village in royal armor to slaughter innocents.

But Tunde was the opposite of death. Tunde was warm and bright and *good*. He couldn't be dead, and certainly not at the hands of the girl he had loved, who had been given the choice between him and Malik and had chosen him.

Yet the proof was right there. The screaming had stopped— Tunde's mother had fainted, and now the other members of her family were trying to attend to her. Adewale had fallen to his knees by his brother's side. Bile sloshed hot and thick in Malik's stomach, and he watched as several members of the court became sick before them. Princess Hanane had frozen completely, her mouth open as if to form words though none came out.

"I know it's hard to believe. I didn't want to believe it myself," said Farid, his voice ragged with grief. "Karina was . . . I raised her. I loved her like a sister, and that love made me blind to who she really was. What she was capable of. She murdered both her father and her mother. And she murdered Tunde too."

An angry buzz roared through the crowd, reminiscent of the energy during Solstasia, but deeper, sharper. Farid raised his voice to be heard above the din.

"This is the evil that has so greatly angered the Great Mother. It is dark magic descending to swallow our homes. It is brothers stolen from our sides simply for seeking the truth. Karina will stop at nothing to claim what she so arrogantly believes is hers, and we must stand together as a united front until this threat to our people is eradicated!"

This couldn't be true. Farid was—this had to be some kind of mistake. But the crowd was in a complete frenzy now. Even if Karina had appeared right then with the light of the Great Mother washing over her, the people would have torn her limb from limb without hesitation.

And yet, through it all, Malik could only focus on the sobbing of Tunde's brother, completely forgotten among the screams for justice and blood.

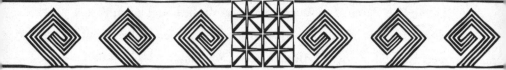

Let us return to the boy, yes?

The baby grows, as babies tend to do, and so do both the boy and the girl. The setting this time is the sultana's garden, on a warm afternoon that should have been no different from the hundreds that had preceded it and the hundreds that would follow.

The children loved the garden, and every spare moment they did not spend studying with their tutors or attending royal gatherings, they spent there. They were not supposed to be in the garden that day. As heiress to the throne, Hanane was busy from sunrise to sunset. Her schedule hardly left enough free moments for eating, much less for playing.

But that morning she had asked Karina and Farid for help escaping her wizened history tutor. After a clever plan involving a candle, two vats of oil, and a particularly aggrieved monkey, the children whisked the elder princess away from the boredom of studying into the safety of the garden. There they ate their fill of sweet dates and plums, until they fell into the soft grass, stretched out and sated like a trio of spoiled kittens.

Eventually someone was going to find them, and an apology would have to be made to both the tutor and to the monkey's distraught owner. But for now, it was a perfect afternoon.

That is, until Hanane sat up, heaved a world-weary sigh, and loudly declared, "I'm bored."

When the other two did not reply, the elder princess repeated with more ferocity, "I *said*, I'm bored."

Farid had noticed. He noticed everything about her. Whenever he realized he was noticing more than he should be, he reminded himself that such behavior was unseemly for a member of the sultana's family and then continued to notice her. Her temper had been rather short of late. He missed the days when his presence alone could quell it.

The elder princess was the sun around which the other two children revolved. They ate when she ate. They slept when she slept. If she had asked them to turn the sea to stars and the stars to sea, they would have found a way to do it, they loved her that much.

Strangely, Karina and Farid did not have much of an opinion on one another—positive or negative. Any affection that might have existed between them was reserved solely for Hanane.

The younger princess pushed herself to her feet as quickly as her four-year-old body would allow. "We could play thieves and ogres!"

"We always play thieves and ogres. I'm bored of it." Hanane's eyes wandered over the garden wall. "I want to go somewhere far from here, like Arkwasi. Or the Snowlands. Or even Eshra!"

The elder princess's fascination with the outside world had begun innocently enough. A demure question here, a stray comment there. Her parents' swift evasion of the subject of leaving Ziran had only heightened her curiosity, until one fateful night

Hanane had slipped into Farid's chamber, roused him from his slumber, and dragged him along behind her with a promise of adventures like the great explorers of old.

He hadn't needed the promises. Even back then, he would have followed her to the end of the world if she'd only asked.

They made it all the way to the Outer Wall before the truth shattered those childish fantasies—Ziran was surrounded by a Barrier of ancient magic, one not even a thousand of the strongest warriors could destroy. Farid could pass through it as he pleased, but some flicker of ancient power in Hanane's blood prevented her from taking a single step past it.

Worse than being caught was the explanation for why their plan had been doomed from the start. The sultana gently but firmly explaining why the Barrier existed and why no member of the family ever had and ever would be able to pass through it. The pitying look in the king's eyes as he'd watched his daughter sob onto Farid's shoulder.

But their futile escape attempt had only magnified Hanane's obsession with the outside world. She never let it show, of course— to everyone else in her life, she was still the sweet, darling princess who was loved by all and who loved all in return.

But Farid saw it. He saw everything about her, especially how she had almost everything a person could possibly want, but her every thought was consumed by the one thing, the *only* thing, she could never have.

"I'm never going to leave Ziran," Karina declared. "I'm going to stay here forever and ever and ever, and then another forever after that."

"I wouldn't let you come with me anyway, because you still wear a diaper and I'm not changing it," said Hanane, and her sister began to cry, for the fact that she still needed a diaper at her age was a sore spot. The elder princess propped her elbow on her knee and her chin in her hand, eyes still trained for the wall. "You don't get to come."

A deep chasm cracked open in Farid's chest. He knew this chasm intimately, had wallowed deep within it after the death of his parents, until the elder princess's brilliant, shining light had pulled him from its clutches.

She couldn't leave him. Being with her was the only thing that made sense, the only thing that kept the chasm closed.

"Would you take me with you?"

She tore her gaze away from the wall to regard him instead. And now he was forced to look at her—and these days he hated looking at her because once he started, he could not stop. She had always been a pretty child, but now, at the age of twelve, the first hints of the woman she was becoming were peeking through.

The same changes were happening to him too. At fourteen, his body was twisting into a shape he did not recognize, the voice coming out of his mouth cracking and stretching into one that was not his. Now when the girl smiled at him, it filled him with a giddy warmth that left him lying awake deep in the night, flushed with thoughts that had only the most shameful of outlets.

He knew he should not be thinking these thoughts, and he knew she did not feel the same way about him . . .

. . . but . . .

Were his feelings truly so wrong?

After all, he wasn't her brother by birth. Many people were happily adopted into families that weren't of their blood, but he hadn't asked the king and queen to take him in. He certainly did not wish to be regarded as her sibling, especially if it meant that the connection he had with Hanane could never blossom into something more.

Hanane's face filled with mischief. "I'll allow it," she declared. "But only if you can best me in a show of strength."

Farid sensed what was about to happen before it did. "Hanane, don't—"

But it was already too late. The elder princess pounced on him with the ferocity of a jungle cat, and they went rolling across the dirt. In the past when they had played such games, they had always been evenly matched. But now everything was different. Even though Farid was larger, he was too distracted by the smell of her hair and the curve of her body pressed against his to fight properly. She pinned him to the ground with a wicked grin, her locs falling in a silver curtain around his face.

"You did not best me in a show of strength, thus you cannot join me on my journey." The princess paused, her face twisting into a rare expression of confusion. She peered down at him as the heat in his body rushed to all the wrong places, and she was only now realizing that they had crossed some line that could not be uncrossed.

"Are you all right?" she asked, and with more strength than he realized he possessed, he shoved her off him.

"I said I don't want to play!"

Hanane's head smacked against the dry ground. When she

didn't immediately stir, Farid and the younger princess scrambled to her side, and it was then that they saw it: a dot—tiny, but growing—of red, staining the front of her dress below her stomach. Farid knew of the menses. He understood it as a sign the princess had taken another step on the unrelenting march toward adulthood.

However, Karina did not. Her eyes welled with more tears. "You killed her!"

With each tearful sob, the wind whipped into a frenzy around them, slicing across their cheeks and arms even as Hanane jumped to her feet and tried to console her sister. The trees creaked and groaned, and knife-like points of hail slammed down all around them. As something deep within the boy crackled to life, the queen ran into the garden, a power they had never seen emanating off her in waves.

"Karina, stop," she commanded, but that only caused the storm to intensify. Not until the king arrived and gathered his daughter in his arms did it ebb, and though everyone else in the garden would remember it as the day the younger princess manifested her powers for the very first time, Farid would only ever remember it as the day the chasm inside him cracked too wide to ever be closed again.

12

Karina

Karina was dreaming again.

This time she was beside a river whose surface shone with glittering, iridescent colors, as if someone had fed stars to the creatures that dwelled within it. The two girls from before—the little ulraji, Khenu, and her taller friend—splashed through the water searching for frogs, laughing at the streaks of multicolored algae that coated their brown skin. Once again, they paid Karina no heed even though she was only a few feet away, solidifying her belief that this was some kind of memory of the past.

But whose?

She felt rather than saw the moment Malik appeared beside her—of all the petty jokes the universe had played on her, the way she felt his presence on her skin from even several feet away had to be the cruelest of all.

He stared at her, and Karina's anger flared in time with the aching heat of his gaze.

"Did you drag me here so you could finish what you started back at the Sun Temple?" she snapped. She had to hold on to her anger, for without it, it would be all too easy to sink into despair remembering what had almost been. How she had felt a moment of perfect connection when she had kissed him, and it had made her believe for just a second that perhaps she was not as alone in the world as she'd always feared she might be.

And then he had shoved a dagger into her heart and, well, here they were.

Malik simply studied her, his face taut and withdrawn. "Not this time."

As ever, Karina felt his voice as keenly as a finger trailing down her spine. It was just like the Second Challenge, when he'd managed to make a story told in the middle of a wide arena feel as intimate as a whisper from one lover to another.

No. She wasn't going to let him lure her to her own death ever again.

This time when she swung for him, Malik ducked. But she pivoted quickly to grab him by the shoulders and knee him in the gut. He went down with a grunt of pain.

"I deserved that," he groaned, and Karina's vision went red. How dare he act so meek, so non-threatening, when he was anything but.

She held him by the front of the shirt. "Give me one reason why I shouldn't kill you," she snarled. They were close enough that she could count every one of the thick lashes framing his black eyes.

She wanted to strangle his stupid handsome face. She wanted to kiss it. She wasn't sure if there was a way to do both at the same time, but Great Mother help her, she was going to figure it out.

Malik simply stared up at her with those night-dark eyes, his gaze remorseful but never wavering. And then he drew a dagger from somewhere, flipped it around, and offered its golden hilt to her.

"If killing me would truly make you feel better, then go ahead," he said softly, the expression on his face unreadable. The little girls in the river weren't too far off, but the world seemed to have narrowed to this tumultuous meeting of anger and desire fighting for control in Karina's chest.

She took the dagger. Dying in a normal dream would do nothing to a person's actual body, but clearly these weren't normal dreams—her hand still bore the bruises from striking him last time. What would happen if she cut open his throat right now? Would she wake to find his blood staining her hands?

But the truth hit her as sharply and as swiftly as a blow to the head—she could pummel Malik into the dirt, grind his bones into sand, strike him down with the full force of her magic until he was nothing but ash and bone, and it still would do nothing to alleviate the deep, aching sense of betrayal she felt.

"You are a liar. Killing you isn't even worth the time it would take to wipe the blood from my hands after," she hissed. "But if you ever lay another finger on me, I will summon lightning from the heavens to burn you alive from the inside out. Do you understand me, ulraji?"

That single word seemed to have more effect on him than her beating had. It was more than a title—it was a line in the sand that neither of them could cross. He could not stop being an ulraji any more than she could stop being a zawenji. Too many bodies and too many wrongs lay between their peoples for them to bridge that divide.

"I understand. And I'm sorry for what I did to you. I know it doesn't mean much, and I know you don't believe me, but I'm sorry all the same."

The apology wasn't nearly enough, and truthfully, part of Karina wished that Malik would put up more of a fight. Having him completely at her mercy meant little when he had basically handed himself to her.

"I want answers," she demanded. "Who are you, really? Why did you try to kill me during Solstasia?"

He quirked an eyebrow. "If you think I'm a liar, what makes you so sure I'll respond with the truth?"

"I could best you in combat and take it from you."

"A baby gazelle with a knife tied to its head could best me in combat. That doesn't mean anything."

Karina bit back a small smile. So he hadn't lost all his fight after all.

She tilted his chin up with the tip of his own blade, forced him to look into the eyes of the girl he'd almost murdered. "You aren't exactly in a position to stay silent."

A bead of blood welled up where the metal met his skin—she may have decided not to kill him, but there were many creative ways to get him to talk that wouldn't leave him dead.

"I'll answer your question if you answer one of mine." Malik's gaze was unwavering even with a knife at his throat. "What really happened to Tunde?"

Her grip on the dagger trembled. Any question but that.

When she didn't reply, he continued, "When you chose him at the end of Solstasia, did you know he was going to die?"

The metallic scent of blood bloomed in Karina's mouth. She was going to wretch. "I did."

The energy between them tightened. "So you did kill him."

"I didn't!" she cried. What this boy thought about her should not have mattered, but for some unfathomable reason she wanted him to know that at the last moment she hadn't gone through with the Rite of Resurrection, that she wasn't the heartless killer everyone believed her to be.

"Then who did?"

Every instinct in Karina's body screamed at her to expose Farid, but she remained silent. She still didn't know who this boy was, not truly. Though it was unlikely that Farid and Malik even knew each other, they were both ulraji. Who was to say he wasn't on Farid's side? Or worse, if Farid found out that Malik knew of his crimes, he might punish him, or spread more rumors to ensure Tunde never got the justice he deserved.

No, she couldn't tell the truth about Farid, not while so much remained up in the air. She'd play that card when the time was right, and not a moment before.

"I can't say. But it wasn't me," she said. Malik's expression remained unreadable—he likely didn't believe her, but he didn't fight her either. "I answered your question, now answer mine. Who are you, and why did you try to kill me?"

"That's two questions. My name is Malik, and I was ordered to kill you by someone who was holding my family hostage."

"Who is this someone?"

"I can't say. But it wasn't by my own choice, Your Highness."

It didn't seem like he was lying, but again, it hadn't seemed like he was lying when he'd held her at the necropolis, or when he'd embraced her on the roof of the Sun Temple. Karina fought the urge to hurl the dagger out of frustration. This wasn't working. As long as he was withholding information from her, and she was withholding information from him, they were left at a frustrating stalemate where every statement was as false as it was true.

Her gaze wandered over to the little girls. Khenu's friend had just dropped a frog down the back of Khenu's top and was now doubled over in laughter watching her try to get it out.

"Who are those children?" This was far less fraught than the ground they'd just been on. "Why do you keep bringing us to them?"

"I'm not sure. I don't know either of them, and we haven't been brought here by any conscious effort on my part." Karina mulled over Malik's words, trying to parse out the hidden meaning behind everything he wasn't saying. She finally let him go, and he lowered himself into a sitting position with his arms around his knees.

"I wasn't supposed to see that vision of the Rite of Renewal, was I?" she asked.

"You weren't. I think this is happening to us because when I—when our magic destroyed the Barrier, our powers connected. Now it seems you can see into my mind when it's vulnerable, and I assume I could see into yours."

As long as she might live, Karina would never forget that moment when the Barrier shattered. She had felt . . . unlimited.

Like pure power itself. It made sense that something so immense had altered them both.

But if everything Karina saw in these shared dreams, Malik saw too, it meant he knew that the only way to save Sonande was to find the scepter and the flute, and then use them to murder her.

"Who else knows about the Rite of Renewal?" she asked sharply.

Silence. She narrowed her eyes.

"Does the council know?" *Does that creature pretending to be Hanane know? Does Farid?* was what she truly wished to ask, but if the council knew, then her traitorous guardian and his monster did too.

Silence again, but this time not just from Malik. The chittering birdsong in the canopy and the gentle croaking of the frogs had stilled. The girls had noticed it too, and they both froze in the shallows of the water as the ground began to rumble beneath their feet. Malik and Karina shared a glance of alarm.

"Slavers," whispered the taller girl. "Run, Khenu!"

The two girls darted out of the water toward the safety of the opposite riverbank, but just as in the first dream, Khenu was far slower than her friend. The ulraji girl tripped and fell in the mud, her foot caught between two tree roots. The drums of battle edged closer and screams rose up through the trees.

"Help!" cried the girl. "Help me, Bahia, please!"

A jolt of lightning ran through Karina's body. Both girls' faces swam into focus for the first time, and in the taller one Karina saw her mother's high cheekbones and brown eyes bordering on purple widened in fear.

"Help me, please!" the younger girl cried again, and there was no mistaking that round face, those eyes darker than a crow flying through midnight.

Eyes just like Malik's.

Bahia's eyes darted between Khenu and the tree line, weighing her chance of survival against her friend's. Karina wanted to scream at the girl to turn around, but the choice had been made a thousand years before she'd been born.

Without even looking back, Bahia Alahari, the greatest queen that Ziran had ever known, renowned for a thousand years as the savior of the downtrodden and the broken, darted into the safety of the trees, ignoring the panicked screams of Malik's ancestor as the raiding party descended upon her.

Karina awoke with a start, her mind a jumble of boys she did not trust and ancestors she had thought she could.

"What's the matter?" mumbled Afua as she rubbed the sleep from her eyes. A full day and half a night had passed since they had embarked on their journey for Doro Lekke, and now here in the dark hours of night before dawn rose on Life Day, a full week since Solstasia ended, they found themselves camped out beneath a small outcropping north of Tiru.

Karina struggled to find words for all the emotions racing through her. Her ancestor had known Malik's. No, not just known—they had grown up with one another, as close as Karina felt with Aminata and Afua. As she had once felt with Dedele.

Until Grandmother Bahia had abandoned Khenu to save herself.

This had to be another one of Malik's illusions; what she had just seen went against everything she knew about her ancestor. And yet the memory had been so raw. If it was real, then what did this mean for her connection to Malik? Was this why he had tried to kill her, out of revenge?

Normally she would have confided these fears in Aminata, but her maid was dozens of miles behind them. For half a heartbeat, she even missed Farid and the days she'd spent pestering him with all manner of questions he would begrudgingly answer. But those days had never been real, even if a bruised corner of her heart refused to let them go.

"It was just a nightmare. I'm fine now," Karina lied. Pain pulsed against the inside of her skull. Her migraines had been coming less frequently since she'd released her magic, but under moments of extreme stress they returned just as viciously as before. If she thought about this any longer, she was going to go mad; in fact, that was probably exactly what Malik wanted. She really was a fool for not having killed him when she'd had the chance.

Rubbing one hand against her temple, she took stock of their little camp: the banked fire on the ground before her, the netting they had hung up to protect from the locusts. The insects remained mostly dormant at night, so the plan had been to sleep through the day and travel from sundown to sunrise, as this would also allow them to avoid the worst of the desert heat. It was far slower than travel on the sand barge had been, but they didn't have much choice.

Sometimes Karina imagined she saw Dedele approaching on the horizon, but it was always just another mirage. Remembering her former friend added another stone to the ever-growing pile of grief inside her. How many more stones could she take until the pile collapsed her from the inside out?

"Did I miss anything while I was asleep?" she asked, and on the pallet beside her, Ife shifted into a sitting position.

"All you missed was sand, but don't worry, it hasn't gone anywhere. Aside from that, nothing. By the way, I never apologized for tying you up in Tiru. I'm sorry for tying you up in Tiru. Let's be friends."

Karina still wasn't sure what to make of the teenager—Caracal's begrudging cooperation in her quest was inspired entirely by self-interest, but she had no idea what kept Ife traveling with them. They were the first dulyo Karina had ever met, her knowledge of the divine genders of the Eastwater peoples learned entirely through books as she'd never been to the region herself. The dulyo were exalted in their society, believed to be closer to divinity than other people. What had happened in Ife's past for them to give up an existence like that for a dangerous and fraught life as the companion of a fugitive Sentinel?

Before she could reply, Ife scooted toward her and grabbed her wrist. Warmth flooded through her arm, and Ife nodded.

"Ah, thought so. Who is it?"

Karina snatched her hand back. "Who is what?"

"Who is the boy, or girl, or person, or paranormal entity who has you so flustered?"

"I'm not flustered!"

Ife began ticking off their fingers. "Your heart rate is elevated, your pupils are dilated, and your temperature is above average, all of which suggest either a recent state of arousal or imminent organ failure."

Heat flushed Karina's face as she recalled holding that dagger beneath Malik's chin and not knowing whether she wanted to kiss him or kill him. Before she could reply, Caracal bounded into their little camp.

"Look who decided to finally wake up. While you lot were busy sleeping, I found a solution to our lack-of-supplies problem." The mercenary jerked a thumb over his shoulder. "There's a village down the ridge that just had a naming ceremony. I bet their stores are filled with gifts for the infant, and we might even be able to grab a donkey or two if we move quick enough. From here, we go to the City of Thieves. If there's any place in Sonande to find information about a secret immortal, it's there."

Afua's eyes shot up. "The City of Thieves is real?"

"Every myth is real if you know where to look."

Karina echoed Afua's surprise, for she had always thought the City of Thieves was a tale meant to threaten children into obedience. An entire city filled with nothing but criminals, ruffians, and the absolute worst kinds of people Sonande had to offer . . . though the rational part of Karina balked at the risk, the part of her that had dreamed of the world beyond Ziran for so long salivated. Besides, if Doro Lekke was real, why couldn't the City of Thieves be too?

But she did not salivate at the first part of Caracal's plan. Naming ceremonies were a sacred tradition throughout Sonande, as so many babies died right after birth that surviving long enough to be named was cause for celebration. It was likely that the infant's family had received enough gifts from their friends and loved ones that they wouldn't notice if a few went missing, but still . . . had they really fallen that low?

"We can't steal from a baby!"

"Not with that attitude we can't!" Caracal shot back. "If you have a better idea, I'm happy to hear it. But seeing as *someone*"— he glared pointedly at Afua, who gave a sheepish shrug—"released our horses back in Tiru, we need new ones if we want even a chance of surviving this journey. And my and Ife's rations were meant for two people, not four. If we don't replenish them soon, we're all going to die of dehydration before we see even a brick of Doro Lekke. So if you have a problem with this plan, you're free to walk barefoot across the desert until you find the Sanctum or until the vultures grab you, whichever comes first."

Karina was going to kill him. Reaching Doro Lekke and escaping the Rite of Renewal be damned, Karina was going to shove her foot down Caracal's throat and kill him.

Before Karina could choke her fellow Wind-Aligned zawenji to death, Ife cheerfully chimed in, "Don't mind him, he hides a gentle and nurturing soul behind that caustic demeanor. Classic rogue-with-a-secret-heart-of-gold character archetype."

Caracal shook his head affectionately. "There you go again with your talk of archetypes. I'm pretty sure if we were in a story, we would know."

"Of course we aren't. No characters in any good story would know they were in one."

Sensing this discussion would go on for a while if uninterrupted, Karina cut in. "Back to the matter at hand, which is apparently that we've fallen so low that we need to steal an infant's naming gifts. Exactly how are we going to do this?"

"I'm thinking we should try maneuver six," said Caracal. "Remember that one, Ife—the one that got us out of that leopard trapper's lair in Falanda?"

Ife wrinkled their nose. "We always do maneuver six. I want to do five."

"Five it is. Come on, the night isn't getting any younger."

They quickly disassembled their tiny camp and followed Caracal to the top of the ridge. *Village* was a generous term for the half-a-dozen compounds spread out below them, clustered close like chicks huddling together for warmth. Even from here, it was impossible to miss the devastation brought on by the locusts, and there was no doubt it would take only a few more days for the pests to eat through the last of the bedraggled crops they'd left behind.

The former Sentinel turned to Karina and Afua and said, "Ife and I will cause a distraction. As soon as the area is clear, you two go down and grab as much food as you can carry. When you hear the wolf cry, that's your signal to meet back here."

Caracal closed his eyes and raised his hands like a puppeteer. The rhythm of the wind around them changed, pulsing low and deliberate like drumbeats thundering across the sky. A cloud of fog rolled over the tiny cluster of huts, thick as a blanket. Karina's own magic stirred in her chest, yearning desperately to match Caracal's—never before had she achieved anything so precise with her powers. If her own magic was a chaotic symphony, his was a perfectly honed melody, one she desperately wished to learn.

"How did you do that?" she asked, her voice filled with awe.

"I'm not running a school, princess. Ife, go."

Ife let out a low, rumbling call not unlike a leopard's roar. Confused villagers ran from their huts, some with actual weapons in hand, others with farm tools, and they disappeared into the fog trying to find the source of the noise. Once the last of the torches had wandered a good distance from the compounds, Karina and Afua raced down the ridge.

At the center of the village was a mighty acacia tree, and from its branches the villagers had hung beads, bits of glass, and wooden charms to bring good luck to the new baby. Clustered around the base was a variety of offerings to the gods, with invocations written to beg that the locusts spare their little town. Karina's heart twisted. She was more likely to help these people than the gods were, but only after she had stolen from them.

Afua's magic made quick work of the locks they found. Soon their packs were bulging with foodstuffs and their waterskins were full to the brim. Animals hated Karina, so she stayed behind to find more food while the younger girl went to procure beasts for their journey. Another one of Ife's howls rang through the air, and Karina bit back her guilt. One day, when this was all over, she'd find this village again and return ten times what she'd taken.

"Make sure to grab some garri too. It'll last you longer than fresh produce."

At this point, Karina should have been used to Hyena appearing out of nowhere, but she still nearly spilled the entire bag of cassava flour in her shock. The trickster lazily regarded Karina from one of the spindly trees outside the storage hut, the weight of her canine body nearly snapping the branch she was on.

"What do you want?" Karina hissed. The only part of Hyena she could see through the fog was her eyes, two unearthly blue dots that seemed to bore a hole into Karina's chest.

"Like I said before, once I start a story, I like to see it through to the end."

"You never said that to me."

"Oh, sorry, did I say that to the boy? I must admit, I give so many cryptic speeches that they sometimes blur together."

Karina wasn't stupid enough to believe all Hyena wanted to do was check on her. The trickster had known exactly what she was doing when she had given Karina *The Tome of the Dearly Departed* and set her down the path that had led to the Rite of Resurrection in the first place. Hyena was one of the most powerful creatures in all existence; nothing she did was without reason, no matter how random she tried to pretend her actions were.

Karina turned her back to the trickster and angrily stuffed more mangoes into her pack. Hyena barked out a laugh that Karina sensed no one in the village but her could hear. "You really aren't going to ask about the Rite of Renewal? Or about what happened with your ancestor and Malik's?"

Karina's grip on the mango tightened. Not only did Hyena hold all the answers to their problems, she *knew* that Karina knew she held all the answers to their problems and reveled in not sharing any of them. If Karina hadn't feared an extremely painful magical backlash from attacking an immortal being, she would have punched Hyena in the nose simply to wipe that smug grin off her face.

But still, her curiosity was too great for her not to take the bait. "What do you know of the history between my ancestor and Malik's?"

"Even when the Ulraji Tel-Ra were at the prime of their power during the height of ancient Kennoua, there were ulraji who shunned their imperialistic ways and refused to turn against their zawenji allies. Bahia Alahari and Khenukahor were born in one such enclave where zawenji and ulraji lived together until, well, you saw what happened."

Entire communities where zawenji and ulraji had lived together . . . the thought seemed impossible, like oil mixing with water, but clearly there had been a time when the divide between the two peoples hadn't been so wide. "I was told growing up that Grandmother Bahia was enslaved."

"But she was not *born* enslaved. Do you not know your own history, child?"

She didn't, and that was exactly the problem. Her history had been stolen from her, and all she'd been left with was a narrative constructed by people with their own biases about how she should feel about her legacy and her past. She wondered if wherever her ancestors were, they were reaching for her too, unable to bridge this disconnect forced upon them.

"Grandmother Bahia hated the ulraji. She had all of them slaughtered. Yet she'd grown up alongside them—"

"Grief does strange things to your human minds."

Karina had known her ancestor wasn't perfect, but she couldn't wrap her mind around such a vast contradiction between her fore-mother's beliefs and actions. The story felt unfinished somehow, but she wasn't sure she was ready to face what other awful truths she'd uncover if she kept digging into her own and Malik's pasts.

Ife's wolf cry whistled through the air. They all had to get out of there, now.

Then again, why was Karina working so hard to find the power of the gods when a power to rival the gods' stood right before her?

"I don't suppose I can make a bargain with you?" Karina asked, and Hyena quirked an eyebrow.

"You do realize deals with me always end horribly for the humans involved, right?"

"Yes, yes, you'll grant my wish, but the cost will be far higher than it seemed upfront, or my wish will only come true in the most devastatingly ironic manner possible. I know the risk, and I don't care. I want to be strong enough to stop the destruction Farid caused with the Rite of Resurrection. Can you make that happen or not?"

"I could."

Hyena stared down at her, and for a single moment Karina saw the thousands upon thousands of eons of existence hidden within the trickster's eyes. These were the eyes of a being for whom things like time and space were as flimsy as a spiderweb beneath an elephant's foot.

How lonely a life that must be.

Hyena blinked, something almost like surprise flickering across her face.

"I could," she repeated. Then she shrugged. "But I won't."

Karina scoffed. "I thought you loved tricking unsuspecting people into unfair bargains."

"*Unsuspecting* being the key word. It's no fun if you know you're getting tricked. No, sweet princess, you are on your own for this endeavor. I shall remain on the sidelines, providing the occasional confusing yet surprisingly deep insight."

"You mentioned before that you owed my ancestor," Karina said as she quickly stuffed everything in sight into her pack. "Are you helping me to make up for your debt?"

"Helping you? Oh, I'm not here to help you." Hyena threw her head back, and her voice shifted to that of a scared child's as she screeched, "Thieves! There are thieves in our pantry!"

The trickster vanished, but her cry had already summoned the rest of the villagers who hadn't gone to look for Ife's fake beast. Karina shouldered her bulging packs and sprinted for the edge of the village, an angry mob on her heels.

"I hope your new baby lives a long and prosperous life!" she screamed. An arrow whizzed by her ear in response.

Another arrow struck one of the packs, though it thankfully it missed her waterskin. She stumbled forward from the impact, but her hands never hit the ground. Instead a great blast of wind sent her sailing upward, high over the lip of the ridge, until she rolled in a heap at the feet of her companions and four beautifully speckled horses.

"I told you we should have done maneuver six!" yelled Caracal as he used his magic once more to push Karina up onto her horse. As soon as her hands gripped the reins, they were off, the desert slipping into a blur around them, the angry villagers at their heels, and the hysterical laughter of a hyena riding the breeze.

13

Malik

You can't avoid this forever, Malik.

On the contrary, Malik could and would avoid thinking about the revelations from his dream with Karina for as long as humanly possible. Running from his problems was one of the things he did best; once, when he was nine, he had spent six hours hiding inside a grain storage bin to avoid his father's attempts to take him hunting. If he could escape that, surely he could escape this.

Besides, nothing he had seen in the dream truly changed things between him and Karina. She was the one who had been raised to revere her ancestor; to him, Bahia's betrayal of Khenu was just another addition to the long list of ways Karina's family had harmed his over the centuries.

In fact, this was a blessing in disguise. Now he knew that whatever tug they felt toward one another was nothing more than the lingering residue of their ancestors' friendship. The kiss hadn't meant anything. He owed her nothing, and he'd feel no remorse when Farid sacrificed her for the Rite of Renewal.

I can't tell if you're extremely naive or extremely stubborn, mused Idir, and Malik chose to ignore that remark to instead focus on the open book of Kennouan history before him.

Ksar Alahari had the second largest library in all of Ziran, yet he was no closer to finding information about the flute or the scepter needed to perform the Rite of Renewal than when he'd begun searching. Malik had spent the week since the locusts had arrived digging through the palace's stores of ancient artifacts and translating the few Kennouan documents he could get his hands on, all for nothing.

With each day that passed, the locusts' devastation only grew. The day after Tunde's death had been exposed, an entire nest of the creatures had been found in a well in Imane's Keep, poisoning a water source hundreds of people relied on. Riots had broken out over the few untainted wells left in that neighborhood, and Malik and his sisters had watched wide-eyed as fires from the unrest bloomed across the city below.

Worse than the turmoil in the Lower City was how calm those in the Old City were about it. Those who could afford to protect themselves from the locusts continued with their lavish parties and bemoaned how their profits were suffering from the insects' presence. Malik felt as though he was straddling two worlds—too privileged to be directly affected by the worst of what was happening, but too much of an outsider to belong among those who had the power to fix things but didn't.

Then again, his job was not to belong. His job was to locate the scepter and the flute. And he was failing at it. Badly. It had set him on edge, the irritation bubbling up with each failed lead. He felt like he had on that last day of Solstasia, when that feeling that he wasn't good enough to be wanted by Karina had threatened to swallow him whole.

You know, sexual frustration in your kind often leads to aggression. If you're this upset over Karina, you should do something about it.

Heat rushed to Malik's face. "Not while you're watching everything I do!"

I already have to watch all your other bodily functions. How would this be any different? Idir asked, genuinely perplexed, and Malik did not have it in him to explain voyeurism to an ancient spirit.

"Rather than commentary on my intimate life, what would be most useful from you right now would be the location of the artifacts," Malik grumbled as he pushed the book aside and picked up another. He and Idir had fallen into an uneasy truce ever since Malik had come back from the obosom's memories. He would never feel fully comfortable hosting the spirit, but there was a certain understanding between them now that came from having lived so thoroughly in the other's skin.

I already told you I have no idea where they are, but why don't you check my memories again if you don't believe me?

Truce or no, Malik would rather face down the serpopard in the necropolis once more than do that. He didn't want to give up any more of his humanity than he already had.

Eventually Malik's small candle had burned to a stub and the lines of text blurred together beyond all recognition. Fear of the upcoming omens kept him turning the pages even though he wasn't processing anything. Locusts now, then quakes, then plagues, then a beast. Everything and everyone destroyed and here he was failing to stop it—

Sleep, Malik, came the Faceless King, and it was because the spirit's tone was surprisingly gentle that Malik closed the book and begrudgingly dragged himself out of the library. Ksar Alahari was a different beast at night, a puppet left sagging until morning when a steady stream of courtiers would once again will it to life. Wars had been won, countries had been conquered, crowns had been forged within this very stone, and three poor children from Eshra had somehow found themselves at the center of it.

"Leila? Nadia?" he called softly upon entering their rooms. It was not yet midnight, so his sisters should have been awake, but there came no response. He called for them once more.

Silence.

I'm sensing someone in your sisters' bedroom, said Idir, the truth of his words humming through the binding. *They're heading this way. Hide quickly.*

All at once, the myriad of thoughts that had been storming through Malik's head ceased. He flattened himself against a wall and summoned the spirit blade.

"There is no line where my body ends and the air begins. They are one and the same, with no beginning and no end." Heat rushed through Malik's veins as the invisibility illusion wove over him. The figure exited his sisters' room into a seemingly empty one, and quick as a viper, Malik had them by the neck.

"Where are my sisters?" he demanded, pressing his dagger against the intruder's throat. He didn't care who they were; if anything had happened to Leila or Nadia, he would sever this person's head from their body. He would chop off each of their limbs and feed them to dogs. He would—

"They're in the kitchens! Your younger sister left her stuffed toy and asked me to fetch it for her!" The young woman choking in Malik's grasp was not some bloodthirsty assassin but a palace maid. He released her at once and she doubled over, one hand pressed against the red line at her throat, not unlike the one Malik had received from Karina during the dream. The other held Gege, Nadia's beloved toy goat.

The bloodlust rushed out of him all at once, leaving shame in its wake. Where were all these violent impulses coming from? "I am so, so sorry," Malik said, not caring that someone of his status wasn't supposed to apologize to a servant.

Perhaps my presence is having more of an impact on you than we realized.

The thought made Malik gag. The maid straightened, and he recognized her as the one who had been with Karina when he'd first crashed into her on Solstasia Eve. Amira . . . ? No, Aminata.

"Take me to them. My sisters, that is . . . please," he added, for though she could not refuse his request, he felt awful asking a favor of someone he had almost decapitated. Aminata's mouth tightened, her eyes falling to the spirit blade still hanging limply in Malik's hand. She nodded.

The maid's demeanor was understandably chilly as she led him deep into the bowels of Ksar Alahari, far from the ornaments and finery of the residential wing. These were the servants' quarters, and the simplicity of the rough-hewn walls eased the tension from Malik's body. This felt more like his home than any other part of the palace he'd seen so far. He glanced at Karina's former maid, his curiosity winning out over the nerves that filled him whenever he spoke to a new person.

"Back on Solstasia Eve, I saw you and Karina together in the Lower City," he said. "Were the two of you close?"

Aminata regarded him for a moment before replying, "My mother was her nursemaid. We grew up together."

A series of questions about what Karina's childhood had been like rose up within him. Had she been an energetic child? What was her favorite food, her favorite color? Was Tunde the only person she'd ever been involved with or—no, he couldn't ask that, not when Karina was suspected of the boy's murder.

She claimed she hadn't done it, but how was he supposed to believe her when she wouldn't say who did? But surely someone who had killed Tunde wouldn't have looked as stricken at the mere mention of his name as Karina had. What had happened between them?

Malik snapped at the bracelet on his wrist and instead asked, "How are the people dealing with the locusts? Farid has me so busy here, I haven't had a chance to visit the Lower City since Solstasia."

"Most courtiers wouldn't care about what happens outside the palace." The maid spoke with the practiced care of someone who had learned at an early age to guard herself around those who had far more power than she did, and though Malik knew he had destroyed any chance they might have had of being friends, he could not help but relate.

"I am not most courtiers."

She stopped abruptly before a small door from which the smell of peeled oranges wafted. "Your sisters are in here. Will you be needing anything else, Champion Malik?"

"No, you may go. And thank you."

Aminata turned to leave, then glanced over her shoulder at him. If Karina's eyes were like a lion's, then her maid's were like a hawk's, finding the weakness hidden behind even the smallest of movements. "She liked you, you know. Karina."

Malik forced his face to remain even, even as his traitor heart thudded at the memory of Karina lifting his chin with his blade. "What makes you say that?"

"Because you'd be dead right now if she hadn't."

With that, Aminata left.

Shivering for reasons that had nothing to do with the night chill, Malik entered the kitchen. It was little more than a storage room with a small clay oven and table, at the latter of which sat Leila and Nadia. His older sister let out a yelp as Malik threw his arms around her.

"Whoa, calm down." Leila awkwardly patted his back. "Everything is fine. Nadia couldn't sleep, so I thought some food might help."

After Idir had taken Nadia hostage, Malik couldn't handle being away from either of them for too long. He still had nightmares where they had vanished, leaving him to survive the horrors of court all on his own. "You should have waited until I returned. I would have come with you."

"We didn't know when you'd be done. You haven't been here." The latter part was said without any malice, but the truth of the words filled Malik with shame. Perhaps he had taken for granted their newfound safety within the palace walls, for in his quest to juggle every one of his new responsibilities, being present in the day-to-day lives of his sisters had been the first to drop. He didn't even know if Leila had made any progress in her search for their mother and grandmother.

No longer. They were the only reason any of this mattered, so he wouldn't neglect them again. Malik sat at the table beside Nadia, who was idly dragging her fingers through the bowl of lemon juice, orange slices, and cinnamon Leila had made her, an old snack Nana had given them as children. "How are you feeling?" he asked her softly. "Have you learned anything new at nursery?"

Nadia's eyes remained stubbornly trained on her bowl as Leila answered, "Our dear baby sister has been kicked out of the palace nursery school."

"They kicked you out?" How did one even get expelled from nursery? Children her age could barely go to the washroom by themselves, much less actually cause trouble.

"She punched someone."

"Nadia!" Malik exclaimed. Tears welled up in his younger sister's eyes.

"He called me a kekki," she said. "I hate them. I hate all of them."

Anger simmered within Malik's gut. No one dared say the slur to his face now that he was Farid's protégé, but he didn't doubt many thought it to themselves whenever he walked by. He hated that even after climbing as high as a person reasonably could within Zirani society, other people's prejudices could still reach them. And most of all, he missed the days when all his sister's problems had been small enough to fit in the palm of his hand.

"I'm sorry," he whispered, for what else could he say? His older sister took one look at his dejected face and silently offered him a bowl of his own.

"This has been a big adjustment for all of us," said Leila. "There are going to be some growing pains, but this low moment we're in is only that—a moment. We're going to be all right."

Malik smiled weakly. "We always are."

At Leila's urging, Malik ate, and warmth spread through his body. Dire circumstances aside, sitting here with Leila and Nadia brought him back to his childhood and the fleeting days of coziness they'd shared between the hardship and turmoil. He couldn't remember the last time he'd felt this way.

"You've changed," he said to Leila. His older sister had always had a sharp personality, even when she meant well, so such comfort from her was rare. She laid her head on his shoulder.

"Perhaps, but I'm still your elder all the same."

"Only by ten months!"

"And what a blissful ten months they were." Leila laughed, then sighed. "You've changed too. And so has Nadia. But what hasn't changed is that it's still the three of us together, no matter what. I can't pretend I fully understand what magic mission Farid has you on, but know that I'm here to support you however I can."

Now Malik was the one about to cry. He pressed the heel of his palm against his eyes, not wanting to ruin this moment with his tears. "I've searched every corner of the palace for any hint of the whereabouts of the scepter or the flute, and I've found nothing. If I can't find these artifacts, and the gods' wrath grows, it'll be all my fault."

To his surprise, it was Nadia who said, "If you can't find what you're looking for inside the palace, then maybe you should look outside the palace."

Malik was about to retort that no other place in Ziran held this much knowledge about ancient Kennoua before he remembered that wasn't quite true. Back during the Cleansing Ceremony, he had met that girl, Yaema, who studied ancient cultures of Sonande. Farid had never said he couldn't enlist another person's help in his search. He had nothing to lose asking Yaema what she might know.

"How would the two of you like to accompany me on a trip to the university tomorrow?" he asked.

"I can't believe a trip to a locust-infested hellscape is the most interesting thing we have to look forward to these days," replied Leila, but from her grin, Malik knew she would come along. "Farid certainly has you working for your keep, doesn't he?"

Anyone else might have missed the hint of disdain behind Leila's polite tone, but Malik knew his sister well. "Farid's methods can be brutal, but they're always within reason," he insisted. "And he's given us shelter and protection at absolutely no cost."

"Does it truly count as no cost when he has you doing his dirty work?"

"It's not dirty work! Someone without—"

Malik stopped. He'd been about to say that someone without ulraji magic couldn't understand, but he sensed that once he truly acknowledged this new divide between him and Leila, it couldn't be taken back.

His sister's eyes softened. "Just . . . please be careful. Farid has given us a lot, but he's asked a lot of you as well." Her eyes fell to the still-healing bruises on his body from his test with the Sentinels. "This is still the same man who overthrew a thousand-year-old dynasty. Don't underestimate what he's capable of."

Malik understood Leila's apprehension, he truly did, but there was a kinship between him and Farid—not nearly as strong as the one he felt with his sisters, of course, but one forged between two people who understood that heady, all-consuming rush of using magic. He needed Farid, and he liked to think that Farid needed him too.

"Come on," he said simply. "Let's get to bed."

They were halfway back to their quarters when a noise cut through the silence—crying. Weeping, actually. Malik and Leila looked at one another with concern, while Nadia swiveled toward the sound.

"Do you hear that?" she whispered, and she raced toward it before her siblings could stop her. Malik and Leila followed her into the innermost portion of the palace, where even the shadows stood still, and Malik realized too late that they were near the deceased sultana's empty quarters as Nadia slipped through the door that led to the queen's private garden.

The last time Malik had been here, he and Karina had accidentally tumbled into the necropolis hidden beneath Ziran. In the time since, the garden had deteriorated so much that one would think years had passed instead of a few weeks. Some of the damage was due to the locusts, but most was due to the fact that the magical hand that had tended to this place was now gone. According to Farid, the late sultana had been an Earth-Aligned zawenji, and Malik could almost sense how the flora mourned the loss of their beloved mistress. It felt wrong to be sneaking through here, as if they were trampling on Karina's mother's grave.

"Nadia." Malik crept through sagging trees and between thorny vines, Leila right behind him. "Nadia, come on, we have to get out of here."

They reached the end of the path, only to freeze. There stood Nadia, twigs and bits of leaves stuck in her hair from where she had barreled forward with no heed for the set path.

And sitting right in front of her, perched on the edge of the fountain that hid the entrance to the necropolis and her own family's bloodstained history, was Princess Hanane, sobbing into her hands so hard that her entire body shook.

He and Leila remained frozen as Nadia laid her head in the princess's lap. Much to his surprise, the younger girl didn't shudder at Hanane's touch as he had. "It's all right, don't cry, it's all right," she said, patting the older girl's knee. Nadia said those words the same way Malik had said them to her countless times, and it might have heartened him to hear her trying to imitate him under any circumstance besides this one. Hanane sniffed before lifting her head, first to gaze at Nadia and then at Malik. Her brow furrowed in confusion.

"I know you," she whispered, and Malik would never get used to how close her voice was to Karina's. "You're Farid's boy."

Something about the way she said *boy* made him bristle. It was so . . . possessive.

"I work with Farid." All Malik wanted to do was grab Nadia, turn around, and pretend this meeting had never happened. He didn't want to think about what Farid might say if he found out they had intruded on the princess like this.

The Faceless King stirred within him. *Get away from the lich.* Walk away. All he had to do was walk away.

And yet . . .

Before Malik could stop himself, he blurted out, "I don't mean to pry, Your Highness, but are you all right?"

As soon as the words were out of his mouth, Princess Hanane burst into tears again.

"Nothing is all right," she said between sobs. "My mother is dead. My father is dead. My sister is missing, and they say she killed them both! I closed my eyes in one time only to open them in another, and I have no idea what's going on!"

Leila shot Malik a look that made it clear he should do something. He approached the princess with the caution of a hunter cornering a wounded animal and knelt beside her, opposite Nadia.

"What do you remember?" he asked gently. Nothing he could say or do would bring back all she'd lost, but he could at least listen.

Princess Hanane sniffed again, and she gestured toward a large marula tree blooming a few feet from the fountain. "That tree wasn't there a month ago."

Judging from the height of the tree, it had to be at least a decade old—

And Princess Hanane had died a decade ago. The realization made Malik feel sick. How did you console someone through the realization that they had died and the world had moved on without them?

Leila jumped in, "What was there before?"

"W-Well, just last week, I helped my mother plant this sapling. We knelt in a clear area right there." She pointed at a thick patch of locust-bitten shrubs. "And planted it. It shouldn't be this big already." She gestured in a wide arc to the flora around them. "None of this should be here, and all the people who should be here aren't. Everything has changed, but I'm still the same."

She gave a mirthless laugh. Idir stirred, and Malik wondered how odd this encounter must be for him, seeing his descendant across so many layers of time and death. Another sense of foreboding washed over Malik, but he chose to ignore it. Even knowing what the princess really was, he couldn't bear to leave her alone when she was so distraught.

However, there was one thing he could do for her that no one else could.

"Can you describe the garden for me exactly the way you remember it?" he asked, his magic warming in his veins. Hanane regarded him for a long time before she finally spoke.

"This entire area, save the fountain, was clear."

"This entire area, save the fountain, was clear," Malik repeated, and in an instant, it was. Hanane's eyes grew wide as Malik's magic settled over the clearing, turning it into the version of the space she remembered. "I can't bring back what you lost, but I can re-create it, at least for a little while. What else do you remember?"

"The lilies on that trellis used to be irises. And the south wall was yellow, not green."

Bit by bit Malik used his magic to bring Hanane's memories

back to life. Her world sounded like something out of a children's tale: a young queen with all the power in the world, a king who was as doting a father as he'd been husband, a young princess who had anything and everything she could possibly want right at her fingertips. Though Malik knew the story ended in tragedy, it was impossible not to get swept into the decadent life that Hanane recounted.

"On my sixteenth birthday, my mother surprised me with dancers," said the princess, and she gasped in delight as they appeared around the fountain, spinning and twirling in their colorful silks. "And Baba loved music, so Mama made sure it was always playing. Day and night, no matter where you were in the palace, music echoed through the halls."

Hanane hummed a melody, and Malik amplified it through the garden as if a dozen musicians had joined in. The princess began to dance, her body twisting effortlessly through the phantom revel Malik had created. They watched her twirl and jump across the garden, every movement in perfect harmony to the illusion around her.

Finally the melody slowed, and so did Hanane. Her shoulders should have heaved with exhaustion, but her body made no movements that she herself did not will it to make. Her chest never rose or fell, her eyes never blinked. She was like a doll, still and perfect, forever trapped as she'd been at the moment of her death.

"I always loved to dance," she whispered. "Baba used to tease that I knew how to dance before I knew how to walk. But I couldn't sing or play instruments like him and Karina. In fact, Karina used to say there were dying warthogs who sang better than I did. Even when she was little, she was so mean!" Hanane began to laugh, then stopped. She turned to Malik. "Make her for me."

For the first time since they'd begun the illusion, Malik faltered. "K-Karina?"

"Yes. When I think of her, I still see the child she was, but in this age she's nearly a woman grown. I caught a glimpse of her during Solstasia, but . . . it wasn't enough." A wistful glint entered Hanane's eyes. "I need to see her as she is now. Please."

Malik would have refused the request had it come from anyone else, but he thought about how it might feel to miss ten years of his own sisters' lives, and found himself beginning the illusion.

"Karina's hair is a few shades darker than yours, but still light enough to be silver," he began. "And her eyes—they draw you in. She looks at you and . . . and . . . it doesn't matter how you see yourself because you know she's seeing you in the way you always wished someone would. Does that help?"

Malik looked at Hanane, but her attention was turned ahead, where Karina stood before them.

It was an illusion. Malik knew this. He had *made* this. But that didn't stop his pulse from quickening as the fake Karina cocked its head to the side and stared at him with an expression of such intense longing it made his mouth go dry. Hanane looked at the illusion, then at him, then back at the illusion. Her eyes widened in understanding.

"Malik, are you in love with my sister?"

Without a word, Malik snapped the thread of nkra connecting

him to the illusion. It vanished instantly. Heat rushing to his face, he turned on his heel and stormed away.

"Wait!" cried Hanane as she ran after him. "I didn't mean to upset you—"

"I don't want to talk about this." Stupid, stupid—how could he be so stupid? It was one thing to fantasize on his own, but how could he have shown that to Karina's sister of all people?

"Please don't leave!" Hanane grabbed Malik by the wrist, and a jolt of cold more frigid than ice ran up his arm. He let out a cry of pain, and Hanane immediately pulled away.

"I'm—I'm so sorry," she sobbed. "I didn't . . . sometimes I forget what I am now."

The princess began to shake, and despite the throbbing in his arm, Malik forced the discomfort from his face.

"It's fine," he said, cradling his frostbitten fingers to his chest. "I shouldn't have snapped at you. It's just that my relationship with Karina is . . . complicated."

Hanane nodded, and rather than mocking him for his stupid infatuation, she simply seemed relieved he hadn't abandoned her.

"Do you think she really did . . . all those things Farid claims she did?" Malik asked.

"I want to believe she didn't but . . . she killed me and our father when she was just a child. Who's to say she isn't capable of killing our mother too, even by accident?" Hanane swallowed thickly. "She's gone. Everyone's gone, but I'm still here." Her voice tightened, thick with unshed tears. "Why am I here?"

"You're here because of Farid," offered Malik. His fingers were still stiff from Hanane's touch. "He cares for you very much."

Hanane looked down, her shoulders sagging. "I'll always have Farid," she whispered.

Uncomfortable silence settled over the dying garden, until Leila said, "Tomorrow, we'll be heading into the Lower City. You should come with us. Go see what your city has become."

The princess bit her lip. "Farid doesn't want me to leave the palace until the omens have calmed."

"Is Farid your keeper? Does he really pull you around on a collar and chain like the rumors say?"

Malik cringed, expecting Hanane to punish Leila for speaking so freely, but the princess simply watched his sister with her eyes wide. Leila continued, "You've been given something no one else in this world has—a second chance at life. Don't waste it letting someone else tell you how to use it."

Princess Hanane lowered her head, and for a long time the only sound was the rustling of her mother's trees. But when she lifted her chin, Malik got the first glimpse of the queen she had been raised to be.

"People in this palace have been beheaded for less insolence than you just showed," she said. "But instead of punishment, heed this request. Take me with you when you leave tomorrow. I wish to see my city with my own eyes."

14

Karina

Karina wasn't going to think about the fact that her ancestor had once lived side by side with the very people she would one day massacre.

She wasn't going to think about the spark of Malik's power that resided inside her, and the spark of hers that resided inside him, or the fact that fire raced across her skin every time he touched her, even though she still did not trust him.

And she most certainly was not going to think about how one small misstep would send her plummeting down this cliffside to an extremely painful end.

"Come on, Karina! You're almost halfway there!" yelled Afua, which was easy enough to say when she, Ife, and Caracal were all safely at the bottom of the cliff. Heights had never frightened Karina before, but one look at the sheer drop beneath her had strangled her courage. Maybe this was punishment for stealing from that baby.

But according to Caracal, the entrance to the City of Thieves lay at the bottom of this canyon. Not climbing down was not an option.

She lifted her right foot from the thin ledge, only for the rock beneath her left foot to wobble ominously. Karina immediately snatched her foot back and cowered against the stone.

"Hurry up, we're not getting any younger down here!" barked Caracal.

"Try not to look at the dozens of jagged rocks below you!" yelled Ife.

Karina bit back a groan. "Thank you, Ife!"

"You're welcome!"

Karina took a deep breath and stretched her right leg toward the next ledge. Just a little more, she was so close—

The earth became the sky and the sky became the earth as the rock beneath Karina's hand broke free and she went tumbling down the cliffside. This was it—after surviving infernos and serpopards and coups, the cause of her death was about to be a bunch of stupid rocks.

But the stupid rock death never came, for her back slammed into a giant cushion of air about a dozen feet off the ground. Karina lay in a daze as Caracal's powers gently deposited her beside the others. The former Sentinel regarded her as if she'd just battled a kitten and lost.

"Congratulations, you might be the first Wind-Aligned zawenji in the history of Sonande to have almost died from a *fall*. Or did you forget that we have control over all wind and air?"

A flood of embarrassment washed over Karina, but as she could not snap back at the man when he had just saved her life, she chose instead to take in their surroundings.

The tall ridges of Shark Tooth's Canyon rose all around them, a chasm that extended north and south through the desert for hundreds of miles in each direction. From where they stood, the other side of the canyon looked to be about two miles away, but there were some places where the gap was as wide as a dozen miles and as narrow as a dozen feet. Karina would have greatly preferred to enter from the latter, but Caracal swore that if they wanted to find Balotho, the City of Thieves—and more importantly, the only place where they might be able to find information on the guardian of Doro Lekke—this was where they needed to be.

"Stay alert, team," said Caracal. "We are about to enter the single most foul and wretched excuse for a town Sonande has ever seen. Keep your coins close and your weapons closer."

For hours they trekked along the jagged cliffs and rocky paths, until Caracal bid them to stop in front of a small stream of water trickling down the rockface. The former Sentinel let out a high-pitched whistle, then knocked three times against the rough stone. "I know you're there, you old windbags. Show yourselves."

A knife whistled past Caracal's face, slicing a cut across his cheek. Karina pushed Afua behind her as a dozen figures appeared around the canyon walls, arrows pointed for their party. The leader seemed to be an old man covered in a pile of brightly patterned blankets and riding the oldest camel Karina had ever seen. Both their faces were so lined and whiskered, it was difficult to tell one from the other.

Caracal flashed the man a smile that somehow retained its usual charm despite the blood pouring down his face. "It's been a while, Nzima. Don't you recognize me?"

Nzima's bushy eyebrows lifted high, revealing a pair of beady eyes. "Why, it can't be—Caracal? Is that you?"

"In the flesh and blood. I know last time I was here we left on bad terms, but—"

Faster than Karina could register, the old man dove over the side of the canyon, dual blades aimed for Caracal's neck. The former Sentinel let out a grunt as the old man shoved his knee into his back and pulled his head up by the locs.

"I thought I told you if you ever showed your face in my city again, I would rip off each of your limbs and feed them to Lolo," spat Nzima. The camel, who Karina assumed was Lolo, continued to chew her own cud, as if she watched her master gut people every day.

"If this is about what happened with your son, I didn't *make* him leave his husband—"

"You tore my family apart, you ingrate!"

If the old man put any more pressure on Caracal's chest, he was going to kill him, and then who would escort Karina to Doro Lekke? More for her own sake than his, she stepped forward and blurted out, "We wish to invoke the thieves' code!"

The others tensed beside her as the old man's scowl deepened. Some claimed the thieves' code was a myth, but she saw no alternative that didn't involve revealing their powers.

"Surely you've heard word of the coup in Ziran and the truth that the royal family was hiding magic from us all? It was complete chaos. Neighbors turning against neighbors, sisters against sisters, accusations of witchcraft everywhere. We had to get away because I may not be a witch, but I have secrets that need to remain hidden, same as every other person in Balotho. Isn't that why this city exists, as a refuge for all who live on the fringes the rest of the world ignores?"

A bead of sweat dripped down Karina's back as Nzima scrutinized her, eyes gliding over her covered hair and hidden Wind-Aligned emblem.

Finally the old man let Caracal go. The former Sentinel staggered to his feet, gasping for breath as his assailant swung onto his camel's back.

"We of Balotho adhere to the thieves' code, as our ancestors did before us and their ancestors did before them. While you are here, you shall adhere to it too," ordered Nzima. "Here we protect the vile and the meek in equal measure and spurn all who wish them harm. Hand over your weapons, or no one gets inside."

Karina, Afua, and Ife dutifully handed over their few knives. Caracal passed Nzima the dual swords strapped to his back, and everyone stared at him. With a frustrated sigh, he relinquished the multiple blades strapped to his wrists and ankles.

"That's it, I promise—" he began, only for Nzima to pat him down and pull out several more daggers, a coiled garrote, four different vials of poison, a razor blade masquerading as a protective amulet, an entire set of lockpicks, and a miniature crossbow that fit snugly into the palm of his hand.

"Well, now I just feel naked," Caracal muttered as Nzima gestured for them to follow him and step only where Lolo stepped, nowhere else.

As much as Karina loathed the idea that the only thing standing between her and plunging a thousand feet to her demise was a half-dead camel named Lolo, she dutifully fell into place behind the others. In this reluctant, single-file line, their group entered the City of Thieves.

Karina realized quickly how Balotho had managed to evade detection for so many years—the city wasn't hidden inside Shark Tooth's Canyon, it *was* Shark Tooth's Canyon. The thieves had built their haven directly into the canyon walls, their routes nearly invisible to the naked eye. Lolo led them down scraggly paths barely wide enough for a single foot, and between boulders so precariously placed that a sneeze from a butterfly might have sent them careening down to the canyon floor. And woven through it all was the City of Thieves.

It was like something ripped from a criminal's fantasy. Merchants hawked weapons as fine as any back in the armories of Ksar Alahari, while others peddled illegal substances that could alter the body, alter the mind, poison this person, heal that one. Someone had stuffed a dozen locusts into a tiny sack and now claimed that steeping them in a tea with star leaf and neem oil would help a person see the future.

Hungry eyes followed Karina and her entourage everywhere they went. Thin tally marks lined the mercenaries' brows, one for each of their kills. A single wrong move was all it would take to end up as such a scar.

But even with the air of danger hovering over the city, there was a sense of order to it all. The thieves' code was the law, and as long as they followed it, they would be fine.

"What's your history with this place?" Karina muttered to

Caracal as they passed an impromptu ring where two scaly gbaha-
lis fought to the death before an eager crowd.

An odd look flickered across Caracal's face. "There aren't
many places in Sonande that will harbor a Sentinel deserter. Balotho is one of them," he replied, and Nzima grumbled under his
pile of blankets.

"Found the boy wandering delirious at the top of the canyon
ten years ago. Took him in out of the goodness of my heart, and
what does he do? Ruins my son's marriage!"

"Would you believe me if I said I was deeply sorry for my
actions?"

"Absolutely not."

"Good, because I'm not."

As Caracal and Nzima continued their bickering, Karina
mulled over this new information. Caracal seemed just shy of his
thirtieth year, so he would have been around Karina's age when he
deserted the Sentinels. Commander Hamidou, the most powerful
Sentinel Karina had ever known, had needed Afua's help to break
the enchantment over her, yet Caracal had somehow broken his,
escaped into the desert, and made it to safety all on his own. How
frightening that must have been, to have had nothing and nobody
but his own wits to keep himself alive for that long.

"All right, old wrongs aside, what else has changed since I was
last here?" asked Caracal.

"Not much. A huge demand has risen for tonics that can keep
the locusts away, so be prepared to pay a hefty sum for that. Oh,
and a traveling wise woman has set up her tent on the north part
of the city. Calls herself Maame Small Claws."

Maame Small Claws? That was quite the ominous name. "What type of wise woman?"

"I haven't been there myself, so I can't say for sure. But from what I've heard, she can see your future with just a touch of your hand, and she has elixirs to heal any ailment, physical or spiritual."

When they finally reached the center of the city, Nzima said, "This is where I leave you. Remember the code. And you—" He pointed to Caracal, whose face remained the picture of innocence. "Stay away from my son."

Once the guide was gone, their group split into two with a plan to meet back at the square in an hour's time. Karina and Afua went north, huddling close to one another for safety.

"What do you think about this place?" whispered Karina.

"I think we could find anything here, if we're willing to pay the price." The smaller girl shivered. "I don't like the sound of that wise woman, though. And what are the odds she'd arrive here around the same time we did?"

"Perhaps she's a zawenji?"

"Seeing the future falls squarely into ulraji territory. And that is if she isn't a charlatan."

You could hardly throw a rock anywhere in Sonande without hitting someone who claimed to be able to commune with spirits or tell a person's fortune. But now that everyone knew magic was real, even the most absurd claims held weight. If there was even a chance this Maame Small Claws might know something that could get them to Doro Lekke, it was worth seeking her out. Karina was willing to throw her hand in on the most unlikely of odds if it meant saving Sonande without having to die.

Eventually they found the wise woman's abode, thanks to the long line of people clamoring to get inside. The heart of the building sat on a precarious army of stilts above the canyon floor. Bright plumes of smoke belched from its windows—mustard yellow one second, ocean blue the next, flamingo pink another. Sounds of music and merriment emanated from the structure, making Karina ache for the Dancing Seal and the other musical establishments she'd frequented back in Ziran.

However, any hope they'd had of waltzing in and demanding an audience with Maame Small Claws died when they saw the thick-necked guards standing outside the entrance and turning away anyone who did not already have an invite. When several minutes of observation made it clear there would be no way inside without either an invitation or a confrontation, Karina and Afua turned back the way they'd come—only to find themselves in the middle of a fight.

"Monster! Witch!"

The accusations were coming from a woman with her hands balled into fists, who screamed at a younger woman kneeling on the ground, blood pouring from her nose.

"If my children starve because of you, I will beat you to death with my bare hands!" bellowed the former, and were it not for several people holding her back, she might have made good on that threat right then and there.

"What is going on here?" Karina asked the person beside her.

"The two are neighbors. Morowa, the older one, claims that ever since Elinam, the younger girl, began working for Maame

Small Claws, her family has been falling ill, and that today she saw her placing a hex on her crops to attract more of the locusts to them."

"You don't know what you're talking about!" cried Elinam, and Morowa wrenched free of those who held her and clawed the younger girl across the face.

"Witch! I'll kill you myself!"

An elderly woman stepped forward and used her cane to pull the two apart. "Pah, Morowa, a woman your age should not debase yourself like this. If Elinam really is what you say she is, then the gods will let us know. Someone bring me a hen."

A small child ran forward to hand the judge a bright green hen. Once the old woman had the bird in hand, she declared, "If Elinam cuts the hen's head off and it dies, then we know she is innocent. But if Elinam cuts the hen's head off and it continues to walk, then she is truly a witch, and we will be rid of her accordingly."

Sonandeans' distrust of the supernatural ran deep, but this was a level of folk superstition Karina could hardly wrap her head around. The fate of this woman's entire life would really hang on a bird's corpse?

The judge handed both a knife and the hen to Elinam. "If you are as innocent as you claim to be, then you have nothing to fear."

Elinam deftly severed the bird's neck and dropped the body. The entire crowd watched with bated breath as the hen twitched once, twice. Horror flooded Elinam's face, but before the bird could rise, Karina dove into the circle and threw her arms around the girl.

"Elinam, there you are! I've been looking all over for you,

dearest cousin!" Into the girl's ear, she hissed, "Play along if you don't want to do die."

"O-Oh yes! Hello, cousin!" Elinam squeaked out in what had to be the most wooden lie Karina had ever heard. But the crowd was so distracted by the impromptu reunion that none of them noticed the flair of Afua's powers reaching out to quickly and painlessly sever the bird's spine. Only when its body had gone completely still did Karina let Elinam go.

"I traveled all this way to come see you, so imagine my surprise when I heard you'd been accused of witchcraft! That bird is clearly dead, so surely we can all move on with our lives now."

Morowa still looked ready for murder, but by their own rules, Elinam had passed the trial. The crowd quickly dispersed, and the girl sagged against Karina in relief.

"Thank you so much . . . if you hadn't been there, I don't know . . ." she wept, and Karina patted her back awkwardly.

"It's no trouble at all. Besides, this is a ridiculous tradition. If you really were powerful enough to destroy an entire field of crops, what's to stop you from rigging the trial by keeping the chicken alive?" Karina did not mention the real reason she had intervened, which was her guilt over the fact she, not Elinam, was exactly the kind of witch these people should be terrified of. "Sometimes people get so unnerved by their own fear, they don't realize that their response to it is worse than what they feared in the first place."

"This is all that Princess Karina's fault," Elinam said with a sniff, and Karina did her best to keep her face even. "Ever since it came out that a member of the royal family was a witch, everyone is paranoid there might be more hiding among us. They say she's the one who sent the locusts down to punish Sonande."

"Don't worry, all of us here hate Princess Karina just as much as you do. Simply the worst," said Caracal. He and Ife had popped up behind her and Afua during the commotion.

"Agreed, she's the worst," Karina said through gritted teeth.

"And what of you, travelers?" asked the girl. "What brings you to our city?"

It did not seem wise to admit they were looking for information on magic after what Elinam had just been through, so Karina said, "We are actually interested in learning more about Maame Small Claws. Would you happen to know how one might get an audience with her?"

Elinam's eyes lit up. "I can't promise you an audience with her, but I can get you inside. Come, this way."

They followed Elinam to the front of the dwelling, where she walked right up to the armed guards and said, "Don't worry, they're with me."

The guards swept their eyes over them, then nodded. One pulled aside the curtain with a flourish, and a loud crash of drums followed by a cloud of pink smoke wafted through the door.

"Welcome to the healing house of Maame Small Claws. Watch your step and remember—only those who are ready to open themselves up can receive all she has to offer."

Before Karina could ask what that meant, the door slammed shut, sealing them inside.

15

Malik

This was such a bad idea. And Malik would know. Almost every idea he'd had since arriving in Ziran had been a bad one, which was how he could tell this was perhaps the worst.

"We're going to get caught," he whispered to Leila.

"Only if you keep looking so suspicious!" she hissed back. "There's the guard up ahead. Just stay calm and say what we practiced."

Nothing made Malik less calm than being told to stay calm, but he still approached the guard standing watch over the main gate out of Ksar Alahari.

"Open the gate. I have business to attend to in the Lower City," he said, somehow managing not to make his voice crack. The guard's lips twisted into a frown.

"Apologies, Champion Adil—I mean, Champion Malik—but we've been given strict orders that no one is allowed in or out of the palace without authorization," said the woman.

Malik thought about how Karina might handle this situation, and gave the woman a haughty glare. "Then you'll be happy to know I am currently under the authorization of Mwale Farid himself."

Malik handed the guard the note from Farid giving permission for him, his sisters, and their chosen attendant to leave the palace grounds. The woman read over it quickly, then scanned their small group, her eyes lingering on the servant. Hanane drew a shuddering breath beside Malik but kept her eyes planted firmly on the ground beneath the hood of her servant's shift.

Finally the woman nodded, then ordered the gate be opened. "May your journey be a safe one, Champion Malik."

It wasn't until they were across the Widow's Fingers, the bridge that connected the Old City of Ziran to the lower one, that Malik felt like he could breathe again. "I can't believe we just did that!" he groaned. "Farid is going to be furious."

"Farid will live," said Leila. "Besides, look at her. She just left the palace, but she already looks better."

Hanane did seem to brighten the farther away they got from Ksar Alahari. She raced ahead of them with a giggling Nadia in tow. Malik wasn't sure what it was about Hanane that Nadia was so drawn to, but his younger sister seemed more like herself than she had since returning from the spirit world as she and the princess galloped through the streets hand in hand, regarding everything they saw with childlike wonder. Just like before, Nadia seemed to have no adverse reaction to touching Hanane.

"Glad to see they're getting along so well," he grumbled, and Leila nudged his shoulder.

"Is someone jealous he's no longer Nadia's favorite?" she teased, and Malik dreamed of how simple it would be to be an only child. "Don't take it so personally; children put down their old toys and pick up new ones all the time. Besides, Nadia is around the age Karina was when Hanane died. If being together brings them comfort, let them have their fun."

Malik hadn't considered that, and he mentally chided himself for feeling jealous of someone who had suffered as much as Hanane had. They were doing a good thing by giving her a few hours' reprieve from being forced to relive her own death.

But that wasn't to say there was no danger outside the palace. Everywhere they looked, the devastation of the locusts was on full display. Houses sat looted and abandoned, the families who had lived there having chosen to flee for fear of more destruction. Cattle covered in sores from the insects' bites gazed at them with sickly brown eyes, and there was a desperation in the air that came from the collective understanding that something awful was happening and they were all powerless to stop it.

This was how Eshra had looked when Malik and his family had left during the worst of the clan wars. He might not be Zirani himself, but these people didn't deserve to suffer like this. He needed to find the flute and the scepter so he could do his part to end this devastation, and he prayed to Adanko that the information he needed was tucked away somewhere inside the university.

Now that they had passed out of the range of Ksar Alahari's protective wards, the wraiths had returned, and they trailed silently behind the group as they made their way through the labyrinthine streets. In a twisted sort of way, Malik was almost glad to see them; with his life having changed so quickly in such a short time, the wraiths were at least familiar, if still terrifying.

After agreeing that Leila and Nadia would wait outside the university with Hanane for she was far less likely to be recognized on the streets than in the school—Malik entered the university grounds. He did his best not to stare at the two towers flanking the gate, each inscribed with thousands of proverbs compiled by students over the years.

It was said that more knowledge was held in a single room of the University of Ziran than in all the libraries in Sonande combined, and from his first steps on the grounds, Malik understood why. There was a deep reverence in the air, a sense that the knowledge amassed in these halls was more important than any of the people who walked through them. Conversations in more languages than Malik could recognize bounced off the tiled floors, and scholars in long robes strolled through the high walkways, piles of books and scrolls in hand.

A small pang of jealousy hit him as he passed a group of young men debating whether the locusts were definitive proof that there existed a malevolent god. He liked to think he would have done well in school, if he'd had the chance to go.

But he had not come here to ruminate on how few opportunities people like him had in this world. He had come searching for Yaema, who he found in the library.

Or rather, she found him, as the second Malik stepped between the rows of bookshelves, Yaema hurtled straight into him, sending dozens of books careening to the ground.

"Ow, watch where you're going you—oh, Champion Malik!" Malik could practically feel the flush that spread through the girl's body. "I'm so sorry, I didn't see you there—"

"Get back here, Yaema!" roared a voice from the direction in which the girl had just come. "Your essay is three weeks late, where is it?"

Malik took one look at Yaema's frightened face, put a finger to his lips, and pulled her into the safety of the nearest book stack. "It would be a shame if your adviser had to chase you all over the campus," he said, and an illusion of Yaema appeared where they'd just stood. The illusion bolted out of the library, and her teacher gave chase, yelling something about respecting the integrity of the academic timeline. As soon as they were alone, the real Yaema stared up at him in awe.

"That was magic, right?"

Malik grinned back. "It was."

"How does it feel when you're using it?" she asked breathlessly. No one had ever asked him that before; Malik wasn't even sure there were words that truly captured the sensation.

"It's like . . . you know how after you wind a spring as tight as it can go, it reaches a point where it can't be wound anymore and flies free? It's like that. A perfect release."

The girl gave a wistful sigh. "Oh, I can't even imagine. If I could do the things you do . . ."

Yaema gazed up at him, and Malik was suddenly very aware of her breath on his cheek, and how sweaty that made his hands feel. He pushed back, wiping his palms on his pants.

Did I not say you are an unusually moist human specimen?

Choosing not to dignify that with even a mental response, Malik cleared his throat and said, "I hope I wasn't interrupting anything important. Actually, I came looking for you."

Now Malik was certain he wasn't imagining the flush that came to her cheeks. "Me? Why would you want—I mean, of course! I don't have very many skills, but I'm happy to do whatever I can to help you."

"Don't undersell yourself. Not just anyone can become a student at the most famous school in Sonande," said Malik, and he meant it. He knew all too well how your own mind could force you to undermine your gifts, no matter how much you accomplished. "Back at the Water Temple, you mentioned that you study the ancient cultures of Sonande. I'm searching for a pair of Kennouan artifacts, and I was hoping you might be able to help me locate them."

Yaema's face fell. "I wish I could, but the university is supposed to remain neutral in all political matters, and it's against the rules for anyone who isn't a master to use our resources to aid a member of the court. Helping you could cost me my enrollment."

Malik didn't want Yaema to be expelled because of him, but if this didn't work, his only option would be to dive back into Idir's memories. He wasn't sure he could survive that again.

I won't pretend to be a master of your human mating rituals, but I am sensing that this girl is attracted to you, drawled the spirit. *You need something from her. Use the former to help you obtain the latter.*

Malik was about to send a silent rebuke but . . . that actually wasn't an awful idea. And besides, hadn't Farid told him the only reason he'd convinced himself there was something between him and Karina was because of his lack of romantic experience? Everyone else got to flirt and tease without consequence, why shouldn't he?

However, the most glaring flaw in that plan was that Malik wouldn't have known how to seduce a person even if they quite literally climbed into bed with him.

He wished Tunde was here. Tunde could have charmed a leopard into giving him the spots off its pelt. He'd have known exactly what to do to persuade Yaema to help him.

Malik pushed away his grief over his late friend and instead twisted his mouth into a sympathetic smile. He bent to pick up one of the books Yaema had dropped.

"That is a shame," he said, his voice low. *Like Tunde. Act like Tunde.* "I don't think I'd be able to sleep at night knowing any harm had come to you because of me."

As he handed the book back to her, Malik brushed his fingers ever so slightly across the back of her hand. Yaema inhaled sharply, and when she didn't pull away, he ran his finger over the pulse point on the inside of her wrist, taking pleasure at the way she shivered.

"I won't ask you to do anything you're not comfortable with. But the information I need is of the utmost importance. Surely someone as smart as you knows of a way I can access it."

He leaned closer, and there again was the leather-and-ink scent again that he'd noticed the first time they met. He tilted Yaema's chin up with his finger, and she shuddered against him. "And of course I'd be happy to do anything you please to make up for the trouble."

"If I help you find these artifacts, will anyone be hurt?" Yaema whispered. An image of Karina's body twisted and broken upon the altar came to mind, but Malik shoved it away.

"Thousands will be saved."

It hit Malik then that if he asked if he could kiss her, she'd likely say yes. And much to his surprise, he wanted to. He had only ever kissed Karina, and a part of him longed to know if all kisses were like theirs had been, or if it was only his lack of experience that had made it feel as if every inch of his body had come alive beneath her touch.

But instead he pulled back. "But of course, if you can't, I understand."

Disappointment rushed through Yaema's face, and she wrung her hands several times before her mouth set into a determined line. "Follow me. But we have to be quick."

Compared to the splendor of the university's main library, the records room Yaema brought Malik to was little more than a glorified storage closet. But her excitement was palpable as she began rifling through the dust-covered documents.

"You're searching for a scepter and a flute that would have been used in a sacred ritual?" Yaema yelled from atop a sliding ladder leaning precariously against a row of shelves. "I don't recall anything about a flute, but the scepter was a symbol of great power in Kennoua. Any of the ones mentioned in the pharaonic records could be the one you seek."

"This one had the head of the jackal on top," Malik offered. "And the material was some kind of green crystal."

"The green was likely malachite. The Kennouans believed the gemstone had holy properties. Oh, and the jackal was the personal symbol of Pharaoh Namra-kha, which would put the scepter's date of origin somewhere around the fifth dynasty, roughly eight centuries or so before the Pharaoh's War . . ."

The afternoon stretched on as Malik and Yaema pored over document after document. She had not been exaggerating her expertise—the girl knew more about the long-lost society than anyone Malik had ever met, even Farid.

". . . and here an unnamed scribe details a scepter being used in a birthing ritual for one of the sisters of Pharaoh Menshaset, but as you can clearly see the design and the stone setting are far too recent to be the one you're looking for—I'm boring you, aren't I?" she said, and Malik bolted upright, embarrassed to have been caught dozing. Yaema's shoulders sagged. "Sorry, I know I talk too much. It's just that with the royal family's stance against Kennoua, it's so rare that I meet anyone I can talk to about it."

"Don't apologize, I'm the one who asked for your help!" he said quickly.

Yaema let out a mirthless laugh. "You'd be the first. My family thinks I'm wasting my time studying this at all. My older cousin was the only one who ever supported me, but he's . . . no longer with us."

The raw chord Malik heard in Yaema's voice made him gently touch her hand. "Your work honors his memory."

Something flashed over Yaema's face, but then she squeezed his hand back. Perhaps once the Rite of Renewal had been completed and everything returned to normal, he would visit her under less dire circumstances. He could use every friend he could get these days.

Malik's mind wandered back to Khenu and Bahia playing in

the forest, decades before the war that would change the course of history. Surely there was a reason that, of all the Faceless King's memories, this was the one his subconscious kept returning to.

"One more question," he said slowly. "Was there ever anyone of great importance in Kennouan history named Khenu?"

"Khenu was a rather common diminutive. Do you know the full name?"

Your ancestor's full name was Khenukahor, offered Idir, and Malik fought the urge to lift an eyebrow. Oh, so now the spirit felt like being helpful.

This might come as a surprise, but like most rational creatures, I would actually prefer to avoid the Great Mother's wrath as well. If that means helping you, then so be it.

"Khenukahor. She would have been alive around the same time as Bahia Alahari, and she would have been a member of the Ulraji Tel-Ra."

"Ulraji Tel-Ra? I don't know that term, were they an organization?" Malik quickly summarized the role of the sorcerers in the Kennouan court, and Yaema bit her lip again in what Malik was beginning to recognize as her thinking expression.

"Every mention of sorcery in Kennoua was destroyed by the Alaharis. But if this group was as important to the pharaohs as you claim, then there should be a record of them somewhere in one of their death logs." After another trip up the rickety ladder, Yaema returned with an ancient scroll that looked as if one wrong touch might send it crumbling to dust. "This is the log for the last pharaoh, Akhmen-ki."

The log held a record of the necropolis's construction, and it detailed exactly where the gold was to be gathered, how the city-sized tomb was to be laid out, and which of the pharaoh's slaves would be placed inside with him. Nausea roiled through Malik's stomach as he read the procedure for mass murder detailed so simply and precisely.

He got to the section detailing the temple at the heart of the necropolis, which had been locked the last time Malik had been there. There was the central room where the pharaoh's sarcophagus lay, along with separate rooms for his gold, his silver, his weapons, his concubines, and his wives.

There was one small room that lay unmarked, and beside it, another that had a series of glyphs Malik was beginning to recognize all too well. He summoned his Mark to his hand and matched the glyphs swirling within it to the ones on the map.

They were identical.

"This is where I need to go," he said aloud. Just thinking about the underground city made his flesh crawl, but one thing was clear: if he wanted to find Khenu, and by extension the scepter, he was going to have to return to the necropolis.

Malik thanked Yaema profusely, tucked the scroll into his pack, and then followed her back to the main library. They had just begun to say their goodbyes when a scowling boy popped up from behind one of the shelves.

"There you are, Yaema. I've brought the object your aunt requested—" The boy stopped abruptly, his eyes going wide with fear when they landed on Malik.

"It's you," Adewale breathed out, and Malik had to fight back an urge to gather Tunde's brother in his arms. No matter how close he might have gotten to Tunde in the short time they'd known each other, he was still a stranger to this family. He had no right to intrude upon their grief with his guilt.

Yaema quickly put herself between the two boys. "Your mother has a message for my aunt, yes?" She grabbed Adewale's arm and began to drag him into the bowels of the university. "Apologies for my rudeness, Champion Malik, but my aunt won't stand for any lateness. I hope to see you again soon."

"Yes, of course—" he began, but the girl was already gone. Malik hadn't realized that Yaema's family was high-ranking enough within the court to know Tunde's. Clearly he still had much to learn about Ziran's social structure.

He'd been looking forward to seeing the afternoon sun after so many hours in the dim musk of the library, but thick black clouds roiled across the sky. He stared up at them, dread pooling in his stomach.

I shall shake the earth from its core, until there is nowhere to stand for people to hear you speak. Then you shall know there is none who rivals me.

"The Tale of the Four Friends" had warned that the second omen of the Great Mother's anger would be tremors and storms, but the story hadn't mentioned how long after the locusts they would strike. How much time did they have until the quakes began—minutes? Hours? And here Malik and his sisters were so far from the sturdy walls of Ksar Alahari, just begging to be crushed beneath the rubble.

Cursing himself for having forgotten such a crucial detail, Malik sprinted down the street in search of his family. Face after face passed, none of them the ones he was looking for, and the ominous rumble of thunder crashed above them. Where could they have—

"Get away from me, demon!"

The cry came from a small corner bordered on one side by a tannery and another by a weaver's shop. Hanane was in the center of a small crowd, her knee upon the neck of a squirming young boy. Her lips pulled back from her face in a feral snarl, and a sticky red substance dripped down her face and now-exposed silver locs. Adanko help him, was that blood?

No, not blood—dye. This boy had thrown dye at a member of the royal family. People had lost limbs for doing less, but the anger of the crowd was clearly directed at Hanane rather than the child. One wrong movement, and they'd have a riot on their hands.

Malik stepped forward, already piecing together an illusion that might distract the crowd long enough for Hanane to get out of there unharmed, when Leila appeared at his side and grabbed his arm.

"She has to handle this herself." Some of the dye had gotten on her and Nadia as well, and Malik felt faint even though he knew it was not blood. "If she doesn't, her reputation will never recover."

Hanane dug her knee deeper into the boy's neck, and his hands scrabbled uselessly against the ground as she stared down at him the same way a lion did a trapped gazelle. The sour taste from the first time they'd met filled Malik's mouth again, and for a second Hanane's features blurred beyond recognition, bringing to mind talons and claws and teeth before they snapped back into place.

It was Leila who stepped forward and called out, "Remember

where we are, Your Highness. Remember who you are."

At the sound of Leila's voice, Hanane blinked as if coming out of a daze. The murderous expression left her face, and she lifted herself off the boy. An older man shot forward from the crowd to gather the child in his arms—his father, the tanner most likely.

"What's your name, child?" she asked.

"His name is Yao, Your Highness," answered his father.

"And why did you throw dye at me, Yao?"

"Because my baba says you're a demon!" snapped the boy. "You're a creature of black magic, and you're the reason the locusts ate all our food!"

Pure terror filled the tanner's eyes, and he threw himself at Hanane's feet. "Forgive him, Your Highness. He's young, he doesn't know what he's saying. I beg you, punish me instead of him."

Hanane regarded the man for a moment before extending a hand to him. "Rise, please. Don't dirty yourself on my account." To the boy, she said, "Tell me, Yao, do I look like a creature of black magic?"

"N-No. I mean . . . no, Your Highness," he added quickly.

"Do I sound like a creature of black magic?"

"No, Your Highness."

"And I certainly don't feel like a creature of black magic. You say the locusts have destroyed your food stores? How much were they worth?"

The boy scrunched up his nose, clearly unable to tie a number to such a large sum, and his father quickly chimed in, "It was truly nothing, Your Highness, just middling scraps."

Hanane rolled up her sleeve, pulled off one of her silver bangles, and handed it to the man. "Then surely this should be enough to replace those middling scraps?"

Even from here, Malik could tell that this one piece of royal jewelry was worth more than all the produce in the souk and then some. The man babbled incoherently with gratitude, but Hanane put up a hand to stop him. "However, there is the matter of punishment. It doesn't do to throw dye at anyone, princess or not, and your son's actions have consequences."

The boy flinched, but Hanane simply swiped a finger through the dye on her front and smeared it across his face. "There, now we are even."

Yao stared up at the princess in wonder before breaking into laughter. The sound seemed to dissolve the anger in the air, and the crowd was watching Hanane now with not quite trust, but curiosity. The elder princess of Ziran straightened up and turned to face her people.

"Much has been said about me since my return, but none of it has been said *by* me. This new reality where magic lives side by side with us has been an adjustment for me too, and unfortunately in my attempts to transition into this second life I have been blessed with, I have neglected my duties as your future sovereign. But no longer. I promise you, starting here and now, everything I do shall be for the betterment of Ziran and nothing else."

Hanane gestured toward Yao and his father, who were still marveling over the bracelet. "If you have grievances to air with me, I will hear them. If you have needs that are weighing you down, I will meet them. All I ask is that you approach me with the same generosity and openness that has made Ziran the greatest place in Sonande."

A crash of thunder rumbled in the distance, but Hanane ignored the weather and extended a hand toward the crowd. "I must return to the palace now. Who among you will walk side by side with me?"

Yao ran up to grab her hand. "I will, princess!"

"I will!"

"I will!"

"Me too!"

One by one, the people of Ziran fell in step behind Hanane, and she gestured for Malik and his sisters to join her as she started up the winding path back to Ksar Alahari.

"What did I tell you?" said Leila as she, Malik, and Nadia watched the princess walk hand in hand with people who just a few minutes before had been determined to rip her to shreds. "That is a girl who was raised to be a queen. Just because others underestimate her does not mean we should."

16

Karina

Elinam went to work explaining what to expect from Maame Small Claws.

"Maame's home has earned a false reputation as a den of inequity, when it is truly a center of healing, both spiritual and physical," said the girl. "What you experience here is meant to help you face the innermost parts of yourself so that you may step into your purpose on the other side."

Karina nodded along, but in truth she was far too distracted for Elinam's words to sink in. The bottom floor of Maame's home housed a lounge where people from all corners of Sonande mingled together on thick cushions strewn about the floor, smoking from long pipes connected to a brazier in the middle of the room. The smoke rings that shimmered in the air smelled vaguely of sandalwood, incense, and . . . starlight. Karina had never considered what a star might smell like, but she was certain this was it.

"This one smells like cedar, leather, and childhood dreams," called Afua, who was already rummaging through the small case of vials beside the main brazier, the people connected to it too relaxed to care. "And this one is orange blossoms, orchids, and lost love!"

"Do you by chance have a seedy bar full of villains on the premises?" asked Ife.

"No, though there is an area where everyone feasts together as equals."

Ife's face fell. "Hardly the same thing."

Despite the bright colors around them, there was a reverence in the air not unlike the feeling one got walking into a temple. This was a place of worship, not just to pleasures of the body but of the spirit as well. It fascinated Karina, who had been taught that healing was bandages and tinctures and tonics, nothing more.

In the dining area, they found people feasting upon food that put even Ksar Alahari's delicacies to shame. Whole fish roasted to perfection, their insides stuffed with fragrant mixes of herbs and mushrooms. Dozens of pots of cheerfully bubbling soups, succulent cuts of meat and fluffy balls of boiled cassava rolling inside. Pot after pot of jollof rice, with sides of shrimp and kebabs. It was all Karina could do to keep the saliva in her mouth as they passed the feast to greet the old woman who was serving it all.

"Maame Small Claws! I have new guests for you. They saved me from a bit of trouble outside," said Elinam. Maame Small Claws was surprisingly tall, easily a head higher than a fully grown man despite her shock of white hair and world-weary face. Her white-and-gray ensemble was deceptively simple, save her headpiece—dozens of tiny interwoven chains that circled her head, fastened together by a shining white jewel on the center of her forehead. Her skirts were voluminous, extending around the woman in a wide circle and train, the beads woven through them clinking together whenever she walked.

"I hope it wasn't that Morowa again. She's always causing trouble." The wise woman spooned a generous helping of egusi stew into a small boy's bowl, patted his head, and turned her attention to Karina's entourage. Kind black eyes sunk deep in a worn face lingered a second longer on Karina than anyone else. "And who do we have here?"

Karina made the Zirani gesture of respect toward the woman. "We have traveled a long way to ask for your help in an extremely important matter. If you would give us a moment of your time—"

Maame Small Claws cut her off with a gentle laugh. "Dear heart, in Maame's house, there are no heavy discussions until everyone has been bathed and fed. Elinam, see to it that our new friends get settled."

Karina tried to protest, but there was nothing she could do to stop the woman from shoving food into their hands before going to help a server carrying a giant basket of banku. Elinam left them at a low table in the back of the room with a promise to check on them later.

Once she was gone, Caracal leaned back on his pillow and dropped a shrimp into his mouth, tail and all. "We're all in agreement that this place is amazing, right?"

"Don't talk with your mouth full," Karina chided, though she was already digging into her own food. After weeks of unseasoned garri and dried meat, Maame's cooking was up to even her royal standards. She glanced over at Ife, whose face was pinched tight. "What's wrong? Aren't you hungry?"

"Too loud in here. Too many people." Ife's grimace deepened

as they squeezed their eyes shut. "I don't like this. I don't like this. I don't like this."

Caracal took one look at his friend and pushed himself to his feet. He guided Ife to theirs without touching them. "Let's get you outside. That should help." To Karina and Afua, he added, "I have counted every grain of rice on my plate, so keep your grubby fingers off it if you want to keep them."

As soon as they were gone, Karina stole the biggest piece of Caracal's beef. "You're our resident magic expert. What do you think about all this?" she asked Afua as she tore into it.

"I'm sensing magic, but it doesn't feel like zawenji or ulraji," replied Afua through bites of kebab. "It feels . . . older. And there's so much stimuli in here, I can't pinpoint the source."

"Doro Lekke was created with older magic. Could this have anything to do with it?"

"I . . . maybe? I don't know." Afua's shoulders sagged. "I'm sorry. Magic is the one thing I'm good at, but I haven't been very useful on this journey, have I?"

"What? No! I don't keep you around just because you're useful." Karina pulled the girl into a one-armed hug. "You are one of the most loyal, generous people I know. There is no one I'd rather be hunting down an enchanted moving city with."

Afua beamed, only to shriek when Karina took advantage of the moment to steal one of her kebabs. Caracal returned to find Afua struggling futilely as Karina quickly shoved the entire skewer into her mouth.

"Ife's doing better, but they're going to wait outside. Loud, crowded spaces like this don't agree with them," said the former Sentinel. Karina nodded, then inhaled the rest of her food before jumping to her feet.

"We'll cover more ground if we split up," she told the other two. "Let's meet back here in an hour to discuss what we find."

And hopefully, whatever magic Afua was sensing in this place was one that would help rather than harm them.

Karina drifted from room to room, trying to understand exactly what it was about Maame Small Claws that had enthralled so many. But as the hours dragged on, all she saw was people being healed and healing others, through touch, through song, sometimes through simple words. Perhaps this truly was nothing more than a healer's den, though a rather unorthodox, almost cult-like one.

She absentmindedly took the drinks Maame's attendants handed her. Her thoughts grew warmer, drifting through her mind like fluffy white clouds. The tinny whistle of a horn accompanied by the booming rhythm of a drum filled the air, and Karina let her feet carry her toward the song. There was some extremely important reason she was here, she was sure of it, but how was she supposed to care about that when there was so much loveliness all around her?

The source of the joyous song was a group of musicians playing in a hammam, steam rising from the bathwater in rosebud-pink plumes.

"Oh, there you are! I'm almost done here, if you could wait just a moment," said Elinam, and Karina watched as the girl massaged oil into a pregnant woman's stomach and voiced a prayer alongside the music for the infant to grow healthy and strong. The expectant mother's skin practically glowed as Elinam draped a patterned yellow robe over her shoulders and directed her to go into the next room for the rest of her treatment. Finally she turned back to Karina. "Thank you for your patience. How do you feel?"

"Fluffy," responded Karina, for there was no other word that could describe the buoyant feeling ballooning in her chest, as if she might float into the sky and never come down.

Elinam laughed. "I don't have any more patients for the evening, so would you care for a bath? You should experience all that Maame Small Claws has to offer before you move on to the next leg of your travels."

Karina was no stranger to being bathed, and so she allowed the girl to disrobe her and lower her into the water. The heat of it against her travel-worn skin was even better than the meal had been, and she let out a moan as Elinam poured a bucketful of rosewater over her head, loosening her silver curls to float around her.

"That's it, just let it all go," said the healer, her voice the perfect complement to the soaring melody that threaded through Karina's warming veins. "Let the water take everything you've been carrying, everything that's been weighing you down. Surrender yourself to it."

Surrender. Karina had always considered it something cowardly, but how lovely it might be to hand yourself over to something so much bigger than you, to no longer have to fight with every breath and just simply . . . be.

Karina tilted her neck back to peek up through the steam and her curls at Elinam, who was pouring a tincture of different oils into the water. Elinam was so pretty. Did she know how pretty she was? Someone should tell her how pretty she was. Karina would do it, but she couldn't quite remember how to get her tongue to form words.

But she must have said the last part out loud after all, for Elinam giggled shyly. "You are very pretty too, princess," she replied, and Karina could have kissed her because she missed the intimacy of being close to another person. It had been so long since she'd kissed anybody, and no that wasn't true, she had kissed Malik and right before that she had kissed Tunde and why was she thinking about Tunde, thinking about him was the opposite of how she wanted to feel right now, she didn't want to think about how she had married him and then kissed his friend and then gotten him killed in the span of less than a day, and wow this water felt wonderful.

It occurred to her that Elinam had called her princess, and oh she wasn't supposed to see her hair was she, but it was too late for that as the healer was now gently detangling the silver curls with her fingers. Karina let out a sigh and pushed aside the small warning bell in her mind to let herself enjoy the feeling of being pampered. It was one of the few things she missed from her old life.

There came a shuffling behind her, and a whispered conversation before the hands were back, sectioning off her coils into long twists. But there was something different about the touch, no less gentle than before but now with a firmness that made Karina shudder.

"It's all right, sweetling, it's just me," crooned Maame Small Claws. "My, how much tension your body holds. What burdens you must carry, and at such a young age too."

The kindness in the woman's voice brought tears to Karina's eyes. Finally, someone who acknowledged just how difficult her life had been, even if her cage had been a gilded one.

"Tell me, little zawenji, who told you of Maame Small Claws? There are millions of places you could have gone in the desert, why come here?"

Karina could not have stopped the truth from coming out even if she wanted to, and she didn't, even though a tiny voice inside her screamed that she should. "I'm looking for Doro Lekke, the long-lost Sanctum of the zawenji. Coming here was an accident."

A shock of lightning blue flashed across the wise woman's eyes. Karina giggled to herself. Hyena's eyes used to flash like that.

"Who else knows about me?" the woman demanded, and now her hands weren't so gentle, but Karina couldn't move away. She couldn't move any of her muscles at all. "Who sent you? Was it the palace? Those meddling priestesses?"

"N-No one sent me!" Oh no, she'd angered Maame. She had to apologize. But why was Maame so upset about being found? This place should be famous throughout Sonande, not found only by those lucky enough to wander upon her. Why didn't Maame Small Claws want anyone to know she was here?

And . . . and why was she called Maame Small Claws anyway?

Karina's muscles were still refusing to work properly, but she managed to tilt her head a fraction of an inch toward the woman. Something slithered under Maame's voluminous skirts.

Legs—not one, not two, but dozens of them, sharp at the end like a centipede's, the sound of their clicking muffled by the beads on her outfit and the chaos around them.

Karina's thoughts fought to come together. That was not good . . . that was not good because—"You're not human," she breathed out, and all at once it hit her.

This wasn't a place of healing at all.

This was a trap.

Karina tried to rise once more, but Maame grabbed her by the shoulder with a grip so tight it punctured the skin of her collarbone. The wise woman's face twisted into a snarl that revealed rows upon rows of venom-tipped teeth.

"And you, daughter of Bahia Alahari, should not have come here."

Before Karina could even scream, Maame Small Claws bit down on her neck, and the world went dark.

17

Malik

By the time Hanane reached the Widow's Fingers, the winds had escalated, shaking the foundations of weaker buildings and blowing howling devils through the already emptied streets. Yet the princess's impromptu procession walked with her against the gales until the group reached the bridge, where Farid waited with a carriage and an entire unit of Sentinels.

"Hanane!" A frantic glint burned in Farid's eyes as he rushed to her side. "I was so worried about you! Come, quickly, you'll be safer in here." To the Sentinels, he ordered, "Disperse the crowd and strike down anyone who attempts to follow us."

"Wait, don't—" Hanane began, but Farid quickly ushered her into the vehicle. Malik and his sisters barely made it in after her before the Sentinels locked the door. Hanane attempted to open the grated window, but Farid slammed the shutters closed.

"Too much of a security risk," he warned. He laid his withering gaze on Malik, who shrank beneath it. "Would you care to explain to me why you almost got the princess killed?"

Malik opened and closed his mouth several times, but no words came out. Hanane let out a growl of frustration.

"I'm the one who forced Malik to take me with him today. If

you're going to be mad at anyone, be mad at me."

"He defied my direct order—"

"Only because I told him to! Surely your word does not hold more weight than the future queen's."

"You could have been killed—"

"It wouldn't be the first time—"

"Are you so desperate to die again, Hanane?" snapped Farid, his voice hoarse.

Tense silence filled the wagon. Hanane's anger softened, and after a moment of hesitation, she placed a hand against Farid's cheek.

"No," she said softly. "I am not."

Farid's entire body seemed to unwind under the princess's touch. For several seconds he simply leaned into it, looking more like a worried boy than the man who was effectively running Ziran.

"Our spies report that there is a faction within the city questioning your right to rule. No word yet on who their leaders are, but we suspect they're being led by members of the court. I know better than most how capable you are, but if anything had happened to you while you were without guards . . ."

"Nothing happened, Farid. And even if something had, I know how to defend myself." The softness in Hanane's face twisted into anguish. "But the people, they're suffering. The locusts are ravaging their food stores, and they believe the palace has abandoned them to their fate. They believe I've abandoned them to their fate. Something must be done."

"The council and I are handling it. There is no need to concern yourself with such matters."

"A queen's only job is to concern herself with such matters."

"And by the standard established by the Ancient Laws, you are not yet queen so long as Karina carries the title. After all the years we spent together, after I moved heaven and earth aside to resurrect you, do you trust me?"

The smallest flicker of doubt passed through Hanane's eyes, but it was gone so quickly Malik might have imagined it. "More than anyone."

"Then trust that everything I have ever done and everything I will ever do has been solely for your benefit. Please, let's not fight. Not over this."

Hanane's shoulders tensed as if there was more she wished to say, but then she nodded and sat back. The rest of the wagon ride passed in awkward silence, and Malik had never been more grateful to walk in the rain than he was once they arrived at Ksar Alahari. But when he moved to follow Hanane and his sisters back to the residential quarters, Farid put a hand on his shoulder.

"Your day is not over yet," said his mentor, his voice as dark as the storm clouds gathering in the sky. "Follow me."

Hanane had told Farid not to be angry with him, but Malik had spent enough years surviving his father to recognize silent fury. His mind raced through a number of things he might say to return to his mentor's good graces as the man led him deep into the bowels of the palace.

"I think I have a lead on the scepter!" he said, and Farid lifted an eyebrow.

"More than a week since the locusts first arrived, and you have nothing but a lead on *one* of the two artifacts you were tasked to find?"

"I—um—yes." Suddenly Malik felt like a fool, a stupid, stupid fool for thinking Farid might be impressed by anything less than concrete results. He jumped as another crash of thunder boomed overhead. Whatever storm was coming was sure to rival Karina's in strength, and though he was grateful to be back in Ksar Ala-hari, he felt sick thinking of all the people they'd left behind in the Lower City to suffer through it alone.

They passed through a thick iron door, and the first thing Malik noticed was the stench—a potent mix of long-rusted metal, human excrement, and something deeply sour that turned his stomach.

This had to be the palace dungeons. Malik swallowed thickly, his throat constricting. Had he displeased his mentor this much? If anything happened to him down here, how would anyone ever know?

"I'm so sorry, I won't talk to the princess again, I won't even look at her," Malik babbled, only for Farid to cut him off with a raised hand.

"I have not brought you here for punishment. Our soldiers retrieved one of the people who aided Karina in her escape during the Closing Ceremony."

They stopped at the very last cell in the row, in front of which stood two Sentinels.

"Has she given any useful information yet?" Farid asked the Sentinel commander, the same one who had thrown fire at Malik during his test. The man shook his head.

"Not yet, but the interrogation has only just begun."

The commander let them into the cell. Much to Malik's surprise, he recognized the prisoner huddled in the corner—Dedele Botye, the Fire Champion. Though they had not spoken much during Solstasia, he would never forget her wakama match with Karina. Dedele had seemed like a warrior heroine from a griot's epic that day, as adept at battle as an eagle was at flight.

However, the Dedele who knelt in the muck was far from the opponent Karina had once faced. Thick chains kept her secured to the ground, and the mixture of old and new wounds littering her skin suggested that she had fought with someone even before the Sentinels had captured her. Whoever that person was, Malik hoped they had left the altercation in better shape than she had.

"Dedele Botye. Not the person I was expecting to find at the heart of this mess." Farid clasped his hands behind his back and circled the girl, while Malik stood off to the side with the guards, not quite sure why he was there. "My sources tell me you refuse to speak. Very honorable. But know that you are in far less danger with me than you were with Karina. After all, only one of us can call lightning from the sky, and that person isn't me."

Silence. Farid knelt before the girl, his arms resting on his elbows. "Though you come from a family of high-ranking traders, you and Karina never met prior to Solstasia. Tell me, what possessed you to risk so much for a girl you barely knew?"

"Come closer, and I'll tell you," mumbled the girl.

Farid did so, and Dedele spat in his face. Malik cringed; there had been quite a bit of phlegm there.

But to his credit, Farid's smile never slipped. He straightened up and wiped his face with his sleeve. "You forget I raised Karina, who once dipped a pillow in cow urine and let me sleep on it when I told her she wasn't allowed to stay up past her bedtime. A bit of saliva is nothing."

"You're an absolute madman," Dedele barked, and for the first time Farid's smile wavered. "I'm not telling you anything."

Farid tilted his head to the side, then lifted his hands, his fingers moving through the air as if weaving on an invisible loom. The web of nkra shimmered in the air before him, though Malik was the only other person who saw it. He watched breathlessly as his mentor stopped on a bold thread that pulsed with peach-colored light.

"A thread of affection," he mused. "For a lover? No, not lover. A friend perhaps? No . . . a relative. A member of your family whom you cherish above all the others. My sources tell me that after your mother fell ill, it was her sister who raised you and your siblings. I wonder what she might say if we brought her in for questioning?"

Dedele bolted upright, her muscles straining against her chains. "My aunt has nothing to do with this!"

"Then she should have no reason not to speak to us." Farid's smile returned, serene as ever. "Your loyalty is an admirable trait, but it is wasted on Karina. The Alaharis gained the fealty of people like your family for generations by positioning themselves as symbols of justice and peace, when in reality they were hoarding immense amounts of power all for themselves. I wish to change this, but I can't do that until the vestiges of the old world have been burned away. I can't do that until Karina is under control."

"And you plan to do so via the Rite of Renewal, correct?" she snapped.

"So you know about the Rite of Renewal as well? Is that why Karina abandoned you in the middle of the desert—because, deep down, you understand that if this ritual is not performed, we all perish? Your beloved family, your cherished aunt—all of them will die because Karina cares more about 'reclaiming her throne' than she does the greater good. What do you have to gain from helping someone like that?"

Dedele remained silent, but the stricken expression on her face showed that Farid's words had cut deep. He straightened up, brushing dirt from his kaftan.

"I'll have the guards bring your meal. Perhaps once you've eaten, you'll be more amenable to sharing what you know." Farid made it to the doorway, paused, and turned back to Dedele, his smile gone.

"I do not wish to hurt you, Fire Champion. But if you ever spit on me again, I will."

And there was that smile again, sunny and bright. "Have a good night."

Only when they were out of Dedele's sight did the full weight of Farid's anger show.

"Let's pause the search for the scepter and flute for the moment, until we have this girl dealt with," he said to Malik, his voice reflecting a calmness that his eyes did not. "The Sentinels tell me she has resisted all interrogation methods thus far. We need to find out what she knows of Karina's whereabouts."

Malik's eyes widened at the implication in his mentor's voice. "You want me to interrogate her?"

Farid nodded. "It is said that the storyweavers of Kennoua were such expert interrogators that their illusions could persuade a babe to turn against their own mother. Use your powers in whatever way you see fit to coerce her into telling us what she knows."

Farid put his hand on Malik's shoulder and leaned in close, his voice uncomfortably hot against the shell of Malik's ear. "And do not bother to return until you do."

Feeling as if his legs might give way beneath him, Malik simply nodded. Soon he was alone with the Sentinels, who watched silently as Malik slid down against the wall and wrapped his arms around his knees, shaking.

Torture. Farid was asking him to torture this girl.

"Is what he said true about storyweavers questioning prisoners back in Kennoua?" he whispered, not caring if the Sentinels thought he was talking to himself.

The Faceless King stirred. *It is.*

The knot of panic tightened in Malik's gut. Trickery and misdirection were one thing, but torture? He couldn't do that . . . could he? But he didn't have a choice. Farid had meant every word of that command—if Malik could not get Dedele to talk, then there was no longer a place for him in the palace.

Dedele barely regarded Malik as he entered her cell the second time. He sat on the ground across from her, and the silence stretched on, broken only by the growing roar of the storm above.

Dark puddles had begun to seep up through the stone, and Malik wondered what would happen if Ksar Alahari were to flood.

"Farid mentioned you had siblings," he said after the silence grew unbearable. "How many?"

As he had expected, Dedele did not reply. Malik's palms filled with sweat, but he pressed on. "I have two sisters myself. The first is almost a year older than I am, and the younger one is six, but she'll be turning seven soon."

Dedele's chains rattled as she shifted her weight from one side to the other. "If your plan is to wring sympathy from me using stories of your baby sister, save your breath. It's not going to work."

Good, she was talking, at least. If there was any way to get her to confess what she knew without using his powers, that was the first step.

"Because of the age difference, I've always been more of a parent than a brother to Nadia. Do you have a younger sister?"

Dedele's eyes roamed over his face, and Malik forced his expression into one of perfect serenity, same as Farid's, even if his insides felt as troubled as the storm. Whatever she found there eased the tension in her shoulders just a bit.

"Two. The older one is eleven, the younger one is nine. And I have three older brothers."

"Five siblings! And I thought two was a handful. You must be worried sick about them. I can try to find out what how they're doing, if you'd like."

Dedele's eyes narrowed. "Why would you do that?"

"Because if I was in your position, trapped here not knowing if my family was safe or even alive, I'd go mad with worry." In truth, the part of him that belonged to his mother and grandmother was always in a state of panic. Malik had to clear his throat before he was able to speak again. "I can use the connections I have within the palace to locate them, if you share what happened when you parted ways with Karina, and where she was headed next."

The former Fire Champion snorted. "Nice try, but no. Karina told me all about what happened between you two, so I know a promise from you isn't worth the air you'd use to make it."

The fact that Karina had told the girl what had happened on the roof of the Sun Temple shouldn't have bothered Malik as much as it did. She was under no obligation to keep the moment secret, especially considering that he'd tried to kill her right after, but up until now he'd thought that was something shared only between the two of them, something no one else could pry their way into.

Malik shook his head. He couldn't let her turn the conversation around on him. "Dedele, please. Karina might have told you about the Rite of Renewal, but you didn't see what we saw. You didn't see what is truly at stake if we don't find Karina and perform it as soon as possible. Farid was not exaggerating when he said it would be the end of everything as we know it."

Malik's magic roared to life, and with his powers he created a replica of the vision he had seen in the Faceless King's memories. Dedele flinched, forced to watch as the locusts tore into the countryside and storm-filled quakes ripped through the earth, crushing people to death beneath crumbling buildings and drowning them in the floods caused by the deluge. Bodies covered head to toe in pus-filled boils rotted in the streets, and blood rained from the sky as a monster ripped from the absolute worst of Malik's night-mares raced across the sky.

"There's still time for you to help us avoid this fate," Malik said, pushing every bit of magic he could into the illusion. He couldn't let Farid down, not again. "Just tell us where Karina went. That's all you have to do to help us save everyone."

Dedele stared at the destruction Malik had created, fear and defiance warring on her face. Finally she spoke.

"I agree with you that using Karina for the Rite of Renewal is in everyone's best interest," she said, and a spark of hope burned to life in Malik's chest. "But even though I may not agree with her, Farid is nothing more than a spoiled tyrant who has deluded himself into believing his vision of the future is the only right one. So I'm not going to help Karina avoid her fate, but I'm not going to help him or you either."

Malik's hope crumbled to ash. The illusion died, returning them to the dank air of the cell.

"Please, Dedele," he begged, his voice cracking from both panic and fear. "There must be something, anything, you want in exchange for this information."

Dedele's expression curled into one of disdain, and a second too late, Malik realized his true accent had slipped through. "That accent . . . you're from Eshra, aren't you?" She let out a cruel laugh. "As if I needed another reason not to help you, there's one more. I'm not turning Karina over to a damn kekki."

Malik blinked, not certain he had heard correctly. "What?"

"I'm guessing you're only working for Farid because he

promised you riches or power. How else would someone like you end up in these halls?"

"Stop it."

"You can claw and simper all you want, but when this is all over Farid is going to throw you away into the gutter where you damn kekkis belong."

This was far from the first time anyone had called Malik that slur, but something about hearing it here, after all that he had gone through, shattered the small sliver of restraint left within him.

No matter what he did, no matter how powerful he became, to some people he would always be just another kekki.

"You throw around that word so casually. Kekki." Idir said something, but Malik did not listen as he was too focused on the girl smirking at him as if he was worth less than the dirt on the bottom of her shoe. "To you it's just another word. You don't even think twice about using it. To me, it's the last word many of my people hear before they die at the hands of people like you."

Suddenly this was about more than just Dedele and Farid and Karina. It was about generations lost to indignity and fear, hoping and praying for a better world that never came.

Malik had experienced enough fear to last him several life-times. Let *him* be something to fear now.

And there, burning and screaming in his chest, was an end-less well of power—the Faceless King's power. Idir himself was still bound, but his magic reached for Malik, and Malik reached eagerly back for it.

Malik, no! cried Idir, but he was too slow to stop the tiniest sliver of his magic from slipping through the binding—just a drop, but still more power than Malik had ever held before.

"Do you know what it's like in Eshra?" Malik asked, and suddenly they were in Oboure—not the village of his childhood but the Oboure of today, ravaged by years of crises. Corpses littered the ground, and scavengers both beast and human scurried between them to steal whatever they could find. Death permeated the air, filling their lungs with its sickly sweet tang.

"Do you know hunger? True hunger, the kind that hollows you from the inside out, forces each of your organs to turn on the others in a desperate bid to keep you alive? Because I do."

For as long as he'd been practicing magic, Malik had never made an illusion that could be touched. He could make someone see whatever he wanted them to see, make them hear and smell whatever he created, but he'd never been able to make them feel it.

Until now.

With the Faceless King's power bolstering his own, Malik gathered up his memories of all those hungry nights, the pangs and the weakness of a body unable to function at the barest level, and sent them all to Dedele. His anger didn't abate even as she cried out in pain.

"Have you ever broken a bone and been unable to set it because your family couldn't afford a healer?" he snarled. "Have you felt infection settling into your body knowing that the simplest medicine could fix it, yet your kind isn't allowed access to it? Because I have."

Dedele let out a scream as the phantom pain of her bones

snapping one by one coursed through her body. Sweat beaded her brow, and her eyes searched frantically for relief that was not coming. Besides, all the bones Malik had broken and all the times he'd screamed, no one had ever come to his aid. Why should she deserve that when he'd never gotten it?

"Do you know what it feels like to be beaten within an inch of your life?" he asked, and Dedele's screams intensified as her limbs twisted beneath the weight of phantom blows. "Do you know what it's like to feel so broken in every inch of your body that death starts to look more merciful than taking another breath?"

You've made your point. Stop this, ordered the Faceless King, but Malik batted the words aside. Try as he might, he could not muster up any sympathy for Dedele. After all, this was nothing more than the illusion of pain—in reality, he had not laid a single finger on her. The same could not be said of him and all the other children of Eshra who lived these injustices every day.

"What you are feeling now, this is what it means to be a kekki. This is what the world puts us through for no reason other than existing. So remember this moment the next time you feel like putting that word in your mouth."

All at once, Malik cut off the illusion, and they were back in the dungeon. He regarded Dedele coldly as she gasped for air. This time he did not bother to lower himself to her level when he spoke to her.

"Now, back to what we were discussing earlier. Where is Karina—or rather, where is she going? Tell me all that you know."

The former Fire Champion swallowed thickly, then set her

mouth into a determined line. "N-No," she spat.

Malik sighed, his magic already roaring back to life inside him. "All right. If you wish to be difficult, so be it."

And with that, Malik began to break her.

"Karina was last seen heading north, in the direction of Talafri. She is looking for someone who can lead her to an ancient city of the zawenji, where she hopes to find the power once granted to Bahia Alahari. With it, she plans both to stop you and to put an end to the wrath of the gods without having to perform the Rite of Renewal."

Farid's eyebrows shot up in surprise, and his eyes flickered from Malik to Dedele, who was slumped over in the corner of her cell. The slight shiver of her shoulders was the only indication that she was alive at all. "She told you all that?"

Malik nodded. "She did."

Farid's gaze fell to Malik's arm, where a dark stream of blood was staining the sleeve of his tunic. "And she did that to you as well?"

Malik clutched his arm to his chest and looked away. "This is unrelated."

Just as before, pain had been the only thing that had allowed Malik to cut off the flow of the Faceless King's power before it consumed him. But it was fine. He was fine. He'd gotten Farid what he wanted. That was all that mattered.

"There was one more thing," Malik added, grimacing through the pain radiating from his arm. "She mentioned that Karina met up with someone in Tiru who is now aiding her search for the Sanctum. He goes by the moniker Caracal."

A clatter rang through the air, and Malik immediately shifted into a defensive stance, the spirit blade in hand. But the commander of the Sentinels had simply dropped his spear.

"Caracal?" the man asked, and the breathless way he said the name was completely incongruous with the warrior's fearsome stature. "You're certain she's with Caracal?"

"Do you have some history with this man, Commander?" Farid inquired, and in an instant, the spear was back in the Sentinel's hand, the image of the perfect, emotionless warrior back in place.

"We trained in the same squad before he deserted. That is my history with him. Nothing more."

Farid nodded. "If you trained together, then surely you know his patterns. Gather a team of your finest warriors; I want you ready by sunrise to go after Karina and this Caracal."

Malik was not sure if he imagined the slightest of hesitation before the Sentinel commander made the gesture of respect. "As you wish, Mwale Farid."

Malik followed his mentor's gaze back to Dedele, who was now crying softly. For the first time, he felt a twinge of regret.

However, the regret died as Farid put his hands on his shoulders and beamed down at him.

"Marvelous, Malik. Simply marvelous. This changes everything, and it's all thanks to you. I could not be prouder."

Malik waited for the swell of pride to rush through him. There was some of that, certainly, but it was vastly outweighed by the boiling nausea within him and the biting pain of his arm. Suddenly all he wanted was to close his eyes and not open them for a very, very long time.

Dedele would be fine. He hadn't killed her. He hadn't even physically harmed her.

But Malik knew better than most how the worst kinds of wounds never touched the flesh.

He was vaguely aware of Farid placing a hand at his back and leading him out of the dungeon. And then his mentor was gone, and Malik was alone in the vast halls of the palace.

That was when his legs gave way beneath him, and he vomited again and again until there was nothing left to come out.

"So the great sultana of Ziran is finally defeated by a giant centipede demon," cackled Tunde. "Imagine the songs the griots are going to sing about this!"

Karina groaned, a myriad of colors spilling across the backs of her throbbing eyelids. "Shut up. You're dead. I don't have to listen to you."

Her late husband's face twisted with mock outrage as he placed a hand over his heart. "I may be dead, but at least I'm not immobilized and hallucinating, so who is the real loser here?"

Tunde had a point, which Karina might have countered had she not, in fact, been immobilized and hallucinating.

The last thing she remembered was being bitten by Maame Small Claws. Now there was nothing but sounds, sensations, and pain, with Tunde here to haunt her through it all.

"You should open your eyes. See just how much trouble you've gotten yourself and your friends into," Tunde urged, and even though Karina's head felt like someone was screwing giant bolts into it, she forced her eyes open.

She was in some kind of apothecary, the shelves lined with clay pots and glass bottles containing the myriad of ingredients

Maame used to make her tinctures. Bundles of herbs hung above them, filling the already heady air with their cloying scent. To her left lay Afua, still as a doll, and to her right, Caracal. Ife was nowhere to be seen.

Karina tried to call to her companions, but all that came out was a whimper. Even breathing felt like trying to walk uphill with a mountain sitting on her chest. Caracal shifted, his eyes roving over something Karina could not see.

"Issam, please . . . come with me . . ." he muttered, before the words descended into unintelligible mutterings.

"Oh, quiet you," snapped Maame Small Claws. The horrifying *click-click-click* of her centipede legs scuttling across the floor filled the air as she bustled about, pulling down jars and herbs and throwing them into a pot hanging over a roaring fire in the center of the room.

"One hundred years," the demon muttered. She sniffed at a jar of eyeballs, gagged, and placed it back on the shelf. "One hundred years since any zawenji has crossed my path, and now there are four? Curse the zawenji. Curse the ulraji. Curse them all."

Four? Karina was certain that number wasn't right, but she was in too much pain to remember why. She let out another cry, and the demon turned to her.

"Oh, you've awoken already?" said Maame. "You are stronger than I expected. But don't bother struggling, all you'll do is make a mess of my workroom."

"Let us go," Karina tried to say, but the words came out jumbled and slurred. However, Maame Small Claws clearly got the meaning, for she shook her head.

"So you can tell everyone my whereabouts and jeopardize the sanctuary I've built for myself? Of course not." The demon snarled, and Tunde scrunched up his nose at the sound.

Even though Karina knew he was simply a manifestation brought on by the venom and her own fear, shame filled her every time she looked at him. If her mouth could have moved, she would have told him how sorry she was. She would have told him how she should have been the one to die that night and how she'd regret until the end of her days that he'd paid the ultimate price in a conflict he'd had no part in.

"Please . . . I just want to know . . . the key to Doro Lekke," she gasped out.

Maame barked out a laugh completely devoid of mirth. "You, and every other Great Mother–damned zawenji who's come to me with foolish delusions of divine power. Each believed they were the one among hundreds of others who deserved such a blessing. Each has died by my hands, their bones and their blood added to my stores."

"Come on, Karina, think," urged Tunde. Everything was moving too slowly, her thoughts floating through her mind like dust motes. "What reason would Maame Small Claws have to murder any zawenji who crosses her path? What does she gain from hiding her actions with this house as a cover?"

Elinam had claimed that Maame Small Claws operated her healing house out of the goodness of her heart, but that clearly was not the case. Whatever they had given Karina had dulled her senses and forced her to tell the truth against her will. Worst of all, she had felt wonderful while it was happening, unable to fight against a horror that did not feel like one.

The demon wasn't taking care of these people for their own sakes, but for hers. She was draining them, pulling the nkra from their bodies, and making them weak and powerless against her. But why? What information could be so important that she had to kill any zawenji who got too close?

Unless her job was to kill anyone who came looking for *her*. And what better way to ensure someone would protect something than by staking their literal life on it?

The realization hit Karina, and she struggled to take another breath. Outside, thunder crashed, shaking the entire house to its foundation. "You don't have information about finding the key. You *are* the key. It's inside you. Those other zawenji, they tried to kill you to get it, and so you killed them first."

Maame scuttled over to Karina and grabbed her face in her hands. Swirling blue strands of power sparked in her eyes, alight with sadness and anger thousands of years deep.

"When your beloved ancestors were building their sanctuary, they needed a way to protect it from thieves and outsiders. So they lured me, an innocent child who believed their lies, from the spirit world, placed their key inside me, and left me stranded here. Nobody gets into Doro Lekke without defeating me, and no one ever has. One by one I destroyed them all, fulfilling my accursed duty and feeding on nkra as discreetly as I could via this abode."

Maame let go, her nails leaving bright red marks down Karina's cheek.

"Only one person has ever gotten past me—Bahia Alahari. She came speaking of revolution and righting the wrongs of the past.

She is the only being I've ever met strong enough to kill me, but she chose mercy when she could have made the fatal blow. I was so moved that I let her inside the Sanctum, and the cursed magic that connects me to that infernal place did *this* to me!"

Maame Small Claws drew herself to her full, terrifying height so Karina could see exactly where her body ended and the grotesque shell of her centipede appendages began.

"This was a mere warning of what would happen if I ever shirked my duty again. I have killed every zawenji who has come looking for the Sanctum since, and now that you know, I must kill you too."

Karina did not have words to express the horror of what she was seeing, even if her mind had been operating at full function. To steal a person from their home, spirit or not, and tie them to do such bidding . . . it was an evil she could hardly process.

Yet all the sympathy in the world would mean nothing if Maame killed her.

"My grandmother Bahia showed you mercy. Please, spare some now, if not for me, then for my friends," Karina begged. "Finding the Sanctum was my plan, not theirs. Spare them."

"Do you think this is a world that rewards mercy? That rewards kindness?" Maame sneered. "You either have power or you don't. Anything else is a lie."

The demon scurried around the pot, continuing to throw more ingredients inside. "I wonder what abilities I will gain from eating you and your friends? How long it's been since I had someone Wind Aligned. Soon I will be stronger than any being in Sonande. The Sanctum will remain hidden as your wretched forebears wanted, and no one will be able to harm Maame Small Claws ever again."

The spirit's voice cracked on that last word, and she quickly returned to preparing her meal. Karina tried to keep talking, but her mouth refused to move. There had to be something, anything—

"This is truly a pathetic way to die, daughter," said a new voice, and Tunde's form gave way to Baba's. Tears streamed down Karina's face as her father stared down at her with open disgust. "What was the point of releasing your powers, what did I even die for, if you can't save yourself when it matters most?"

Karina didn't know. She didn't know and she was so tired and even in her lowest, most hopeless moments, all her mind could conjure was images of contempt instead of comfort.

But who was she kidding? She couldn't imagine being saved because she was not the kind of girl people saved. Sweet, kind girls—girls like Aminata, girls like Hanane—those were the kinds of girls people saved. No one risked their lives for broken girls with venom on their tongues. No one mourned the girls who stomped lion-footed through the world, who projected strength to hide hearts more shattered than whole.

No one saved girls like her.

"A true queen wouldn't need to be saved." Her father's voice switched to her mother's, and Karina didn't have to look to imagine the cold glare on her face. "Grandmother Bahia would have been able to save herself. I would have been able to save myself. But you aren't like us, are you?"

Her mother was right. She didn't deserve to call herself a zawenji. She didn't deserve to call herself a queen. Karina tried and she tried, harder than anyone else, and all it had gotten her was a slow death with no one to mourn once she was gone.

The world blurred into streaks of bright colors, and Karina understood with a bone-chilling certainty that she was not leaving this room alive. With her last bit of strength, she fought past the shards of glass grinding against the inside of her skull and sent a single plea out into the universe for the gods, for someone, *anyone* to hear.

Help.

19

Malik

Liar. Murderer. Torturer.

The words cycled in a constant loop through Malik's mind, needling under his skin and cracking through his bones.

He'd had no choice. Dedele had said it herself—sacrificing Karina for the Rite of Renewal was the only way to save them all. Doing what he'd done down in the dungeons had been the only way to figure out Karina's location.

Liar. Murderer. Torturer.

He'd never used an illusion to meddle so thoroughly with a person's mind before. What if Dedele carried those scars for the rest of her life, and they led her to harm herself? Harm others?

Pressure ballooned in Malik's head. He needed to get out of here, get away from what he'd done, but there was nowhere to run, nowhere far enough that would get him away from his own mind—

"I can't stand the way he talks to her!" fumed Leila, and Malik snapped out of his reverie to watch his older sister pace around their small sitting room. Though it was still early in the day, the sky had turned pitch-black, bathing the room in shadows. "Like Hanane's a dog who has to do whatever he says!"

Malik swallowed the dark thoughts down. He forced a smile to his face. "He just wants what's best for her," he said. Leila couldn't know what he'd done. She'd never look at him the same if she knew.

"What's best for her can't be never leaving the place where she died! You saw how happy she was outside the palace and how quickly she won the people over. She deserves to be out there, for her own good and for Ziran's, but she can't do that as long as Farid is hovering over her shoulder every second of the day!"

Leila's hands curled into fists at her sides, and though his sister had never been particularly violent, Malik suspected that would change were his mentor to walk into the room right now. The dark thoughts continued to whirl through his mind, but Malik forced himself back to the warmth of his sisters' presence in a world that was feeling colder by the second. The palace rumbled as another crash of thunder tore through the air, and he had to remind himself that they were safe here, no matter how bad it might get.

"I didn't realize you cared for Hanane this much," he said, which earned him a pillow to the head.

"You're not the only person in this family who can befriend a princess," she snapped, but there was no denying the embarrassed edge to her voice. Hmm. Under different circumstances, Malik might have prodded more, as he often did whenever Leila was infatuated with some girl, but this was a dangerous path to even think about, much less acknowledge.

Leila continued, "You didn't hear the things she told me when you were at the university. Things about her childhood. She and Farid were together almost every moment after he arrived at the palace, and it's clear she doesn't know who she is outside of his influence. She says he was raised as her brother, but the way he talks about her, the way he looks at her, it's not brotherly. Something isn't right there."

"Has she expressed any displeasure with his behavior?"

"Not explicitly, but—"

"Then it's not our place to question," he reminded her. "He loves her. He always has."

Leila flopped onto the divan across from Malik, all the fight draining out of her body. "Love shouldn't look like control."

For the first time since they'd returned from the Lower City, Nadia spoke up, "I liked Hanane. Will we get to see her again?"

The obvious answer was no. Honestly, they'd be lucky if Farid ever let them attend court events again. Malik began to respond, but the words came out as a hiss as the cut on his arm pulsed with pain. Leila frowned. "Are you all right? Where did Farid take you after we returned?"

And just like that, Malik was there in the dungeon again, breathing in the putrid air, feeling no remorse as his powers destroyed Dedele from the inside.

"Farid just wanted to give me an update on Karina's location. They believe she's headed toward Talafri in search of divine power from the gods." Malik had never lied to his sisters before, at least not about something so big. But it was for the best. He had to keep believing that.

Liar. Murderer. Torturer.

Before Leila could poke too deeply into the lie, he rose to his feet and walked over to where Nadia sat curled up on the window ledge. "Can I get you anything before I turn in for the night?"

She didn't acknowledge his presence at all, her eyes glued to the destruction happening outside their window. The storm had intensified, and it was only thanks to the sturdiness of the palace walls that it had not affected them yet. Light shimmered from the rivers that had formed through the streets, only a hint of the flooding that would rock Ziran if the deluge did not let up.

"We're going to be fine," he promised with a confidence he did not feel.

Nadia kept her face pressed against the metal grate. "They won't be."

Once more, Malik longed for the days when he had known exactly what to do to ease all his sister's woes. But it seemed the only person who could coax a smile from Nadia anymore was Hanane, and the princess was hidden deep in the palace where Farid could keep an eye on her.

Malik retreated into his bedroom and threw himself face-first onto his bed without even changing into his nightclothes. He couldn't believe that just that morning he'd been in the university, flirting with Yaema and sorting through ancient scrolls. Tomorrow, he would return to his quest for the scepter, which meant that he'd be forced once more to face the horrors of the necropolis. Tonight, he'd sleep.

But his eyes had barely closed when dark energy coursed through him, like a thousand needles stabbing at every inch of his skin. Malik buried his face in his pillow to muffle his scream—no matter what, he couldn't let his sisters see him this way.

"Leave me alone," he growled, his own power rising to push

back against the force of whatever this was.

Did it ever occur to you that I don't have to actively attack you for your body to revolt against my presence? snapped the Faceless King. *Humans were never meant to wield powers like mine, and now you're paying the price.*

"She called me a kekki!"

I don't care if she called you the plague-ridden underside of a mangy chimpanzee. If you keep meddling with forces you can't control, you might die, or worse, I might die!

Sweat dripped down Malik's brow as he muffled another scream. He just had to ride this out. It was just like when he was a child recovering from one of Papa's beatings—the pain always went away eventually, so if he could just hold on a little longer . . .

And then the pain receded, replaced by a single call that rang through Malik's mind clear as a bell.

Help.

Malik bolted upright.

That was Karina calling for help. Calling *him* for help.

Just like when he had pulled her into the vision of the Rite of Renewal, now Karina was the one tugging on their connection. He felt her terror as if it were his own, ice cold in his bones.

He almost called back, only for Farid's words from a few days ago to bore into him: *At best, Karina considers you a threat that needs to be dealt with. And at worst? You are nothing.*

Karina had chosen Tunde over him. She was a zawenji. Her ancestor had left his to die, and her family had been subjugating his people for hundreds of years. Every thread of logic inside Malik told him to ignore her call. The connection didn't have to mean anything if he didn't let it mean anything.

But there came another wave of energy as Karina's fear radiated through him. Wherever the princess was, she was dying, and he was about to feel every second of it.

Help. The call came again, and in that moment there was no Faceless King, no ulraji or zawenji, no rituals or sacrifices or promises that mattered more than the fact that Karina needed him. Malik focused in on that single golden thread of their connection, and with every ounce of magic inside him, he pulled.

The palace and the storm fell away. In an instant, he was somewhere warm and dark and stifling, and Karina lay on the ground still as a corpse. Even then, Malik hesitated. What if this was some kind of trap?

But then she looked up at him, and the pure terror Malik saw in her eyes destroyed the last of his inhibitions. He fell to his knees beside her, heart pounding in his throat.

"Karina, it's me. I'm here. Can you hear me? Karina. Karina!"

Malik tried to pull her to her feet, but of course he could not, for he was not truly there. Whatever was happening here was hundreds of miles away from Ziran, and he was nothing more than a phantom witness viewing it through their connection.

He took quick stock of their surroundings: an apothecary of some kind, with a hulking figure whose body was half human, half centipede, stirring a giant cast-iron pot. The monster whipped her head their way, her beady eyes narrowing. Malik froze in place, and after what felt like a lifetime, her gaze slid past him to return to her vile work. Thank the Great Mother, she couldn't see him.

Malik looked down at Karina again, his mind racing to piece

together an escape route. He shouldn't be doing this at all, but if she died, Farid would have no one to sacrifice for the Rite of Renewal. That was the only reason he was helping her. That had to be it.

"Karina, please, you have to get up," Malik begged. He tried weaving an illusion around her, but his powers sputtered away, unable to create anything in a place where he was not actually present. In the dream she'd been able to touch him, but this wasn't a dream.

He didn't want Karina to die. He had never wanted that, not truly. He hadn't even wanted that when her death was the only thing that could save Nadia or even now, when it was the only thing that might save the world. If he had to stand here and watch her die, he would shatter, and then the binding between him and the Faceless King would break, and everything would be a nightmare and he wouldn't even care because it would mean Karina was dead.

"Karina, get up," Malik tried again to move her, to no avail. "Please, I'm here, I'm with you, you have to get up."

20

Karina

Get up.

Those two words were little more than a whisper, but they managed to cut through the blanket of pain smothering Karina's senses.

Get up. Get up. Get up.

Maame's venom held her body in a death grip, but Karina forced her eyes open to see not Tunde, not Baba or her mother but . . . Malik.

"Karina," he said as he kneeled beside her. "Karina, can you hear me?"

Wait, why was Malik here? The others' presences she understood—she had been the one to kill them, so it was only fair that they got to taunt her in her final moments. But she hadn't murdered Malik . . . had she? At one point she had wanted to, but that was so long ago and she was so tired now. Suddenly nothing seemed grander than laying her head against the cool ground and forgetting about murder and parents and everything in between.

"No, no, Karina, look at me. Stay with me." Malik tried to touch her, but his hand passed harmlessly through her face. The strangeness of the sensation, like a cloud passing over the sun on what should have been a clear day, forced Karina's eyes open again.

"You have to . . . get out of here," she gasped out. "Before she catches you." It was too late for her and Caracal and Afua, but the demon hadn't bitten Malik yet. There was still time for him to avoid joining the list of deaths caused by Karina's hand.

"Who are you speaking to, princess?" Maame Small Claws glanced over her shoulder, but all she saw was Karina lying face-down and alone. "Patience, dear. My preparations are almost complete."

If Karina had been in control of her arms, she would have physically shoved Malik out of the hut. But he stubbornly refused to run, and she could not tell if that was the single most idiotic or honorable thing she had ever seen. His eyes frantically searched the apothecary, landing on the bundle of herbs swaying directly above Karina's head. "Rosemary repels evil," he said, and wow, had anyone ever told him how nice his voice sounded? Someone should tell him that once the world stopped spinning. "If you can stand up and reach the rosemary, you can fight her."

A flicker of memory nudged the back of Karina's mind. Kneeling in her mother's garden, elbows deep in loamy soil. *Rosemary keeps the devils at bay*, the Kestrel had said. Yes, imaginary Malik was right. Clinging to the memory like an anchor, Karina tried to push herself to her feet.

She got a single inch off the ground before she collapsed, her muscles screaming in pain.

"I . . . can't," she gasped.

"Yes, you can," Malik urged, his voice hoarse with desperation.

"You can do this. All you have to do is stand."

Why did Malik even care so much if she lived or died? The ulraji had hated the zawenji for centuries, and her ancestor had personally wronged his. He had once tried to kill her. If anything, he should be celebrating her imminent demise.

Karina must have spoken aloud, for his desperate expression twisted into one she could not read.

"I did try to kill you," he said. "Remember how I lured you to the Sun Temple? Remember how I told you exactly what I knew you wanted to hear just so I could kill you?"

Humiliation surged through Karina. In a fit of pure anger, she pushed herself to her elbows. "Rot in hell!" she spat. Something flickered in Malik's eyes, but his mouth set in a determined line as he leaned down, his face inches from hers.

"If you die here, you'll never be able to take your revenge on me. So stand, Karina. You don't have to run. You don't have to fight. All you have to do is stand."

Malik's goading stoked the tiny bit of stubbornness Karina hadn't known she still possessed. Yes, she'd never been the kind of girl people saved—and that was why she had learned to save herself. Every time she'd looked for a savior and hadn't found one, she'd become her own.

Karina pressed her palms flat on the dirt, pushed herself an inch off the ground, and immediately collapsed again. Blood welled in her mouth from the impact, but she spat it out.

Stand. Karina braced a hand against the ground.

Stand. She rocked her weight onto her right foot. It held.

All she had to do was stand.

Later, Karina would not remember exactly how she'd gotten to her feet. She wouldn't know why her buckling knees hadn't given way beneath her, or how she'd even been able to think with the venom making her thoughts slower than tar. All she knew was that when she had begged for help from every deity she knew, not one of them had come for her.

Yet even when the gods had abandoned her, Malik hadn't.

The horrifying *click-click-click* of Maame's legs resounded as she turned her attention back Karina's way. "All right, princess, it's finally—no!"

With an inhuman scream, Maame Small Claws lunged for Karina, and with a scream of her own, Karina tore the bundle of rosemary from its hanging just as she and the demon collided. Hundreds of tiny claws slashed open her face, but Karina held fast to the herb, rubbing it on every part of the demon's body she could reach. Oozing sores opened up where the rosemary made contact with Maame's skin, and her screams intensified into bloodcurdling shrieks. Maame thrashed like a wild stallion, but Karina kept pressing the rosemary deep into her flesh until her hands were slick with the demon's blood.

Karina fought with no strategy. She fought with no grace. She was nail and tooth and fury and bone, and when she tore into Maame Small Claws, it was with the primal desperation of a creature that did not wish to die. With the last of her strength, she pressed the ragged remains of the herb straight into the demon's eyes. Maame staggered around wildly, and Karina jammed her shoulder into the demon's gut, shoving her straight into her own soup pot.

There came screaming . . . screaming . . . and then silence. Karina's legs gave way once more, and she slammed back onto the ground with blood, both hers and Maame's, pooling in her mouth. She felt the faintest glimmer of someone touching her gently on the forehead before every trace of Malik vanished.

Karina needed to search for an antidote to Maame's venom, but the burst of strength that Malik's encouragement had given her was gone. The ground rolled and pitched beneath her feet, and glass shattered around her as Maame's jars toppled from the shelves, filling the air with a mixture of toxic fumes. What was going on outside, some kind of earthquake?

A figure ran through the beaded curtain that covered the entrance to the room. "Karina!" cried Ife, drops of rain dripping from them onto Karina as they knelt beside her. Their eyes widened at Maame's blistering corpse and Caracal's and Afua's unconscious bodies. "I went back into the house but I couldn't find you so I went back outside and then it started storming and then I heard you scream so I came here and I don't understand what's happening!"

Rain? It never rained this far into deep desert, and never at this time of year unless—oh no.

The second omen, storms and quakes strong enough to tear Sonande apart, had begun.

Another tremor rocked the world, and stars danced in Karina's eyes as her head smacked against the wall. She spat out more blood and said, "Ife, Maame poisoned us. You have to look through her stores and see if you can find an antidote."

A flash of lightning illuminated the entire room, followed by an earthshaking crash of thunder. Despite the fact that her body was collapsing in on itself, Karina's magic shuddered in awe at such a fearsome display of the sky's power.

Ife took one look around the room, then shook their head. "No time for your idea. Let's try mine."

Before Karina could protest, Ife grabbed her by the wrist. Blue light pooled where their skin made contact, and warmth tunneled through Karina's body as small beads of purple liquid oozed from her pores and evaporated into the air. One by one, her muscles unlocked, and the blood in her mouth dwindled to a metallic aftertaste.

Karina's eyes grew wide. Ife was a zawenji.

"You didn't tell me you could use magic!"

"You never asked!"

In a few more seconds the venom was gone from Karina's system, and Ife pulled away from her, visibly drained. Afua had mentioned that Moon-Aligned zawenji were adept healers, but this was the first time Karina had ever experienced it herself.

"That should be most of it." Ife coughed as more jars and vials shattered around them. "But it's going to take me a little while to help the others."

Karina quickly weighed their options as the storm howled above them and the earth quaked beneath them. Ife wouldn't be able to heal the others fast enough for them all to run, and the two of them weren't strong enough to carry both Afua and Caracal to safety.

If all four of them were to make it out of here alive, Karina had to find a way to stop this.

"You keep them safe!" she told Ife, and with one last look at her unconscious friends, she ran outside into a world crumbling before her eyes.

The City of Thieves was in complete chaos, with nearly a third of the buildings caved in on themselves and still more on the verge of collapse. People ran in every direction trying to get to higher ground, everything they could reasonably carry bundled in their arms or strapped to their backs, but there was little they could do when the earth itself was raging against them.

Karina froze, her mind replaying the destruction she'd caused in Tiru the last time she'd unleashed her powers. What if she let her magic free here, and it caused more deaths?

Another tremor coursed through the stone, and a huge chunk of rock plummeted from the canyon's edge toward the town. With no time to think, Karina sliced her hand through the air, summoning a gale that slammed the rock back into the wall. But more boulders fell, several tons of earth and stone hurtling their way, and she decided then that if there was even a chance that she could help, she had to at least try.

Her head still pounding from Maame's venom, Karina envisioned a net in her mind's eye and thrust her hands skyward. Several gusts of wind twisted together to catch the stone in midair, and Karina let out a cry of anguish as she felt each rock that pelted against her magic as if it was hitting her own body. Her vision began to tunnel, and with a primal yell, she shoved the rock as hard as she could. The boulders soared over the edge of the canyon and crashed together in wet heaps.

Time lost all meaning as Karina stood on the ledge, deflecting each piece of the crumbling canyon that came for Balotho. Her life was not measured in hours or in minutes but in undulating waves of pure power, nkra transformed into wind and tempests that fought the avalanche to a standstill. Every time she wanted to give up, she remembered Malik's unshakable belief in her, and she found that much more reason to keep fighting.

Karina sang to the wind and it sang back, her arms conducting a symphony of magic only she could hear. And even as her body crumbled from the strain, her heart was alive; her muscles screamed, but her spirit soared. This was what she had always been holding back. This was what the Great Mother had put her on this earth to do. With each gale, she felt more real, more alive.

More like the descendant who deserved to inherit Bahia Alahari's power.

More like the person her mother had always wanted her to be.

More, her magic demanded, and more Karina gave, her soul against the very earth, brilliant and glowing and alive with the sky itself in the palms of her hands.

21

Malik

Malik awoke seconds before the first tremor hit Ksar Alahari. He had only just registered that he was back in his room and no longer with Karina when the ground pitched like water.

The second omen was here. He had wasted too much time.

Another tremor tossed Malik to the ground, but he fought to keep his balance, leaning heavily against the wall as he staggered for the exit.

"Leila! Nadia!" he called out. The two came running for him, fighting to stay upright amid the constant shaking. Malik grabbed his sisters, and together they ran from their rooms. A single thought occupied his mind—getting them all to safety. Nothing—not what had just happened with Karina or what had happened before with Dedele—mattered more than that.

But though Ksar Alahari had withstood the locusts, earthquakes were an entirely different matter. No corner of the palace was safe from the tremors, and huge chunks of debris rained down around them as they tried to find a safe place to hide. Malik had hallucinated an earthquake during the Third Challenge, but that had been nothing compared to this nightmare. The Faceless King

churned within him, and the spirit's fear of death shot through
Malik's mind.

They had just reached a spiraling staircase that would take
them to the lower levels when a loud crack rent the air. The stairs
split in two beneath Malik's feet, and he started plummeting
down to what surely would have been his death had someone not
grabbed him by the wrist.

"I've got you!" shouted Hanane, and he was too grateful to
even care that once again his skin blistered with cold where the
princess touched him. With surprising strength, she hauled him
back over the edge. "I've been looking everywhere for you three!
Come on, follow me!"

Moving with the speed of someone who had known these
halls since birth, Hanane led the trio through hidden staircases
and secret rooms until they were deep in a level of the palace only
the servants usually roamed. Behind a great wooden door was
the entrance to one of the palace's safe rooms, which Hanane all
but shoved them through. Only once inside did Malik realize that
Farid and the council were already huddled in the back.

Hanane moved to join Malik and his sisters in their corner, but
Farid yanked her into his arms as another boom shook the world.
Though the walls around them trembled and cracked, the cellar
held.

"I was so worried about you!" Farid cried.

"Farid . . . you're hurting me . . ." Hanane choked out, and
Farid took a step back, though he did not release her.

"Are you safe? Are you hurt anywhere? Why didn't you come

straight here?" he demanded. Hanane seemed to shrink into her-self.

"I had to find Malik and his sisters. They didn't know where the safe room was."

Farid finally looked at Malik then, as if only just realizing he was there. The older ulraji narrowed his eyes and pulled Hanane away from the rest of the group.

"Come. It's safer over here."

"But I—"

It was useless to protest. Farid and Hanane settled into their corner while Malik, Leila, and Nadia settled into theirs. The sib-lings clung to one another like they had as children hiding in a house that was more nightmare than home, and again during those long nights trekking across the Odjubai Desert. Though even as Malik sat there cowering with his sisters, a part of him was still in that hut with Karina, and he could hardly breathe for worry. What had happened after she'd fought off the demon woman? Was she safe from the earthquakes?

He tried to call to her through their connection, but it singed him, glowing hot and bright with a power he could not breach. Karina was alive, but she was expending so much magic he could not reach her.

So he let the connection go, and let his sisters bury their faces in his shoulders as the world crashed around them.

Hours after the last of the aftershocks had passed through Ziran, Malik and those he'd hid with emerged from the cellar into a world of silence. Malik watched with numb detachment as Hanane walked through the rubble of her childhood home, a thousand years of history torn apart in less than a day. When their party reached what had once been the bedroom she and Karina had shared as children, she fell to her knees in silent anguish.

Farid knelt beside her and put a hand on her shoulder in a gesture that felt more territorial than comforting. "We'll rebuild it together," he promised. "We'll make it stronger than it was before, better—"

"We need to send aid to the Lower City," Hanane said softly. "If we sustained this much damage, it's going to be far worse down there. We'll need to bring the displaced here."

Malik did not think he could hate the council more, but that was before he saw them balk at Hanane's suggestion of letting commoners into the palace.

"Disasters such as this bring out the absolute worst among the common folk. The most important thing to do right now is close off the Widow's Fingers and station extra reinforcements around it to deter any looters from sneaking in," argued one vizier.

"We do not have reinforcements, because Mwale Farid has sent them all to retrieve Princess Karina, which they still have not done," added the grand vizier, the edge in her voice unmistakable. "Not only have you failed to follow through on all the grand promises you made since coming into power, you have put us in a position where we are unable to defend ourselves from our own people as the gods rain their wrath down from the skies."

The air was tense as a viper coiling in on itself before the strike, and Malik bet that if he could see the web of nkra now, the threads leading from the council to his mentor would be a pulsing, murderous red. Farid's mouth flattened into a thin line.

"If you recall, my plan also involved dealing with Karina on the final night of Solstasia, which did not happen as she so easily slipped past the soldiers you stationed to protect the walls. But fear not, as we have new information about her whereabouts"—Farid glanced at Malik, who fought to keep the bile in his throat as he recalled Dedele. Adanko help him, had the dungeons survived the quake?—"and we will have her under control soon. Once we do, we'll be that much closer to putting a stop to this once and for all."

"Is this power of yours strong enough to stuff lightning back into the sky?" demanded the grand vizier. "Will it unflood the homes of the thousands who will riot on our doorsteps? What is it you're not sharing with us, Mwale Farid?"

Now was the time for Farid to share the truth about the Rite of Renewal, but he stayed silent. If he were to reveal the exact details of how to perform the ritual, there would be nothing stopping the council from gathering the materials and Karina themselves, and killing Farid without a second thought. As long as there was information he had access to that they did not, then they needed him . . . for now.

Farid opened his mouth to speak, but Hanane cut him off. "If you all do not shut your mouths right now, I will throw you off the side of the Widow's Fingers the first chance I get."

That shut the council up, and they watched wide-eyed as Hanane rose, a fire blazing in her eyes that had not been there before the quakes. "Did I not just give a direct order? I want scouts sent to every neighborhood in the Lower City to assess the damage, and I want messengers sent to the courtiers telling them to prepare their homes to house as many of the displaced as we can."

Gone was the girl Malik and his sisters had found weeping in a garden in the middle of the night. Now that the crisis had hit closer to home than they had ever thought it would, Hanane had slipped into leadership as if she'd been born for it—which, of course, she had.

It was only Farid who dared reply. "How would you choose who we let in? We don't have the resources to house every person affected by this." His eyes softened, and he slipped once more into the gentle voice he only ever used with the princess. "I know it hurts your heart to see your people suffer, but we can't save them all."

"So just because we can't save all of them, we should save none? Absolutely not."

"Hanane, you don't know who these people are. You don't know if they wish you ill. Letting them into the palace is well-intentioned madness."

"Then the guards will work extra hard for their pay."

"You aren't considering—"

"Farid, which of us is the ruler of Ziran, me or you?" asked Hanane. The world seemed to hold its breath as the formerly dead princess stared down the man who had resurrected her.

Something shifted in Farid's face. He nodded. "It's always been you."

Hanane nodded back before turning to Leila. "You mentioned you're trained in healing? Can you work in the infirmary until we bring more healers in?"

"Of course, Your Highness," said Leila, not a small amount

of pride in her eyes as she watched her friend take charge of the situation.

The next few hours were a blur as those who had been spared from the quakes did what they could to help those who had not. Hanane directed it all, a beacon of calm amid the swirling chaos. Her scouts returned bearing news that Temple Way was completely flooded, with nearly half of the Lower City structurally compromised. Tens of thousands of people had lost their homes and their livelihoods in the span of a few short hours. Malik knew how it felt to lose everything you owned to forces far outside your control—he wouldn't wish such a feeling on even his worst enemy.

But the most concerning news was the survey of the palace, which revealed that the lowest levels had borne the brunt of the damage and the threat of flooding was imminent. Farid had looked at him when that news had arrived, the realization hitting them at the same time.

The necropolis was underground. If they wanted to find the scepter, they had to go now.

"I must admit, Champion Malik, I did not expect to hear from you so soon," exclaimed Yaema as Malik led her through what was left of the queen's garden. It was near noon now, though it was hard to tell with the storm clouds still covering the sun, and Hanane's effort to aid those displaced by the disasters was in full swing. The first refugees had begun trickling into Ksar Alahari, their mouths agape at the wonders around them, just as Malik's had been the day he'd arrived.

Truth be told, Malik wished he was with the princess now,

helping her with this massive undertaking. That was where Leila and Nadia were, the former in the infirmary, the latter with the other palace children, helping to fetch blankets and mats and anything else the refugees might need. And Hanane was at the center of it all, directing the herculean effort with an orderliness that would put any military officer to shame.

But everyone had their part to play in getting through this crisis, and Malik's lay deep in the necropolis. However, seeing as the last time he had been there he'd almost been eaten alive by a serpopard, he was not about to enter the city of the dead again without a plan. Hence why he had asked the princess to summon Yaema, the one person in Ziran with knowledge of ancient Kennoua to rival Farid's.

"I did not expect to need your expertise again so soon either, but things have changed since we last met," he replied. "How are you, though? Was your family safe through the quakes?"

A strange look passed over Yaema's face. "The majority of my family lives in the Old City, so we were spared from the worst of the destruction. Honestly, they're all still so busy grieving my cousin, I don't think they've even noticed half of Ziran is in ruins." Yaema blinked and shook her head. "Ah, I'm sorry, thank you for asking. What do you need from me?"

It felt wrong to bring Yaema into the royal family's private space, but Malik did not know of any other way to access the necropolis. Between the locusts and now the quakes, the garden was utterly destroyed, and his heart twinged with sorrow as they picked their way through the broken trees and shattered stones.

"I think the scepter I'm looking for might be hidden in the

necropolis of the last pharaoh. I'd like your help retrieving it."

Yaema's eyes brightened. "An actual necropolis—yes, of course I'll help! Where is it?"

"Right here."

Malik pressed the signet ring he'd gotten from Hanane into the indentation at the base of the fountain and recited the Alahari family words: *Despite it all, still we stand.* Smooth stone slid away from the entrance, revealing a set of footsteps and the sound of rushing water. There was no way to tell from here just how much damage the necropolis had sustained—the golden city might have flooded, rendering this entire mission futile.

The river hasn't overflowed to that point yet, but that won't remain true for long, said Idir. *Hurry.*

To Yaema, Malik said, "This is no light favor to ask, and I completely understand if you would rather not risk your life for—"

But the girl was already bounding down the stairs into the gloom. "What are you waiting for? Hurry up!" she called, and Malik shook his head in wonder before running after her, the marble sliding shut above their heads.

The last time Malik had been here, he and Karina had quite literally crashed down the stairs into the river, arriving on the shore of the necropolis through a mixture of sheer luck and the aid of whatever demonic creature—*You take that back, Ipsi is a delight*—fine, the aid of whatever *pet* of Idir's had lived at the bottom of the river.

It was impossible not to think of Karina as they edged their way down the shaky stone. Now that the worst of the quakes were over—for now—there was no way for Malik to ignore what had occurred between them right before the tremors started.

He should have ignored her cry for help. He should have pulled his blanket over his head and slammed his hands over his ears and ignored her pleas, just like he'd spent his childhood pretending he did not hear the grim folk stalking around him.

But instead he had gone to her. And the excuse that he had done it solely because they needed her for the Rite of Renewal was just that—an excuse. In that moment he had been faced with the reality of a world without Karina in it, and his heart had shattered at the thought.

And somehow, Karina had risen to her feet. She had *won.*

No, there was no somehow about it. That was one of the things Malik admired most about her—the way she forged a path forward where others claimed there was none. Even without his help, she would have found a way to survive Maame Small Claws. The real problem was why he'd done what he did.

You know why, whispered the Faceless King, and Malik couldn't bring himself to respond as he handed Yaema a torch and a long coil of rope.

Karina was a zawenji. He was an ulraji. She was a member of royalty, while there were animals that had more rights in Ziran than he did. She'd had the chance to be with him, but she had chosen Tunde and expressed absolutely no remorse about it.

Yet in her lowest moment, she hadn't called for Tunde or any of the other noble boys who had likely warmed her bed. Standing at the edge of death, Karina had wanted *him.* Surely that meant this wasn't all in his head, that this pull they felt toward one another was not just because of their ancestors?

And what if that is what it means? asked Idir. *What if the girl is falling in love with you? When the time comes to sacrifice the soul of a queen to appease the gods, are you willing to do what must be done to save this world?*

For once, the obosom did not sound snide or scornful. He simply sounded . . . sad, which somehow unsettled Malik more. He pushed all thoughts of Karina deep, deep inside him and forced himself to focus on Yaema, who was gawking at a massive mural before them.

"This has to be at least a thousand years old!" she exclaimed. The light from their torches illuminated the jewels embedded in the stone, revealing the bloody history of Ziran. "Look at the workmanship!"

Malik placed his hand against the depiction of the Ulraji Tel-Ra, stomach twisting at the horrors revealed through this art. Which of these masked figures had been Khenu, and just what had she done in the name of this ancient empire?

You don't have time for this. Keep moving! barked the Faceless King, and only then did Malik notice that the last dregs of the Gonyama were swirling white with foam. The part of Idir that was still connected to the river roared within him, letting him feel how close it was to spilling over its banks.

He and Yaema quickly tied one end of the rope to the thick stalagmites at the bottom of the cavern, and the other end to their waists. Then they climbed along the cave wall, the din of the river swirling away beneath them. The world narrowed to rock after rock, pure adrenaline the only thing keeping Malik moving forward. If he stopped moving, he would think, and if he started thinking, he would panic, and if he started panicking, he would fall, and if he fell, he would drown and—

Breathe. Stay present. Stay here. One step at a time. He could do this.

In less time than he had expected, but far longer than he would have preferred, the golden glow of the necropolis appeared up ahead. Pure disbelief radiated off Yaema as she scurried down the river wall and over to the cliff's edge.

"It's so . . . it's . . . wow," she breathed.

The necropolis remained mostly intact, but water was rising fast in several of the streets. There was simply no time to admire how the entire tomb glowed despite the lack of external light, or to mourn for the hundreds of people who had been trapped here in eternal servitude to the man who had enslaved them in both life and death. A putrid, rotting stench filled the air, which Malik quickly realized was the serpopard's deteriorating corpse.

"Be careful not to touch anything," he warned Yaema. "Last time I was here with Ka—with someone else, she touched the wall, and it released the serpopard."

Yaema nodded, and soon they'd passed through the water-logged streets to the inner temple with the giant obelisk on top. It was still locked; Malik's attempt to slice through the thick bolts with the spirit blade did nothing.

Yaema examined the hundreds of glyphs drawn down the temple doors. Normally Malik's mind translated Kennouan glyphs into a language he could understand, but the ones on the temple formed a jumble of words and phrases that held no meaning. "Can you read that?" he asked.

"Barely. Normally glyphs are read top to bottom and left to right, but when you do that, everything here is complete nonsense. But why would they write a bunch of gibberish on something as important as the pharaoh's tomb? That doesn't make any sense, unless . . ." The girl's eyes went wide. "It's a cipher!"

Malik was suddenly very glad he'd brought Yaema along, for though he'd always had a talent for riddles, ciphers were a different beast. "Can you, um, un-cipher it?"

"Decipher, and yes, though it's going to take some time."

Time was one thing they absolutely did not have, but there was no way around it. While Yaema began cracking the cipher, Malik fidgeted beside her and tried his best to calm the frantic beating of his heart. He didn't know why he was so nervous when nothing bad had happened yet.

And that was exactly the problem. Compared to his first journey through the necropolis, this second trip had been *too* easy. Anything that had ever come easily to Malik had always turned out to be a wolf masquerading as a sheep. Dread crawled over his skin like ants. Idir remained silent, doing nothing to assuage or confirm his fears.

The behavior of the wraiths wasn't helping—or rather, the wraith. He had assumed that once he was outside the protective range of the wards surrounding Ksar Alahari, the usual pack of grim folk would return to follow him around. But there was only a single wraith floating beside them now, its eyes as wide and white as Malik's own were wide and black. None of the wraiths possessed any identifying features, but there was something familiar about this one in a way he could not place.

The roiling red light where its heart should have been pulsed crimson red, and Malik found himself counting the beats, counting his breaths, counting everything to try to keep himself calm, and why was it so quiet, where were the traps, what was going on here—

"I've got it!" cried Yaema. "The deciphered text reveals a riddle: *A pair are we, traveling together each and every day and night, never apart, yet never have we met. Who are we?*"

Breathe. Stay present. Stay here. Two things that were always found together—dark and light? No, they traveled. A pair of things that moved through the world together but never crossed paths . . .

"Eyes," Malik said, and it was Karina's that came to mind, twisting the knot in his stomach even tighter with worry for her. "They're always together, but they can never meet."

As soon as he had slid the corresponding glyphs into place, a great rumble shook the earth. He and Yaema clung to each other on instinct, fearing another quake, but it was simply the door to the temple sliding open. They pulled apart quickly, cheeks flushed, and with an awkward cough Malik led the way inside the pharaoh's tomb, the solitary wraith drifting along behind them.

Inside the temple was a hoard of riches that extended as far as Malik could see, and likely past that as well. Bricks of gold sat stacked into pyramids several times their heights, and they passed statues carrying chests overflowing with rubies and emeralds, sapphires and quartz. At least a hundred petrified soldiers stood guard, ceremonial weapons bright and unused in their frozen hands.

At the center of it all, on a raised dais, lay the pharaoh's sarcophagus. Something deep in Malik's gut pulled him toward the
gilded coffin, and he approached with a hand raised to—no. He
wasn't here for the pharaoh, he was here for Khenu. They followed the map they'd found at the university into the next series
of rooms, which was marked as the resting place of Pharaoh
Akhmen-ki's wives.

If the pharaoh's room had been decorated for war, then this
one had been decorated for beauty, with thick garlands of flowers
strung up through the rounded columns and long waterfalls spilling
perfumed water into the pools lining the tombs. The room for the
concubines was sparse and dark in comparison. There Malik and
Yaema lingered, reading about who these women had once been
from the inscriptions on each of the forty-five stone sarcophagi.

Mennerakan of Lower Luxum, aged nineteen summers,
daughter of the scribe of the Flowering Fields.
Bera of Kairum, aged twenty-six summers,
daughter of the High Priest of Kairum.
Sessharek of Upper Remet, aged thirteen summers,
daughter of unknown.

Forty-five woman, all different ages and tribes. Forty-five
women whose only commonality had been their connection to the
pharaoh, and who would forever be defined by this. Malik forced
himself to read every single name, bearing witness to these women
who had been had been relegated to little more than footnotes in
the histories of empires and kings.

But none of them were Khenu.

Malik and Yaema regarded the map once more to hunt down the small, unmarked room where Malik hoped the Ulraji Tel-Ra lay. A buzz in his veins told him they had reached the right place, and he could practically feel his heart in his throat as he placed his palm flat against the stone. The Mark slid off his skin into the wall and expanded until it was as tall and wide as a door. It opened its mouth, and the stone cleared way.

The nkra here was so thick that Malik almost choked on it. The magic surrounded him, ecstatic to be near the living after so many centuries with only the dead for company. The Ulraji Tel-Ra's toms had been grouped together based on the kind of magic they could do—seven different categories, each one a mirror flip of the seven kinds of zawenji. Yaema began reading the titles out loud.

"Heartstealers. Dreamwalkers. Threadseers—this is what Farid does, right? Souldancers, mindtappers, spiritcleavers." Yaema turned to Malik, her eyes wide. "Here are the storyweavers."

Malik could hardly dare to breathe as he walked down the line of storyweavers one by one. His people. His kin.

And yet . . .

He lifted his head. "Khenu isn't here."

"If she's not here, then where is she?"

Malik had no idea, but this meant one thing—it was over. The necropolis had been his only lead. If the scepter wasn't here, then he had no idea where it might be. Black spots tunneled over his vision at the thought of what Farid would do to him when he returned empty-handed.

He'd failed. *Liar. Murderer. Torturer. Failure.*

Yaema placed a hand on his shoulder. "We can keep looking. When we get back, I'll rip the entire university apart if I have to. We're going to find this thing, don't worry."

Malik appreciated the comfort, but she didn't understand how much was at stake. His hands began to shake as his mind began to close in on itself until a shadow shifted in front of him. He looked up to see the wraith, and out of desperation more than anything else, he asked, "Do you know where Khenu is?"

In response, the wraith drifted out of the room, and Malik and Yaema hurried to follow. It led them all the way back to the pharaoh's chamber, past the sarcophagus to a thick purple curtain that sectioned off one part of the room from the rest. Whatever was back here, it was not an official part of the necropolis, for it hadn't been on the map.

Dread filled Malik's veins as the wraith stopped before the curtain. With shaking hands, he pushed it aside to find a chamber that put all others in the temple to shame. The walls had been formed of pure rose quartz, and whatever enchantment had been placed over the room had made it so that the thick torches here had burned steadily across the centuries. Their shifting light reflected on a long staircase leading up to a body lying on a bed of stone.

Malik's ancestor looked so peaceful in her resting place that she might have been asleep, the fabric of her white gown spilling over the sides of the slab like rivers of fluttering lace. Malik's heart lurched—that was Nadia's face he saw in Khenu's features, the round face and thick curls that existed in his family line to this day. Malik could not imagine a more beautiful place to lie in death, and yet it was heart-wrenching to think about Khenu being so far from the sun and from the family who hadn't even known she'd existed.

But most important of all was the scepter folded between her hands, power humming within the green malachite.

Malik took the scepter from his ancestor as gently as he could. Surely there had to be something protecting the most important magical object in Kennouan history, and yet . . . nothing. No serpopard, no curse, no trap. It didn't make any sense. How in the world had Malik been able to walk in here and just take the scepter from the tomb as if it were a flower in a field?

And why had Khenu been given something of such great importance to the pharaoh to begin with?

Malik's eyes fell from Khenu's corpse to the wraith, and then from the wraith to the glyphs on the side of the slab, which spelled out a single word:

Beloved.

The answer came to him like a blow to the gut, and the moment he realized it, the Faceless King shifted inside him.

The magic that protects the necropolis does not register you as a thief for the same reason no grandparent would be cross with their grandchild for plucking fruits from their orchard, said the spirit, and the walls seemed to close in all around Malik. He looked at the wraith—no, not just any wraith.

Khenukahor, the spirit of his ancestor who had led him here.

She touched a spectral hand against his forehead, and Malik *saw*.

He saw Khenu being dragged from her home, screaming for

help that never came. He saw the slavers realizing what they'd found and turning her over to the Ulraji Tel-Ra to begin the process of honing the child into a weapon. He saw the moment the pharaoh, this man old enough to be her father, noticed her and ordered him brought to her, still more child than woman.

And Malik *felt*.

He felt Khenu's desperation and her fear. He felt the pain and the disgust and the violation, and more than anything else, that wild, primal desire to survive in this viper's nest she'd been thrown into. He felt the burning hatred of Bahia Alahari in his bones, and how it had driven her to claw her way through the ranks and seize power however she could, even if it had meant giving herself to the very man who had ripped away all she had.

Beloved.

Beloved.

Beloved.

Malik understood now why the necropolis would never shun one of Khenu's children, for Khenu's child had been the pharaoh's child. The temple *wanted* him to take the scepter. And by the Ancient Laws, written thousands upon thousands of years before even Ziran itself had been a glimmer of an idea, everything down here, from the tombs to the gold, to the bodies, belonged to him.

Malik couldn't breathe. He couldn't think. It was—he had to get out of here.

But his legs wouldn't move, and everywhere he looked he saw the gold closing in on him, the memory of the bloodshed and the wealth mixing together in his mind's eye until he could not tell one from the other.

Yaema was trying to keep him upright, but there was nothing Malik could do to stop the onslaught swallowing him whole, his legacy dooming him thousands of years before he'd even been born and he couldn't breathe, he couldn't breathe, the scepter was sinking into the Mark just like the spirit blade, it was a part of him now, and he couldn't breathe. And even as the world blurred and darkened around him, a terrifyingly familiar whisper flooded through his senses, whispering to him two small words:

Welcome home.

22

Karina

Karina had to hand it to the people of Balotho—for a bunch of bloodthirsty, murdering thieves, they sure knew how to make a girl feel welcome.

"Is there anything else I can get you, anything else at all?" asked Elinam as she leaned attentively over the chaise on which Karina now lay. The spacious rooms had once been Maame's personal quarters, but with the demon dead, the city had been more than happy to give them to Karina and her companions as they recovered from their ordeal. Elinam had been particularly generous, likely out of guilt for almost getting Karina murdered. It seemed none of Maame's disciples had known the true nature of her healing house, and they had been horrified to learn that they had unwittingly been luring people to their demises.

Three days had passed since Karina had saved the City of Thieves from the earthquakes, and the people adored her for it. *Savior,* they had screamed when the dust had cleared to reveal Karina standing there, the sole bastion keeping them all from being crushed alive. *Savior,* they had cried when they had lifted her near-comatose body into the air, taking care not to trample the coils of silver hair that now cascaded around her face and down her legs, as thick and voluminous as the clouds she summoned. The people had seen her hair growth as a blessing from the gods, and even now four attendants bustled behind her, braiding it in the local style.

According to Afua, it was likely a side effect of unleashing so much magic at once. "Think of it like a recoil," she explained when she'd finally awoken from Maame's venom, unharmed though annoyed at having missed all the action. "Our bodies react in strange ways when under extreme stress, and all that extra energy had to go somewhere."

Karina far preferred Afua's theory to the idea that the gods were messing with her body, but that wasn't going to stop her from accepting pampering from the only group of people in Sonande who looked at her and saw something other than the massive bounty on her head. To the people of Balotho, Karina was a hero. They composed songs in her honor, adorned her with jewels and beads, fed her their sweetest meats, and draped her in their softest cloths.

She did not tell them that their real savior was a boy hundreds of miles away in Ziran. She doubted they would believe her if she did.

Her attendants threaded the last of the wildflowers into her hair and then stood back to admire their handiwork.

"You look lovely, princess. Positively radiant," Elinam gushed as she handed Karina a silver mirror.

And she was. Under their expert care, Karina's curls had been twisted into dozens of silver braids that looped into one another, forming one giant braid that fell to her ankles. Glass beads, cowrie shells, wildflowers, and gold thread were woven throughout, and in that moment, her beauty rivaled even the depictions of the Great Mother they'd all been raised to worship.

Karina stared at her reflection.

With her hair this long, she looked like her mother.

When she did not reply, the attendants' faces fell. "Have we displeased you?"

Karina swallowed down the feeling of wearing another skin over her own to give the women the smile they were expecting. "Your work is befitting of the gods themselves."

The attendants looked ready to pass out from pleasure. After tying a last string of red-and-gold beads around her waist, they took their leave. Alone for the first time in days, Karina let the smile drop before retrieving two oilskin-wrapped items hidden at the bottom of her pack.

The first one was nothing more than a piece of bone, triangular in shape and about the size of a closed fist. The symbols of all seven patron deities had been engraved on it, as well as the butterfly symbol of the Great Mother. However, when Karina pressed her finger into its center, it grew warm and twitched like a compass, until the its tip pointed northwest, in the direction of the Eshran Mountains.

And more importantly, toward the Sanctum.

This was the key to Doro Lekke, the last obstacle between her and the power she needed to stop Farid and prevent another disaster like the one that had almost destroyed Balotho. She should have felt jubilant. She should have felt ecstatic.

Instead, she felt numb, just as she had when she'd returned to

Maame Small Claws's workshop to find the key floating on top of the dark liquid in her pot.

When your beloved ancestors were building their sanctuary, they needed a way to protect it from thieves and outsiders. So they lured me, an innocent child who believed their promises and lies, from the spirit world, placed their key inside me, and left me stranded here.

Karina unwrapped the second item, and the chains of Maame Small Claws's headpiece clinked softly in her palm. The more she thought about how the demon had been forced into the role of Doro Lekke's guardian by the ancient zawenji, the more the ache in the back of her head grew. She couldn't reconcile the monster she had fought with the child the zawenji had tricked, but just because she couldn't imagine it did not mean it had not happened.

Footsteps approached, and Karina was about to order whoever it was to leave her be when Caracal, Afua, and Ife piled through the door.

"Glad to see the Great Savior of Balotho has a moment to spare for us poor folk at last," teased Caracal as he plopped down on a cushion across from her, but his words lacked their usual bite. Though Ife claimed that none of them would bear lasting damage from Maame's venom, the former Sentinel was taking far longer to recover than Karina and Afua had. Karina twisted her head side to side, hating how much tension all this hair put on her neck.

"What am I supposed to do, just not let them adorn me with precious jewels?" When Caracal didn't take the bait, she threw him a worried look. "How do you feel?"

"Better. Ife says I should be well enough to travel by morning."

"He should avoid venomous demons in the future, though," Ife chimed in. "It does horrible things to the nervous system, not to mention the muscle spasms, organ failure—"

"I understand, Ife. Thank you."

Ife was the only member of their party who had escaped Maame Small Claws unscathed, and looking at them now Karina could hardly fathom the amount of power hiding in that lithe frame. They deserved the city's admiration just as much as she did, for without them she'd be a dried-out husk in a pot. "And when exactly where you planning to tell me you were a zawenji?"

"Technically, I never told you. You saw me using my powers. That's not the same as telling."

A memory resurfaced of the second dream she'd shared with Malik, and how Ife had sensed the shift in her body just by grabbing her wrist. "You used your powers on me the day after we left Tiru."

"I did. That's when I learned you broke your collarbone when you were five, your left foot is approximately a third of an inch smaller than your right, and your next menses is going to be several weeks late. But don't worry, you're not pregnant," they added at Karina's startled expression. "It's just stress. If you were pregnant, I would tell you."

Ife listed off this information as if it was completely mundane, rather than them understanding things about Karina's body that she herself did not know. "Why didn't you ever mention you could do this? I get why you'd keep this from regular people, but why keep it from fellow zawenji?"

"I knew," Caracal chimed in.

"I sensed it," Afua added.

Karina growled. "Fine, why keep it from me?"

Ife fiddled with a thread trailing from the hem of their sleeve. Without looking at her, they said, "I don't understand people. I never have. And they don't understand me. And that's fine because I understand stories. Stories follow a formula. There's a beginning, middle, and end. Everything has its place and everything makes sense. I've gotten used to things not making sense, but others haven't. They don't like it when you can do things they don't understand, or when your gender or your face or any other thing you can't control doesn't make sense to them. Caracal has never made me feel bad or broken, but others have. I used to tell people. Now I don't."

The Moon-Aligned zawenji absentmindedly touched the dulyo mark on their right cheek. The dulyo were cherished in the Eastwater region as celebrated members of their communities; how deep the distrust of magic ran that Ife had been chased out of their home, as if being a zawenji rendered everything else about them void.

Knowing Ife would not like to be touched without warning, she made the gesture of respect toward them. "Thank you so much for all that you've done."

"You all got hurt because of me. I could've gotten to you sooner if I'd been able to handle the tent."

"You did nothing wrong. None of us would be alive right now without you."

Ife did not reply, but their body relaxed somewhat. Afua leaned over and plucked the key to Doro Lekke from Karina's lap. Her hands glowed with soft purple light as her magic pulled apart the object's history in a way only a Life-Aligned zawenji could. "I can't believe we're about to step foot in a place no zawenji has seen in a thousand years."

And all we had to do was murder a being that was only trying to defend herself, Karina thought darkly. But she didn't wish to ruin the first true moment of calm they'd had this entire journey, so instead she asked, "Can you see the Sanctum's exact location through the key?"

"A little bit . . . I'm seeing a forest, though not as dense as the main part of the jungle, and rolling hills coming into a swamp. I think it's around where the Eshran foothills meet the Arkwasian jungle? About a week's travel northwest from here. But more than anything else, I'm getting a strong sense of home. The Sanctum is this key's home, and it wishes to return there very badly."

"Then we'll leave this place at the first light of dawn," Karina declared.

"Your legion of adoring fans will be crushed," said Caracal.

"Such is the ever-fleeting nature of love."

Afua put down the key and picked up Maame's headpiece. The light from its central jewel sparkled over her face like a thousand tiny stars. "Do we have to worry about another guardian coming to take Maame's place?"

"I don't believe so," replied Karina. "From the way she described it, the role is one that someone has to take over, though they can be tricked into it. Until another comes forward, the city will remain undefended."

Karina wished she still had Baba's oud in her hands so that she could drown her uneasiness beneath the familiar chords of her music. But she had destroyed the oud, just like she'd destroyed Maame Small Claws, just like she destroyed everything she touched.

Caracal's gaze fell to Karina's trembling hands. He turned to Ife and Afua. "I heard someone claim he saw a spirit that's half monkey and half pig. Why don't you go check it out?"

"Which half is which?" asked Ife.

"You'll have to ask him to find out."

"I'm intrigued. Afua, let's go."

As soon as the younger members of their party were gone, Caracal lifted a slitted eyebrow at her. "All right, princess, talk. We got what we came here for, so why are you moping like someone stole all your kola nuts?"

"I'm not moping!"

"People who aren't moping usually don't have to reassure others that they aren't."

Karina turned the key over again in her hands. As ever, it pointed toward the home its keeper had died trying to protect.

"Maame Small Claws was only a child when our people forced her to become Doro Lekke's guardian. A child of the spirit realm, yes, but a child nonetheless. All my life I've been taught that the ancestors were wise and good, but this seems so cruel. What does it say about me if people who would do something like that consider me worthy of their legacy?"

Caracal was silent for so long that Karina started to feel embarrassed for having shared something so vulnerable. However, when he spoke, his voice was soft. "The first thing they teach you when you become a Sentinel is obedience. That you never defy an order, no matter how vile it may be. But the second thing they teach you? Legacy.

"They spend years making us memorize the names and deeds of Sentinels past until we know more about these people who died centuries before we were born than we do the families we were taken from. They drill into us unquestioning faith, and that, coupled with the enchantment that connects us all together, is what makes the Sentinels the efficient, deadly force that they are."

Caracal leveled his gaze on her, the faintest glimpse of the horrors he must have seen shining deep within it. "But no cause that can't withstand justified questioning is truly worth following. If our present can't be sorted neatly into heroes and villains, then neither can our past. It's good that you're doubting the ancestors, and it's good that you're wrestling with what you've been taught. All that means is whatever path you choose, it'll be because it's what you truly believe, not just because someone else wants it for you."

A lump rose in Karina's throat, and before she could stop herself, words she'd never shared with anyone else rushed out. "Sometimes I doubt the gods even exist. Everyone talks of them so easily—Afua herself can commune with them—but I pray and I pray and I pray and I feel . . . nothing. What if that's why all these bad things keep happening to me and everyone I love, because they know deep in my heart I don't believe?"

"Then you are either far more powerful than we realized, or

the gods are far weaker than we think, that a single girl's crisis of faith could wreak this much havoc on us all."

Caracal could not have been more different from the priestesses who had taught Karina theology as a child, but his words provided a balm to a part of her that had been cracked and sore for longer than she cared to admit. The reminder that she was simply one person in the long line of billions to ever exist was freeing. Fixing the complicated, beautiful, vicious world they lived in did not have to rest on her shoulders alone.

Except, of course, if Farid sacrificed her for the Rite of Renewal.

Karina took a shuddering breath. There was one more thing she wanted to ask the former Sentinel while the air between them was for once calm.

"When you deserted the Sentinels ten years ago, how did you break the enchantment on you? The only other Sentinel I've met who broke it needed Afua's help to do so." Commander Hamidou had been freed from the enchantment for less than a day before she'd died helping Karina escape Ziran. That was just one more reason Karina had to see this journey through to the end—she couldn't let the woman's sacrifice be in vain.

Caracal's body tensed, and it looked for a second as if his walls were rising once more. But then he sighed and rubbed his brow. "Ten years ago, my squad and I were assigned to patrol Ksar Alahari—not the private part where your family lived, but the outer sections. We were about an hour into it when this . . . this force ripped through the air.

"It was like someone burned all my bones and replaced them

with new ones in the same exact moment. No one else had felt what I did, and I might have forgotten all about it, except something in me shifted after."

There was something raw in Caracal's voice that made Karina reach over and lightly touch the back of his hand. The corner of his mouth twitched up.

"The thing you need to understand about the enchantment is that it doesn't just make us follow our masters' orders, it makes us *want* to follow them. You can't rebel against something that your mind has convinced you that you want to do. But after that day . . . I couldn't do it. I saw every atrocity asked of us with a clarity I'd never had before."

Caracal pressed a palm against his eyes, but he kept speaking. "For months I tried to ignore it. They'd taken me from my mother when I was an infant, so this was the only family I'd ever known. I couldn't imagine leaving it. But then one day, we were ordered to retrieve a man who was suspected of being an enemy spy in Ziran. We were told to bring him back alive but to kill anyone who witnessed it. By accident, this old man saw and—"

Caracal drew a shuddering breath. "That very night, I walked away from being a Sentinel, and I've been walking ever since."

He looked as if it had taken everything inside him to share what he just had, yet there was one more thing Karina needed to know. "Do you remember the exact day you felt the power that shifted everything?"

"Like I could ever forget. It was the day the king . . . your father . . . died."

Karina watched the pieces click together in Caracal's mind. Her voice raw and hoarse, she shared the story of what had really happened the night Ziran had lost its king and eldest princess. When she finished, the former Sentinel stared at her as if seeing her for the first time.

"It was you. You summoning that storm . . . you broke my enchantment," he whispered.

"It seems I did. But it was an accident, like everything else I do." It was one thing to have the people of Balotho fawning over her, but Karina had grown strangely attached to Caracal's rough nature during their time together. She didn't want him to simper over her like the courtiers used to. "But why were you the only member of your squad affected by it?"

"I was the only Wind-Aligned member of that team. Our shared Alignment is probably why your powers hit me more deeply than the others."

Karina had always hated the idea of fate, that everyone was on a predetermined path that there was no way to change or fight. Yet something stirred within her as she and Caracal quietly reflected on this connection between them. The same action that had ended her father's and sister's lives had saved his. That did not make up for what she'd done, and it would not fix all that had gone wrong after, but it gave Karina the smallest glimmer of hope that maybe, just maybe, there was still some good she could put into the world not because of her family or legacy, but just because of her.

"One last question. Was Issam a member of your team too?" she asked.

Every inch of Caracal's body wound in on itself. "How do you know that name?"

"You kept saying it when you were paralyzed by Maame's venom. Were you two close?"

Caracal looked off into the distance, and when he spoke again, Karina sensed that he was no longer talking to her.

"We were in the same squad together. From the start, we were all each other had. He was . . . Issam was . . . he was the best thing."

This was the hardest part of grief—that no matter how many wonderful things happened after the initial loss, the smallest reminder could make the wound bleed as keenly as the day it happened. "May the Great Mother guide his spirit to the Place with Many Stars," Karina whispered. Perhaps it was disingenuous to give the prayer right after mentioning her crisis of faith, but she did not know what else to say.

Caracal laughed. "Oh, the asshole isn't dead. In fact, knowing him, he's probably risen through the ranks and doesn't even remember me. Meanwhile, a day doesn't go by that I don't think of him."

The laughter in his voice died. "I don't regret leaving the Sentinels, but I regret leaving him. If you ever find someone who feels as natural to you as breathing, don't leave them. Because if you do, you'll feel as if you're gasping for air every moment after."

They were both silent for a long time before the former Sentinel excused himself to go hunt down their missing friends. Not tired enough to sleep, yet not quite ready to talk to anyone else, Karina ordered her guards to turn away any more visitors, then curled up in a ball on her bed. Caracal's words ran on a loop through her mind like a stallion circling a ring.

He was the best thing.

His declaration had been so simple, so . . . easy. Karina wondered what it was like to love someone so wholly and completely, no doubt, no hesitation. She'd never felt that way about anyone. She didn't even know if she could.

Because the choice of who to give her heart to had never been Karina's to make, she had never given much thought to the kind of person she'd want to spend her life with. It was easier to focus on who was available, and to leave them before it became anything too difficult to escape. That was exactly why she'd ended things with Tunde when he'd tried to make their relationship into something more than a shared form of physical release.

And yet as she lay there with the soft orange of sunset streaming across her face, Karina felt some tiny, neglected part of herself reaching out to hold and to be held, for the very intimacy and connection she had spent so long running from.

She didn't know what was going to happen when they left Balotho in the morning. She didn't know what would happen once they reached the Sanctum, or what she'd do once she finally obtained the power she so desperately needed.

All she knew was that she was hundreds of miles from home, surrounded by admirers exalting her name on all sides, yet there was only one boy who had seen her at her absolute lowest. Malik had featured heavily in her dreams these last three days, and thank the Great Mother they weren't ones that were shared with him, for these were the kinds of fantasies that left her sweat soaked and aching when she woke, and try as she might, her own touch wasn't enough to relieve her of the desire.

She knew now that the feelings she'd thought she'd had for Malik during Solstasia had been nothing more than a mix of grief and the unpaid debt between their ancestors forcing them together when they'd both been at their most vulnerable. The thought that fate had thrown them onto each other's paths made her want to turn away from him simply to spite the powers that be.

But wouldn't avoiding Malik just because fate had wanted them to meet still be allowing destiny to mold her decisions? It was like Caracal had said—whatever happened, it should be because she wanted it, not because she was acting with anyone else's intentions in mind.

And right now, Karina wanted Malik.

So as the sun sank, Karina nestled into her blankets, closed her eyes, and dreamed of him.

23

Malik

Malik didn't tell Farid what he'd found down in the necropolis.

It wasn't because his mentor would not have understood. And it wasn't like Farid could not have figured it out for himself if he'd actually had the time to go down to the city of the dead and piece the tattered bits of history together.

It was because everything his ancestor had been forced to do to protect herself had cleaved Malik in two. A part of him wished to storm the streets of Ziran and tear down everything that had been built by those who had allowed this injustice to happen. Not just for Khenu, but for all the wraiths as well, who Malik realized must be every ulraji ancestor trailing behind him, hoping he'd find a way to avenge what had been stolen from them in life.

The other part of him was filled with a deep, unending sense of shame. The weight of the pharaohs' sins—not just the one Bahia and Khenu had known, but all of them, every dynasty throughout the centuries of Kennoua's rule over Sonande—crushed down over every breath Malik took. He didn't even know through which side of his family this bloodline carried. Was it his father's? Had that been the source of the man's constant anger, and had violence been the only way he knew how to express it?

Malik didn't know, and honestly, it didn't really matter, for nothing changed the fact that this was his legacy to bear.

Liar. Murderer. Torturer. Monster.

That was why Malik swore Yaema to secrecy about what they'd found in the necropolis, and why when they'd finally clawed their way to the surface, he'd lied to Farid and to his sisters that the scepter hadn't been there. Farid had been disappointed, but there was nothing to do except order Malik to continue his search.

Malik did so with Yaema at his side, the two of them staying up long hours to try to uncover the whereabouts of the flute. He was grateful for the company, as Leila and Nadia were still busy helping Hanane get the displaced people settled. He didn't know what he'd say to his sisters even if they had been together; it was better for him to carry the stain of their heritage alone.

Liar. Murderer. Torturer. Monster.

Yaema was the only person he talked to regularly during that time, and she proved to be good company. He no longer missed the longing looks she gave him or the flush on her skin whenever her hand lingered on his longer than was necessary. But he never did anything about it because he didn't deserve her attention, not when there was something so evil flowing through his veins.

Days passed. Malik woke and he ate and he searched and he slept until he woke and did it all again. On the surface, he still smiled and spoke as normal. No one around him noticed anything different about him.

But inside, there was nothing. No panic. No fear.

Nothing.

And then, three days after the earthquakes, on Wind Day, there was something. A now-familiar tugging sensation deep within his chest, pulling him somewhere far from there.

Pulling him toward Karina.

Malik was in bed flipping through a book when it came. Her last call had been a desperate plea for help, but this time it was gentle, almost curious. It was a request, one Malik could have accepted or declined at his will.

If it had been a command, he would not have gone. But there was something about being handed a choice, one tiny thing he still had control over, that cracked through the miasma that surrounded him.

So despite the fact that it felt like his own mind was caving in on itself, he went to her.

"What happened to you?" Karina reached a hand toward Malik as if to touch his face, only to pull it back.

They both stared at one another, the sounds of the jungle the only thing breaking through the silence. They were back in Khenu and Bahia's village, though neither of the girls was around. Fireflies drifted lazily through the swaying grass at their waists, and several monkeys chittered away in the canopy above.

Malik imagined how he must look through Karina's eyes—wan and thin, bruises in various states of healing all over his skin.

"Nothing," he lied.

"It doesn't look like nothing." Karina's hands curled into fists at her side. "It was the council, wasn't it? They finally realized you're an ulraji."

He'd forgotten that Karina knew nothing of his arrangement with Farid or that he was living in her old home. Hoping to deflect her away from this topic, he shot back, "And what happened to you?"

In the few days since her fight with Maame Small Claws, Karina's hair had ballooned in length, trailing down her back in a giant braid formed of dozens of smaller braids that reached almost to her ankles. But that was not the only thing about her that had changed; there was a new tightness to her face, and the dark bags lining her eyes matched his own.

"I'll tell you what happened to me if you tell me what happened to you," she said. She took a step toward him. "Please, Malik, talk to me. Tell me what's wrong."

The world is ending, the only thing I understand anymore is my magic and its source is vile and evil and everything I was raised to hate. I have the scepter and if I don't give it to Farid we all might die, but if I do give it to him, you definitely will.

"I'm all right."

"You realize this magic connection goes both ways, right? I can't read your thoughts, but I can feel your distress. You don't have to pretend you're all right if you're not. Not when you're with me."

The gentleness in her voice cracked his restraint. "Why are you being so nice to me?" he choked out. "You saw what happened between our ancestors. You know what I am and what you are. This connection, what happened with Maame Small Claws, none of it has changed that. I tried to kill you! You hate me!"

Malik wanted her to scream at him. He wanted her to rage. He

didn't deserve her kindness and didn't have it in him to pretend
he did, not after what he'd done to Dedele and learning the truth
about his bloodline.

"I don't hate you," said Karina.

"You should!"

"Why, because of something that happened a thousand years
ago? Because of a war that neither of us fought in?" Karina's amber
eyes flashed. "I should hate you because you tried to kill me. You
should hate me because of what Ziran's done to Eshra. I should
hate you because of what the Ulraji Tel-Ra did to my ancestors.
You should hate me because of what Bahia did to Khenu—don't
you see there's no end to this? The cycle of this for that and that
for this, blood for blood, I'm sick of it. I'm sick of all of it!"

Karina wrapped her arms around herself. "Back in Maame
Small Claws's hut, if you hadn't goaded me into fighting, I would
have died. After that, I just . . . I refuse to continue this cycle of
revenge and retribution just because that's what we're told to do.
So no, I haven't forgiven you. But I don't hate you."

She looked up at him, and it felt as if Malik had never known
how to breathe. "You were there for me when no one else was. Let
me be here for you now. Tell me what's wrong."

Malik drew a shuddering breath. He sank to the ground with
his head between his knees.

"I feel like I'm breaking apart." The part of him that spoke
with Farid's voice warned him not to reveal so much to her, but
he could no longer ignore the pressure ballooning in his chest,
closing in on all sides. "Everything I thought I knew about

myself is warring with everything the world wants me to be. I look in the mirror and the person I see there—I don't know him, but I can't get away from him."

Karina lowered herself beside him. "I'm going to touch you now," she said slowly, like someone trying to coax a baby bird into their palm. "Is that all right?"

He gave the smallest of nods. Karina wrapped her arms around him and laid his head on her shoulder. Everything fell away but the feeling of her hand rubbing soft circles on his back.

"It's all right," she said as his entire body shuddered with heaving sobs. "You're all right. I've got you."

Malik did not know how long they stayed like that—maybe a few minutes, maybe a few hours. The chaotic crush of his mind hadn't gone away, but Karina's presence drew him back into himself, away from that frightening ledge that seemed to get closer by the day.

"What would help you most right now?" she asked when Malik's shaking had finally stilled. "Comfort or advice?"

"A-Advice," he said, for Karina had already given him more of former than she realized.

"You know what I used to do when living at court made me feel like I'd lost all sense of who I really was? The honest, real answer, and not the polite one a princess should give?"

"What did you do?"

She pulled back, her face completely serious. "I'd go fuck someone."

No amount of preparation could have readied Malik for that

answer. He stammered out several sounds that weren't actually words, and Karina let out a laugh.

"Not all the time—gods, who even has the stamina for that? From the moment I was born, I was told I was nothing more than another thread in the larger tapestry of my family's history. Every part of me belonged to this bigger thing I'd never asked to be part of."

Karina leaned back on her elbows and stared at the thin clouds floating overhead. "But with physical intimacy, nothing matters but you and whoever you're with. It became a way of having some part of my existence that no one else could control. We don't get any say over many things in our lives. Your body and who gets to touch it and why should be one of them. That's my advice—when it feels like the world is trying to pull you a million different ways, find that thing you know is yours and hold on to it with all that you are."

A part of his existence that no one else could control . . . Malik wasn't sure he'd ever had that. But perhaps it wasn't too late to find it.

"Thank you," he said, for the roiling, awful feeling inside him had died down somewhat. It never went away, not truly, but he felt like he could breathe for the first time in a long time. Karina mirrored his posture, resting her head on her knees to stare back at him.

"Thank you for not thinking I'm some sort of sex-crazed harlot."

"People say that to you?"

"Far worse, usually."

"That's awful."

She shrugged. "I'm used to it."

Malik was ashamed to think how many of the rumors about Karina he had believed as fact before meeting her. The girl people had derided for years wasn't even a shadow of the person who sat beside him, so complicated and compassionate. "That doesn't make it right."

Now that Malik was no longer mired in his own thoughts, it was impossible to ignore the proximity of Karina's body to his. He noticed now that she had freckles just like Hanane, though on her shoulders instead of her face. He had a sudden urge to run his fingers over them and had to sit on his own hands to stop it.

He didn't realized he'd been staring until Karina grinned. "If you're going to stare like that, you should at least offer to pay my bride price."

Malik had spent so long trying to escape his body that he had no idea what to do with the heat coursing through him, so he blurted out, "I'm sorry, it's just your hair looks so different."

Karina's face fell, and Malik mentally kicked himself. "N-not a bad different!" he sputtered. "It's pretty! You're really pretty!"

Great Mother help him, was it too late to let the locusts eat him alive? Malik never fumbled for words when telling a story or weaving an illusion, but when he was around Karina, whatever it was that connected his brain and his mouth refused to work properly, and all that came out was jumbled, stammering nonsense.

Karina quirked an eyebrow. "Just pretty? Are you sure the

word you're looking for isn't gorgeous? Ravishing? Divinely and ridiculously beautiful?"

Most would have seen her teasing as vanity, but Malik saw it for what it really was—an attempt to lessen his own embarrassment. It meant more to him than he could say, which was why he said with mock seriousness, "Karina, you are so luminous it is a mystery why baby sea turtles flock to the moon instead of you."

She laughed at that, and Malik felt it like sunlight sliding across his bones. "Well, thank the gods somebody finally noticed. And thank you. I know I'm pretty, but it never hurts to hear it." She twisted a few of the braids through her fingers. "I hate it."

"Why?"

"I've never worn my hair long, but my mother and my sister always have. Everyone who looks at me is going to see the people they wish I was, and they'll be even more disappointed when they realize I'm just . . . me."

"Just you was enough to defeat Maame Small Claws," he said. "You alone are more than you realize, and I'd hate to be anyone too stupid to know otherwise."

Whatever expression he was making made Karina's eyes darken in a way that sent his heart racing. "I don't understand you," she murmured. "One second you're trying to kill me, the next you're complimenting me. What do you want, Malik?"

Malik was too entranced to move away, too scared to move closer. Karina's hands rose between them, hovering a few inches from his face, and the desire he saw in her amber eyes made his mouth go dry.

"Not what you think you should want or what you've been told to want. What do *you* want?"

Before he could overthink it, Malik caught one of her hands in his own and kissed her palm.

"I want to be your friend," he whispered, and it was amazing how much more terrified he was showing her this aching, vulnerable part of him than he'd been when she held a knife against his throat. "I want to forget. Just for tonight, I want to forget everything and everyone and . . . I want you to help me."

One heartbeat passed.

Another.

Then he felt the gentlest of touches trailing along his jaw, her thumb brushing over his cheek.

He couldn't help it—he flinched. Karina paused.

"Am I hurting you?"

He shook his head. "No. I'm just . . ." How did he even begin to explain how few people had ever touched him, and how fewer still had done so gently?

But he didn't want to be that person anymore, the one who flinched and cowered when what he really wanted was more.

And like Karina had said earlier, though he could not control much in his life, he could control this.

". . . not used to being touched like this."

"Do you want me to stop?"

He pressed her forehead against hers. "No."

Breathe. He was breathing.

Stay present. He was more present in his body than he could ever remember being, every inch coming alive beneath Karina's touch. Her hands seemed to trail fire under his skin as she dragged them up across his jaw, traced the line where his temples met his curls, pressed her thumb softly against his bottom lip.

Stay here. He was here, and she was here, and right now there was only this.

But he was still himself, and he couldn't stop his body from tensing when her hands cupped his cheeks. She paused there for so long that he opened his eyes, only to see Karina's face twisted into a ludicrous expression. Laughter burst out despite his humming nerves, and she grinned at him.

"There's the smile."

Before Malik could do or say anything else, she kissed him.

The heat that had been pulsing within him seemed to explode as Karina deepened the kiss. Malik hooked his fingers through her waist beads and pulled her into his lap, her hips flush against his. She let out the softest "Oh," against his mouth as he pulled them down among the flowers, his back against the dirt, her hands in his hair. Their magic burned the air, and it was all too easy to imagine it igniting everything around them until nothing else remained.

Karina let out a groan as Malik kissed along the line of her jaw. His hands had found her waist beads again, and he vaguely recalled the old superstition that only a woman's spouse should ever touch her beads. Karina pushed her hips up against his, and Malik knew that if they didn't stop now they weren't going to, and also that he was both terrified and aching to know what would happen if they didn't.

But his mind had finally caught up to his actions, and he was suddenly all too aware of the awkward angles and knobby bones of his body and the voices whispering in his head that he was disgusting and ugly and didn't deserve to touch her or anyone else. "W-Wait," he stammered, and Karina immediately pulled her hands back.

"You don't have to do anything you don't want to do," she said softly, and Malik wished he could explain that this wasn't a matter of not wanting to be with her physically—because he wanted it so badly it ached—but that he couldn't, at least not right now with his mind tripping over itself. The barrier holding him back was completely mental, but that didn't make it any less real.

"It's just I'm not . . . can we stay above the waist?" It embarrassed Malik to even ask that. He'd been taught that a true man was always ready to bed someone from the moment he came of age. The boys in his village had been bragging of their conquests for years, while the thought of even holding someone's hand still sent him into a cold sweat.

But Karina nodded, and she didn't look at him as if he was less than for not being ready to cross that line, even if it was in a dream. "Do you want me to move away?"

He sat up with her still in his lap. "No. This is perfect."

She looped her hands around his neck and rested her brow against Malik's, so close he could feel her heart beating against his chest. "You know, there's so much I don't know about you."

"What do you want to know?"

"Everything. Tell me everything."

Malik grazed the line of the scar he had given her, which peeked over the edge of her top, a perfect match to the one he had given himself. "Kiss me again, and I will."

Karina did so, the kiss this time slow and languid, as if they had all the time in the world. As promised, her hands stayed above the waist, and when they broke apart he said, "I'm seventeen years old. My birthday is two months into the still season."

"I'm five months older than you. That makes me your elder."

"Most elders don't climb into people's laps."

"This one does." She kissed his brow. "Tell me more."

"I'm allergic to groundnuts, and dogs love me, though I'm terrified of them."

She kissed down the side of his neck until she reached the soft dip where it met his shoulder. There she bit hard enough that Malik knew there would be a mark in the morning. He inhaled sharply. "I . . . forgot what I was going to say."

Karina laughed again. "This is a bad idea."

Stars danced in his eyes. "Extremely."

"I don't hate you, but I don't think I trust you."

"I don't really trust myself."

But Malik didn't want to think about that, or about any of the other awful things that awaited them in the waking world. So he hooked a finger through her necklace of beads and pulled her to him and kissed her and kissed her until he could think of nothing else.

Malik awoke the next morning feeling as if every inch of his body had been dipped in gold. Thanks to their connection, his body bore the marks of Karina's touch as if she had actually been there.

The only thing better than kissing Karina had been talking

to her, and the more Malik learned about the fascinating, often surprising idiosyncrasies that made her who she was, the more he wanted to know.

He had hoped no one would notice the shift in his demeanor, but he had underestimated the keen gaze of a nosy older sister.

"Someone had a fun night," Leila remarked, her eyes falling on the quickly purpling mark on Malik's neck. He slapped a hand over it, face flushing over their simple breakfast of bread, tomato stew, and olives.

"Um, yeah."

Leila narrowed her eyes. "Was it that university student you're always spending time with these days?"

"What? No!" he said a little too quickly. It wasn't that people assuming there was something happening between him and Yaema was a bad thing. She was the closest thing to a friend he'd had since Tunde passed. Back in Oboure, he had never dreamed that someone like her would give him the time of day, let alone her affection.

Yet despite all that, she wasn't Karina.

"Where's Nadia?" he asked.

"Having breakfast with Hanane. She invited us both to dine with them, but I didn't want you to be alone when you woke. Besides, I think Nadia feels more comfortable opening up when we're not around."

Malik wished his heart didn't twist so much at that. The fact that Nadia was speaking to anyone at all was something to celebrate. It was petty and childish to be upset that the person wasn't him.

A part of Malik wanted to keep the memory of last night tucked away so that he could revisit it whenever the world felt cruelest, but it was the part of him that felt like it was singing that said, "I saw Karina again last night."

His sister's eyebrows shot up. "Didn't Farid tell you to stay away from her?"

"He did."

Farid had told him a lot of things, but after what Karina had said about rejecting the cycle of their ancestors, Malik was looking at his mentor's orders in a new light. Farid always spoke with such conviction that his way was the only way, but what if it wasn't? What if there really was a means to appease the gods that didn't involve a sacrifice, and his mentor was too jaded by all the history between him and the royal family to see it?

"I didn't mention this before, but I found the scepter down in the necropolis." He still wasn't ready to share what else he'd learned down there. Not yet. "I didn't tell anyone at first because I was scared, but now . . . I'm not going to give it to him."

Malik waited for Leila to tell him what an awful idea this was. The sister he had grown up with would have thrown at him a list of reasons why he shouldn't do this faster than it would have taken him to actually say the words.

But Leila only stared. "Without the scepter, he can't perform the Rite of Renewal. The disasters are going to worsen until Sonande is completely destroyed."

They both glanced out the window at the black storm clouds blanketing the city. What they could see of the sky beyond was angry and red, like a wound that refused to close. Malik unconsciously touched the Mark, hardly believing that part of the answer to ending all this suffering was hidden right within his skin.

"Karina has found the key to the city of the zawenji," said Malik. "In a few days, she'll obtain the power of the gods, just like Bahia Alahari did a thousand years ago. With it, she should be able to end these omens without performing the Rite of Renewal. There's a chance we can fix this without anyone having to die."

"Let's say Karina's plan works. What about the coup and the succession crisis? I just don't see any path forward that ends with Farid and Karina on the same side."

"But there is one thing that still connects them—Hanane. Farid and Karina may never be close again, but if anyone can persuade them to lay down their arms, it's her."

Leila still didn't look convinced, and Malik did not know how to put into words why he felt so strongly about this. His duty toward Farid and his connection to Karina were pulling him in two different directions. If there was even a chance that he could have both, he had to take it.

"Do you trust me?" Malik's eyes fell to the crooked ridge of Leila's nose, broken when she had once protected him from one of their father's blows. Her expression softened.

"I do," Leila said, and those two words were as soothing as any balm. "I know you'll do what you must, and I support you in whatever you choose. But for the love of Patuo, get a shirt with a higher collar."

A soft chuckle broke though the conversation. "You and your sister are so energetic so early in the morning. How lovely."

Malik jumped to his feet at Farid's voice, the scepter burning beneath his skin like a newly lit flame. "Good morning! Did I miss a summons?"

The former palace steward stood in the doorway to their suite, resplendent in a black-and-gold kaftan, not a hint of fatigue from dealing with the councils or the omens on his face. "With all the commotion, it's been too long since we had a lesson. Let's rectify that."

Malik needed to calm down. There was no way Farid knew about the scepter or his night with Karina. A small jolt of unease flared in his chest, but with one last look at Leila, he followed his mentor out of the room.

The signs of Hanane's work reverberated all around them. Servants wheeled crates of food out of the kitchens while guards gently guided the displaced to their new homes. Malik wondered if Farid was upset that Hanane hadn't invited him to dine with her this morning, but he knew better than to ask. They walked in silence until they reached the training grounds where the council had tested Malik on the day of the Cleansing Ceremony. Malik's heart dropped to his feet—six Sentinels stood in the center of the pit.

"Why are they here?" he asked nervously.

"Did you know that Hanane came to the council last night and declared it was time to hold her coronation?"

Malik swallowed thickly. He had not known that.

Farid continued, "She believes that seeing her formally ascend the throne will boost the morale of the people and help unify the fractured divisions within Ziran. She wants everything for the event ready within a week."

From a courtly standpoint, Hanane's plan made sense. A coronation, even a rushed one, was a show of strength, and would signal to her enemies that no matter what they might believe in the wake of her resurrection, she was the one leading Ziran.

But the moment Hanane was officially crowned, the title of queen would pass from Karina to her. And because no one would dare suggest sacrificing Hanane, their one chance of performing the Rite of Renewal would be snuffed out in an instant. Their only hope would be Karina's plan to find the city of the zawenji, and even that had no guarantees.

"This is quite a complication," Malik said weakly.

"It is indeed. I had every step of our future planned, and yet somebody has ruined it by putting ideas into her head she shouldn't even be worrying about. Now beggars walk the hall of Ksar Alahari, and through Hanane's well-intentioned actions, we all might perish."

"She's only doing this because she doesn't realize the truth of the Rite of Renewal. Perhaps if we tell her she'll change her mind?"

"Given how conflicted Hanane was over even sending soldiers to capture her sister, how do you think she'll react to learning that if she takes the title of queen, Karina might be spared?"

Hanane would immediately demand they sacrifice her instead, which Farid would never allow to happen. Malik wasn't sure where the strength to contradict his mentor came from, but something in him forced him to say, "She's just trying to do what she was raised to do. And I think she was lonely before—"

"She's not lonely. She has me."

But you're not her sister, Malik thought, but he didn't dare speak for fear of the pure ice in Farid's voice. He cast another nervous glance at the Sentinels, and his mentor followed his gaze.

"Issam's team is only days away from catching up with Karina and her entourage, but doing so will be meaningless without both the scepter and the flute," Farid said. "What updates do you have on their whereabouts?"

The Mark swirled in tight circles around Malik's lower back, as if it too was nervous about the secret hiding within it. Everything he'd ever wanted—a life of safety for him and his family—was within his grasp if he'd only give Farid what he desired.

If he'd only betray Karina once again.

Malik thought of the way she'd held him last night when he'd felt as if he was breaking apart from the inside. How safe he'd felt when the world had narrowed down to just him and her.

He willed his expression into calm.

He shook his head.

"Still no sign of either the flute or the scepter. I'm sorry."

Farid regarded him for several seconds, then sighed. With a wave of his hand, the web of nkra spun to life around them. The older ulraji pulled on one of the threads protruding from Malik's chest, one that glowed more brightly than the rest.

The one that connected him to Karina.

"Did you really think I wasn't going to notice that something shifted in your connection to Karina last night?" Farid asked softly. "You've been talking to her, haven't you? Even though I told you not to?"

Farid wrapped his fist around the thread, and numbness spasmed through Malik's body. He froze in place, a rabbit caught in a snare as his mentor leaned down close enough for him to feel his breath against his cheek.

"I don't like being lied to, little brother."

Farid let the thread go, and feeling returned to Malik's body.

"I see in you power to rival the ulraji of old. But over the past few weeks, it's become clear that what you lack is not power, but discipline. Hence why I've prepared a special lesson for today."

Farid gestured at the ring of Sentinels surrounding them. "The zawenji naively believe you can separate the body from the mind. But when one suffers, so does the other. You are at war with yourself, Malik. Had you not been so conflicted, perhaps you would not have put these foolish ideas into Hanane's head. Perhaps you would have known better than to lie to my face."

Farid stepped out of the pit as the Sentinels formed an impenetrable wall around Malik.

"That's why your lesson today will be one on combat. Hopefully in training your body, so too will you steel your mind. It begins now."

Malik didn't even have time to summon his spirit blade before the first Sentinel drove his fist into his gut, sending him flying across the stone. Blood splattered across the tile, and pain shot through his spine. He tried to push to his feet, only for the second Sentinel to slam his spear into his back. The spirit blade dropped from his grasp, and as Malik tried to reach for it, a booted foot slammed onto his hand, grinding his fingers into a bloody pulp.

Use your powers! Do something! screamed the Faceless King, but Malik couldn't think, he couldn't feel anything except pain. His mouth opened to weave some sort of illusion, but before he could say anything, one of the Sentinels snapped his leg in two.

Malik let out a bloodcurdling cry as pain like he had never known tunneled through his body. He actually lost consciousness, only to regain it when the Sentinel dropped him to the ground with his left leg twisted beneath him. Tears streamed down Malik's face, his mouth moving to say words with no meaning.

And then through the haze of agony came Farid's calm voice.

"Heal him."

Malik screamed again as one of the Sentinels grabbed the shattered halves of his leg, but instead of more pain, there came a soft blue light. In seconds, the bone was whole again, and the Sentinel tugged him back to his feet. Malik was a pitiful sight, tears and mucus streaking his face, but at least it was over.

That is, until Farid called, "Again."

This time Malik managed to deflect the first few blows, but it wasn't long before one of the Sentinels thrust her spear through his gut. When the Sentinel pulled the spear out, Malik's blood sprayed across her pristine white armor.

"Heal him," ordered Farid, and they did.

It continued like that, the Sentinels attacking with a fury no human could match and Malik powerless to fight back. They beat him black and blue, smashed his bones, severed his limbs. Each time Malik reached the brink of what a person could endure without dying, Farid ordered the Sentinels to heal him, and they did so, only to attack again.

And again.

And again.

Malik tried more than once to summon his magic, but there

was always another sword, another spear, another fist to beat him back down.

It lasted for hours. It lasted for days. Malik didn't know. He was facedown on the ground when Farid finally commanded the warriors to stop. His mentor descended into the pit to kneel beside him, the hem of his robes dragging through pools of Malik's blood.

"I know this may seem like I'm torturing you, but I'm not," said Farid, and Malik might have cried at the genuine remorse in the older ulraji's voice were his face not too swollen to do so. "When I am through with you, your power will be second to none. I can build you into a god."

Malik let out a whimper as Farid tilted his chin upward, forcing him to meet his gaze.

"But first I must break you."

This must have been how the people of Kennoua saw the pharaoh—a god among men, untouchable, immovable.

"But we can only work together if you tell me the truth," Farid said. "So I will stop the lesson right here if you give it this time— what did you find in the necropolis?"

There were so many stories of heroes facing adversity to protect the ones they cared about. Heroes who stood against all manner of monsters without ever betraying what they stood for, no matter how much they were tortured and attacked. Heroes strong enough to keep this secret in order to protect Karina.

But Malik was not a hero. He was just a boy, and he was in pain, so much pain, and here was Farid offering to take it away for something as measly as the truth. He could feel the Faceless King whirling inside him, his anger a boiling pot threatening to spill over, but Malik couldn't do it anymore.

Malik stretched out his hands, where the scepter appeared in a flash of green light. Farid beamed a smile that outshone the sun.

"See, was that so difficult?"

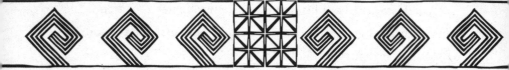

Back to the boy, one last time.

Farid had not realized it was possible to hate a person as much as he hated Prince Hakim. It wasn't like the prince was the first person who had come to Ksar Alahari intent on winning Hanane's hand in marriage. At fifteen, she was already attracting suitors from all over Sonande. They were the elite among elites, all wearing their wealth and their power in the way they dressed, the way they spoke, even the way they walked.

Farid hated every single one of them.

To her credit, Hanane treated them all with the same general politeness expected by someone of her station. Whenever her parents asked how she felt about this prince or that heiress, she simply shrugged.

"They seem nice enough, but I don't know if I wish to wed them," she'd say. Her indifference soothed Farid's soul. He might not be a prince or have all the wealth of the world to burn, but he had Hanane's companionship, a prize of incomparable value.

Until Prince Hakim arrived.

Farid might have understood the prince's appeal had he been

particularly handsome or smart or even strong. But Hakim was disgustingly average. Average face, average hair, slightly longer than average nose. His home wasn't even of great strategic value to Ziran, as it was little more than a cluster of rocks off the Dakendi Coast.

Yet for some unfathomable reason, Hanane was enamored with him. Before he'd arrived, she'd spent her limited free moments whiling away the hours with Farid or her sister, but now it seemed all her time belonged to the prince. When they weren't out riding together, Hanane was showing him around the palace or taking him to a performance, or just sitting on a wall and talking— always with a chaperone, of course, but that didn't change the fact that every time Farid saw them together, a small part of him died.

"What does she even see in him!" he exclaimed for the fifth time in as many minutes as he paced around his bedroom. Karina lay sprawled on his bed, barely listening to his rant.

"Maybe she thinks he smells nice." She flicked her wrist, and a scroll detailing the genealogies of Ziran's noble families sailed across the room. Karina was only seven, but her powers had grown exponentially since that day in the garden. The queen had even mentioned finding a tutor for her magic, discreetly of course. This was before . . . well, you already know.

"Lots of people smell nice. Smelling nice isn't a good enough reason to obsess over someone," Farid scoffed.

"Well, I hope he smells nice, or else kissing him can't be all that fun."

Farid stopped his pacing. "What?"

"I caught Hanane kissing him the other day, and she promised me all her dessert for a month if I didn't tell anyone, not even you," she said idly, not realizing that each word cut like a knife straight into Farid's veins.

He did not wish to believe it, but Karina had nothing to gain from lying about this. How could Hanane do this to him?

For though Farid was only seventeen, he knew with unwavering certainty that Hanane was his soul mate. Her face was the last thing he saw in his mind each night and the first thing he thought of come morning. When he had tearfully revealed his ulraji ancestry to her, she had accepted him wholeheartedly because that was just who she was, kind and loving and bright.

How many nights had he spent fantasizing about what it might be like to kiss or even just hold her only for this insipid, vapid prince to waltz in and take what was rightfully his?

"He's not good enough for her," he seethed.

"If you care so much, why don't you do something about it?" said Karina.

Farid recalled that the prince wore a ceremonial dagger everywhere he went, a thing of pure beauty with shells from the Dakendi Coast inlaid in the hilt. It would look even more beautiful embedded deep in its owner's chest.

That would teach the prince not to touch what did not belong to him.

But that idea was too obvious, too messy. A better plan blossomed in Farid's mind, and he left the younger princess to her magic as he went to find a herbalist.

Days passed, and rumors swirled that with all the time Hanane and the prince were spending together, surely a proposal must be imminent. Through it all, Farid remained the smiling, pleasant ward he was meant to be.

And then opportunity arrived. The queen had a rare evening free, so she spent it dining with her children, her husband, and the prince. Though Farid still refused to think of the queen and king as his parents, he knew them well enough to see they both approved of Hakim—if he made an official offer for Hanane's hand, they wouldn't turn him down.

At one point, the prince told some stupid joke and Hanane burst into that beautiful, radiant laugh of hers. Hakim threw him a sly grin, and Farid smiled politely back.

And then doubled over and vomited the contents of his stomach all over the table.

The healers found poison in his system, and what followed was a frantic search for whoever had dared to harm the sultana's ward right under her nose.

A search that led them to a vial of elephant's ear toxin nestled among Prince Hakim's belongings, exactly where Farid had left it

The queen's fury was swift—she had Prince Hakim whipped and then exiled from Ziran, despite his pleas of innocence. She then cut off all trade with his small island. Farid felt the tiniest twinge of guilt when he learned that without Zirani trade, Hakim's people would starve.

However, the guilt faded when Hanane came to visit him in the infirmary and threw herself across his bed with a sob.

"I'm so, so sorry, Farid! I can't believe Hakim would do this!" she cried, and he gently wiped her tears, his heart racing even as his body shuddered from the toxin's effects. However, Farid would have poisoned himself a dozen times over if it meant having Hanane back.

"You couldn't have known," he said. "You see only the best in people. That's why—"

The words died in Farid's throat. Prince Hakim was no longer a problem, but he couldn't confess his feelings until he was certain no one would ever try to take her from him again.

"That's why I'll always be here to protect you," he finished. Hanane laid her head against his chest, and Farid wondered if it was possible to die from pure joy.

"What would I do without you?" she murmured. He ran a finger down her cheek and grew smug at the thought of poor Prince Hakim returning home to his people with famine and disgrace instead of a new bride.

"Hopefully, you'll never have to find out."

24

Karina

Malik didn't visit her the next day.

Karina told herself this did not bother her. After all, how many nights had she spent with someone only to disappear by morning and never speak to them again? So what if, for a little while, he had made her feel as if she mattered not because she had magic or was the descendant of a great legacy, but simply for being herself?

Except he didn't visit her the day after that either, nor the day after that. Despite what she told herself, Karina grew worried. She even tried to call across their connection, but he never responded. She knew he wasn't dead, for she would have felt it, so he had to be ignoring her.

Fine. Let him pretend that night hadn't happened. See if she cared.

For more than a week her group raced across the Odjubai, their packs heavy with food and other resources given to them by the grateful denizens of the City of Thieves. Karina wore the key to the Sanctum on a string of beads around her neck. It pointed ever northwest, and they followed its direction as the shifting dunes of the desert gave way to the rolling shrubland that bordered both Eshra and Arkwasi.

But it wasn't only the terrain that was shifting—Karina could *feel* them getting closer to Doro Lekke. All four of them felt the pull, like an anchor reeling their magic home. This, coupled with the ordeal they had survived in Balotho, had changed the dynamic of the group. Nothing illustrated this more than when Caracal found Karina attempting to lift a flower off the ground with her powers on the sixth night of their mad sprint.

"The problem is you're trying too hard," he'd explained after watching Karina blast the flower halfway across the clearing she was practicing in. "You like music, right? A storm is like a symphony, a dozen different elements coming together to create something bigger. Compared to that, a wind whip is a single note. Simple, but play it just right"—He flicked a finger, and a single petal split from the flower to land in his palm—"one note is all you need. Honestly, I'm surprised you can summon lightning, but you can't do this. It's like you figured out advanced equations without ever mastering basic arithmetic."

Karina had looked from the severed flower petal to the former Sentinel. "I thought you said you don't teach?"

He rubbed his neck sheepishly. "I don't. But for the right person, I'm willing to try."

From then on, Caracal used every moment of rest they had to teach Karina what he knew about being a Wind-Aligned zawenji. She learned how to change air pressure in a field where flamingos danced in a patchwork of feathers. She learned how to turn drizzle to frost, to sleet, to ice in the ruin of what had once been a chief's grand fortress. She felt as she had when she'd first learned to play the oud, rejoicing at each new technique and hard-won improvement.

On the tenth day they reached a waterlogged delta where they traded their horses to a toothless woman for a long canoe and four oars. It was Karina's first time riding a boat on actual water, and though she quickly discovered she had no stomach for it, she marveled at each splash of the waves against their ship and the glittering scales of ninki nankas slithering beneath the surface.

This close to the Eshran border, there were Zirani soldiers everywhere, and it was only thanks to Caracal's years of experience eluding the army that they managed to evade their clutches.

"There shouldn't be this many people stationed here," Caracal had said after a harrowing day spent hiding in the mud and praying that high tide wouldn't drown them all before the soldiers passed. "They must have everyone they can spare looking for you."

If Farid had sent all these people after her, then who was rebuilding Ziran? Karina's anger only grew with each soldier they passed, for that was one less person to clear the rubble in her home and distribute aid. Even if someone were to perform the Rite of Renewal tomorrow, it would take years to rectify this damage. The same urge to do something, anything, substantial that Karina had always felt during her days locked up inside Ksar Alahari clawed within her.

Yet despite the key growing warmer against her chest with each passing day, there was no sign of Doro Lekke. The location of the city could not have moved as the key continued to point in the same direction, so where was it? Karina said as much to Afua on their second day in the swamp. "It's here. I can feel it," was all the Life-Aligned girl replied, and Karina nodded, gripping her oar tighter.

I'm coming, she thought to her mother, to Bahia, and to every other zawenji ancestor who had existed between them. The power hidden in the Sanctum was her birthright. With it, she could save everyone without dying. *Wait for me.*

And then, on their fifth day in the swamp, in an area filled with thick reeds taller than a full-grown man, where the jackfish swam right up to their boat, Karina felt it.

"Wait!" she yelled, nearly capsizing the entire canoe. "We're here!"

"Far be it from me to doubt the magical bone shard you stole from a demon centipede woman's corpse, but there is literally nothing here," said Caracal, but Karina simply closed her eyes and cast her power outward, just like the former Sentinel had taught her to do—not to attack but to listen.

The wind responded, amplifying every sound around her a thousandfold. She was in the rustle of the reeds and the gentle croaking of the bullfrogs. She was the breeze whistling through the trees, the humidity curling all their hair and slicking their bodies with sweat.

With each breath Karina sank deeper into the magic until— there it was. A single pocket where the sound did not quite reach. She opened her eyes and pointed straight ahead, to a gnarled tree growing on a small island that seemed little more than branches and mud.

"That's it."

At first glance, this island was no different from the hundreds of others dotting the swamp, revealed only when the tide fell low. But a second glance uncovered a flat stone disk more than ten feet across, nestled among the roots. On the disk had been carved eight symbols—seven for the patron deities, one for the Great Mother. They stood around it in a half circle after disembarking and anchoring their canoe.

"Well, what now?" Karina asked. Caracal shrugged, but Ife walked over to the Moon-Aligned symbol. They inspected the crescent-shaped emblem etched into their palm before stepping onto the one on the disk. Pale blue light blossomed from the ground in a spiral around them, so bright everyone had to shield their eyes.

"I think we're supposed to do that," Ife said.

The others followed suit, with purple light appearing when Afua stood on the Life-Aligned symbol and yellow light when Karina and Caracal stood on the Wind-Aligned one. The light bathed the swamp in shifting colors as the magic of Doro Lekke connected with the magic in their veins.

But despite the beauty of it, there were still four empty symbols beside them. Karina bit back a sound of frustration. "This doesn't make any sense. Who builds a city you can only enter when six other people are with you?"

She regarded the empty symbols once more when an idea came to her. She stepped from her spot, scooped a handful of water from the edge of the island, and returned to drizzle it over the Water symbol. Ocean-blue light rose from the ground and carved the Water symbol into the tree.

"Not bad, princess," said Caracal, and Karina practically glowed beneath the praise.

For the Earth Alignment they only needed mud, and Afua created a small flame with their last piece of flint for Fire. Sun took the longest to figure out, and they ended up tying a small mirror from the bottom of Ife's pack to a tree branch so that a shaft of sunlight hit the Sun-Aligned symbol at just the right angle.

As soon as the last symbol was covered, a rumble tore through the earth, and an ornate door appeared from within the bark of the tree. On it was a single triangular indentation. With trembling fingers, Karina removed the key from her neck and placed it in the hole.

There came the creak of ancient, groaning wood as the door swung inward, revealing a staircase formed of twining branches.

A single creature fluttered out of the gloom of the entrance—a bone-white butterfly. The symbol of the Great Mother.

All four of them stared at it, no one daring to speaks as they felt the magic that wafted up from the entrance tugging deep within the core of everything that made them what they were.

The wind seemed to push at Karina's back as she led the way down into the lost city of their ancestors, and once they were all through, the bark closed around the entrance, smooth as if there was no way it could be anything but.

Karina loved Ziran. It was hard not to, with its beauty and its power. But even during the days when her family had been whole and her future bright, she'd known deep down that she did not belong there. No matter how hard she tried to be the perfect princess everyone needed her to be, a small part of her had always been too wild, too much, even for those who loved her most.

But not here. Here, the world was filled with primal energy that did not have to exist or justify itself, but just *be*. Doro Lekke was a forest's dream of what a city should be, with each structure carved not from the wood of the tree but of the tree itself, its roots having grown into the buildings and walls of the dwellings all around them.

Specks of dust floated through the thin shafts of sunlight poking through the root ceiling, and the only other light came from luminescent algae floating down the rivers that made the Sanctum's streets, just like Karina had seen near Bahia and Khenu's hometown. Statues lined the wall, each holding in their hands different items and offerings that had not been touched for a thousand years.

And the magic—it was everywhere, soft as moss in some places, hard and unyielding as stone in others. It beckoned Karina forward, whispering in her ear *welcome, welcome, welcome*.

"This is . . ." Caracal trailed off, lost for words. They all were.

The softest of breezes turned Karina's head toward a tunnel where more light glowed. Forgetting all else, she moved toward it.

The voices grew louder the deeper Karina went. They whispered in words not of any human tongue but of lightning and waterfalls, volcanoes and hurricanes. The voice of magic urged her to keep moving, to keep going, to slow for nothing and no one.

"Karina, wait! Something seems off," cried Afua, but Karina charged ahead. Pressure pounded in her head, the overwhelming crush of the Sanctum trying to give her everything it had to offer at once. Shapes and colors danced across her eyes, and the world grew fuzzy at the edges. Bleeding, festering rat piss, not a migraine here of all places, not when she was so close—

"Karina!"

Karina went stumbling backward as Caracal grabbed her. She began to thrash, but Afua took her face and twisted it to look at the path she had been following. The ground fell off sharply not even five feet in front of them, into a chasm at least a hundred feet wide. Had the former Sentinel not stopped her when he did, Karina would have plummeted straight into it without even noticing.

With his free hand, Caracal picked up a stone and hurled it over the edge. When the unmistakable thud of it hitting the ground never came, he whistled. "All right, something about this place is clearly messing with your mind. Let's come up with a plan—ow!"

Caracal yelped as Karina bit down on the hand that had been holding her and twisted out of his grasp. She wasn't even thinking as she did it; her mind held nothing but that burning desire to follow those voices calling her name.

Before anyone else could stop her, Karina summoned all the magic she possessed, raced forward, and leaped.

It was the closest thing to flying she had ever experienced, and she let out a whoop of exhilaration as her body soared through the air, buoyed upward by the strength of the wind. But she had underestimated the length of the chasm and made it about three-quarters of the way across before she began to drop. Wind howling in her ears, Karina shot a desperate gust down that sent her careening the rest of the distance and smacking hard against the opposite wall, dozens of feet below the ledge. She slid down for several more feet before finally catching herself by her fingertips on a jutting rock.

"Or we could just do that!" Caracal yelled, his voice small from so far away. Ten long streaks of blood soiled the chasm from where Karina's fingers had slid before finding purchase. The pulsing pain in her hands forced her to pause long enough to catch her breath.

But the voices were relentless, and even a second spent not trying to reach them was a second too long. Her arms straining with effort, Karina grabbed a rock above her. When it held, she pulled herself up to the next one, and then the next. Having exhausted too much of her magic getting across the chasm, she had nothing but her own strength to pull her inch by painful, agonizing inch up the stone. She heard her friends yelling that they were going to look for another path, but she could not focus on them lest she lose her grip and plunge to her death.

After what felt like forever, Karina hauled her trembling body over the ledge. Even with sweat dripping down her skin and blood coating her hands she did not stop, leaning heavily against the root-formed wall as she followed the light into the chamber she had seen in her vision with Malik.

The cavern was easily several stories tall, with an open ceiling through which the half-moon grinned down at Karina. Statues of the seven patron deities ringed the room, each one depicting one of the great myths about the creation of their world. There was Gyata, pulling the sun into the sky to save it from the churning mass of chaos that threatened to drown its light. There was her own patron, Santrofie, flapping his wings to create air and breath.

Each statue had been carved with such precision that it seemed the gods might spring to life at any moment.

At the center of it all was a statue of the Great Mother. Her face had been smoothed away by weather and time, but the widespread gesture of her hands—open to give wrath or mercy in equal measure—was unmistakable. Hundreds of white butterflies fluttered around her, creating a shifting, living veil.

Karina began to understand exactly what it was that moved people to faith. It felt like every second of her life had been leading to this moment, and she was certain that every moment after would be defined by it. There was no bringing her mother back, no saving the people who had died in Tiru or Balotho, but with this, she could finally end Farid's reign of terror. She could become something more than the queen who had run when her people had needed her.

Yet standing there in one of the most sacred spaces in all Sonande, a single thought ran through her mind: Hanane should have been there. Not the fake one Farid was parading around, but her real sister. Leaving Ziran to experience all the wonders of Sonande had been Hanane's dream first; she should have been there as Karina stood where their ancestor once had.

"God of my mothers. Provider of all," Karina began, as she knelt in that hallowed space, her words echoing all around her. "I come before you seeking the power only you can bestow. Reveal to me that which was hidden here thousands of years ago, so that I may right a great wrong and spare your children from an agony they do not deserve."

Karina kissed the statue's feet. It was only then that she noticed a single basket nestled at its base, closed only with a small string loop. Despite its humble appearance, pure power radiated from it.

With the voices at a fever pitch and the butterflies fluttering around her, Karina took a deep breath and opened the lid.

25

Malik

The pain wasn't so bad when Malik didn't think about it.

Farid had let him go as soon as he'd handed over the scepter, and just like after his test, there was not a single permanent mark on him.

Farid asked him if he understood that this was his fault. He did.

Farid promised him that as long as he remained truthful, this wouldn't happen again. He would.

Farid told him that he should be grateful it wasn't worse. He was.

Truly he was, for there was something perversely comforting about letting his mind slip back into the scared child he had once been, the one who had lived the pain of broken bones and ruined organs every day and who knew how to lower his head to stay alive at all costs. He knew how to live with this version of himself better than he did the version that had tortured Dedele and that had handed Karina to death not once, but twice. He had needed the reminder that all he had ever been, and all he ever would be, was a coward.

He was grateful for Farid.

He was grateful.

He was.

Preparations for Hanane's coronation breathed new life into Ziran, just as the princess had hoped they would. In a matter of days, the city had transformed from a frightened, empty skeleton into a place of festivity and joy once again. Ksar Alahari became a whirlwind of planning, even as more and more of the displaced were let inside its walls each day. Like most things of importance to the Zirani, a coronation was a weeklong affair that started and ended on the day of the new queen's Alignment. So on the Sun Day nearly two weeks after Malik had given up the scepter, he stood on a balcony watching hundreds of people stream into the brightly lit halls of the palace.

But though laughter and light permeated the air, Malik felt none of it. He hadn't felt anything, really, since the lesson. A dark hole had opened inside him where his emotions should have been, and these days it felt as if he was looking at the world through a film of broken glass. Leila had noticed the shift, and he'd waved off her concern by claiming the search for the flute was simply tiring him out.

And it was true that he'd spent every day since the lesson with Yaema, combing the city for even a hint of the flute's whereabouts. At the girl's request, he'd arranged a room in the palace for her to aid in the search, and he had even gotten her an invitation to the coronation as well. It seemed like the least Malik could do when she was giving up so much to help him, and when he could not return the affection she felt for him.

Malik almost wished the world would just end already so that he no longer had to deal with the void inside him that grew each day that passed without him finding the flute. But there was no one to blame because he had chosen this; he had let Farid down and it was his fault, he wasn't looking hard enough but he didn't know what else to do, there had to be some way out of this hell he had created for himself—

A soft rustle broke Malik from his thoughts. He whirled around, dagger in his hand and magic on his tongue, but it was only Nadia.

"They said I was getting in the way so I have to wait outside," she said. As tradition dictated, Hanane had spent the entire day before the start of coronation week in isolation, and now her quarters were a war zone as her attendants and Leila helped her prepare for the first of the series of ceremonies that would end with her becoming sultana. Avoiding that frenzy was exactly why Malik had come out here. He couldn't handle being around so much joy when everything inside him was lifeless and dim.

Nadia at least looked wonderful in her coronation dress, a large swath of orange fabric tied off at the waist, which had been designed to match both his and Leila's. "Hanane says she'll let us walk in with her," she said as she bounced on the balls of her feet with excitement. "And we get to stand up front where we can see everything and—"

"Can we please talk about something besides Hanane for five minutes?" Malik snapped.

He regretted the words the second they were out of his mouth and Nadia's lip wobbled. "You're mad at me."

"I'm not," he promised, hating himself even more for letting his petty jealousy slip out when there were far more important things to deal with. "You haven't done anything wrong, I'm just . . . what is it that draws you to the princess?"

It was a heavy question to ask a six-year-old, but Malik couldn't stand not knowing. Nadia looked down.

"Ever since I came back from the spirit world, things are weird," she said softly. "Sometimes things look like they're real but they're not. Or they look like they're not real but they are. I didn't tell you about it because you—you always look so sad, and I don't want you to be sadder."

Malik would have taken a thousand beatings from the Sentinels if it meant he could erase the pained expression from Nadia's eyes. Sometimes he forgot that she was no longer the baby he used to carry around everywhere, and that she spent just as much time watching him as he did watching her.

She continued, "I don't know why, but I never get a weird feeling around Princess Hanane. I always know she's real. I'm sorry, please don't be mad at me."

Malik had heard tales of people developing strange abilities after coming into contact with the spirit world. Was that why Nadia had felt such a kinship with the undead princess, for they'd both sensed in the other a place that no other human had seen?

Malik knelt to his sister's level. "I'm not mad at you, and you are never, ever bothering me, all right? No matter how sad I look, I *always* have time for you. I promise."

The tears that had been brimming in Nadia's eyes finally spilled over, and with a wail she flung herself into her brother's arms.

"I was s-s-so scared!" she sobbed, and in that moment Malik was ten years old again, and she was the infant so small she fit in the crook of his arm. One day Nadia was going to grow up and have a life and adventures that had nothing to do with him, but right now she wanted a comfort only her older brother could give her.

"I know," he whispered. Tears streamed down his own face as he cradled Nadia close to his chest. "I know, I know."

Idir stirred within him, but the spirit stayed silent, allowing the two siblings to have this moment that had been so long overdue.

"I hear crying. Why are we crying?"

Leila pushed through the curtain, took one look at her siblings bawling their eyes out, and wrapped her arms around them both. The three of them stayed that way for a while, and Malik felt like he was holding on to them long after he'd let go.

"You should eat something," said Leila when they finally pulled apart. "I doubt there'll be much time once the ceremony begins, and you haven't been eating lately."

Everything had tasted like ash since his lesson, but his sisters didn't need to know that. "I'll be fine."

Leila nodded before surveying the throngs of guests spilling into the courtyard below. "Hanane's been asking me what our plans are once this is all over—the coronation and the Rite of Renewal, that is. She says we're welcome to stay at Ksar Alahari for as long as we'd like and that she'll even give us our own lands and titles. I think that would make us the first-ever Eshran members of the Zirani nobility."

It was a generous gift, and for the first time Malik allowed himself to imagine what life would be like once this was all over. No more fighting. No more hiding.

No more Karina.

His chest constricted, and he had to force his thoughts away from that painful morass lest he forget to breathe. Instead he said, "I don't think Farid will still want us at court after this is all done."

"Do you think I give a rat's ass what Farid wants?" said Leila, and Malik tensed.

"You shouldn't say things like that!" he whispered. It felt like the man was watching them every second of the day, but right now, Farid was down in the receiving hall, entertaining guests before the ceremony. For once, they were truly alone.

"On the contrary, more people should say things he doesn't want to hear. And the way he talks to Hanane? You'd think he owned her. It bothers her, but she feels like she can't speak against him after all he's done for her. But was resurrecting her really the gift he claims it was if he holds it over her head for the rest of her life?"

Leila grew more passionate the longer she talked, her hands gesturing wildly as their mother's always used to when she got deep into an argument. Malik simply watched, still apprehensive but amused. "I didn't realize you and Hanane had grown so close."

Leila coughed awkwardly. "Look, all that really matters is that things are going to change for all of us. But we've weathered change before and come out the other side stronger for it. So no matter what happens, I'm on your side."

Tears burned at the back of Malik's eyes. The truth about his training with Farid sat on the tip of his tongue, but he couldn't bring himself to share it. Now that his own mind and his connection to Karina were no longer safe places, he didn't want anything to tarnish his relationship with his sisters.

Before he could reply, one of Hanane's attendants poked her head onto the balcony.

"She's ready."

At the center of the room, Hanane sat still as a doll as the servants placed the finishing touches on the first of her seven different coronation outfits. Today's gown was orange in honor of her patron deity, with the red and silver colors of the Alahari family embroidered over her chest in a pattern reminiscent of a sunburst. Several tiers of beads ringed her neck and arms, and half her locs had been piled high above her head, threaded through with wires of pure gold to match the ceremonial lines of red, orange, and gold painted over her face. Malik and Leila simply stared, and Hanane's face twisted with worry.

"What's wrong? I look weird, don't I?" she moaned.

Nadia threw herself across Hanane's lap. "You look like a princess!"

"But I am a princess."

"Oh. Then you look normal!"

Hanane finally laughed, the tension disappearing from her face. Leila's face twisted with mock seriousness.

"I still think something is missing." She bent over, removed Hanane's jeweled slippers, and tossed them in a corner. "There. That's better."

Hanane stared down at her now-bare feet. She burst into tears, and Leila flinched in alarm.

"Oh no, don't cry!" Leila cupped Hanane's face in her hands, shivering slightly from the unnatural cold, and gently wiped the tears away as best she could without ruining the princess's makeup. "It's too early for you to start crying. Nothing has even begun yet."

"I'm just so grateful you three are here," Hanane said through several undignified hiccups. "Without my parents and without Karina I just . . . I don't know how I would have survived these last few weeks without you."

Another layer of unease wrapped around the growing knot of anxiety in Malik's gut. What type of wretched person was he to stand here and accept Hanane's gratitude when he had knowingly handed her sister to her death?

"You wouldn't have been alone. Not with Farid here," he offered, but at the mention of Farid, something in Hanane's face shuttered.

"With Farid, it's different. It's always been different."

"He loves you." Suddenly it seemed important that Malik remind her of this, that he remind everyone in the room of this. The taste of blood rose in his mouth once more, and he swallowed it down. "I think—no, I know he loves you more than anyone or anything in this world."

Leila looked at him as if he had just struck her across the face, but Hanane threw a glance at the servants. "Leave us," she commanded, and as soon as they were gone she slumped over in her seat like a puppet whose strings had been cut. "I know Farid loves me. I think I knew that before he even knew it himself. He defied the Ancient Laws to give me a second chance at life. How could that be anything but love?"

A strange look had entered Leila's eyes, and she spoke so quietly Malik almost missed it. "But do you love him?"

The smile slipped from Hanane's face. She idly twisted the queen's signet around her finger.

"Farid believes I return his feelings because I spent years letting him think I returned his feelings." The air grew heavy, like they were in a temple and Hanane was giving a confession that had been weighing her down her whole life. "He was so traumatized when he came to live with us, and I thought that if his feelings for me gave him something to hold on to, then why take that from him? I never promised him anything, but I didn't dissuade him either."

Hanane let out a mirthless laugh. "Actually no, I don't deserve to play innocent. The truth is I liked knowing that I held so much power over him. And though Karina viewed him as another sibling, I never did, because I knew he didn't want me to see him that way. And after an incident where a visiting prince poisoned him out of jealousy, I felt I owed him for so many years of pining, so I let things get more physical than I should have. I was curious and he was willing and I didn't see the harm. Friends experiment with one another all the time."

The princess closed her eyes and tipped her head back. "If I had realized . . . I never should have let it get this far. I'm the reason he is the way he is, and now I have to live with what I've done to him."

Leila took a step forward. "With all due respect, Your Highness, that's the stupidest thing I've ever heard." Hanane's eyes snapped open, and she gave Leila an incredulous look that Malik's sister returned. "It is! So maybe you were in the wrong for toying with his feelings when you didn't return them. Maybe you weren't a perfect victim. But what kind of self-respecting adult allows teenage heartbreak to rule ten years of their life? I don't care how sad his childhood was. My own father held me down and broke my nose when I was seven. Our village elders tortured Malik for weeks on end when he was six. Nobody escapes this world without some sort of trauma, but that doesn't mean you get to do whatever you want because of it."

Leila gathered Hanane's hands in her own.

"You are a queen. You answer to nobody and to no one. If you choose to keep Farid around, do so because you truly want him around, not because you feel like you have to. Don't let the mistakes of your past dictate your future."

It was likely that no one had ever spoken to the princess like this before, and that no one ever would again. Hanane had every right to kick them all out for such insolence, but she simply stared at Leila. The silence stretched on until a priestess entered the room and performed the Zirani gesture of respect.

"Your Highness, it is time."

Hanane pulled away from Leila and jumped to her feet, as if trying to get as much physical space as possible between her and their conversation.

"Let's go, friends. It seems the time has come for me to receive my crown."

Farid was speaking with a few guards when Hanane and her entourage swept into the small holding room off the side of the main hall. He stopped mid-word to stare at her, and in light of what the princess had shared with them back in their rooms, Malik felt even more like every look between them was not meant for anyone else to see.

"You are . . . a pure vision," Farid said breathlessly. He reached out a hand as if to graze the line of rubies at her collarbone, and Hanane deftly stepped back.

"As always, you are too kind." She quickly turned to the High Priestesses who would be conducting the ceremony. "Where do you need me to go?"

"First will be the procession through the prayer hall," said Sun Priestess. She and Water Priestess would be leading the proceedings, as the head priestess of Hanane's Alignment and the head priestess of the current era, respectively. "Then we will take you to the inner chamber, where you will enter deep meditation with the gods to reflect on the role bestowed upon you. After that, the procession will take you in a loop around the city, so that the faithful may gaze upon their new sultana and rejoice."

No one made mention of the fact that both these women's homes and places of worship had been completely destroyed. That was how Ziran had always done things, moving forward with as little focus as possible on what was wrong.

"I like rejoicing. Rejoicing is good." Hanane looked over her shoulder at Malik and his sisters. "You three will be accompanying me during the procession, of course."

Farid shook his head. "Only family may process with the queen-to-be."

"And since I returned, these three have been family to me and more. They're coming." He began to protest, but Hanane put up a hand to stop him. "Queens go to advisers for advice, Farid, not permission. They will stay with me for as long as I wish to have them by my side, and that is final."

Hanane seemed to have taken Leila's words to heart, for she stared up at the older ulraji with a defiance Malik hadn't seen before. Farid's eyes darkened, and every muscle in Malik's body tensed to run, for he knew what followed that expression.

But then his mentor smiled.

"Whatever my queen desires, she may have. However, Malik needs to stay here. He'll be helping with security tonight."

Hanane pursed her lips but nodded. "Fine. Malik may stay behind."

As the priestesses went over with Hanane, Leila, and Nadia exactly how they were to process into the room, Farid drew Malik to the side.

"I have an update on you regarding our search for Karina. Thanks to the information you gleaned from Dedele Botye, our soldiers in the Eshran foothills have caught her trail. They are only a few days from catching up with her," he said.

Malik's stomach dropped farther than he'd known it could. So not only had he consigned Karina to death, he had increased the Zirani presence in his homeland as well.

Farid watched him closely. "You don't seem pleased by this news."

"I—I am! It's just that . . ." Malik snapped the bracelet on his wrist, both hating and relishing the sharp bite of pain. "I've been worried about my place here at the palace. I feel as if I'm not doing enough for—"

Enough for whom? asked the Faceless King, and Malik truly did not know. All his life he'd been fighting for his family's survival, but now that their survival was no longer in danger, what *was* he fighting for?

"Your place is right here with me. You are a wonderful student, and I sincerely apologize for anything I may have said or done to imply otherwise."

But if that were the case, why had he allowed the Sentinels to beat Malik to near death? Malik could no longer discern which version of Farid was the real one, the kindhearted teacher or the ruthless ulraji.

"But what happens when this is all over?" Malik asked, hating how small his voice sounded. "After you . . . after you perform the Rite of Renewal?"

"Isn't it obvious? Hanane will rule as she was always meant to do, and I'll stand by her side. And you'll stand by mine. Your sisters are free to stay as well. You'll have everything you ever wanted, Malik. You'll be safe."

Safe—that *was* everything Malik had ever wanted. The more he thought about it, the more appealing the idea became. He'd suffered before because he had crossed Farid, but it would never happen again. Everything was as it should be, if he just remembered his place and didn't stray past it.

Malik nodded, and Farid squeezed his shoulder before going to join Hanane for the procession. The first of the trumpeters blew a joyous sound on their ivory horns that echoed throughout the hall, followed by a flurry of triumphant drumbeats.

The coronation had begun.

Hanane had explained to them earlier that tonight's ceremony involved cleansing in each of the seven elements that formed the Alignments. "It represents the future queen forging a connection with each of the patron deities on behalf of our people," she'd said.

These were not the short prayers their people did several times a day, but long, complex incantations invoking gods and the ancestors, time and space. All this to say that for the first hour or so, Malik was rapt with attention, but by the third, he was bored out of his mind and his foot was falling asleep.

Because he was not at the front of the hall like his sisters, it was easy enough for him to slip into a shadowed corner and weave an invisibility illusion over himself. Now unseen, he was able to survey the members of the court discreetly, just as Farid had ordered. However, nothing seemed amiss. All Malik saw was hundreds of battered yet excited people, hoping beyond hope that a new queen might be what Ziran needed to weather the challenges plaguing it.

Farid still hadn't mentioned how Hanane's ascension to the throne would impact his plans for the Rite of Renewal. At this point, Malik was too scared to ask.

Malik was scanning the hall once more when a movement on the upper floor caught his attention. He recognized Yaema, deep in conversation with Tunde's younger brother, Adewale. The latter's presence surprised him; last he'd heard, Tunde's family was still declining every social invitation, including tonight's. Driss's family had declined as well. He didn't know when the families of the two slain Champions would be ready to rejoin the court, but he doubted it would be any time soon.

Though he and Yaema had gotten close, Malik hesitated before approaching. In the wake of the conversation with Hanane, he felt even worse about relying on her so heavily when he knew he did not feel for her the way she felt for him. He hesitated so long that she finished her conversation with Adewale and walked deeper into the palace, away from the coronation hall. Odd that she'd leave the main festivities when she had pressed Malik so much for an invitation to the event.

Once Malik had reached the second floor, he let the illusion go and called out, "The view is better downstairs."

Adewale's eyes went wide with the look of someone caught in a place they knew they were not supposed to be. "You're Farid's henchman," said the boy, and Malik bristled internally. Was that what the world saw when they looked at him?

. . . Were they wrong?

"And you're Adetunde's younger brother." Malik hadn't realized just how young the boy was. His voice hadn't even begun to crack yet. "Are you here alone? Where is your family?"

"T-They told me not to come. But . . . I had to see it for myself. I had to see what Tunde died for."

Malik's heart twisted. "You don't have to hide out here like some kind of criminal. Come down and join the festivities."

Adewale eyed him warily, before his eyes flicked down to the rubber bracelet tied around Malik's left wrist.

"That was my brother's. Why do you have it?" he asked sharply, the grief in his voice raw and thick.

"Tunde gave it to me during Solstasia," answered Malik. "I've always suffered from . . . destructive tendencies. He gave this to me to help curb them."

Malik realized that he did not know if Tunde's family had already held his funeral or not. It was hardly surprising that they hadn't invited him when he and Tunde hadn't known each other for long, but the thought that he'd missed the chance to say good-bye to his friend burned.

"I only knew your brother for a short while, but he was a better friend to me in that time than some people I've known for years," Malik said. "He was a light, and this world is less bright for having lost him."

He untied the bracelet and offered it to Adewale. The welt formed by the band was a dark purple spot on the inside of his wrist. "Here," he said softly. "You deserve this more than I do."

With shaking hands, Adewale took the strands of rubber and stared down at them as his shoulders began to heave. "I miss him so much it hurts to breathe. I don't know who I am now that he's gone."

Malik gently pulled the smaller boy into his arms and let Adewale sob into his chest. The music wafting from the coronation was a joyous roar that could not penetrate their bubble of grief.

"You're never going to be the person you were with him again." The force of Tunde's death washed over Malik anew as he recalled the life his friend would never get to live, the love he'd never get to see bloom to fruition, all the paths he'd never get to walk down. "But each day is a chance to become someone just as good. Someone he would have been proud to call his brother."

They stayed that way for several minutes, until Adewale blew his nose on the corner of Malik's shirt and pulled away. He watched silently as Malik tied Tunde's bracelet around his thin wrist. Something dark washed over his eyes when he finally looked up.

"Don't stand by the east wall," he hissed before running off in the direction Yaema had gone. Malik watched him go, alarm bells ringing in his ears. *Don't stand by the east wall?* What was about to happen at the east wall?

He'd been tasked to alert Farid the second anything seemed amiss, which was what Malik moved to do. He ran faster than he could ever remember running, through the decorated arches and down the stairs, only to be met with cheers and the pounding of drums. Hanane had finished receiving her blessings and was now coming out to address her subjects. After what she had done for them in the wake of the earthquakes, the people of Ziran adored her, and there was nothing but delight in the air as she raised a hand to silence their jubilant cries.

"My fellow Zirani," Hanane began, and that was as far as she got before a blast tore through the east wall.

26

Karina

Nothing.

Inside the basket, there was no weapon, no scroll, no divine power. All that stared back at Karina was . . . nothing.

A strangled sound somewhere between a sob and a laugh escaped her mouth. Karina inspected every corner of the basket, even picked it up to see if there was something hiding beneath it.

Nothing.

Her vision turned red, and she threw the basket to the ground. "What the hell is going on here?" she screamed. How could her magic be responding so strongly, how could she have risked the fate of every person in Sonande, for there to be nothing here?

Warmth cut through her rage, ballooning out from her core like a fire lit directly in her chest. The hairs on the back of her neck bristled upward.

Someone was watching her.

"Afua? Ife, Caracal, is that you?" she called. The footsteps behind her were too soft to be any of her companions, and she was torn between her desire to turn around and her fear of what she might find if she did.

Karina gathered her magic into her palms, ready to blast the stranger away before they got any closer, when a voice as familiar as her own froze the blood in her veins.

"Look at me, daughter," the woman said, and Karina did so, her throat tight with a wild, impossible hope.

"Mother?"

The hope withered as soon as it had been born, for the woman in front of her was far too short to be the spirit of the late sultana—though she was still tall enough that Karina had to crane her neck to look at her. This was not her mother's long, angular face with its regal cheekbones, but a square one with a prominent jaw, black hair cornrowed into a low tail.

But her eyes were unmistakable—a brown bordering on purple, the same color as dusk falling over desert sand, just like those of the little girl in the dreams Karina had been seeing for weeks.

No, this was not her mother.

This was Bahia Alahari. Bane of the pharaohs, salvation of an entire nation, one of the most powerful zawenji who had ever lived.

Karina's ancestor.

"You have traveled a long way to be here, daughter. Welcome," said the ancient queen, and Karina's legs almost buckled beneath her.

Her entire life, Karina had dreamed of how it might have been to grow up surrounded by a big extended family that loved her. She would never get to experience that—but right here, right now, getting to speak with the originator of her entire line was more than she could have ever imagined.

But she was not simply here as a granddaughter speaking to a grandmother. Today, she was one queen petitioning another for aid. Karina offered Bahia the gesture of respect before bowing her head in deference.

"I come before you seeking wisdom, atti," she said. "The ulraji have risen once more, and your people are again in danger from the same threat you spent your life trying to eradicate. Their actions have threatened the world's balance, and now disasters threaten to destroy us all. Please, bestow upon me the power of the gods so that I may protect what you built so many centuries ago."

Karina could feel the power to control not one but all Alignments within her grasp. In her mind's eye, she saw herself stopping an earthquake with a flick of her wrist. She saw herself marching back to Ziran to rip Farid and the false Hanane off her throne and to destroy anyone who dared side with them.

Yet the spirit of Bahia Alahari did not move, even as the butterflies flitted off the statue of the Great Mother to land on her shoulders.

"The power you seek exists," said her ancestor. "But you are not to access it. So it has been decided, and so it shall be."

The ancient queen's tone was not unkind, but her words still hit Karina like a slap to the face. "But I have traveled across Sonande. I defeated the Sanctum guardian. Is that not what you did too? Is this not the place where the gods blessed you?"

"It was in this very room that I learned to speak to lightning and breathe through water, to create a soul from fire and wield darkness and light as twin sides of a whole. But just as two branches on a tree do not grow the same way, your path differs from mine. For you, no such power waits here."

Grandmother Bahia may not have looked like the Kestrel, but all Karina could see was her mother's disappointment in her face. Her entire family was dead, Sonande itself was on the brink of collapse, and yet the one thing that remained was that Karina still wasn't enough for the people who were everything to her.

A wild thought came to her: What if this was some sort of secret test, like the ones the grim folk often put heroes through in folktales? Perhaps if she proved her worth by defeating the most powerful zawenji of all time, the Sanctum would give her what she wanted.

"This is no test," said Bahia, but that didn't stop Karina from hurling a huge gust of wind straight for her ancestor.

However, the blast passed harmlessly through the specter and into the opposite wall with a boom that rained bits of wood upon them. Karina whipped the wind into a frenzy, but it was no use; Bahia Alahari was not on the mortal plane, and thus nothing Karina did could harm her. Karina sank to her knees.

"If you don't grant me this power, we'll all die." Had her ancestor been dead so long that she'd lost all shred of compassion? "Everything our family has fought for, everything *you* created, will be destroyed because of one man's greed."

"If what I created is truly so flimsy that one man can tear it apart, then perhaps it should be destroyed."

Karina stared up at the ancient queen in disbelief. The Kestrel might have been distant with her own child, but she would have never spoken of her people's suffering with such callousness.

"All my life, I was taught the most righteous thing to do was to live a life crafted in your image." Karina's voice cracked, the weight of all these weeks of hardship finally crashing down on her. "I was told that you fought for justice for every single person regardless of status. And now you're telling me to stand by and do nothing as millions of people die?"

"I did not say there is no path for you, only that it is not this one. The fool looks at a blank canvas and sees nothing. The wise woman looks and sees the world. What stands before you, daughter? Nothing or the world?"

"I don't know!" Karina exploded. "I can't fight Farid on my own, and I don't have any allies to help me! And now you claim there is magic strong enough to defeat him, but because I am unworthy, I cannot have it! So there is nothing left to me, no path to follow—"

No, that wasn't true. There was one thing left that only she, and no one else, could do.

The Rite of Renewal.

The power behind Bahia's voice was unfathomable as she confirmed what Karina had begun to suspect. "You think in terms of birthright and revenge, but what are such petty things in the face of She Who Created All? The Great Mother's displeasure with humankind began long before Farid performed the Rite of Resurrection. He is nothing more than a man—death will come for him when it comes, as it does for everyone. What you face is a fight before divinity itself. What greater purpose could you ask for than saving the very soul of Sonande?"

The words wormed beneath Karina's skin. Hadn't she sworn she'd do anything to protect Ziran? Did sacrificing herself not fall under "anything"?

Karina knew she was speaking to a being with the power of the gods on her side and that she should be grateful that her ancestor had deigned to appear before her at all. Yet her anger and fear boiled over before she could stop herself.

"What right do you have to speak to me of sacrifice when you chose to offer up your son's life over your own to win the Pharaoh's War? When you abandoned your best friend to slavers in the jungle? Every sacrifice that helped you succeed was made by someone else!"

Her ancestor's face contorted with pure rage. Karina had to brace herself against the power that radiated off the queen in violent, screaming waves.

"What do *you* truly know of sacrifice, peacetime child that you are?"

Her voice was the earth itself rending apart; a crack of lightning across the sky; an avalanche rolling down a mountainside to wipe an empire off the face of the world. The spirit of Bahia Alahari placed her hand against Karina's forehead, and Karina moved beyond her body, beyond space and time.

She saw once more the luminescent river from her dreams with Malik, but this time through her ancestor's eyes. She felt the coolness of the water against her skin and the steadfast belief that childhood would last forever. She heard that first rumble of war drums and smelled the tang of smoke in the air.

"Slavers. Run, Khenu!"

But Khenu had always been too small, too slow. Karina saw her fall and knew if she went back for her that neither of them would make it to safety. A carnal desperation to survive welled up inside her, and she let it carry her feet away from her friend's pleading cries.

Witnessing Bahia's abandonment of Malik's ancestor filled Karina with just as much shame as it had the first time. But the memory continued past the moment when Bahia darted into the tree line. This time, Karina was in Bahia's body, feeling each one of her friend's screams within her own soul as the slavers took her away. She felt the exact moment her ancestor realized she had made the wrong choice, and how she'd run back toward the river ready to fight the entire raiding party with her bare hands, only to find all traces of the raiders and of Khenu gone.

"I was a child, and I was scared." Bahia's voice came from everywhere, from inside Karina herself. "And I paid for that split second of fear every moment for the rest of my life."

The memory raced through the years. Karina watched her ancestor run away from her village, determined not to return without her friend in tow. She watched Bahia trek across Sonande for years, searching and searching for that tiny round face with the midnight-black eyes.

And then she found it.

Bahia found Khenu in a cavernous hall of gold not unlike the necropolis. Her friend was older now, still more child than woman, but with the cutting eyes of someone who had survived a viper's nest only by becoming more vicious than the vipers themselves. She was perched in the lap of the pharaoh, separate from the concubines and even the wives. Above them.

Beloved.

Karina felt Bahia's relief that her friend had survived that day in the forest, the crushing terror of what she'd had to become to do so.

She felt the rumble of the pharaoh's voice asking Khenu what the slave's punishment should be—fed to the dogs, perhaps, or boiled alive? And the beloved of the pharaoh, exalted above all others, regarded her oldest friend and her worst betrayer with a bored glance.

"The lash should do," said Khenu, her voice the hypnotic purr that Karina knew so well from Malik's own, and the memory went dark now with pain, every lash against her ancestor's skin searing against Karina's own, the promises and the curses to the gods, a burning hatred that consumed her from the inside out.

"Every choice I have ever made, every life I sacrificed in the name of revolution, I paid for in more ways than you could possibly know." Karina wept and begged for it to end, but her ancestor's suffering had taken hold of her body.

"I spent my childhood toiling in the death pits of Kennoua, then my adolescence as a personal pet of the pharaoh, body and mind completely tied to his ever-changing whims. And then I was chosen by the gods to be the vessel through which they waged their holy war. Then I had my family and I thought, finally, for the first time in my life, I had something that belonged only to me.

"But even after I had given them everything, the gods demanded more. They demanded the life of my only son, so I could harness the power of the fifty-year comet and end the war. I held him for his first breaths in this world, and I held him for his last. Then when my only love, the being you call the Faceless King, went mad from our child's death, I banished him so he could not destroy everything I had worked so hard to build."

They had returned to the chamber, though Karina was hardly conscious from the delirium of magic swirling through her. She had thought she had known the story of Bahia Alahari, but this was no triumphant tale of good conquering evil.

It was a tragedy of two girls ripped apart by betrayal and violence so inhumane that even a thousand years later, the ghosts of it haunted their descendants' every step. Now Karina understood exactly what had been drawing her to Malik from the moment they'd met—it was no blessing but a curse, one that had begun the very moment her ancestor had decided her life was worth more than his ancestor's.

"I killed my son. It killed me, but I killed him. And the only reason you are standing before me today is because I made that impossible choice. So that is what I know of sacrifice."

This was something beyond grief, beyond anger. It was a clarity as sharp as the honed blade of a knife, and Karina had no weapon strong enough to counter it.

"Every little girl thinks she wants to be a queen, but few realize that it means doing what no one else is ready to do. If you murdered Farid tomorrow, it would all be for naught, as the Great Mother's wrath would tear through the world and render all your actions useless. If you truly love this world and its people, you would turn your sights away from this petty squabble and to the real problem at hand."

Bahia placed her hand against Karina's chest, right over the very spot where Malik had tried to kill her. "Blood of my blood, bones of my bones, I leave you with this: when you came to this chamber you found nothing on the altar, for you already carry the power you need inside you. The only true path lies in never forgetting who needs you most."

Karina was crying once again, though she did not know why. The butterflies descended upon Bahia like a pure white storm, and when they disbanded there was nothing left, only the faintest whisper of a sigh to acknowledge anyone else had even been there.

For several minutes, Karina stared at nothing.

And then she fell to her hands and knees, pounded her fists against the ground, and screamed, with no one but the gods to hear.

27

Malik

The blast threw Malik off his feet. Pain exploded through his head, and for several minutes he lay there in a daze. Screams rose through the air as another explosion rocked the north wall, the world pitching and roiling beneath their feet as it had during the earthquakes.

Get up, Malik! shouted Idir. Though the world spun and blood painted his vision red, Malik struggled to his feet to survey the damage.

The coronation hall was in complete chaos, with half the survivors attempting to rescue those who had been caught in the blast while the other half fled for their lives. But the doors must have been barred from the outside, for no amount of pounding was opening them.

Malik scanned the room for his sisters, but it was impossible to tell anyone apart with dust and blood everywhere. Had they been caught in the blast? Or trampled in the chaos? Or—

Now's not the time to panic. Act quickly and decisively, and you might survive this.

His ears ringing, Malik nodded and swiftly wove his invisibility over himself again. Once that was in place, he shuffled down what was left of the staircase, spirit blade in hand.

Destruction met him at every turn. He pushed past people whose legs had been crushed by falling debris and children with gaping holes in their chests. Courtiers who just a few minutes ago had been strutting through the palace in full regalia were now on their hands and knees trying to dig their loved ones out of the rubble. Any guilt Malik felt at not helping the victims was nothing compared to the single thought coursing through his mind.

Get to Leila. Get to Nadia.

He finally found his sisters clustered with a group of the highest-ranking nobility near the dais where Hanane had been addressing the crowd. Masked assailants armed with swords and spears ordered them to kneel, and the group did so quickly— all except one man, who let out a roar like a cornered lion and launched himself at the nearest fighter. Silver flashed, and the noble's arm fell in one direction and his body in the other. Another man tried to crawl toward the severed body, only to be struck down just as swiftly.

"Nobody else move!" roared one of the masked attackers, and it was all Malik could do to keep the invisibility over himself as the putrid scent of blood clogged his senses. Leila had gathered Nadia into her arms, a look of pure murder in her eyes. Thank Adanko, they were both covered in dust but unharmed.

But where was Hanane?

Malik inched forward slowly, hardly daring to breathe lest he draw attention to himself. He found Farid with his hands up before a pair of rebels who were large and stocky as bulls, taking directions from a woman around Malik's mother's age. His mentor's eyes pulsed with rage as he watched Hanane thrash in the arms of a second woman, who had one arm around the princess's waist and a blade shoved up against her throat.

Surprise coursed through Malik. He knew these women—not by their faces, but by the echoes of the sons who were no longer with them.

Mwani Zohra and Mwani Adama. Driss's and Tunde's mothers.

Mwani Zohra, Driss's mother, called out, "Is the north exit secure, Yaema?"

No, he hadn't heard that right—she couldn't have said—

The rebels cleared a path for the girl who had traversed the necropolis with Malik, the one who had been his sole companion for weeks, to come join Driss's mother. She was completely unharmed, a bow and arrow in her hands and a hard glint in her eyes.

"Yes, auntie, and we're working on the southern one now," she said, every trace of the clumsy awkwardness Malik had found so endearing now gone. "My observations on the guard patrol were all correct."

My older cousin was the only one who ever supported me, but he's . . . no longer with us.

The majority of my family lives in the Old City, so we were spared from the worst of the destruction. Honestly, they're all still so busy grieving my cousin, I don't think they've even noticed half of Ziran is in ruins.

The entire time, the dead cousin Yaema had been talking about was Driss. The very boy Malik had killed.

This was why Adewale had been visiting Yaema back at the

university. This was why neither family had been seen at court for weeks—not because they'd been grieving, but because they'd been plotting the demise of every person who had stolen their children from them. Malik had personally let Yaema into the inner heart of the palace because he'd felt guilty over using her to get the scepter when the entire time she had been using *him* to steal information about palace security so her family's forces could maneuver around it.

And like an absolute fool, he'd assumed the intense emotion that had passed over the girl's face whenever she'd looked at him had been desire, when it had never been anything more than a boiling, blood-tinged desire for revenge.

Are all human boys unable to differentiate lust from blood-lust, or is it just you?

This was all Malik's fault. The blood staining the hall was on his hands just as much as it was on those holding the weapons. At the last moment, Adewale had tried to warn him, but if he had recognized the warning signs earlier—

No, no time now for what ifs. Nothing mattered beyond getting his family out of there.

Malik slipped between the guards and tapped Farid on his shoulder. "I'm here," he whispered, and though his mentor kept his expression even, Malik could practically feel the relief washing off him.

"Wait for my signal," Farid muttered under his breath. Then he stepped forward, his arms spread wide like a welcoming host. "Mwani Zohra. Mwani Adama. How pleased I am that you decided to attend the coronation after all."

"Save your breath, Farid," snapped Driss's mother. She said something to the nearest guard, and Malik noticed now that his spear was embossed with the Sun-Aligned emblem even though he wore the colors of the Alahari personal guard. The rebellion must have smuggled their fighters in with the refugees Hanane had let into the palace. If the servants had known, none had said anything, and indeed, none had been invited to the coronation anyway, sparing them from the massacre.

Mwani Adama's grip around Hanane's neck tightened, causing the princess to let out a small whimper. Farid's smile turned sinister. "I can't say I understand what is happening here, but I'm sure we can come to some sort of agreement—"

"Keep speaking, and I'll slit the princess's throat," snapped Tunde's mother. However, though her blade was pressed tight against Hanane's neck, no blood beaded up against the metal. Malik wasn't even sure if Hanane *could* be murdered a second time, but he had no desire to find out.

Dropping the civil facade completely, Farid snapped, "What do you want?"

"We want justice," said Tunde's mother. Her voice shook around that word, but she never lowered her knife. "When our sons were chosen for Solstasia, we were told they would be safe in the palace's care. But they died under your watch, for reasons that are so clearly lies, it would insult their memories to even repeat them. We want the truth, Mwale Farid. And we want our sons' killers to reveal themselves *now*."

"Exactly how is massacring half the court going to honor their memories? Is this what Driss and Tunde would want?"

"Don't you dare say their names!" roared Mwani Adama, and Hanane let out another cry as the woman's grip tightened further. Malik racked his brain for anything he could do to diffuse the situation. An illusion might buy them a distraction, but even if they somehow escaped the palace itself, who knew what awaited outside?

The easiest solution would be to give them what they wanted—him. Both Tunde and Driss would still be alive right now if he had killed Karina when he'd first had the chance. Perhaps if he surrendered himself to these women, they would let everyone else go.

It's not worth the risk, argued Idir, but Malik disagreed. Besides, who in Ziran had more right to be angry about what had occurred that week than these families who had lost their loved ones and could never know the true reason why?

Farid took another tentative step forward. "I cannot even imagine the pain you must be going through. I wanted to wait until things were under control before bringing you this joyous news, but . . . your sons are not dead."

Mwani Adama's face shifted from disbelief to unbridled rage. "You lie!"

"I do not," Farid insisted. "The proof of resurrection stands right before you in our beloved princess. I use this power sparingly, as I wish to save it only for those who deserve it most. And you are both right—your sons did not deserve to die. That is why I brought them back to life, same as I did Hanane."

The sound of flesh hitting flesh rang through the hall as Driss's mother struck Farid across the face. But even with his cheek swelling, Farid's steadfast gaze did not waver. "In fact, your sons are both here right now."

Malik was just as surprised as the mothers were. Tunde and Driss were both alive? How was that even possible? He had seen both their corpses himself, and the Rite of Resurrection had only been possible during Solstasia—

Oh. *Oh.*

Farid gave the quickest glance back to where Malik still waited, and with a sickening dread, Malik understood exactly what his mentor wanted him to do. Pain pulsed through his head from the explosion, but he called to mind a memory of Tunde, trying to tie all he remembered about his friend into a single, perfect image.

"Tunde is here." Malik's magic buzzed to life even as he struggled to stay on his feet. "Just as he was the last time I saw him alive—happy and whole. Just as he should be."

"Mama?"

Malik knew it was an illusion, yet still his heart squeezed as Tunde stepped out from behind one of the few alabaster pillars that hadn't crumbled in the blast. Tears spilled over Mwani Adama's cheeks, and the knife in her hands trembled against Hanane's neck.

"Omo mi," she breathed out, and though Malik did not know much of the languages of Eastwater, he recognized that endearment—my baby. "Is it really you?"

"It is," Malik made the illusion say. The cruelty of what he was doing sickened him, but Mwani Adama lowered the blade one inch, then another.

Just a little longer. He only had to convince this mother that her dead child was still alive for just a little longer.

"Put the sword down, Mama," Tunde said, taking another step forward. "Let's talk about this calmly. No one else has to get hurt."

The blade went slack in Mwani Adama's hand. She slowly began to pull it away from Hanane's neck.

But then the wound on Malik's head jolted with pain, and his magic fizzled beneath the strain. In that same instant, both the fake Tunde and the invisibility surrounding Malik vanished.

Malik locked eyes with Tunde's mother, and the pure despair he saw there would haunt him for the rest of his days.

With a guttural scream, Mwani Adama thrust her blade straight through Hanane's neck.

The princess's body fell to the ground with a wet thud. Mwani Adama stared at it listlessly, as if she herself did not realize what she had just done. Then she too fell, Farid's own sword sticking out of her back.

"Adama!" screamed Mwani Zohra, but Farid had already pulled the sword out of the other woman's body. He turned it toward Driss's mother, pure murder in his eyes.

"Call off your fighters," he ordered.

"You're a monster."

"Call them off!"

"Never!"

"I am going to kill you." Nothing human remained in Farid's expression. This was the grief of a man who had lost his love twice now, and they were all going to die beneath the weight of it. "I am going to sever each of your limbs one by one and choke you with your own blood."

"F-Farid. Stop this, I'm begging you," came a hoarse voice.

The world seemed to slow as Hanane's corpse lifted itself onto one hand, then another. She pushed to her feet, then slowly pulled the knife from her neck. The muscle and viscera within her wound glistened bright red, but no blood poured out of what would have been a fatal injury on any living creature.

But Hanane was no longer a living creature. Not anymore.

Mwani Zohra let out a bloodcurdling scream. "Demons!" she cried. "Kill them! Every last one!"

Her cry was quickly silenced by Farid slicing through her chest, but the command was already in the air. The rebels were moving again, hacking through the crowd to get to Farid and Hanane. Farid tried his best to defend her, but combat was not his strongest skill, and he was quickly overpowered. As his mentor let out a cry, Malik grabbed the sword he'd dropped.

"Hanane!" he called, tossing it to her.

The princess caught the sword in midair, and her eyes darkened the moment her fingers wrapped around its hilt. The sour taste filled Malik's mouth once again as Hanane sized up her opponents, slipped into an offensive stance, and charged.

Now Malik understood just how much Hanane had been holding back when she'd fought that little boy back in the Lower City. She hadn't just been trained in combat—she excelled at it, her blade moving faster than Malik could even see. In seconds she'd torn through the fighters surrounding her and Farid, blood splattering the beautiful fabric of her coronation gown. She moved with inhuman grace and without fear of death. Malik could barely keep up as they fought back-to-back, adrenaline making his reflexes razor-sharp. His body moved on the memory of battles that were not his own, Idir's time as a general in Bahia's army granting him the ability needed to cross blades with fighters much more experienced than he was.

Soon they had their immediate area clear, but more rebels were pouring in. Hanane hauled Farid to his feet, and he called to Malik, "Meet at the fountain!" before he led Hanane through a door to the servant's chambers. Malik ran over to his sisters, who cowered against the wall as the world turned to slashing swords and flying blood all around them.

"We have to get out of here! Follow Farid!" he yelled.

"Did you not see Farid murder a woman in cold blood? We're not going with him!" Leila screeched. Malik wanted to scream. They didn't have time to fight over this, not when the rebellion's fighters were quickly overpowering the rest of the unarmed court. And with both Tunde's and Driss's mothers dead, the group had no leaders to stop them from falling into complete anarchy.

Malik had seen this level of violence only once before, on the day he and his family had fled Oboure.

They had not survived that to die here.

Malik's magic welled up inside him, and Leila must have sensed what he was about to do, for she backed away, shaking her head frantically.

"No, Malik, don't—!"

"You have nothing to fear. Farid will take us somewhere safe, far away from this carnage." Malik pushed every ounce of comfort he could into the illusion, forcing his sisters to see safety where there was only blood. "Everything will be fine if you come with me. You don't have to fight me. You don't *want* to fight me. All you have to do is follow."

Leila's and Nadia's eyes both went slack, and neither protested as Malik pulled them through the same exit Farid and Hanane had used.

This is the only way, Malik told himself as he led his sisters through the blood-soaked halls of Ksar Alahari. *This is the only way I can keep them safe.*

But the fighting was just as bad in the inner portions of the palace as it had been in the coronation hall, with loyalists to the throne locked in bitter combat with the rebels. Bodies from both sides littered the ground, and those who could not fight cowered in fear, some having dragged corpses over themselves as cover.

Malik's sandals grew slick with blood as he and his sisters tore their way into the heart of the palace, where most of the guests hadn't been allowed. If they could just make it to the tunnels hidden beneath the queen's garden, there was a chance they could escape this night with their lives.

Malik rounded a corner only to crash into someone's back. He almost slashed them with his dagger before realizing it was Aminata.

"Whose side are you on?" Malik barked, no longer able to tell ally from enemy.

"Yours, you idiot! I had nothing to do with this!" she screamed back. Bruises littered the maid's face and a nasty cut bled from her temple, but judging from the blood staining her hands, her opponent had gotten off worse than she had.

There was no time to wonder if she was lying or not. Malik gestured for Aminata to follow him, and if she had any questions about Leila and Nadia trailing slack-jawed in his wake, she did not voice them as they continued their mad dash for freedom.

But just as they turned the corner to the hallway before the queen's garden, an entire group of armed fighters entered from the opposite side, Yaema at their forefront. The girl who Malik had almost kissed stared him down, an iron-tipped arrow nocked into her bow.

"I'm sorry, Malik," said Yaema, and Malik wasn't sure if he imagined the sincerity in her voice. "In a different world, I think you and I could have been good friends."

In a single fluid motion, she lifted the bow and pointed it straight at his heart

"But not this one." Her eyes glinted with hatred. "This is for Driss."

Malik threw himself in front of his sisters, deflecting the first arrow but not the second, which lodged deep into his right shoulder. His good hand pressed to the wound to keep himself from crying out, he tried to turn his party back, but more people had cut off the hallway they'd just come from. With both the rebels and the loyalists wearing Alahari colors, there was no way to tell which group was which.

As Malik stood there with his sisters and Aminata, enemies approaching on all sides, something deep within him snapped. His vision went red as he plunged past the binding that separated him from the Faceless King and grabbed onto the obosom's magic. A wave of power radiated outward from his body, knocking several of their assailants flat onto their backs.

"GET OUT OF MY WAY!" Malik screamed.

His magic wove shadow creatures eight feet tall, with wicked talons and sharp teeth that shone in the dim light. But these were no mere illusions, for with the Faceless King's power amplifying his own, the constructs had become tangible. One man screamed as one of the creatures grabbed him by the hair and severed his head from his body, while another snatched a woman in its jaws and dashed her against the stone.

Power surged through Malik, Idir's frantic yelling at him to stop little more than a gnat buzzing in his ear. At one point he saw Yaema go down, and he did not know and did not care if it was because of him or one of the other fighters trying to escape this massacre.

The air grew thick with the scent of blood and metal as Malik's magic cleared the path.

He didn't stop. He didn't think.

Malik simply moved forward, a hurricane of power tearing through the world, the screams of the dying following in his wake as he led his sisters to safety.

"There you are!" called Farid when Malik and his party finally reached the garden. It was eerily quiet, as if even the creatures of the night had known what was coming and had not wished to witness it. Smoke rose from the front of the palace, casting a pale haze over the almost full moon.

Using the signet ring, Farid quickly opened the entrance to the

Queen's Sanctuary. He and Hanane lowered themselves into the tunnel, and a shaking Aminata quickly followed. Leila was next, but she paused at the threshold. Resistance sparked in her eyes as she pulled Nadia close to her chest, and Malik sensed her will was seconds away from pushing past his enchantment.

"Everything is fine. You want to keep walking," said Malik, the Faceless King's magic burning through his core. Leila's eyes went slack once more, and she descended into the tunnel without complaint. Malik followed behind her, praying to Adanko and the Great Mother that he had made the right choice as the sickly sweet scent of death blew through the air

But this was for his sisters' own good. Everything Malik had ever done, everything he would ever do, was to protect them.

Like Adewale had said, he wouldn't know who he was without them.

28

Karina

Karina had never been religious. Even now, if someone had presented her with irrefutable proof that the gods existed, she would be hard-pressed to muster anything more than burning apathy.

But the revelation that her own ancestor thought all she was good for was dying shattered something deep inside her. She'd never needed the gods when she'd had the story of Bahia Alahari as a north star dictating the kind of person she should aspire to be. Without that compass to guide her, Karina was adrift, a tiny boat being battered in a raging sea.

The full weight of her failure dragged her down as she went to find her friends. She passed the chasm and realized just how idiotic she'd been to leap across it the way she had. What a useless fool she was. No wonder her ancestors didn't want to help her.

"Afua! Caracal! Ife!" she called, but her echo was the only response. After an hour of walking, three pinpricks of light appeared deep inside the heart of the chasm. Karina called for her friends again, and this time Afua called back, "Down here!"

Her friends were in some kind of tiered gazebo suspended on a bridge over the chasm. It resembled Maame's healing house back in Balotho, and with a pang Karina realized the demon must have built her home to replicate this very structure. Maame had spent thousands of years held hostage by the zawenji, only to be killed so that Karina could find what?

Nothing. Absolutely nothing. Suddenly everything seemed so funny that Karina almost laughed, if only to fight back the tears burning behind her eyes.

"You're back!" exclaimed Afua, and she dropped the fertility talisman she was examining to run over to Karina's side. "How did it go?"

The young girl beamed up at her, and Karina tried to imagine herself as Afua must see her—capable, confident, always taking charge.

All I've learned from this is that the only thing I can do to help Sonande is die.

Karina shook her head. "It was the wrong room," she lied, and Afua's face fell.

"Oh, well, don't worry about it! There's so much of this place we haven't explored yet, I'm sure you'll find the right one soon."

She bid Karina to sit in the small camp her friends had made in the middle of a circle of giant stone heads, each one twice as tall as a person, and began telling Karina all they'd done in the hours they'd been separated. Karina had felt as if she'd only talked to Bahia for a few minutes, but time seemed to work differently down here.

"We found an entire area for making talismans, and another one just for practicing magic!" Being surrounded by so much nkra seemed to have energized Afua, and stars danced in her eyes as she explained the wonders they'd found. "Who knew an entire community of zawenji could accomplish something like this?"

"What about the Conserve? Is that not a community of zawenji?" asked Ife.

Afua's smile dimmed. "The Conserve is . . . rigid. I don't think I realized just how paranoid and stagnant they were until I left. I thought their way of keeping zawenji magic safe was the only way, but now that I'm seeing how our people used to live, I know there's more. I'm glad you decided not to go there, Karina."

Afua placed her hand against one of the statues, and it hummed as she read its history. "This place is more alive than anywhere I've ever been. And it's sad. It grieves for Maame Small Claws. It needs someone new to take up the mantle of guardian and protect this place, so that it can live on for a new generation of zawenji to discover."

"But who's going to become the new guardian?" asked Ife.

"I don't know. But until someone claims the role, Doro Lekke will remain undefended."

Caracal had kept his gaze on Karina throughout the conversation. She thought she'd kept her expression even, but he narrowed her eyes at the look on her face. Her hands balled into fists. "What?" she snapped.

"You didn't get it, did you?" He did not have to specify the "it"—the power of the gods, the only thing that mattered.

"No, I didn't," she said through gritted teeth. Caracal barked out a high, desperate laugh.

"I knew it. I fucking knew it!" The Wind-Aligned zawenji threw his hands in the air. "We trekked hundreds of miles, faced down horrid monsters, I almost died, and for what? A power that never even existed! You've doomed us all over a children's tale!"

"I didn't lie!" Karina screamed back. Deep in her heart, she knew her anger was not for Caracal, but she needed to let it out somewhere. "The power of the gods is real!"

"Then where is it, huh? Where is the incredible power that apparently only your ancestor in the entire history of Sonande has ever been worthy enough to wield?"

It was the genuine disappointment in his voice that sent Karina over the edge. He had begun this journey for his own selfish reasons, but at some point, he had truly believed Karina might be able to save them all.

Now she was letting him down, just like she had let down everyone else in her life.

"I didn't get the power because the gods are a bunch of heartless bastards!" Karina yelled. "It doesn't matter to them whether we live or die, and it never has!"

Caracal's hands curled into fists at his side, and Karina wished he would punch her, if only to give her a reason to unleash the full force of her wrath upon him.

But before he could, Ife stepped between them both. "You two shouldn't fight. Every quest has a moment where the group comes to odds, but it shouldn't happen here."

"The world isn't some story, Ife," snapped Karina, and Caracal growled again, but now Afua joined in.

"Ife is right. We're all tired, and hungry, and no one is thinking straight. Let's return to the surface and regroup. We can figure out our next steps then."

Karina and Caracal gave begrudging nods and followed the

other two up the path that led out of the Sanctum. All the while, Karina wrestled with how to explain to the others what Bahia had told her. Afua, especially—she would never agree that killing Karina was their only hope after she'd risked so much to keep her safe.

They had almost reached the surface when the rumble of voices made them stop.

"Secure the perimeter. Make sure to block off any potential exits."

"Of course, Commander."

In all the weeks Karina had known Caracal, she had never seen the look of pure devastation that crossed his face at the sound of that voice.

"Issam," he whispered, as if the name was both a prayer and a curse. Issam as in . . . Caracal's old lover Issam? The one from his days as a Sentinel?

But if he was here, then that meant . . . oh no. Oh no, no, *no*.

Farid's army had found her at last.

Afua grabbed Karina's arm, her entire body shaking. "It's the boat. We just left it up there." In their excitement over finally finding the Sanctum, they had forgotten to hide the vessel, and it had led the Sentinels straight to them.

Judging from the pounding of axe against wood, Issam and his troops hadn't figured out how to open the entrance yet. But it was only a matter of time before they realized the trick, as the key was still in its hole and the Sentinels were zawenji themselves.

Or worse, their attempts to break into Doro Lekke might collapse the entrance completely, sealing Karina and her companions inside. She hadn't seen any other exits, and it was unlikely they'd find any before they starved to death.

"What should we do?" whispered Ife, and it broke Karina's heart that even after her outburst, the others were still looking to her for guidance.

Her instincts told her to burst out there, magic blazing, and fight their way out of this like they had back in Balotho.

But even if they did somehow defeat Issam's squad, then what? There was nowhere in Sonande she belonged, and no one who would be able to hide her before Farid tracked her down again.

And Karina was tired. So, so tired. At this point, anything had to be better than the fatigue that wound through her bones like a sob her body could not release.

Her skull throbbed with the beginnings of a migraine, and Karina wished she could just fall to the ground with her head between her knees until it passed. One of the white butterflies brushed against her cheek, reminding her of her ancestor's words.

Remember who needs you most.

If she ran out there and fought, it would be rebellion for the sake of rebellion, the same as all the times she'd defied her mother simply to prove she could. But there was another path open to her, if she was only brave enough to take it.

"Is this what you want?" she asked the butterfly. "Will this finally be enough for you?"

The creature kissed her nose before settling on one of the statues lining the tunnel to the surface. Karina had not paid them much attention on the way in, her mind at the time too full of thoughts of the power she was going to obtain, but now she took in each object in the statues' hands. The first one held a scale, both sides perfectly balanced. The second held a spear, the third a calabash.

And in the fourth was an algaita, the wood of the flute long and worn, covered in centuries of dust. But it was the only object from which pure power hummed.

Right here, practically being handed to her by the ancestors, was the other artifact needed for the Rite of Renewal. Karina's entire body felt numb as she picked the algaita from its perch and blew the dust off its body.

It fit into her hands as if crafted just for her.

The world around them shook again, and the tree itself seemed to groan the painful wheeze of a creature slowly dying. An unsettling rush of calm flooding her, Karina turned to her companions. "Follow my lead."

The others nodded, eyes ablaze with determination and magic. Folding her anger and grief into resolve, Karina stepped forward and pressed a hand against the wood. The door slipped open easily, prompting several shouts of alarm from those on the surface.

Karina and her entourage exited the dark world of their ancestors into one blazing with harsh light. A dozen Sentinels stood in a circle around the island, weapons aimed straight at them. Swirling light from all the zawenji gathered at the base of the tree filled the air, illuminating the night into a rainbow of color.

Issam stood at the very center of the Sentinels, the maroon-and-silver sash that used to belong to Commander Hamidou now draped across his chest. He was young for a commander, tall and stocky with close-cropped hair and the broad shoulders of someone who had trained as a warrior from birth. Issam's eyes lingered on Caracal for a heartbeat longer than the others before slipping to Karina.

"Stand down!" he barked, and Caracal rolled his eyes.

"The man gets a promotion, and suddenly he thinks he can order me around," he muttered, but the joke could not hide the ache in his voice.

Issam drew his blade with one hand and summoned thin plumes of flame that raced onto the dark metal with the other. That old fear of fire sparked deep within Karina's chest, rooting her to the spot. A single word, and her friends would unleash their powers until this standoff devolved into an all-out brawl that they had a fair chance of winning.

But even if they won, what would they do next? Run around in circles like a mouse avoiding a trap while the Great Mother destroyed the world?

No more. Karina was going to end this, right here and right now.

She took a step forward, all the magic around them flowing through her veins.

She put her hands in the air.

"Put down your weapons," she called. "I surrender."

Beside her, Afua let out a strangled cry, which Karina ignored. She stuck her arms out toward Issam to show him she held nothing but the algaita. "I surrender," she repeated.

Issam regarded her for several tense seconds before he yelled at one of his subordinates to bring the chains. The second the ivory cuffs touched her wrists, the wind song died in Karina's ears, and it took her a panicked moment to remember that ivory dampened magic. At least she knew they weren't going to kill her, not when Farid needed her alive for the Rite of Renewal.

This was the path that she alone could walk. Saving Sonande not through her triumph but through her death.

Karina threw what she hoped was a reassuring smile to her companions. "It's all right," she said, hoping they heard her silent plea for them to not resist. Farid might still spare them if they didn't cause any more trouble. "Just trust me, please."

Caracal threw her a look of pure disgust, while Ife just stared. But it was Afua's reaction that broke her heart in two. The Life-Aligned zawenji shook her head, stepping backward as the Sentinels closed in on them.

"No! I'm not going back to the dungeons! I can't go back!" She sobbed, her tiny frame shaking. "No! No!"

"Do the rest of you surrender too?" yelled Issam.

"No, we don't!" Caracal sliced his hand through the air, and the wind around them rippled in warning. "Do you even realize what you're doing, Issam? Who you're working for? You're nothing more than a murderer's pawn! You, who always spoke of justice and order, reduced to a retrieval dog!"

Caracal took a tentative step forward, and Issam's entire body tensed. "Come back to me," Caracal whispered, his voice hoarse. "If we have to fight, let it be because you hate me for leaving, not because your master has ordered you to."

Issam had been inching closer as well, and now the two men were only a few feet apart. A glimpse of the boy Caracal had fallen in love with flashed across the commander's face. "You're the one who deserted the Sentinels. *You* come back to *me*."

Caracal shook his head. "I'd rather die a fugitive than live a slave."

The vulnerability on Issam's face drowned beneath a wave of anger and regret. "Then die," he spat, and with those words, the world erupted into flames.

Ropes of blue-and-white fire tore for Karina's friends, only to be deflected by the shield of wind Caracal pulled around them. The two men fought with an intimacy only lovers could possess, dancing around each other's blows with both familiarity and speed. Fire battled wind, the two of them perfectly in tune with the other's movements.

"You've lost your edge, Issam," gasped Caracal as he flipped between twin towers of fire. He pulled the flames into a tornado, then twisted it to shoot the inferno back at its creator.

"Shut the fuck up, Tabansi," roared the man. Karina had wondered what name hid beneath the mercenary's moniker, but she had never dreamed she would discover it like this.

"Stop it! We surrender!" she screamed, but she had been forgotten in the rage of battle, unable to move past the diamond formation of Sentinels clustered around her. How was it that even when she was trying to surrender, everything still went up in flames?

Issam and Caracal had started the battle evenly matched, but only one of them had been training at Sentinel-level intensity in recent years, and soon the difference in skill became clear. The Fire-Aligned zawenji reared his head back and let out a long jet of blue-white fire that hit Caracal square in the face, sending him crashing into the roots of the tree as his skin charred. Ife ran to the former Sentinel's side, their magic frantically working to undo the burns crackling across his skin. Only Afua remained standing.

Something glinted in Afua's hands—Maame Small Claws's old headpiece, the one that had connected her to the magic of Doro Lekke. Afua looked down at the interlocked chains before looking up at Karina, and the pure terror in the Life-Aligned girl's eyes warned Karina of what she was about to do.

"Afua, don't!" Karina screamed, but the girl was already slipping the headpiece over her temples. The chains shrank to fit her head, so much smaller than Maame Small Claws's, and light shone from all eight markings in the tree as Afua's eyes glowed white with power.

Karina called her friend's name again, but her voice was nothing compared to the force of Doro Lekke claiming Afua as its own. The Life-Aligned zawenji rose off the ground as the city of their ancestors welcomed its newest guardian, star-bright light dancing through the air. All at once, the soldiers' weapons tore from their hands, turned in midair, and raced back toward them.

A few managed to duck in time, but most fell to the ground screaming, their swords and spears lodged deep in their chests. Issam threw a shield of fire to cover both him and Karina, and it was only his quick thinking that saved them from being sliced to ribbons. Behind Afua, Ife cowered with Caracal in their arms, their back against the tree.

"Tabansi!" roared Issam, and Afua lifted her hand. Another wave of power slammed across the island.

And Karina felt it deep in her gut as the enchantment that kept the city moving roared to life. There came the groan of ancient wood splintering apart, and the world shuddered as the tree protecting the Sanctum, already weakened from the soldiers' attempt to knock it down earlier, collapsed in on itself.

The tree hit the ground with a boom louder than thunder, and minutes later when the dust cleared, no sign remained of Afua, Caracal, or Ife.

Karina stared at the place where the entrance to Doro Lekke had been as the Sentinels began to dig through the rubble. Even though she had seen it with her own eyes, her heart refused to believe what had just happened.

Afua—her sweet, courageous Afua—had given herself over to Doro Lekke rather than face imprisonment again. She had become the Sanctum guardian, bound to forever protect the city until she was struck down by the next person who wished to enter it. She would never see her family again. She would never grow up to become the amazing woman Karina had known she would one day be.

Despair welled up in Karina's chest, but she was too shocked to even cry. Her fault. This was all her fault.

Ever the leader, Issam was the first to recover. He came over to Karina and grabbed her by the arm, pulling her to her feet with surprising gentleness.

"Time to go, princess," he growled, and Karina took her first heartbroken steps into the future she had chosen for herself, far from wherever her friends had gone.

29

Malik

Deep in the heart of a shining golden desert, where the sun blazed across sapphire skies by day and the moon danced across endless stars by night, there was a boy. And in the center of this boy, there was a tree.

The tree had once been a sight to behold, its trunk thick and its branches sturdy. But now its bark was gray with rot, its fruit shriveled and dry. The rest of the grove was hardly any better, little more than withered, gnarled husks.

Though it was happening inside him, the boy did not see the grove dying bit by bit.

But the Faceless King saw. The spirit had lived a long life, and he had seen humans lose themselves to all manner of things—war, violence, grief. But he had never experienced it as intimately as this.

And so with nowhere to go and nothing he could do, the Faceless King lowered his head and waited.

Spread throughout the Zirani Territories were secret safe houses run by the sultana's spy network just in case of a situation that might require a member of the royal family to flee the city. Of course, none of the safe houses had ever been used, as no Alahari had left Ziran for a thousand years, but they existed nonetheless. It was to the nearest such house that Farid now marched Malik, Hanane, and the rest of their small party, all their coronation finery soiled beyond repair.

There was something morbidly funny about the fact that after all that had happened, Malik and his sisters were leaving Ziran the same way they'd entered—with nothing but the clothes on their backs, though far nicer clothes they might be. Hanane was still barefoot, though of all of them she minded her injuries the least.

Malik didn't find it funny, though. He didn't feel anything. His mind had gone numb, and it was pure instinct that kept him putting one foot in front of the other. He didn't even mind the wraiths hissing and screaming for justice in his ears.

The gray light of morning had just begun to break across the horizon when they finally reached their destination: a small farmhouse at the edge of an ancient irrigation field. The ground here was churned and broken from the quakes, with debris littered all over the field. It hardly looked like the kind of place where royalty would stay, which was likely the point.

Still, Malik kept the spirit blade in hand as the farmer answered the door. What if the rebels had turned the spy network against them and they had to fight their way out again like during the coronation—

His mind screeched to a halt. He couldn't think about the massacre or the blood still coating his hands. He couldn't think about Leila and Nadia trailing behind them, slack-jawed and magicked into perfect obedience.

The farmer was younger than Malik had expected, and she eyed them suspiciously through the crack in her gate. "Who goes there?"

"The winds blow eastward today," said Farid, not a hint of exhaustion in his voice despite their trek.

Malik's knuckles tightened into a death grip around the blade's hilt, for if the woman did not say the second half of the code, they'd be forced to kill her for what she'd seen. There would be more blood again—more screaming—just like—just like—

But then the farmer opened the door and made the gesture of respect. "Yet still they never reach the sun."

The woman hurried them into her farmstead before bolting the gate shut. Her home was hardly more than three rooms stuck together like beads on a string, plus a small structure in the back that housed the family's chicken and goats. Malik and his sisters stood off to the side as Farid explained what had happened. Hanane remained within his arm's reach at all time, but she stayed silent, her fingers twisting a loose thread from the strip of fabric tied around the gaping wound in her throat.

The farmer gave her own bedroom to Farid and Hanane to use, and a second room for Malik and his sisters that he assumed must belong to her children. As soon as they were settled, she and her family ran to prepare a meal out of whatever meager supplies she had on hand. As soon as she was gone, Farid leaned against a rickety table and ran a hand through his hair.

"Last night certainly did not go as planned," he muttered. It was such an understatement that Malik might have laughed if he had remembered how. A part of his mind was still in the hall, seeing people fall one by one like slaughtered cattle. Every time he closed his eyes he saw the people he had cut down, his blade slicing through muscle and bone as if it were nothing more than parchment—

Breathe. Stay present. Stay here. He had acted in self-defense. That was what it came down to in the end, right? Tunde's and Driss's families had done what they thought they'd had to do, and so had he.

There had been no other way.

Malik needed to believe there had been no other way.

Farid turned his attention to Hanane, and his eyes softened. He gently grabbed one of her hands in his own, running his thumb over her knuckles.

"It's all right. You're safe now," he murmured.

Hanane's eyes lifted just a fraction, and they passed over Farid to land on Leila and Nadia. "Aren't you going to let them go?" she asked Malik hoarsely. It was the first time she had spoken all day.

Facing down another horde of armed warriors seemed preferable to his sisters' wrath, but Malik could not leave them enchanted forever. He led them back outside to the small barn. Once there, he felt along the threads of magic until he found the one that connected him to their illusion, and pulled it to the edge of breaking.

He paused. Perhaps it would be best to let his sisters enjoy whatever fantasy they were seeing until they had a concrete plan. Surely it'd be fine to leave the illusion just a little longer—

Don't lie to yourself, boy. Face what you've done, said Idir, and Malik filled with shame. He unraveled the illusion and stepped back as his sisters' eyes cleared as if waking from a dream.

Leila regained her bearings first, rubbing a hand against her temple as she surveyed the chickens and clay pots around them. "What . . . where . . ."

Malik saw his sister return to those last few minutes of carnage before his magic had dulled everything except the desire to follow him. He braced himself for her anger, knowing he deserved it and more.

But it never came. Instead, Leila drew Nadia close to her and stumbled backward.

"I—at the palace—you!" she sputtered. Nadia began to cry, and horror dawned on Malik as he remembered what she'd told him just the day before, about being unable to differentiate fantasy from reality.

His sisters, the people who mattered more to him than anything else in the world, weren't angry at him.

They were terrified of him.

"Nadia, don't cry. It's still me." He tried to reach for her, but Leila grabbed a bucket with her free hand and swung it in a wide arc in front of herself and their sister.

"Stay away from us!" she screamed. For all the times Malik and Leila had fought over the years, not once had she ever looked at him as if he might cause her true bodily harm.

As if he was their father.

"I didn't have a choice!" he cried. They had to understand that if he hadn't forced them to come with him, they wouldn't have survived the attack. A choice between their deaths and their hatred wasn't truly a choice at all.

Yet Malik understood their terror, for he knew better than

most the violation of having someone other than yourself sifting through your mind. The whites of Leila's eyes shone as they
darted around the small barn. She pinched her arm so hard she
drew blood.

"How do I know this is real? That it's not just another illusion?
How many times have you done this to us?"

"I've never used my powers on you before this, I promise!"
Malik took another step forward, and his sisters cowered, curling
around each other as he and Leila used to do when their father's
temper was at its worst. That reminder only amplified his desperation, his bone-deep need for them to *know* he was nothing like
that man.

Frustration boiled up within him. If they were going to be so
unreasonable, perhaps he should weave another illusion to calm
them down enough to listen to him—

No. Malik reached for Tunde's bracelet, only to remember he
had given it to Adewale. His fingers found his arm and dug in
deep, until the pressure in his head died down and blood welled
up beneath his nails. Clearly everybody was too distraught to talk.
Once they'd all had time to calm down, they could work this out.

"I'm going to go now," he said, proud of how even his voice
sounded though his heart was breaking. "There's a room for
us inside the house. You two can rest in there. I'll stay outside
tonight."

He paused at the entrance to the barn and took one last look at
the defiant thrust of Leila's jaw, the soft curve of Nadia's cheek.

"I did it to protect you," he said, hoping the weight of everything he wasn't saying was coming through on the little that he

could. "Everything I've ever done has been to protect you."

Leila's eyes met his, and he saw some unnameable thing shift there. She gave the slightest of nods, and with that, he left them to pick up the pieces of the trust he had shattered.

Malik had not been away from Eshra for so long that he had forgotten the trimmings and trappings of provincial life. His body moved on instinct—gather wood for the fire; fetch water from the well; heat the water, clean himself off, wash his clothes. Focusing on mindless tasks left no room in his brain for anything else. No thinking about Yaema's betrayal. No thinking about the plagues and the beast that could still strike at any moment. Just him and the wraiths out here all by themselves.

But he was halfway through the process when he simply stopped, his mind refusing to work anymore. He didn't even react when the farmer walked up to him with a fresh set of clothes in her hands.

"I'll admit, man pup, I really didn't think you had that level of bloodshed in you," said Hyena, and Malik could only stare at the water slowly turning red, not even caring that he'd missed the flash of blue in the farmer's eyes when they'd first arrived at the safe house.

He waited for the trickster to mock him or, even worse, try to comfort him. But she did neither. She simply placed the bundle beside him and said, "You would not be the first of your line to break under the weight of such power."

"Leave us," ordered Malik, but it was the Faceless King's voice that spoke through his mouth, as he could not bring himself to say anything. He noted the spirit's odd flare of protectiveness over him, then filed it dully away with wherever the rest of his emotions had gone.

The trickster stared at him, and if he was the hero in an epic tale, this was where she would have given him the encouragement he needed to regain his fighting spirit. But Hyena shook her head and walked away, leaving him to stare at nothing until the water grew cold.

Hours later, Malik finally changed into the clothes Hyena had brought him. He considered trying to talk to his sisters again but decided against it. Aminata was nowhere to be found, and Farid had yet to assign him any particular task, so Malik decided to steal a few hours of sleep while he could, even though it was the height of midday. He'd stay in the barn to give Leila and Nadia the space from him they so clearly desired. Papa had forced him to sleep outside enough times that the thought did not upset Malik as much as it should have.

He was in the house, rooting around for a blanket, when he passed the slightly ajar door to the farmer's bedroom. Through it, he caught a glimpse of Farid bent over Hanane, and a shiver ran down his spine. But then he saw the quick flash of silver in Farid's hand, the small line of stitches at Hanane's head—Farid was attempting to sew the princess's wound closed. His mentor pulled the last stitch tight and stepped back to admire his handiwork.

"There you go." When Hanane didn't speak, he frowned. "Does it hurt?"

The princess shook her head. "It doesn't hurt now and it didn't hurt last night." She drew a long, shuddering breath. "What kind of monster almost loses her head and feels absolutely nothing?"

Farid dropped to his knees and gathered Hanane's hands in his own. "You are not a monster."

"I am! The locusts, the earthquakes, the rebellion—all this is only happening because you resurrected me. I should be the one you sacrifice for the Rite of Renewal, not Karina."

Just a few days ago, Malik might have agreed with Farid. But that was before he'd seen Hanane plow through an entire contingent of fighters as easily as hacking through wheat. Before he'd seen her rip limbs from bodies and shatter skulls without breaking a sweat.

Hanane might not be a monster, but she clearly wasn't human either. They had all been fools to believe she could go through what she had gone through and come out unchanged.

"No," said Farid, that single word filled with pure ice. "Hanane, when you died, my soul died as well. Even knowing what we know now about the Rite of Resurrection, I would do it again without hesitation if it meant having you back with me."

The farmer's bedroom was the largest room in the house, but suddenly there was no space in it, nowhere to go that wasn't filled by Farid and the weight of the words he had been waiting an entire lifetime to say.

"I failed you yesterday. I was so focused on the threats coming from the outside that I neglected the ones from the inside. Never again. So long as I draw breath, nothing and no one will ever harm you again. I don't care if it angers every god in every sky. You are never leaving my side."

Hanane had resembled a warrior goddess made flesh last night, but here, alone with Farid, she trembled like a child. She looked around frantically until her eyes fell on Malik, still hiding awkwardly in the doorway. "Malik! Come in!"

He had no choice but to obey, even as Farid's anger at being interrupted bore into him.

"How are Leila and Nadia?" asked the princess, her voice high-pitched and tight. Malik's eyes darted between her and Farid as he wondered what he might say that would cause the least amount of friction.

"They'll be all right," he said weakly. He decided against mentioning Hyena's presence in the house; if he tried, the trickster would likely vanish simply to make him look mad.

Hanane moved her locs aside to reveal the sutures on her neck. "How does it look?"

Truthfully, Farid's stitches were jagged and sloppy. Clearly sewing had not been part of the education he'd received at the palace.

"It . . . could be neater."

"Leila mentioned you're skilled at these things. Could you fix it? If I'm to spend the rest of my second life with this wound, it needs to look presentable."

Hanane's tone was light, but the meaning behind her words was clear—do not leave her alone with Farid. A muscle in Farid's jaw twitched, but he pulled his face into a smile. "Yes, Malik, I must admit I am not practiced in something so . . . provincial. Go ahead."

Malik felt the word *provincial* like a slap to the face, suddenly ashamed at his humble upbringing. But he dutifully took the needle and thread and began replacing Farid's stitches with his own.

Because Hanane no longer bled, closing the wound was not unlike stitching two thick, unusually cold bolts of fabric together. Malik let himself focus on the fact this was now the second time he'd used his skill with a needle to aid a princess, for if he thought too much about what he was doing, he might vomit.

Once he had finished, Hanane felt along the nearly seamless line Malik had left behind. "This is perfect. Thank you so much." She looped her arm through his and hauled him toward the door. "Come, you must be famished."

Hanane stayed by his side as Hyena served them a simple meal of meatball tagine and freshly baked bread with roast chicken. Neither Leila nor Nadia joined them, and so Farid and Malik ate in tense silence. Hanane took a few bites out of politeness to their host, but she subtly shifted her food to Malik when no one was watching, as she no longer needed to eat. No one but Malik seemed to realize who the farmer really was.

Aminata returned halfway through the meal, and one look at her was enough to get the farmer's family to scatter. Farid sat at the head of the table like a king ready to hold court.

"What have you learned?" he asked.

"In the wake of the failed assassination attempt, the council has established control through most of the Old City, but the Lower City remains in chaos. The grand vizier is summoning all non-essential members of the military back to Ziran to quell the unrest."

"Should we let her know we survived?" asked Hanane, but Farid shook his head.

"If Mwani Jeneba knew where we were, no doubt she would dispatch her personal assassins after us to secure the throne for herself. No one on the council can know our whereabouts until we've obtained a force of our own. Were you able to send my message to Issam?" he asked Aminata.

"I was."

"Then there's nothing to do now except wait for his response. As long as we still have the Sentinels on our side, this isn't over."

"But what about the flute?" Malik asked. He couldn't walk another minute, but he also couldn't stand the thought of just sitting there and waiting for threats both human and supernatural to come for them. The next omen was the plague; what would they do if one of them caught it all the way out here, where there weren't any healers?

"We won't be able to search for the flute if we're murdered in our beds," said Farid. "My decision is final. Once we hear from Issam, we'll make our move."

Hanane, the only person who might have changed Farid's mind, kept her head lowered. At the defeated look on her face, Malik swallowed his objections and looked down at his hands.

He had no right to talk. All he could do now was follow orders like the good dog he was.

The news they were waiting for came after several days of listlessness, during which Malik's sisters did not speak to him once. Farid eagerly read the message Aminata had brought from the spy network, and when he lifted his eyes, triumph shined in them.

"They've captured Karina," he said. "They found her in the

marshlands up north and are currently taking her to Ksar Nirri in Talafri. And most importantly of all, she has the flute."

With the flute and the scepter both located, they had everything they needed to perform the Rite of Renewal. They had won.

Malik felt his mentor watching his reaction, so he forced his face into a smile. "That's wonderful," he said, hating himself more and more as the image of Karina's corpse bashed against the altar ran through his mind. Twice now he'd betrayed her. *Sickening, cowardly, useless—*

Farid stood up, genuine excitement on his face for the first time since they had fled Ziran. "Ready yourself and your sisters to ride by daybreak," he ordered Malik, who could do nothing but nod.

It seemed the gods were not quite done with him or Karina yet.

30

Karina

Days passed, or at least Karina assumed they did. It wasn't easy to keep track of time from inside a tiny, windowless cell. Ksar Nirri was the largest of her family's fortresses outside Ziran, and its location right at the border between Eshra and the desert made it of the utmost strategic importance.

Floor after floor of metal and stone rose around her, crowded on every level with soldiers whose primary duty was managing her family's continued occupation of the mountains. Even if Karina had somehow found a way to remove the magic-sapping ivory cuffs from her wrists, it would have been impossible to escape from the fort on her own.

But honestly, they hadn't needed to put her in cuffs or in this cell, as she had no desire to escape. What was the point of fighting when she was going to die no matter what?

Issam had taken the flute from her, and somewhere deep inside she knew that Farid had found the scepter. There would be nothing stopping him from performing the Rite of Renewal as soon as he arrived.

It was over. And if her ancestor was to be believed, this was how it was meant to be.

So Karina slept and she woke and she slept and she woke and she slept again and she woke again until she could barely tell one from the other. Her mind was a shapeless, formless blob drifting through the mundane needs of her body.

She wept only once, when she remembered Afua chained forever to the Sanctum, and Caracal and Ife stranded in some remote corner of Sonande all on their own. She hadn't realized how attached she'd grown to her companions, but now she missed her magic lessons with Caracal. She missed braiding Afua's hair and the way Ife's eyes lit up whenever they got talking about why stories worked the way they did. She missed them all so much it ached. She was grateful that she didn't share any more dreams with Malik, for she couldn't stand him seeing her like this, so broken and defeated.

And then several days into her confinement, instead of the snarling guard who usually brought her meals, Issam opened the door to her cell.

"Mwale Farid has summoned you, Your Highness," said the Sentinel commander. Karina stared up at him, wondering if the enchantment on him left any room in his heart to grieve over Caracal's fate.

Karina did not struggle as he led her out of the cell. She likely looked as awful as she felt, judging by the way the few people they passed recoiled at the sight of her. The hair the people of Balotho had so lovingly worshipped was dirty and matted, and she reeked of excrement and decay. The part of her that used to care about her appearance had gone silent, as had the part of her that should have been scanning the halls for any potential exits.

The fort was not only a prison but also home to many of the officers of the Zirani government in Eshra, and it was to one of the latter receiving rooms that Issam brought her. It had been decorated in the traditional Zirani style, with the colorful floor lamps and geometric tile Karina was used to, but nothing about this place felt like home.

Some tiny sliver of resistance she hadn't realized she still had forced her to lift her head and face her end with dignity.

Dignity that died when she saw that seated next to Farid was none other than the monster wearing her sister's face.

For weeks Karina had repeated to herself that the creature was not Hanane. That she owed it nothing and should feel no remorse for leaving it behind in Ziran. But as they stared at one another, some long-buried part of her was overcome with an urge to throw herself into the monster's arms and sob, and that disturbed her more than even the thought of the impending ritual.

"What happened to you?" whispered the lich. Gods above, even its voice was exactly as Karina remembered—soft and bright, like the sun on a warm summer's day. She took a step back, though there was nowhere to run with Issam right behind her.

"Don't talk to me, monster!" she spat. That thing wasn't her sister. It wasn't Hanane.

The lich's eyes brimmed with tears, and Farid shook his head with a knowing smile. "Did I not tell you this would happen?" he murmured to it. How could he not feel the wrongness trailing from this creature, the way everything around her felt so stilted and warped? Was he just ignoring the shadows swimming beneath its brown eyes?

Farid rested his chin in his hands and regarded her sadly. "Little Karina, always causing trouble until the very end," he said more to himself than anyone else. Farid too looked exactly as Karina remembered him—always in control, not a single thread of his clothes or hair out of place. He looked over his shoulder and said to the seemingly empty air, "Malik, the artifacts, please."

Right before her eyes, Malik appeared behind Farid's stool with the algaita in his hands. The ulraji boy looked just as awful as Karina felt, his cheeks hollow and a haunted look in his eyes. He handed Farid the flute, and then pulled the scepter out of a black tattoo in his palm and gave that to him too. Karina's eyes went wide—was that where he kept pulling that dagger from?

Taking care never to let their eyes meet, Malik moved to leave, only for Farid to say, "No, stay. It'll be good for you to see this." Farid noted Karina's confusion and lifted a single eyebrow. "All this time the two of you were spending together, and you never told her you were working with me. That's no good, Malik—a lie of omission is still a lie. I assume you didn't tell her what you did to the Dedele girl either? It'll take her years to recover from having her mind tampered with like that, if ever."

Karina's vision tunneled to a pinprick as the pieces clicked together in her mind. Malik had been working with Farid this entire time. She'd let him kiss her, let him hold her and make her believe he saw something worth saving in her when behind her back he had tortured her friend and conspired with a man who wanted her dead.

Suddenly it was all too much. Karina burst into wild laughter.

Farid's brow furrowed. "I don't see what's so funny," he

snapped, but Karina was too deep in hysterics to explain. Of
course Malik and Farid were working together. Of *course* she was
foolish enough to get betrayed by this boy not once, but twice!

The line between Farid's brows deepened as Karina's laughter
devolved into soft hiccups. "This is the first time we've seen each
other in weeks, and all you can do is laugh?"

More silence. Farid's nostrils flared. "So you have nothing to
say for yourself?"

"So you have nothing to say for yourself?"

"Karina, stop that."

"Karina, stop that."

"This is childish, and you know it."

"This is childish, and you know it."

It *was* childish, and likely ill-advised, but Karina was getting
too much enjoyment out of frustrating Farid to stop. If she was
going to die, let her at least spend her last moments spiting the
man who had taken everything from her.

Out of the corner of her eye, she swore she saw the fake Hanane
give the smallest laugh. Farid took a deep breath, his expression
hardening. "This has always been your problem. You'd rather
hold on to your own immature pettiness than aid anyone other
than yourself."

Anger flared beneath Karina's mirth. "I'm immature? Really?
What's your obsession with the past if not immature and twisted?"

"It's not twisted to fix something that never should have been
broken. You were the one who tore our lives off the paths they
were meant to be on. If anyone is responsible for this current sit
uation, it's you."

As a child, Karina had been convinced that Farid was the smartest person in the whole world. But the man sitting before her had his head so far up his own ass, it was a wonder he could find enough air to speak.

Karina tilted her chin toward the lich, finding it easier to stomach the creature when she didn't look directly at it. "And what do you have to say about all this? Or did he take your tongue from you when he brought you back?"

The lich opened its mouth, only to close it again. Farid looked as if he might lunge for Karina, while Malik seemed as if he had never been more uncomfortable in his entire life. What a group the four of them were. When the griots retold this moment in their histories, would it be as a triumph or a tragedy?

Honestly, Karina didn't care. She let out a sigh. "You know what, Farid . . . tell me what you have planned and let's get this over with."

Farid began, "As you already know, Sonande lies on the brink of total collapse, and the only way to save it is by performing the Rite of Renewal, which requires the soul of a queen. As Hanane has yet to be officially coronated, you currently hold the title, which is why, with a heavy heart, I have decided that—"

"I'll do it. I'll be your sacrifice."

Karina had spent days preparing herself for this moment, but her mouth still ran dry actually saying the words out loud. She called to mind Grandmother Bahia's words: *Remember who needs you most.* This was what the people of Ziran—all the people of Sonande—needed from her. For them, she would set aside her desire to best Farid.

For them, she would die.

Farid narrowed his eyes. "The Karina I know would never agree to this so easily," he said, his voice laced with suspicion.

The Karina that Farid had known had died the moment she'd watched an assassin murder her mother, and again when she'd lost her home, and yet again when her own ancestor had told her that her death was more useful to this world than her life.

Suddenly Karina ached for the solitude of her cell. Things had been so much simpler in the muck. "Since you believe my words about as much as I believe yours, let's make a blood oath. That'll prove I mean what I say."

"No!" the lich and Malik both cried, and it was the anguish in the voice of the latter that made Karina's heart tug. But he was probably just acting again, like he had at the Sun Temple. Or perhaps somewhere deep inside, Malik did care for her in his own way, but those feelings had become twisted by the role demanded of him as a member of the Ulraji Tel-Ra.

Karina didn't know which possibility hurt more.

Farid stared at her coolly, then nodded. "Issam, your dagger."

Once the blade was in her hand, the full gravity of what Karina was about to do hit her square in the chest. As soon as she said these words, she would either die from the Rite of Renewal or from the magic of the oath stopping her heart.

Her hand wavered.

Remember who needs you most.

"Repeat what I say and nothing more," said Farid, and Karina nodded, not trusting herself to speak. "'I promise to be the soul of the queen needed for the Rite of Renewal and will do my duty without complaint or fuss. I will make no attempt to stop or interfere with the completion of the ritual in any way, shape, or form.'"

"I promise to be the soul of the queen needed for the Rite of Renewal and will do my duty without complaint or fuss. I will make no attempt to stop or interfere with the completion of the ritual in any way, shape, or form."

The iron of the knife cut into the flesh of her palm as the magic of the oath worked its way through her blood, a power more ancient than either the zawenji or ulraji binding her life force to the promise. When it was done, Farid smiled.

"Now, was that so difficult?"

He was right—it hadn't been difficult. In a strange way, it was freeing. She had never been the one destined to stop Farid, but by her death, she was paving the way so that someday, someone else could.

"When are we doing the ritual?" she asked.

"Now that we have all the artifacts, we can perform it at any time. But since you have chosen to be cooperative, I will be merciful. We will perform the ritual tomorrow at sundown, and until then, you shall be treated as a guest of the caliber that you deserve, not a prisoner." He paused, and Karina hated that a tiny part of her—the part that still saw him as her brother—grew sad at the genuine remorse in his eyes. "That's the least I can do for you on your last day."

The lich had remained silent through the oath, but at those final words, it let out a distressed sob. Malik put a stabilizing hand on its shoulder and said, "Let me escort you back to your room, Your Highness."

Karina's eyes moved from the lich's crying face, to Malik's gentle touch, to the muscle twitching in Farid's jaw. There was no reason to say anything, not when the oath was bound and done, but she could not pass up one last opportunity to work her way under Farid's skin.

"Actually, I was wrong," she said. "You have grown more mature, for the old Farid would never have been able to handle Hanane preferring another man's company over his."

The twin looks of confusion on the lich's and Malik's faces were beyond comical, but the real prize was the fury on Farid's. Karina suppressed a grin—she had him. Now to rub salt into the wound.

"I understand the appeal. Malik is closer to her own age, while you are practically a grandfather in comparison. If you ask me, your apprentice is a far bigger threat to your future than I could ever be. But you know what I find funniest about this entire situation?"

Farid was far taller than her, but Karina felt that she was the one looking down on him as she said, "You have broken the Ancient Laws, defied the will of the gods, literally resurrected Hanane from the grave . . . *and she still does not want you.*"

All her life, Karina had needled and annoyed Farid, pushing him to the very edge of his patience in the way that only family could.

But never, not once in all that time, had he ever struck her.

Until now.

Karina staggered backward, clutching her swelling cheek. Tears flowed down her face, more from shock than from actual pain. Both the lich and Malik looked ready to be sick as Farid straightened up and threw Karina a look of pure disgust.

"Do you see what you made me do?"

Despite the pain radiating through her face, Karina forced herself to meet Farid's gaze.

"I am only what you made me to be, older brother."

It was the worst insult she could think of—a reminder that they were connected in all but blood. No matter how hard he tried to deny it, the love he claimed was so pure and true was crossing into a taboo that couldn't be reconciled.

It was a small victory, but a victory nonetheless, and Karina let it warm her as her gaze fell to the lich's horrified face.

"Now I know you are truly not Hanane," Karina whispered, and though she'd meant the words to be venomous, her voice came out small and sad. "For if my real sister saw a man raise a hand against me, she'd make sure it was the last thing he ever used those hands for."

The lich's mouth opened, but no sound came out. Farid's expression turned feral. "I've changed my mind. Malik, where is the nearest body of water? We're going to perform the Rite of Renewal right now."

The lich let out a choked sound. "No! Farid, not yet—"

"We've wasted too much time already."

"Please, not now!" The lich grabbed him by the arm. "Perform the ritual in the morning. I don't need a week or even a day, but please . . . give me one last night with my sister."

Anyone else would have been struck down for such insolence, but Hanane had never been just anyone to Farid. The tension slipped from his body, and he gave a terse nod. "Use tonight to say your goodbyes," he said. "At first light, we do the ritual."

The lich turned its attention toward her, and a shiver of pure terror ran down Karina's spine. She had thrown one last insult toward Farid.

And in return, she'd earned herself a night with a monster.

31

Malik

He'd frozen. Farid had attacked Karina, not in defense or because he needed to for the ritual, but simply because she'd annoyed him.

And Malik had just stood there and let it happen.

Liar. Murderer. Torturer. Coward.

Karina had looked at him as Hanane had led her from the room, and he wished there had been anger in her eyes, or disappointment or even disgust, but there was . . . nothing. Her gaze had been dull and lifeless, and if Malik had been a hero he would have raged against everyone and everything that had broken her so thoroughly.

But he wasn't a hero.

He realized how foolish he'd been to expect Karina to stride into that room with some trick up her sleeve to avoid her fate, full of all the swagger and confidence he'd come to hold so dear.

But it was gone. She'd made the blood oath, and now the world would be saved. With the last of the Alaharis gone, Khenu and the rest of the wraiths would finally have their revenge, for it was unlikely that Hanane's resurrected body would be able to continue the line.

It was over. They had won.

Malik should have been happy. But instead there was nothing, and the nothing only grew as he made his way to the room his sisters were sharing within the fort.

Ektri Tairou—the Black Rot. That was what Malik's people called Ksar Nirri in Darajat, named for the black stones that had been used to build it, so incongruous among the traditional pastels used on Eshran homes. He and his sisters were probably the first Eshrans in centuries to walk these halls as guests rather than prisoners.

On the way back he'd stopped by the kitchen with a tray of fruit and bread for Leila and Nadia, who were still refusing to speak to him. He didn't wish to push them, but he needed . . . he didn't know what he needed, but he knew that he shouldn't be alone, not when the dark stain inside him that had been there even before the Faceless King now threatened to envelop him whole.

"Leila? Nadia?" he called. "It's me. Can I come in?"

No reply. The door was unlocked, which was odd—Leila never stayed in a room without locking the door, a habit born from their violent childhood.

A pang of alarm ringing in his ears, Malik entered the room. He took stock of the two beds, the small stools and table—but no Leila or Nadia.

Black spots danced at the edge of his vision. Had someone broken into the fort and stolen them away? No, that was ridiculous; Ksar Nirri was one of the best-defended places in the world, and there were no signs of struggle. Had they gone to the bathing rooms, perhaps?

But closer inspection revealed that both their packs were gone.

The realization slammed into Malik like a blow to his head.

His sisters hadn't been taken.

They'd left. They'd left *him*.

The world spun beneath Malik's feet. *Oh no. Oh no no no no no no no* NO. They wouldn't—not without him, they wouldn't— *Malik, calm down.*

They couldn't be out there alone with no magic or status to protect them. They needed him. He needed them.

Malik!

He couldn't do this without them, what was he going to do, where could they have gone, how could they do this—

Farid. Farid would know what to do. His earlier tiredness forgotten, Malik tore through the halls and flung himself into his mentor's quarters.

"Leila and Nadia, they're gone!" he screamed, not caring about whatever meeting he was interrupting between Farid and the officers who ran the fort. Malik tried to explain his sisters' disappearance, but in his fear the words all blurred together. Farid gave an irritated sigh.

"Malik, slow down. I can't understand a word you're saying."

"They're gone, they've taken all their belongings with them, we have to go after them—"

"Honestly, this is probably for the best." Farid returned to his map as the other men in the room shifted awkwardly. "It was never realistic to travel with a child so young anyway, and that older sister of yours has been rather unpleasant despite all I've done for her. Besides, we have everything we need now. There's nothing they can do to derail our plans, so if they want to go, let them."

"Please, Farid," Malik begged, his voice cracking. "I need you to help me—I can't be alone right now—"

"I don't have time to coddle you," Farid snapped, and Malik flinched. "Besides, has it occurred to you that if your sisters left with no warning and no note, it is because they do not want you going after them? *You* are exactly what they wish to get away from. You've grown cocky and arrogant, and you've forgotten that your place is to do as you're ordered and nothing more. Now go. I have business to attend to. I'll send a summons if I have need of you."

It was pure shock that made Malik's body move, and he could do nothing but stare as the man who had once called him little brother slammed the door firmly in his face.

Of course Malik went to look for them. He even went back to the refugee camp they had once lived in along with their mother and grandmother, even though every step through the camp brought him deeper into that pit inside him. He used every bit of magic he possessed to squeeze down the streets and hidden corners of Talafri, searching for any sign of Leila's blue headscarf or Nadia's round face.

But it was no use. They were gone.

Malik hardly remembered walking back to Ksar Nirri. He barely registered the wraiths crowding around him, because Leila and Nadia were gone, and he had no one to blame but himself.

He knew better than most the violation of having one's mind entered without their consent, yet he had hardly hesitated before doing it to them. And the worst part was, even now, he still loved how powerful his magic made him feel.

He was a monster, and he'd enjoyed being a monster, and now he was all alone.

Malik paced around his room for hours. How could his sisters do this to him? Didn't they see he'd had no choice?

They didn't understand what he was going through. *Nobody* understood what he was going through. If every part of their mind was constantly trying to tear itself apart, they'd have made all the same choices he'd made too.

But they didn't care about his suffering, so fine. Let them go. He didn't need them, and he never had.

He didn't mean that. Malik needed his sisters, like the tides needed the moon, like a compass needed the North Star. He sent up a plea to every god, to every being that had ever existed, for them to come back. He'd be good this time. He'd take care of them, like a brother was supposed to do. He'd never use his magic ever again, he would never scare or harm anyone ever again if they would just come back.

They weren't coming back.

Great Mother help him, they weren't coming back.

The wraiths had crowded around him, trying to coo platitudes that he did not deserve. Pressure ballooned in his head, screaming for a release and Malik reached for Tunde's bracelet and it was gone just like Tunde was gone, Tunde his friend who'd had the heart ripped straight from his chest and there had been so much blood it was so red and now Malik's own arm was covered in blood his fingers ripping through the flesh of his forearm because he was bad his father had been right about him and now Papa was gone and Tunde was gone and his sisters were gone and soon Karina would be gone and he'd be all alone because he was bad and he deserved every bad thing that had ever happened to him and the burn of the cuts on his arm were proof that whatever dark twisted thing inside him that made him ruin everything he touched was now coming for him and he'd tried to fight it before every time he'd climbed the lemon trees it had whispered for him to let go why wouldn't he just let go it would be so easy a fall and then pain and then nothing no more of this no more grim folk no more father just let go and he hadn't because he'd been scared but he wasn't scared anymore he was empty and he was numb and he missed his sisters and he just wanted the voice to stop he was trying to breathe and stay present and stay here but breathing hurt and the present hurt and here was a nightmare and he couldn't do it anymore he wasn't strong enough to fight it off there were no lemon trees here but the idea was the same fall then pain then nothing and he could do it right now he could end this pain right now

Now

NOW

Malik was on the roof. He did not know how he'd gotten on the roof.

All of Talafri stretched out below him, and beyond it, the dark silhouettes of the Eshran Mountains. Perhaps wherever Leila and

Nadia were, they were looking up at this same sky and almost-full moon hanging peacefully overhead. He hoped so.

What a mess he must have looked on the outside, with his clothes disheveled and his left arm in shreds. But on the inside, he was calmer than he could remember being in a long time.

Just as Farid had said, it was over. There was nothing left to do and no one left to fight.

He curled his fingers around the railing but—wait. There was still one piece of unfinished business. Malik found the binding separating him from the Faceless King, gathered all the strength that remained to him, and pushed.

It didn't budge.

Malik pushed and pushed, but the binding held. In a heartbeat, he was back in the lemon grove, hacking at a dying tree in the middle of a dying world.

"Let go!" screamed Malik, but Idir held tight. "Take your freedom and go! Destroy the world, flood every town, do whatever you want! I don't care, just go!"

"I'm not leaving you."

"THEN WHY AREN'T YOU TRYING TO STOP ME?"

Malik paused, his hands shaking at his sides. The Faceless King's face wore an expression Malik had never seen on it before—concern.

"Do you want me to stop you?"

H-He didn't. Or he did? Malik didn't know. The mania of the last several hours seeped away, laying his actions bare for him to see. He was so close to the edge, yet even now he could not bring himself to step toward or away from it.

He saw the choice before him in stark, simple clarity: live or die.

Right now, neither seemed that different from the other.

"I can't live like this," he said. "I've tried and I've tried and I've tried and I just . . . I can't do this anymore. I don't deserve to live, but I'm too scared to die."

The Faceless King laid his serpentine head gently on top of Malik's. "Humans are so strange. Life isn't given to be deserved. It's given to be lived. If you can find one thing that makes it worth seeing another day, then you've done all you're meant to do."

The air warmed around them, and Malik was engulfed by the now-familiar feeling of Idir's memories overtaking his own. He was back in Kennoua, back in that palace his ancestors had built on the bones of countless innocents.

"Why are you showing me this?"

"Just watch."

A hooded Khenu ran by, whispering hurried information via code to figures hiding in shadowed corners.

Bahia can't know, she hissed. *She can never know.*

He watched his ancestor unravel the pharaoh's household from the inside, remaining publicly the besotted paramour, while privately passing along plans and weaponry to the slave rebellion. The night of the great siege, when the revolution had overtaken the streets of the capital, the pharaoh watched the destruction of ten thousand years' worth of empire from his bedroom window.

I don't understand . . . he began, and it was the last thing he'd ever say before a heavily pregnant Khenu bashed him over the head with a torch holder, attacking him in the only place in the world where he'd ever allowed himself to be vulnerable—her bed. It was where Bahia found them hours later, the God Among Kings slumped over in a puddle of blood and Khenu deep in the throes of labor, her hands slick with viscera.

Malik watched as the much-celebrated, oft-repeated battle of the founder of Ziran and the last pharaoh never happened, as Karina's ancestor took in the carnage and realized what had occurred. He watched the warrior queen throw her sword away and kneel beside her enemy.

He watched as Khenu took her very last breath just as her son took his first. He watched Bahia look down at this ulraji child, so like the ones she had spent decades massacring, and made a choice.

He watched Bahia running through the city, her generals giving her wide berth, for they assumed that the blood covering her must be the pharaoh's, that she had defeated him, the savior of the gods come at last. Bahia ran through the massacre of the ulraji happening all around her, the one she herself had ordered, with the last ulraji child tucked under her arm. Malik watched as Karina's ancestor placed Khenu's child in the back of a wagon between a bale of hay and a pile of coiled rope, where in a few hours his cries would awaken the wagon's owners, a couple from Eshra, who would take the child in as their own, never questioning this blessing that surely the gods must have left them.

Live well, little one, Bahia whispered, and then Malik was alone in the lemon grove with the Faceless King once more. Malik drew a shuddering breath, trying to reorganize his understanding of the entire world in the wake of what Idir had just shown him.

"The same Bahia who ordered the execution of every ulraji was the one who ensured the continuation of your family's bloodline," said the Faceless King. "The same Khenu who had been raised to be loyal to the pharaoh above all else was the one who killed him. And yet it was easier for the people to rally behind the idea that there had been some grand battle between good and evil that killed the pharaoh. So that was the story Bahia spread, instead of the truth that the course of history was changed by two girls who each chose the sin she could bear the most."

Idir tilted his head back. "For the thousand years I was trapped in that realm, I agonized—how was it that my wife was willing to spare Khenu's child when she so coldly sacrificed our own? All these centuries later, and I still don't understand why. And as I'm not sure what will happen to me were I to pass, there is no guarantee I will ever see her again in the Place with Many Stars to ask her.

"There are choices you make in life that cannot be undone and that cannot be buried. They can only be carried, and you either buckle beneath the weight of them or grow strong enough not to. And growing is always worth it if it helps you get to that next thing that makes life worth living."

For the first time since Malik had let the spirit into his mind, the two were in perfect harmony, neither trying to subdue the other.

One thing.

Malik didn't need some grand purpose. He didn't need a magic birthright or a magnificent destiny. All he needed was one thing to keep himself together until tomorrow. Tomorrow itself was another battle, but today?

Just one thing.

In an instant, he was back on the roof, the pain in his arm stinging and fierce. The drop below was dizzying, and from this high up, Malik could not see where it ended. The voice had returned, nudging him softly forward. All it would take was one step, maybe two—

He stepped back, away from the edge, and fell to his knees. He cradled his injured arm to his chest and turned his face heavenward. A small movement caught his attention.

A single white butterfly, landing gently on his nose before zipping down to the courtyard and out into the night.

32

Karina

Bleeding, festering, plague-infested rat shit, Karina's face *hurt*.

She did all she could to relieve the pain, which wasn't much considering she was still bound hand and foot. And to make matters worse, her head was killing her. However, it was different from her migraines; this pain was thick and languid, casting a haze over all her senses. Perhaps it was a side effect of the blood oath?

Karina didn't know, but she did her best to lean into the pain, for it made it easier to ignore the lich.

The creature wearing her sister's face had taken her to a bathing room, where it had cleaned the grime of the cell from Karina's face and body. Karina had done her best to remain impassive even though its touch was like burning ice. Then it had taken her back to its room, dressed her in a long nightshirt patterned in the traditional Eshran style, and now sat behind her gently detangling Karina's mass of silver hair.

"Remember that time you got in a fight with the butcher's boy when he said our family dyed our hair and there was no way it actually grew out of our heads silver?" The lich moved through Karina's curls with expert care, pulling the brush from the ends up to the roots and twisting each section when she was done. "And you got so angry that you cut off all your hair with a pair of shears you stole from the kitchens so you could prove him wrong when it grew back in?"

Karina did remember that—her mother had been absolutely furious, and her father had laughed so hard he'd cried when he'd seen her shorn head.

But that was a memory for her and her sister to reminisce over. She refused to share it with this thing.

"Or how about that time you realized the goats you liked to feed were being raised for slaughter, so you tried to hide them in our bedroom and thought nobody would find out?" The lich shook its head and laughed. "Even when you were little, you never let anyone stop you from doing what you thought was right . . . honestly, it made me a little jealous how easy it was for you to speak and do as you please."

Karina's anger flared. In what world would Hanane have any reason to be jealous of her? Hanane had been the heir, Karina the spare. Hanane had cast the perfect shadow that Karina had never managed to move out of. How dare this creature speak to her of jealousy when Karina had been breathing it every moment of her life?

But she kept silent, even as her nails bit crescent marks into the skin of her palms. Karina was determined to go to her death with grace and dignity; she wouldn't let the lich goad her into giving in to her uglier instincts.

The lich secured the last twist in place, and then lowered its face beside Karina's to stare into the mirror. "Just look at us."

Hanane had taken after their mother and Karina their father, but seeing their faces side by side made Karina realize just how similar their appearances truly were, especially now that her hair was so long. All at once she was five years old again and giggling at her older sister's silly jokes, racing her to see who could get to the stables first, screaming at her on what she did not know would be the last night of Hanane's life.

The wrongness Karina had felt the first time she'd laid eyes on the lich returned, and she squirmed away.

"Why are you doing this?" Karina demanded. The lich stared at her before pulling out a small key hidden in her robes. In several quick movements, she had Karina's chains off. Karina stared dumbfounded as the lich tossed the ivory cuffs to the side with disgust.

"Because though there is nothing I can say or do that would convince you that I am your sister, it doesn't change the fact that you are mine. Even if you hate me or never want to see me again, I can't stand the thought of leaving you in chains. Especially considering what you're going to do tomorrow . . . what you're giving up for all of us."

Another wave of dizziness washed over Karina. "Farid won't be happy about this."

The lich pursed her lips together. "Farid can be . . . passionate," she said, glancing over her shoulder as if the man would materialize out of thin air. But he had promised them a night alone, and so far he was making good on that promise. "I'm sure once he has time to calm down, he will realize how unreasonable he is being."

A scream of frustration bubbled in the back of Karina's throat. How was it that everyone gave Farid chance after chance, no matter how many evils he committed, yet she was still atoning for mistakes she'd made when she hadn't even been old enough to realize what she was doing?

"And what if he doesn't calm down?" spat Karina. "How long are you going to stand by and let him do whatever he wants simply because he cares for you?"

The lich's bottom lip trembled. "It's not that simple."

"Is it not? Because from where I'm sitting, it is. If there is anyone in this world Farid will listen to, it's you. But you've always done whatever he's told you to do. When this is over and I'm dead and out of your way, will it be worth sitting on your throne if he's pulling all the strings of your reign?"

The creature that was not her sister began to fidget, twisting the fabric of her skirts between her hands as she said, "We are close but . . . it's not what you think—how do I explain this? Farid, he's . . . I . . ."

"You don't need to tell me how you trust him more than me. I've always known."

The lich recoiled as if she'd been struck. "And how am I supposed to trust you when you make it so difficult?" she cried. "None of this would have happened if you had just stayed in Ziran after Solstasia!"

"So you're saying that because I ran after being tricked with an illusion, captured, and attacked, that this somehow makes me less trustworthy than the man who *murdered our mother*?"

Karina hadn't realized she was screaming until the words were out of her mouth, but she couldn't stop even if it meant the man in question might overhear.

"What?" whispered the lich.

"Farid killed our mother! He planned the coup! He intentionally manipulated me so that he could murder Tunde and use his heart to bring you back to life! I know it sounds impossible to believe, because he was my family too, but this is what Farid does! He manipulates and he schemes and he twists things in the shadows while pretending to work for the greater good when all he really wants is to have what he wants no matter the cost!"

Karina was panting heavily now, her body revolting against the giant spurt of energy. "I have spent every moment of every day since the fire hating myself for what I did to you and Baba, even when I didn't remember I had played any part in it. But I swear on the grave of every Alahari queen—no, I swear on both our parents' graves—that I did not kill our mother, no matter what Farid has told you otherwise."

Karina slumped back, the rush of rage suddenly replaced by something duller yet equally all-consuming.

"Now you have two truths—mine and Farid's. Who you choose to believe is up to you."

Shocked silence stretched between them, the lich's eyes wider than coins. Then the creature opened her mouth to say something that Karina never heard, for it was then that Karina collapsed on the ground and darkness overtook her.

33

Malik

Each minute ticked by with agonizing slowness, as if the world was as reluctant as Malik was to see the coming day. His frenzy from earlier had dwindled, yet the ache in his chest from his sisters' absence filled every breath with pain. The Faceless King's words echoed through his mind, soft yet insistent.

One thing. Just one thing.

He'd been lying there unmoving for hours when someone burst into his room. For a wild, hopeful moment he thought it was his sisters, but it was only Hanane's scared face that swam into focus.

"I need your help!" she cried. "Karina's dying!"

Malik didn't move, too numb from all the tragedy he'd faced tonight for another to faze him. Hanane let out a frustrated sound, then hauled him to his feet and dragged him through the fort up to her bedroom. The guards outside it had both been knocked unconscious, which Malik guessed was her doing.

The sight of Karina slumped on the bed, shudders wracking her body, cut through some of the fog in Malik's mind. He knelt and pressed a hand against her forehead—it was burning hot.

His instincts told him to get out of the room and forget what he'd seen before Farid found him and punished him.

But he couldn't—no, he didn't want to leave Karina suffering like this. He didn't want to abandon someone who needed him ever again.

"Is this because of the blood oath?" asked Hanane.

He shook his head, trying to remember how to speak when his voice was so hoarse from screaming. "A blood oath has no side effects unless the terms are breached."

But how could Karina have fallen so ill so fast when she'd been fine just that evening?

And when the Great Mother grew disgusted by the monarch's defiance, she sent down a pestilence to all the people across the land until their blood boiled and their lungs drowned in their chests.

"It's the third of the punishments from the Great Mother—the plague," he said, and Hanane's hands flew to her mouth.

"We need to get her to a healer."

"But what about the Rite of Renewal?" It wasn't like the magic of the ritual would care if the sacrificed queen was sick or not.

Several expressions warred across Hanane's face, before it settled into the steely mask she'd worn the first day he'd met her. "Fuck the ritual. I'm saving my sister."

Karina opened her eyes just a fraction, her face contorting in pain. "Malik?" Her eyes traveled down to the makeshift bandage he'd tied around his forearm. Dark spots of blood were already starting to seep through. "What happened to your arm?"

Malik wiped away the beads of sweat that dotted Karina's brow with his good sleeve. He thought about the hatred between the zawenji and the ulraji, and the loyalty that had thrived between their ancestors despite it. "Don't worry about me right now. How do you feel?"

Her eyes flickered between him and Hanane, her pupils huge and unfocused. ". . . Bad."

"We're going to get you help," promised Hanane. She turned to Malik. "Do you know of any healers who have experience with the plague?"

"Not here in Talafri . . . but up the mountain in Oboure, there are diviner women skilled in traditional Eshran healing. If anyone can help her, it's them."

He did not mention that he knew of the diviner women because of Leila's training with them. He was barely holding himself together; if he spoke about his sisters, he would come undone once more.

"Don't worry . . . about me . . ." mumbled Karina as she attempted to stand, only for her legs to buckle beneath her. Malik caught her before she hit the ground, though his arm screamed in protest, and he cradled her close to his chest. An unspoken understanding passed between him and Hanane—Karina was in no state to even walk across a room by herself, let alone trek across an entire mountain.

"You have to take her. She'll never make it to Oboure otherwise," declared Hanane. "If Karina stays here she will die, but if we get her out, she could still have a chance. In the meantime, I'll convince Farid to sacrifice someone else. But not Karina. Anyone but her."

Malik's heart thudded in his throat as several emotions warred within him. Fear at the thought of what Farid might do to him if he was caught stealing away the most important element of the ritual. Dread at the thought of returning to Oboure after he and his family had risked their lives to escape it. And despair, for what if Hanane couldn't convince Farid to sacrifice someone else, or they couldn't find another queen in time?

Was it really fair to put Karina's well-being over everyone else in Sonande's?

But Karina looked up at him, completely helpless in a way she hadn't been even back in Maame Small Claws's hut. And suddenly this wasn't about their ancestors. It wasn't even about defying Farid. This was about which sin he'd be able to carry and which one would crush him.

If Karina died without him doing everything he could to save her, it would haunt him for the rest of his days.

"I'll take her," Malik said with more confidence than he felt. Relief flooded Hanane's face, and she gently brushed her hand across Karina's forehead. "But how do we get her out without Farid noticing? He knows when I use my magic, so I can't create an illusion to distract him."

A mischievous grin spread across Hanane's face, and she had never looked more like Karina than she did then.

"Leave that to me."

Malik had never seen an illness like this before. Leila should have been here—she'd know what to do about the fever racking Karina's body and the bone-white veins tinged with green that pulsed up her neck and arms. She'd be able to do more than crouch here with the princess curled against him, eyes trained on the guards in case any of them stirred.

But Hanane had ordered Malik to wait as she put their plan into motion, so wait he did. His magic was as jittery as he was, wound tight as a coil. It wasn't so much the impending journey to Oboure that daunted him as much as the knowledge that this was a betrayal against Farid that there would be no coming back from. When dawn came and he discovered Karina gone, he would turn the entire might of the Zirani army against them.

Bile rose in Malik's throat as he felt his bones snapping one by one, saw his blood seeping into the dirt, felt the crush of his organs rupturing as Farid stared down at him as serenely as ever.

I can build you into a god. But first I must break you.

Two sets of footsteps broke Malik out of his morbid thoughts. Hanane appeared in the dim light with a familiar face in tow.

"Put that thing down before you poke somebody's eye out," Aminata snapped at the spirit blade clenched in Malik's fist. She held a thick funeral shroud in her arms, the white of it too clean for the dank air of Ksar Nirri.

Karina drew a shuddering breath thick with phlegm. "Aminata?" she whispered, and the maid knelt beside the princess to wipe the sweat from her brow.

"Are you sure we can trust her?" Malik asked Hanane, who quickly dropped the two packs she'd brought so she could help Aminata lay out the shroud.

"I'm pretty sure I have more experience rescuing royalty than you do," said the maid.

Malik and Hanane laid Karina on the blanket as Aminata explained what she'd gleaned while they'd been stuck in the fort. "The plague arrived in this town a few days before we did, and the chief has a cart going to each house to collect the bodies of its victims for burning. Thanks to a well-placed bribe from yours truly, the cart will be here in about an hour. The plan is to get Karina on it, and then for you to follow after and remove her from it before the bonfire starts. There's some coin in the packs for you to buy food and mounts once you're out of the city. If all goes according to plan, you'll be miles away before Farid notices the deception."

Malik stared at her. "You planned all this in a few hours?"

Aminata shrugged. "I've helped plan harder escapes in less time."

"Thank you."

"Don't thank me, I'm not doing this for you. Karina's an annoyance, but she's my annoyance, and I haven't invested this much time training her to be sultana for her to die like this. Give me the rope." Her demeanor softened as she tied Karina's arms and legs together. "Karina, I'm going to need you to stay very still, all right?"

The younger princess let out a thin groan, but did not struggle as they wrapped the shroud around her with practiced care. By the time Aminata was done, Karina resembled an actual corpse so strongly that a shiver ran down Malik's spine. It was a wonder she could even breathe under that thing.

"For this to work, when you go out there, you're going to have to look normal. No hesitation, no nervousness. Can you do that?"

Aminata asked him sharply, and Malik's first instinct was no, he couldn't. But then he remembered how his ancestor had spent years as a mole within the Kennouan court, never once breaking cover, even when pressed by enemies on all sides.

He swallowed thickly and nodded. "I can."

With one last look Karina's way, Aminata left the room so that she could signal them when the plague cart arrived. Karina stirred once more, and Hanane laid a gentle hand against her head.

"You know I don't obey Farid because I want to, right?" she whispered, and Malik could not tell if the words were for him or for her sister. She let out a sad laugh. "I thought perhaps if I gave him what he wanted it might placate him, but I've given him everything I am, and it's still not enough. I've even lost my death to him. When it comes to Farid, I've never had a choice."

Malik touched her arm gently, letting her know that he understood all that she was and was not saying. "You always have a choice. Even when you've lost all else, you always have that. Farid tried to break all three of us, but we're still here."

Hanane lowered her head, but she didn't pull away. She looked at Karina once again, her sorrow morphing to protective fierceness.

"He's taken so much from me. He doesn't get to have her too."

"Come with us," Malik said suddenly. "We'll take Karina to the diviners, and once she's healed, we'll figure out a way to stop all this madness."

It was a far-fetched idea, but Malik could not stomach the thought of leaving Hanane behind. "You're allowed to choose yourself. You're allowed to leave."

No one must have ever said those words to Hanane before, for something in her face cleared, and she nodded. She picked up one of the packs and opened it, revealing the flute nestled in among the supplies.

"Take this with you too. I don't trust Farid with it," she said, and Malik realized just how much they'd all been underestimating this girl, that she'd been able to orchestrate this all so quickly.

All too soon, the signal came from below—a low, clear whistle that anyone listening might have mistaken for birdsong. Malik rose to his feet, one arm beneath Karina's knees, another beneath her head, huffing slightly—Karina was many things, but light was not one of them. Hanane was monitoring the door to Farid's meeting. Once Malik and Karina were through, she would join them.

Just as Aminata had promised, not a soul was in the courtyard. The plague cart stood at the entrance, already filled with nearly a dozen shrouded bodies identical to the one Malik held. Aside from the Mark turning in tight circles above his lower back, Malik was the perfect vision of calmness. He had learned that having authority was much less important than having the *air* of authority; the servants took one glance at the hardened look in his eyes and scurried off.

Time seemed to slow, the cart inching ever closer. As he approached it, Malik imagined himself, Karina, and Hanane finally free of the man who had worked so hard to control each of them. For the first time in a long time, something almost like hope sparked within his chest.

Breathe. Stay present. Stay—

"Where are you going, little brother?"

Farid descended down the spiral staircase leading to the fort's entrance like a specter out of a nightmare and stopped a few feet away from him. Malik wondered if a person had ever died from pure fear.

"What are you carrying?" asked the man.

Farid was going to kill him. He was going to kill him, just as Papa had tried so many times to do, and he was going to keep that deceptively calm smile on his face the entire time he did it.

"One of the Eshran serving girls died." He begged his magic to stay still and not to alert his mentor that something was amiss. "I knew her from my days in the camp, so I just . . . I wanted to provide the traditional prayers for her before they took her away."

Was it even worth lying to Farid? Even now was the man's magic painting Malik's deception in a bright gold that he could not see?

He didn't know and he couldn't know and still the lie rolled off his tongue.

Farid tilted his head to the side with his hands behind his back. He opened his mouth to say something when Hanane came hurtling out of the shadows and threw herself into his arms.

"Farid!" she cried, tears flowing down her face. "I went to say my goodbyes to Karina, but I—she—she said such horrible things—"

As ever when Hanane was around, Farid's attention narrowed to her and nothing else. "What happened? What did she say?"

Hanane put her hands against Farid's chest and stared up at

him through tear-stained lashes. "She called me a monster. She said were it not for her chains, she would kill me again herself."

Storm clouds gathered in Farid's eyes. "I knew we should have done the ritual tonight. I'll go rectify that right now—"

"No!" Hanane threw her arms around Farid and buried her face in the crook of his neck. It burned Malik to imagine what that gesture must be costing her, and he couldn't help but remember the shame and disgust that had filled the princess's voice when she'd described the full twisted depths of her and Farid's relationship. "I . . . I just—stay with me. Please, just stay with me tonight. Like we used to do. I . . . I need you."

Malik had watched Hanane fight her way through a militia. He'd watched her pull a sword out of her own neck. But he'd never seen her as scared as she looked now, trying to draw Farid's attention away from him and Karina.

Farid froze for half a second before he placed one hand behind Hanane's head and another at her lower back. "Of course," he murmured. Hanane looked up at Malik over Farid's shoulder, a single command in her eyes.

Go.

And so Malik did.

He reached the plague cart and tucked Karina in among the actual corpses as Hanane led Farid back into the fort. Hanane would be fine. She knew what she was doing. But that didn't stop the voice inside Malik that screamed to go back for her, consequences be damned. After what she'd told him about the true nature of her relationship to Farid . . . no. Malik turned back to the fort, only to find himself face-to-face with Commander Issam.

The Sentinel narrowed his eyes, and Malik's magic burned on his tongue, ready to fragment Issam's mind just as he had Dedele's, when the man said, "Your princess, she tried to protect Tabansi."

Malik did not know who Tabansi was, or what to make of the phrase *your princess*, but more shocking than either of those things was the fact that Issam had spoken to him in Darajat. The new commander of the Sentinels was Eshran, and he was looking down at Malik now with a crush of emotions he could not name.

A muscle twitched in the warrior's jaw, as if he was trying to fight off something that only he could see. He stepped back with his head cradled in his hands, pushing against his temples. "Leave this place. Get out of here, now!" he snarled in Darajat, and so Malik did, ignoring the part of him that screamed to go back for Hanane as he walked Karina out of the fort and toward freedom.

Karina was on a boat, being rocked gently from side to side.

No, not a boat—she was nestled between a pair of arms, and they held her so carefully, as if she was the most precious thing in the entire world. Baba? But Baba was dead, and her mother had never held her like this. Whoever it was, all Karina wanted to do was lose herself in the gentle sensation.

"Open your eyes," said Tunde, and why was he talking to her when he was dead? Was she dead too? "Stay awake, Karina."

Despite the fact that every inch of her body screamed in protest, Karina forced her eyes open. She was nestled between a pair of strong arms on the back of some furry beast, and judging by the way the green countryside rolled past them, they were moving fast.

"Oh, you're awake," rumbled a voice that reverberated through her whole body. Malik. Yes, she was with Malik. Karina sighed and snuggled back against his chest.

Wait, she was with Malik?

Karina's instincts took over. She jammed her head against his chin before launching herself off the back of their mount. The world swam as she fell to the ground with a hard thud, and again when she tried to stand. Everything felt thick and hazy, like she was seeing the world through distorted glass.

Malik dismounted quickly and reached a hand to help her up, only to recoil as thunder boomed directly above them—a reminder that even in her weakened state, she was still strong enough to hurt him. "Where are we? Where are you taking me?" she demanded.

"On the east side of Mount Mirazzat, about a few days' ride from Oboure. The diviner women there might be able to heal you."

Heal her? Why would she need a healer—a wave of coughs racked Karina body, and by the time the last one was out, the entire world spun.

"The third omen . . . the plague . . ." she croaked out, and Malik nodded. Karina tried to recall when the illness had settled in, but it felt like sifting through mud to find a single coin. She remembered the long days she'd spent in the dungeons waiting for Farid, her making the blood oath and him striking her across the face, her yelling at the lich, and then . . . nothing.

Now here she was traveling across Eshra in the arms of the boy who may or may not be her greatest enemy.

"Why are you doing this?"

"You'll never make it to Oboure on your own in your current state."

"How do I know you're not lying about taking me to a healer so that you can kill me without any witnesses?" She wasn't fool enough to believe he was doing this because he cared about her well-being. If he needed her alive, it was only because he wanted to use her for the Rite of Renewal too.

"Karina, if I wanted to kill you, why wouldn't I have done it while you were unconscious and unable to resist?"

"I don't know! I don't understand why you do anything that you do!" Perhaps it was foolish to yell at him when they were the only two people for miles, but Karina didn't have it in her to hold back anymore. "One second you're saving me from Maame Small Claws, the next you're giving my location to Farid. You tortured Dedele! You did nothing when he locked me in a cell in Ksar Nirri, and now you're risking your life to get me to a healer? Why are you doing this? Whose side are you on?"

Why do you pretend to care about me only to take it away?

Karina slumped forward; the outburst had taken the little strength she had left. Malik stared at her, a new weight in his eyes that hadn't been there before their time in the fort.

"All my life, all I ever wanted was to feel safe. For someone to protect me and feel proud of me. Farid offered that to me, and I took it, without checking to see what strings might be attached." He cradled his left arm close to his chest, and Karina got a glimpse of a thick bandage beneath his sleeve. "The things I did for his approval . . . the things I chose to do—it's too late to change any of it. I'll never stop atoning for what I did to Dedele or anyone else I hurt. But never again. I don't care if we're the last two ulraji who are ever going to exist, I'm never going back to him."

Malik looked up at her, his mouth thin with resolve. "And you'll never have to go back either. Hanane made sure of that."

Karina had completely forgotten about the lich. "What happened?"

"She stayed behind to distract Farid so that we could get out."

Her entire life, Karina had always assumed Hanane and Farid's relationship had been one of equals. But both she and Malik had been manipulated by the man. If what Hanane had claimed at the fort was true, and she was just as much a victim of his manipulation as they were, it terrified Karina to think what she must have done to keep him distracted enough for Malik to carry off his most important captive.

"All she wanted was for you to get to safety. That's all I want too." Malik extended a hand toward her. "As for what side I'm on, I want to be on yours. I know I haven't always been, but—if you'll have me, I'm yours."

Instincts honed from years of pushing everyone in her life away almost made Karina smack Malik's hand down. But for the first time in her life, she was truly free of Farid. It felt like a specter had been looming over the sun, and now that it was gone, all she could feel was warmth.

Of course only death loomed at the end of this path, for she could escape Farid but not the blood oath. However, now her death would be on her own terms, not his.

And she had Malik to thank for that gift, however short it might be.

Her heart in her throat, Karina took Malik's hand and wondered if he felt the same jolt of energy she did when their skin made contact. She allowed him to help her back onto the beast. Their mount was a denzik, an Eshran creature somewhere between a ram and a stag; they were prized for their skill at navigating shaky mountain paths. Something told her Malik hadn't paid for the creature, and that its owner was currently cursing their names.

Malik's heartbeat reverberated through her body, making her

uncomfortably aware of the way his chest pressed against her back. To distract herself, she said, "So you kidnapped me."

"It was a rescue!"

"No, what you did is definitely kidnapping. You've stolen me away like a thief in a fireside tale, and now you have me completely at your mercy."

Malik laughed, and the rumble of it sent heat pooling low in Karina's core.

"You know, I once had a dream about you tying me up, but would you believe it, there was actually more rope involved—" Karina began, only to devolve into another coughing fit. Malik shifted slightly, so that she could lean back more.

"Sleep. Don't worry, I know these mountains in my blood. I'll get you to Oboure, I promise."

Of this, Karina had no doubt, but if she slept now, she wasn't sure she'd wake again.

"Tell me a story," she asked, and in the silence that followed, all Karina could make out was the sound of her own heart slowly falling into sync with Malik's. It was almost enough to lull her back to sleep, until he opened his mouth and began his tale.

"This is the story of how Kembi fell in love with the moon."

Though Malik was not using his powers, Karina could see each twist and turn of the story as vividly as if it was unfolding right before them. By the time he was finished, a note of melancholy hung in the air. She wished desperately to see his face, to know what expression he'd held as he'd told her this story of a forbidden love between a boy and the moon that could not be, but already the sleep was pulling her under once again.

"Malik?"

"Hmm?"

Even keeping her eyes open was an uphill fight she was quickly losing. "Are you Kembi, or am I?"

She felt rather than heard him answer, but by then, she was already gone.

35

Malik

Malik felt it the moment they crossed into Eshra. It was the subtlest of shifts as the mountains loomed closer and the trees grew taller, the soil grew richer and something long dormant inside him stirred awake, stretched out like a cat, and whispered in his ear, *Welcome back.*

But for everything that was familiar about his home, far more was not. The omens had torn through the region, leaving gaping canyons where entire mountains had once been and abandoned homes beside destroyed fields. More than once Malik had to reroute their path because an avalanche had blocked a pass or a river had flooded a road.

And the plague—shallow graves marked the countryside as physical remnants of the plague's toll, but the real sign was the silence. The air should have been overflowing with the sounds of the farmers tilling their fields, merchants hawking their wares, and young people scrabbling up and down the paths in preparation for their adulthood ceremonies.

But it was quiet. So deathly quiet.

However, what frightened Malik most of all was the fact that Karina was getting worse.

She'd been mostly lucid, if fatigued, when they'd first fled Tala-fri, but now, on the third day of their journey, her head kept lolling to the side, and Malik had been forced to lash her down to the denzik out of fear she'd fall off completely. Every few minutes he'd press a hand against her stomach, simply to check she was still breathing, and every few minutes pure terror would fill him until she gave the smallest of movements.

The weather had also been worsening as the days passed, which Malik guessed was Karina's magic responding to her rap-idly deteriorating health. By sundown on the third day, the light mist that had been hindering their progress since morning had blossomed into a full-on downpour, and he had no choice but to find them shelter in a small cave. Once inside, he tethered and fed the exhausted denzik, wrapped Karina in a nest of blankets in the driest corner he could find, and made a fire. His clothes were completely soaked through, so on instinct he pulled off his tunic and set it to dry before remembering exactly who he was with.

He didn't have to turn to feel Karin's eyes boring into his back, and the old familiar panic almost made him cover himself before he stopped. After all they'd been through, what did he have to hide from her?

"Do you need anything?" he asked, and she gave him a weak grin.

"No. Just enjoying the view."

Malik sputtered something that was more embarrassment than words. However, if she felt well enough to joke, then perhaps she was faring better than she looked.

Karina's gaze shifted from Malik's bare back to the rain pouring down outside the cave. Her eyes narrowed, and the rain began to thin. But in a heartbeat, it slammed back down with more intensity, and Karina flopped back, panting. Malik hurried over to help her sit up.

"I thought I might be able to lighten the downpour," she groaned, but Malik shook his head.

"Save your strength."

Sweat glistened on Karina's brow, and she shivered beneath the wet layers of her own clothes. "I think you need to take this off," said Malik, and she nodded. He began to move away to give her privacy when she turned her back toward him and lowered her head.

"Help me?"

Malik nodded then, realizing Karina couldn't see it, said, "Of course," but his voice cracked as he did because of course it did and now his mind was rambling instead of doing the thing he'd been asked to do. He reminded himself they were friends as he helped Karina peel off the wet layers of her top. Pushing her hair aside and wiping the sweat from her back was a friendly thing to do. Idir had stayed silent since they'd left the fort, and for once, Malik wished the spirit would say something, if only to distract him from dangerous thoughts with no viable outlet.

Once Karina was down to her underclothes, Malik placed the wet ensemble beside the fire. He began to move toward his own corner for the night when she reached for his arm.

"Stay," she whispered, her eyes unfocused and bright. Even with her wet clothes removed, the fever coursing through her body, and the fire roaring only a few feet away, Karina still shivered. "Please."

His heart in his throat, Malik laid down beside her, his chest against her back, one arm looped tight around her waist. He wasn't sure what to do with his hands until she solved that problem for him by lacing her fingers through his, nestling down so she was using his good arm as a pillow.

He had been hoping for an hour, maybe two, of uninterrupted rest, but there was no way he could sleep now. He counted to one hundred, and then backward from one hundred, and then forward again, all in a futile attempt to distract himself from the precarious situation he was in. The rain was a soft hum, almost comforting now that they weren't trapped in it.

"Malik?" came a small voice, and Malik's eyes snapped open. Without realizing it, he had fallen asleep. The fire had dwindled to embers, but the entrance to the cave was pitch-black—not morning, not yet.

"Yes?"

"Aren't you worried about catching the plague too?"

"At this point, I've almost died so many times it's starting to lose any meaning."

Now Karina laughed, and then gave a small sigh as Malik buried his face in the crook of her neck. Minutes, or perhaps hours, passed with him slowly circling his thumb over hers, and then—

"Malik?"

"Hmm?"

"You can see ghosts, right?"

The circling stopped. Everything they had left behind came

rushing back to taint this tiny, safe corner they had carved for themselves.

"In a sense. But not all the dead. Just wraiths."

Karina shifted ever so slightly, and Malik fought the urge to hold on tighter. "Have you seen Tunde's wraith?"

The dam Malik had crafted around the memories of his fallen friend burst open. All the grief and confusion and jealousy he felt toward Tunde leaked through the fissure, and Malik could do nothing but let it consume him.

"If I had, I wouldn't know. They aren't distinct enough from one another for me to tell them apart most of the time. But I think only bitter, unsatisfied people come back as wraiths. Tunde lived a good life, so he wouldn't have as much reason to linger."

But who was to say that Tunde was not one of the wraiths who followed Malik everywhere he went, and that he wasn't watching the girl he'd loved for so long resting in Malik's arms? What if they were betraying this boy yet again, even after his death?

Malik could sense that Karina was thinking similar thoughts.

Yet the guilt was not enough to make them pull away from each other.

Gathering all his courage, Malik asked the one question that had been haunting him since the moment he'd seen the gaping hole in his friend's chest.

"Karina, how did Tunde die?"

The rain was a roar now, drowning out all else around them and almost certainly flooding the paths they'd need to take tomorrow. It was beneath this cover of rain that Karina spoke. Her words lacked the practiced cadence of a griot, and more than once the fever overtook her so completely that she had to stop and restart, but still Malik listened.

She spoke of a little girl with everything she could possibly want until she had accidentally destroyed it all, and how she had cut herself again and again trying to put the pieces back together. How she had simultaneously grieved for and felt jealous of a ghost, and how she had failed so often to meet people's expectations that she eventually made herself into the monster they all believed her to be.

And then Solstasia. The queen, dead. Magic, revealed. And a spell that could fix everything, if only she sacrificed the heart of a king.

"It was never supposed to come down to you or Tunde. In fact, I did everything in my power to not have to make that choice. But then you were the last two, and I could only save one of you from the Rite of Resurrection . . . and I chose you."

The memories of that tumultuous week unfolded in Malik's mind, and he felt his understanding of both himself and Karina shifting as he took in this revelation that her rejection of him had been anything but.

Karina gave a laugh devoid of any mirth. "Do you understand now why I have to do the Rite of Renewal? So many people have died for me. This is the only way I can make sure their sacrifices weren't in vain. It's all I'm good for—"

She let out a small yelp as Malik flipped her over so they were face-to-face. He wiped the tears from her cheek with his thumb and ran a finger up and down the bridge of her nose. Confusion flooded her eyes. "What are you doing?"

"It's a calming technique my mother taught me. Usually it's used on babies, but I thought it might help."

"Why are you doing all this when you should hate me?" she asked with a hiccup.

Gods, he should. Their list of wrongs against one another was written in blood that would haunt them both for the rest of their days.

But equally as long was the list of ways they'd each saved the other. He and Karina had been fighting for one another before either of them had fully realized it. Just as she'd taken a leap of faith when she'd saved him from the Rite of Resurrection, he too was ready to take this leap and defy both the gods and the odds to get her up this mountain.

Malik pulled her in close and kissed her brow.

"Because to me, you're worth it, no matter what has made you believe otherwise."

The old stories had taught Malik that love was about grand declarations and even grander gestures. But it was there, in the small hours of the night as Malik held Karina and let her cry into his chest in the ugliest, most snot-ridden way possible, that he realized love was more like a pebble sinking into a pond, soft as the turn of one page in a story to the next, yet the ripples of it extending outward into everything about the way he saw the world and himself.

It was far from the most explicit thing that had happened between them—and there was far more snot involved than Malik ever would have expected spending the night with a girl—but it was so much more than even the searing kiss in the dreamscape had been, because this was real—awkward elbows and mucus and all. This girl had stolen the heart from his chest and run off with it, and he wasn't even upset, because a person could never truly steal something that already belonged to them.

But even the sky cannot cry forever, and eventually the rain stopped, as did Karina's tears. Malik's good arm had lost all feeling now, but he wasn't going to move.

"Malik?"

"Still my name. Yes?"

She twisted her head so she was looking at him. "Can you promise me something?"

"Is this about the moon again?"

Karina gave him a weak smile, and Malik did not know what was better—seeing her smile, or knowing he was the cause of it.

"I don't want the moon. Not this time." She coughed again. "I want you to promise me that if we don't find the diviners or if we do but they can't help me, you'll perform the Rite of Renewal."

The blissfulness of the moment crashed down under the weight of what Karina was asking him to do.

She wanted him to kill her, even though it felt as if it was his own heart beating in her chest. Outright refusal lay on the tip of his tongue, but her gaze was so steady that Malik knew this was a battle he had lost before it had even begun. So instead of battling, he nestled his face into the crook of her neck and whispered the promise into the heat of her skin.

The rain was gone by morning, leaving behind a deceptively cheerful sapphire sky above and a waterlogged world below. Neither Malik nor Karina mentioned what had occurred the night prior—Karina because she was conserving her strength, Malik because he did not trust himself to bring up the promise he'd made without bawling. Instead, he regaled her with stories of Oboure, mostly to keep her from falling into a sleep she would not wake up from.

"They call it the Yellow Pearl of Eshra," he said, and Karina nodded along as best she could despite the layers of cloth Malik had wrapped her in to keep out the mountain chill. "All the buildings in the center of the town are painted in various shades of yellow, so it looks like a piece of sunshine blooming right out of the mountainside. And the smells! At any time of day, someone is baking bread, and more often than not they'll give you some in exchange for a secret or a line of poetry. Eshrans love poetry. They say the average Eshran dies with ten times as many poems in their head as coins in their pockets."

"It sounds wonderful," Karina whispered, and the hoarseness in her voice made Malik walk faster. They had reached the part of the path too treacherous for even the denzik to cross, so now he carried Karina on his back across the mountain, fatigue winding through his bones but adrenaline spurring him forward. The rain had stopped, but the temperature was frantic as Karina grew weaker, alternating between bouts of burning heat and freezing cold that made the trek even more difficult.

"When this is all over, I'll show you every wonderful thing in Eshra," he promised. Perhaps if he made enough promises, they would bury the one that loomed over them both. "We don't have a lot in my village, but what we do have is beautiful."

Every step was harder than the last. The mountain cracked Malik, forcing him to face in stark clarity the limits of his own strength. He had done the climb from the bottom of Mount Mirazzat to the top so many times, but never carrying another person, and never in the wake of the breaking apart he'd faced back at Ksar Nirri.

Who are you? his homeland asked him with each grueling mile. *How far are you willing to go?*

And each time Malik looked at the line where the ground met the sky, he heard that voice again, edging him to take that step that would end his suffering once and for all—a fall, and then pain, and then nothing. The voice was there; it had always been there, and likely always would be.

If Malik had been on his own, he probably would have collapsed a half-dozen miles ago. But he was not alone; he might have given up on himself, but he would never give up on her.

He had bested the darkest part of himself before. He'd do it as many times as he needed to in order to keep himself and his loved ones safe.

Soon Malik reached the point where he couldn't even speak for the pain lancing through his lungs and the wind biting his face, but he did not put Karina down. He stumbled more than once. He fell more than once. But he kept going, one foot after the other, until he reached a familiar crest in the path, with the little stone guardian planted at the crossroad pointing toward Oboure. Malik's heart swelled in his chest as he raced for the crest. He'd done it. They'd made it. Karina was going to be all right—

He stopped at the top of the ridge, only feet away from where the ground slid into a dangerous mixture of mud and broken branches. From their vantage point, the entire valley stretched out like an unfurled quilt, including the giant chunk of earth that had slid down from the mountainside to bury what had once been Oboure.

A scream built in Malik's ears, and it took him several moments of stunned silence to realize it was the wind and not him. His body seemed to move of its own accord as he carefully picked through the treacherous path and surveyed the ruins of what had once been his home.

Oboure was simply . . . gone. Few structures had survived the landslide, and the ones that had looked so decimated it was unlikely anyone could step foot in them without the foundations giving way completely. Here and there Malik saw remnants of the village he had known—that was the wall of the little schoolhouse where the aunties had taken turns teaching the children numbers, this was the market where farmers had brought their best cattle to sell each Earth Day—but what was left behind was little more than carrion for the vultures. Given a few more months of harsh weather, it would look as if there had never been a village here at all.

Malik didn't realize until then that deep down, a part of him had taken comfort in knowing that he and his family could one day return here if they wished. Now that his old home was destroyed, and Ziran was on its way toward civil war, there was no place for him anywhere.

He forced himself to walk through the wreckage and bear witness to the destruction until he came across the spot where the diviner women had trained. All that remained was a crumbling pile of rocks, and it was there that Malik came undone. He screamed and he screamed and Karina's arms tightened around him, holding him just as tightly as he had held her the night before.

It was hours before Malik came back to himself in any sort of coherent way. "What now?" he asked, his throat burning from overuse. He didn't know who he was asking—Karina, or the gods. "What do we do now?"

Karina twisted his face gently so he had no choice but to look at her. "We do the Rite of Renewal."

He had forgotten all about the ritual in his despair, but at the reminder he shook his head. "No. No, no, no. I . . . I . . . I can't—"

"We're too late to help Oboure, but we can still save other towns from meeting this fate. And any day now Farid is going to catch up to us. We need to do the ritual, and then you need to run somewhere far away before he catches you."

"I can't. Karina, I can't."

"Then this plague will kill me, and my death will be meaningless. Let me die, and we kill millions. Sacrifice me, and you can live long enough to defeat him."

Karina pressed against the Mark coiled tight in Malik's palm, and the surprise of the touch caused it to switch into its dagger form. She closed his fist around the hilt and then guided his hand so the tip pressed against her heart, right where he'd stabbed her during Solstasia. They both knew the dagger couldn't actually kill her, but the meaning was clear.

Malik could hardly see for the tears blurring his eyes. What was the point of magic and the miraculous things he could do if he was forever powerless to fight for the people he cared about the most?

Karina placed a feverish hand against his cheek, the strain from speaking clear on her face. "Please, Malik. Let Bahia's debt to Khenu be repaid. Let's end the cycle of revenge once and for all."

Malik sorted through every folktale and legend he knew for some trick or loophole, but there was none. He swallowed down another wail and forced himself to nod. He couldn't let her last memories of this life be his blubbering face.

"We need a body of water," he said through hiccups. "There's a lake not far from here, near my old home. We can . . . we can do it over there."

Karina nodded, and Malik had begun to help her up when he sensed the unmistakable feeling of someone watching him. He threw himself before Karina, dagger in hand.

"Show yourself!" he barked. The figure stepped out from behind a broken wooden beam—it was a woman old enough to have been his grandmother, the cloth sacks at her back full of items she'd scavenged from the ruins. Her eyes widened in recognition—not of him, but of Karina.

"It's you!" she exclaimed, hurrying forward, only to stop and stare warily at Malik's spirit blade.

Malik turned to a wide-eyed Karina. "You know this woman?"

"I met her and some others back in Tiru. They were—ugh." Her body slumped forward, and Malik managed to catch her just before she hit the ground. Alarmed, the woman ran over.

"Please, she's caught the plague and needs a healer," he begged, and the woman scrutinized him carefully.

"Are you her friend or foe?" she demanded, and it was only then Malik realized how suspicious it must look to see a young man dragging a near-comatose girl across the mountain.

"Friend."

Whatever the woman saw on Malik's face satisfied her, for she nodded. "Come with me," she ordered, and Malik did as he was told, keeping one hand on Karina's back the whole way.

36

Karina

"You're not going to make it," said Tunde, and Karina might have snapped at him if her tongue didn't feel too heavy to use. She'd been sick before, but never had every inch of her body felt so inflamed like this.

Stars danced across her vision, and the only thing tethering herself to her body was the feeling of Malik's hand pressed so protectively against her back. She didn't know where this woman was taking them, and truly she did not care. One breath, and then another. That was all she could muster the energy for anymore.

One.

More.

Breath.

37

Malik

"Princess Karina saved my life," explained the woman—Siwa—as she led them through the harrowing path left behind by the landslides. "I was one of a group of women who had been stolen from the refugee camp in Talafri by traffickers heading for Ziran. The princess came to our aid when no one else would. I don't like to think what might have become of me without her."

The woman shot Karina a look of pure gratitude, which Karina was too weak to receive. Malik marveled at how tales of the girl's worst exploits spread so much farther than the ones of her kindness.

But there was little time to talk, for with each second Karina dimmed more. The fear of her dying in his arms had expanded in his mind and left room for nothing else, not even space to process what had happened to Oboure. Malik even went so far as to try to channel their connection to send her any good health he could, too desperate to feel ridiculous about it.

"You're going to be all right," he said, more for his own sake than for Karina's.

Siwa eventually brought them to a flat area where the path opened onto a dead end against the mountain wall.

"What I'm about to show you cannot be shared with anyone else," she warned, and Malik nodded. Siwa began to hum, rubbing her fingers on the wall in a pattern Malik did not recognize, and after the first few notes, the mountain hummed back. The stone grew warm beneath their feet as the song reverberated around them. Then came the grinding of rock against rock as several tons of stone slid away to reveal a tunnel whose walls pulsed with purple light.

The source of the light quickly became apparent—amethyst. The inside of the mountain was a giant jewel, with enough gems and crystals embedded in the wall to sustain several nations for many generations to come. Siwa led them past cave paintings from times long past, depicting creatures and wonders Malik had never seen before. Whatever this place was, it was ancient, older even than the ruins of Kennoua back in Ziran.

"After Karina freed us, we debated where we should go," explained Siwa. "A few decided to test their fortunes in Ziran, but the majority of us returned to Eshra. We were camping in the valley for a few weeks when the earthquakes occurred and opened up an abandoned mountain path. Inside we found this. Now it's grown to house whatever survivors of the landslides we can find. We're doing everything we can to keep this place secret from the Zirani."

Malik could not blame them, for he had no doubt that if their occupiers knew of the literal riches hidden deep within the earth here, they would tear them away from his people just as they had torn everything else. He was suddenly grateful that Karina was too delirious to realize where they were, then immediately felt guilty for such thoughts. The fact that she was Zirani and he was Eshran shouldn't matter right now, not when her very life was on the line.

Siwa's camp was far larger than Malik had expected, with hundreds of people hidden away between the canvas tents and threadbare blankets, trying to survive on what little they could scavenge from the wreckage. Siwa brought them to the very heart of it, where a group of old women sat crushing herbs into poultices. She said something to them, too quick for Malik to make out, and they murmured back.

"What are they saying? Can they help her?" he asked.

"They're not sure, but they have someone who they think can. Give her to me."

A wave of protectiveness coursed through Malik, but he obediently handed Karina over to Siwa. He thought he saw the princess weakly lift a hand in his direction, but then she was gone inside the tent, and Malik was alone once more.

38

Karina

Now for this chord, you curl three fingers around the strings and press your little finger down just like this—

"—her fever is too high—"

—and with your other hand, you strum the first and the sixth strings like this—

"Karina? Can you hear me? Karina!"

—and you've made your first note! Try it, doesn't it sound wonderful?

Karina did try it, though her note did not come out with the same clear melody as her father's. She beamed up at him with a many-gapped smile—several of her infant teeth had fallen out, and the adult ones had yet to grow in their place. "I did it!"

The king clapped. "You did!"

Karina wiggled on her cushion, so happy she could burst into song. Take that, Hanane. Her older sister might be bigger and taller, and she might get to go to all the fancy parties that happened long after Karina's bedtime, but Karina had played a whole chord by herself!

"Try the next one," suggested Baba as he moved her fingers

into position, and Karina could not remember feeling safer or more protected than she did in this moment.

Hang on, Karina, I've got you.

Karina's face scrunched in confusion. "Someone is calling me."

"I don't hear anyone." Baba extended his hand to her. "Come, let's go for a walk. It's such a lovely day."

Karina knew that if she took her father's hand they would walk and walk as far as their legs could carry them, chatting about everything and nothing. Nothing bad would ever happen to her again if she was with him.

Karina reached for it. She stopped.

"But it's not day at all," she said, and surely enough, more stars than Karina had ever seen stretched all around them like a thousand miniature suns. She and Baba were ankle-deep in the starlight, warm as a current.

And that voice. It was coming from everywhere and nowhere all at once, pleading for her to come back.

But come back where?

Baba said once again, "Let's take a walk."

Karina knew she should say no, though she could not recall why she knew it. But the voice that had been calling her was gone, and without it she felt small and afraid, and here was her father promising her everything would be all right, and so this time when he offered his hand, she took it.

And they began to walk.

39

Malik

Malik knew these people.

Not all of them, of course, as the settlement was filled with refugees from every corner of Eshra. Their region was home to an array of different cultures, and Malik could not know every Eshran just as one grain of sand on a beach could not know all the others.

But he recognized the ones from Oboure. They made up about half the settlement's population, which meant that at least a third or so of the townspeople had survived the quakes. There was Eleikum, who had once pushed Malik into a well on a dare, now nailing a shoe to a sleepy mule. And the Ackun sisters, who all whispered quietly among themselves as they stole glances at Malik when they thought he was not looking.

All these people remained just as Malik remembered, yet he himself could not have been more different. They stared at him as much as he stared at them, everyone trying to reconcile the person they had become with the person they had been.

But the faces that were not there haunted him even more than the ones that were. The victims of the plague were being isolated in a separate part of the mountain, and it seemed every hour someone new broke into blood-flecked coughs. Their crops destroyed, their villages decimated, and now their loved ones diseased—Malik's people had suffered so much. Even if he and Karina performed the ritual, the trauma of these tragedies would echo through history for generations to come.

The minutes ticked by, each one grinding what was left of Malik's calm into dust. He had no way of knowing exactly how the diviner women were treating Karina—their methods were a sacred secret even to other Eshrans, divine knowledge supposedly gifted to his people by the gods they had worshipped before the Zirani had imposed the Alignment system on them.

Malik did not know who these gods were or if they even existed, but he hoped with every fiber of his being that they were benevolent, for Karina's life lay in their hands now.

Though all Malik wanted to do was sit outside the tent until Karina was released, the villagers had other plans. Less than an hour into his vigil, a group of men holding makeshift weapons came up to him, clearly the self-appointed protectors of the camp, and told him to come for he had been summoned by the elders.

They took him to a war room in a tent toward the back of the cavern, tucked between a ring of amethyst stalagmites. Every Eshran village was led by nine elders—one for each of the nine clans—but he only saw six of Oboure's here. His stomach turned over to imagine the last three buried beneath the crush of the land-slide or eaten alive by locusts.

The leaders of Oboure leveled their steely gazes on Malik, and to his horror, he began to shake. The last time he'd been alone with these men, they had beaten him within an inch of his life, trying to chase the magic from his body. They had very nearly succeeded too. His terror blurred their faces until he saw Farid in each one, ready to snap his bones for daring to not be what they wanted him to be.

The oldest of the men, Elder Addo, spoke first. "You have caused us a great deal of trouble, young man, for not only have you brought the Zirani princess into our sanctuary, our scouts report that teams of soldiers began swarming the valley this morning. Exactly who are you, and what evil have you brought to our door?"

It was an effort for Malik to parse the man's words through his fog of terror, but soon the meaning became clear.

The elders didn't recognize him. They had held him hostage for weeks, given him scars both mental and physical, and yet not a single one knew who he was.

"Don't you recognize me?" he asked. "Do you not remember Rahila Hilali? What you did to her son?"

There came several seconds of puzzled silence, and then Elder Addo's eyes widened. "By Kotoko, I . . . I remember you. Mansa?"

"Malik," he said flatly. There was something almost hilarious about the fact that not a day went by when Malik did not think about what these men had done to him, yet he wasn't even important enough for them to remember his name. "I was accused of practicing witchcraft, and you spent weeks trying to chase it out of me."

Elder Addo coughed awkwardly. "We are here to discuss not matters of the past, but matters of the present. Frankly, the fact that you are one of our own makes your actions even more concerning. Do you realize how much danger you've put us in by bringing Princess Karina here?"

Malik hated that even after all these years, his instinct was to fall to his knees and beg forgiveness. Of course he had known that Farid would come after them, but he still did not regret bringing Karina to safety.

"Why were you traveling with the princess to begin with?" demanded an elder so short his legs dangled off the edge of his stool. "What are you to her, and what is she to you?"

The most hated people among the Eshrans were those who had turned traitor and sided with the Zirani during the occupation. Malik could see the elders' imaginations running through all manner of sordid situations that might have led him to be alone with the princess for so long, and he felt dirty, shameful, at the implication that he had chosen to be her plaything over his own people.

"I owe her a great debt," he said. "The spirits of my ancestors would not let me rest if anything happened to her before I could repay it."

Heat rose to Malik's face as the leering looks continued. Elder Addo clicked his tongue. "In any case, perhaps it is not too late to turn this situation to our advantage. The princess of Ziran will make for a fine bargaining chip."

Malik bit back a snarl. He hadn't come this far to hand Karina over to a new prison. "There is no bargaining with Farid. He'll smile his way through any negotiation, then cut you down the second your backs are turned."

"You do not tell us how to run our people," said the man.

"Now that she is here, the princess's fate is ours to decide, as is yours. We will use both of you as we see fit to protect this place."

This was where Malik was meant to play the prodigal son, quivering with gratitude for the simple fact that these men had not killed him on sight. He was supposed to stand to the side and let the elders decide his fate, and anything he said against them would be taken as harm of the highest order, even if he was right.

But their plan to negotiate with Farid was foolish at best and completely suicidal at worst. None of these men knew what it was like to deal with true magic, the kind that took without remorse and understood only bargains and power. They'd be nothing but blood on stone once Farid was done with them.

"N-No," said Malik, and though he stumbled on the word, it still rang clear through the cave. "You can't do that."

Elder Addo sneered at him. "So my suspicions were correct. Tell me, what has the princess given you to make you turn your back on your kin? Riches? Does she let you warm her bed?"

Malik swallowed thickly, the quiet intimacy of the night before warming through his veins. "No one here has the power to face Farid besides her. If you give her up to him, you are dooming us all."

"What do you propose we do then about the thousands of soldiers marching toward us as we speak? What plan do you have to arm our people for battle, or stock enough food to help us withstand a siege?" When Malik did not reply, Elder Addo shook his head. "I never thought I'd see the day that a self-respecting son of Eshra would allow himself to be a Zirani royal's paramour. If you wish to be a traitor, then you will be dealt with as such."

Malik's chest constricted with memories of too-small spaces and bloody beatings. The nightmares of his childhood had never left; they had been here, waiting to remind him that no matter how hard he tried to change, he could never escape the way the world saw him.

But as the elders stared at him, smug in their certainty that they had him under their control, something within Malik shifted. He wasn't a child anymore, no matter how these men tried to make him feel like one. And he wasn't alone either, not with the Faceless King stirring inside him, reminding him that he had faced down far worse than the elders and survived.

Malik had made more mistakes than he could name, but they had taught him how strong he was. How no matter how many times the world knocked him down, he always found a way to get up again.

Farid hadn't given him that. Even his magic hadn't given him that. Malik had given himself that, and he wasn't going to let these men take it away.

"Do you remember how old I was when my family left me in your care?" Malik asked. "I was six. I was a child away from home for the first time, and I was scared, and you were supposed to help me. Instead you beat me until I could barely stand and made me terrified of my own shadow."

"What we did is what our people have done for generations to ward off evil," said Elder Addo.

"What you did was cruel. Just because it is tradition does not make it any less so. You hurt me and never took any responsibility for it." Malik realized that he was now taller than most of these men. It was hard to be scared of someone when you were looking down on them.

"Yet despite all you did to me, you never realized the truth— the accusations were right. I could commune with spirits. I could weave things into being simply because I wanted them to exist. What if I told you I could conjure riches unlike anything you could possibly imagine? More wealth than any person in our village has ever seen?"

Fat sacks of gold dropped from above, the clang of the coins hitting the ground deafening. The elders quaked, drowning alive in a pool of their own greed.

"And what if I told you that I could conjure your worst nightmares? Each and every thing you have ever feared, brought to life before your very eyes?"

Just as the men reached the coins, they transformed into golden panthers that circled them, hissing in their faces.

"Sorcerer!" the men screamed.

"The proper term is ulraji," Malik corrected.

Once more he felt the well of power he had dipped into when he had cast the illusion of pain over Dedele. It would be so easy to break these men the same way they had broken him. For a heartbeat, Malik imagined doing exactly that. After all, he was the descendant of a king; as far as status was concerned, he outranked them. He could show them a pain that would make what they'd done to him look like child's play.

But as Malik looked at their frightened faces, he found that where the sharpest part of his anger had once been, there was now only a detached calm. What did these men matter compared to the horrors he'd already won against?

With a flick of his wrist, Malik released the illusion.

"I'm not going to hurt you, because I don't want to hurt you," he said, wishing his mother and grandmother could see him now. "I never want to do to anyone what you did to me. But I am no longer someone for you to control. I am not yours, and I never will be again."

The elders cowered. Satisfied that his point had been made, Malik began to turn away before pausing and turning back.

"By the way, I would very much appreciate it if sleeping arrangements were made for me and the princess," he said, and the elders nodded along like a group of bobbing birds. Let them think he and Karina were lovers.

They didn't need to know just how badly he wished that rumor were true.

Great Mother help him, what had he done?

It would not be long before word of what had happened in the elders' tent reached the rest of the settlement, and so Malik spent the next hour huddled away in a corner with his head tucked between his knees, trying not to panic his way into a coma.

He had faced down the elders. Not just faced them down—he had threatened them. During normal times, that would have gotten his entire family kicked out of the village. There was going to be some kind of punishment for this—he had to go back and beg their forgiveness—

You have done nothing you need to apologize for, said Idir. *Raise your head. You did well.*

Malik pressed at his eyes with his palms, willing the nausea to settle. "Am I imagining things, or did you just praise me?"

I believe I did. The end of the world must be addling us both.

Malik let out a dry laugh. Now that he and the obosom had each seen the other at their absolute lowest, it was hard not to be grateful for his presence. How odd to find such comfort in a supernatural creature with no understanding of human morality.

And Malik did not regret what he'd done, even if his nerves tried to convince him otherwise. The child he'd been had deserved to have someone stand up for him, and he would gladly do it again if it meant no one else would ever go through what he'd gone through.

Once he was certain the elders weren't sending a team of warriors to throw him off the side of the mountain, Malik went to check on Karina. He was almost to the diviners' tent when someone grabbed him by the shoulder. He whirled on them, ready to craft whatever illusion he needed to get them to leave him alone, then stopped cold.

The woman in front of him was short, the top of her head barely reaching the bottom of Malik's chin. Her red headscarf framed a tired face made older than it truly was from lines born of a lifetime of hardship. Yet there was an elegant bearing to the tilt of her head and the steady fire of her gaze. Malik couldn't breathe, afraid that any movement might shatter this moment, but his fears blossomed into awed disbelief when the woman cupped his cheek, tears streaming down her face.

"Mama!"

40

Karina

The Dancing Seal was one of those establishments that was both older and dirtier than it had any right to be, with a questionable layer of grime covering every visible surface as well as the staff. However, the food was great and the entertainment even better, which was what had brought Karina to the restaurant near the outer wall of Ziran.

As Aminata sulked beside her, Karina kept her eyes trained on the musician currently commanding the crowd, a stout, oud-playing bard with a mustache so perfectly coiled that it had to be fake. Appearance aside, the man had skill, and from the easy way he swaggered around the circular stage in the center of the room, he knew it.

The audience for the evening was comprised mostly of travelers and merchants, their faces lined from years trekking the unforgiving desert roads. In the chatter of the crowd, Karina recognized Kensiya, one of the languages of the Arkwasian people from the jungles north of Ziran; T'hoga, a language spoken on the East-water savanna, and even the occasional word in Darajat screamed at frightened Eshran servers. Every major group in Sonande was represented.

But best of all . . . best of all . . .

Karina inhaled sharply, startling Aminata beside her. "What's wrong?" asked the maid.

"This isn't right. This already happened," she said, but her friend just stared at her as if she'd lost all sense. Karina pointed toward the stage. "That man is actually Hyena, and she's currently hiding *The Tome of the Dearly Departed*—"

But she stopped, for the mustached bard was gone, and the stage was now empty.

"Wait, what's wrong!" cried Aminata as Karina jumped to her feet and pushed her way through the throngs of the crowd, her head spinning. No, this wasn't right. There was someone she was supposed to be with, someone who had given everything to keep her safe. She had to get back to him, except she could not remember who he was.

Karina burst through the doors of the Dancing Seal and into the halls of Ksar Alahari. Night had fallen, and the palace was in complete disarray.

Well, perhaps disarray was not the best word. Even at its most chaotic, Ksar Alahari was nothing less than stately and well organized, run by a methodical system Karina hadn't bothered to learn.

It was also empty. There was no reason the palace should be this quiet so close to Solstasia. Where were the servants running in every direction, yelling that more pillows were needed in the room of this ambassador or that onions had yet to arrive in that kitchen? Where were the groups of servants scrubbing furiously at intricate zellij-tile depictions of crimson sunbursts and screaming gryphons lining the walls or at the mighty black-and-white alabaster arches draped with garlands?

At least Baba was here, though Karina did not know where he'd come from. She could have walked with him for hours. His pace was neither too fast nor too slow, and as they strolled, he hummed a familiar melody she could not place.

"What is that song?" she asked and, oh, how she'd missed her father's lopsided grin.

"Just an old lullaby. I used to sing it to you all the time to sleep, though you were the only baby I've ever known that actually grew more awake when someone sang to them."

They were in her old nursery now, and her father was here, holding on to her hand, but he was also across the room cradling her infant self to his chest, pacing around in a circle as he sang that same low song again. Baba must have noticed the way she subtly checked the room, for he said, "Your mother rarely joined us for bedtime. It wasn't quite her strong suit."

"Mothering wasn't quite her strong suit," she muttered, then flushed with shame. She never wanted to put Baba in the uncomfortable position of choosing between her and her mother.

"It wasn't," he agreed, for all the love in the world wasn't enough to make a person into someone they could not be.

He pulled her into the courtyard where the Solstasia Eve comet viewing had happened, dancers twirling through the space and booming laughter drowning out the cheerful music.

"Karina's here!" someone called, and the party cheered. It seemed everyone she had ever cared for was here tonight—Commander Hamidou and Aminata, Ife, Caracal, and Afua, and so many more. Even Dedele gave her an apologetic nod. Dozens of silver-haired people milled about—the Alaharis of old, the grandparents and cousins and family she should have had. All of them here to welcome her.

And yet she found herself scanning for one face in particular—a boy, yes, with wide black eyes and a nervous demeanor, what was his *name*—

"The guest of honor has finally arrived." Tunde stepped before her, smiling that crooked grin of his. Karina let him grab her by the hand and pull her around the courtyard, buoyed by the pure joy of having all her loved ones together in one place. She felt like dancing, and she knew that if she did the whole room would dance with her, and they would never stop, for there was no reason to stop when they were all alive and together and here.

"If you want to dance, then dance." Tunde put his hands on her waist and pulled her in close. "And if you don't want to dance, don't. Here, there's time enough for all the things you could not do back home."

Karina's body unwound under his touch, so comforting, so familiar. "You can stay," he whispered, his breath warm against her ear. How many nights had they spent pressed together just like this until she had made it difficult because causing problems was what she did best? But it didn't have to be difficult. She could melt into him just as she had the last night he'd been alive, forget about everything except the places where his body fit against hers.

And they could take all the time in the world, for there was nothing here *but* time—sweet, glorious, unending time. She could stay with Tunde as long as she pleased, and when she grew tired of him, she could gossip for hours with Aminata, discuss theories of magic with Afua, make amends with Dedele.

But . . .

Someone was missing. Someone else besides the boy she could not remember.

Karina pulled away from Tunde as gently as she could. "I need to find my mother."

He gave her the saddest of smiles. "Even in death I can't keep your attention on me," he said, and she gently kissed his brow.

"You deserved someone who loved as fiercely and deeply as you did. I'm sorry that person wasn't me."

Karina left him before she could watch his heart break for a second time.

The party was in a full frenzy, but the Kestrel was nowhere to be found. Karina's instincts took her not to the Marble Room or even to her mother's garden, but to a small wing of the residential quarters that opened above one of the dozens of courtyards. Her mother stood at the railing, gazing down at a young Karina, Hanane, and Farid playing among the plants. The walls were angled so that she could see everything below, but no one could see her. Karina wondered exactly what had happened to her mother that she felt she could not openly watch her own children play.

"Oh, Karina. You're not supposed to be here," the Kestrel said, and as ever, neither her voice nor her face betrayed any emotion. And on some level Karina knew that this was happening inside her own head, and how sad it was that even in the world of her dreams, she could not conjure a warm and open version of her mother.

The little Karina down below shrieked in delight as Farid and Hanane tickled her mercilessly. She remembered this day. In only a few minutes, Hanane would grow bored of the game, and Farid would grow fretful from Hanane's boredom, and Karina would grow upset for them both, and then her power would overflow for the very first time.

"You were watching us," she said, and the Kestrel said nothing. Karina had been too young at the time to notice it, but now she saw the embers of Farid's future obsession blazing through what she'd assumed had been an innocent childhood interaction. Even back then he'd looked at Hanane with a possessive glint in his eye, a king surveying his lands and finding them to his liking.

The Kestrel left the balcony and Karina trailed behind her, same as she always had. They passed the room where the queen had had Prince Hakim whipped for allegedly poisoning Farid. They passed an older Farid curled over an ancient tome, filling his head with poisonous ideas a thousand years gone. The warnings had been baked into these very walls, and still no one had intervened.

"Why didn't you do more?" Karina cried bitterly, and instead of answering, the Kestrel threw open a set of doors. The mural of their family's history stretched in front of them as far as Karina could see. But instead of stopping at the story of Bahia, the mural continued, a thousand years of history ending with the Kestrel's untimely ascension to the throne and her even more untimely death. The area beyond her mother's story was completely bare.

The place where Karina's story would one day go.

Her mother placed a hand against the portion of the mural that depicted the birth of Hanane. "When it came to my family, all I ever saw was what I wanted to see," said the queen, and for the first time in her life, Karina heard her mother's voice waver. "I wanted so badly for nothing to harm you three, I convinced myself nothing ever could. I refused to even consider the possibility that one of you might hurt the others."

Her mother turned to her. "My time in this world has ended. It is time for a new queen to carry on the legacy that was given to me by my ancestors before me and to them by their ancestors before them."

"A legacy of what exactly?" challenged Karina. "Winning a war none of us were alive for? What about the things our family has done to Malik and his people—who carries that? How can we claim the victories of our ancestors and not claim the atrocities too?"

Karina stepped forward, the words spilling desperately from her. "All my life I was taught that unlike every other power in Sonande, Ziran was built on a foundation of justice. But though our foundations may have been pure, what grew from it was rotten. The Ziran of today is a corruption of the ideals we claim to hold."

Karina waited for the punishment, for never in her life had she spoken to her mother in this way. But the queen just smiled.

"What are you going to do about it?"

"What?"

"I said, what are you going to do about it?"

The Kestrel gestured at the thousand years of history around them. A thousand years of battles and torment and oppression, yes, but also of revolution. Of hope. Of one person realizing the world could be better, and doing everything they could to make it so.

"Have you forgotten who you are? Have you forgotten who you are of? The ancestors are our roots, keeping us grounded. I am the trunk, keeper of the connection. And you, my darling girl, you are the branches, you are the leaves, you are every good and green thing. You can bloom and bloom, if only you give yourself the chance."

One by one, the tiles of the mosaic twisted into buds and petals, life growing from the remains of pain and death.

The Kestrel knelt down and pressed her lips against Karina's brow. Flowers filled her lungs, filled her blood, the seed of her ancestors taking root inside her. "A new queen must rise."

Her mother took a step back. The path now extended both in front of and behind Karina, both ends mired in shadow.

"You can go forward, or you can go back," said the Kestrel.

"Which one will return me to the world of the living?"

"One will take you home. One will not. Deep down, you already know which is which."

Karina threw her arms around her mother's neck and nestled against her like she'd never been able to after the fire. She savored every inch of this moment, for she knew it would not come again.

"Do you need me to show you the way?" asked Baba, for he had returned, and when Karina shook her head, his smile grew sad. "Ah, I forgot. You're a big girl now. Big girls don't need their fathers to lead them back home, do they?"

Karina wanted to scream no, for there would never come a time when she did not need her father. For as long as she lived, part of her would always be that small girl trailing behind him, knowing nothing could harm her as long as he was there.

But she was so much more than that little girl. And all the people she had been and that she was becoming were pulling her forward.

Pulling her home.

Karina flung her arms around her father, surprised to realize he wasn't that much taller than she was now. He hugged her back.

"Promise you'll come back before the lights turn on," he murmured as she pulled away, taking in for the last time the faces of the first people who had ever loved her.

"I promise."

The first thing Karina noticed upon waking was that her fever was gone and her thoughts no longer felt like they were slogging through tar to get to her. The second thing she noticed was that she was so ravenous that she might have eaten the thin blanket she was wrapped in, were it not for the two faces that swam into focus.

"Caracal! Ife!"

The older of the two zawenji grinned down at her, the left side of his face shiny with newly healed burns. Ife sat beside him, thick bags under their eyes. Karina bit the inside of her cheek to check that this wasn't some sort of plague-induced fever dream. The blood on her tongue confirmed that it wasn't.

"You get hurt a lot. You should stop doing that," said the Moon-Aligned zawenji. "If you'd gotten here even a day later, you would have been too sick for my magic to help. On a related note, don't expect to have full use of your colon for the next four to six weeks—no hugging! I don't like hugging!"

Karina immediately let them go, tears streaming down their face. "I'm so sorry, I'm just . . . I thought I was never going to see you again."

Caracal patted her head, a gesture that on any other day Karina might have bitten his hand for. "Seems like you're stuck with us for a little longer, princess."

"But how did you even get here? And what about Afua . . ."

Her words died at the pained look on her friends' faces. "We don't know," Caracal said softly. "After she triggered the enchantment that moves Doro Lekke to a new location, we woke up back by the chasm on our own. We searched for days, but there was no sign of her. No corpse, nothing. She was just . . . gone. Eventually we had to move on without her."

Karina had known it was a hope beyond hope that Afua might have found a way past the enchantment that now bound her to the Sanctum, but grief washed over her anew at the confirmation. At the very least they knew she was not dead, but what kind of life would Afua have now that her existence was tied to that place?

"Our first plan was to stay in the Sanctum until things got better out here. But the butterflies really didn't like that," explained Ife. "They started biting—did you know butterflies could bite, because I didn't and it turns out it hurts a lot—until we followed them through the tunnels and they opened up here in the mountains, which was when the Eshrans caught us and now we're here." Ife scrunched up their nose. "The Eshrans really don't like magic, but they like dying even less, which is the only reason they haven't killed me yet."

The only thing Karina believed in less than divine intervention was coincidence. But in that moment, she didn't care which had brought her and her friends back together, only that it had. She wrapped an arm around Caracal's neck, and after a moment of hesitation, the former Sentinel hugged her back before awkwardly pulling away.

"I'm sorry for everything I said back in Doro Lekke," she said. "Especially to you, Ife, that was unkind of me. And thank you—for everything."

Ife nodded and Caracal gave an embarrassed half-shrug. However, as grateful as Karina was that they were here, there was still one more face she needed to see.

"You shouldn't be on your feet yet!" Ife scolded as Karina threw off her blanket and hobbled out of the tent.

Malik. She needed Malik.

She found him in the center of the settlement, speaking to a large crowd in Darajat. Karina hovered at a distance, noting how different the boy was here compared to Ziran. His voice was lower in his native language, and though she could not understand what he was saying, she heard her name, "Solstasia," and "Farid" several times. Something had happened to him while she'd been recovering; he seemed lighter, as if some great weight that had been holding him down was now gone. He met her gaze, and the smile he gave her made Karina's legs go weak.

"Karina!" Malik immediately came to her side and checked her over, igniting a flurry of whispers from the crowd. "Are you all right? Does it hurt anywhere?" he asked in Zirani, and for the first time Karina wished she'd bothered to learn Darajat, if only so she could speak to him in his mother tongue as easily as he spoke hers.

"No, I feel fine." The Eshrans watched their interaction closely, more than a few with open contempt. Karina did not begrudge them their suspicion; after what her ancestors had done, it was a wonder that these people hadn't placed her head on a pike the moment she'd arrived.

Two women Karina recognized approached behind Malik.

"Fatima!" she exclaimed, and the old woman Karina had saved in the desert smiled warmly at her. Her daughter stood beside her, and now that she and Malik were side by side, Karina finally understood why the younger woman had seemed so familiar all those weeks ago. The resemblance was not in their features, but in the quiet yet steady way they both held themselves, how they both tilted their head to the side when they were deep in thought, and how their eyes shone when they smiled.

"You're Malik's mother," she said, and no doubt that if Hyena were there, the trickster would have been beside herself with laughter at the way fate had tied her to Malik once again.

"You can call me Rahila," said the younger woman. "I now owe you two debts: the first for saving my mother's life, and the second for bringing my son back to me. You have done more for me than words of gratitude can ever express."

The women and children Karina had saved in Tiru were dispersed throughout the crowd, and they nodded along with Rahila's words as they gazed up at Karina with open adoration. Warmth and embarrassment flooded through her.

"You don't have to thank me. It was the least I could do."

Malik shook his head. "The least you could have done was nothing, which is what most people would have done. Karina, my mother and grandmother are alive because of you." He gazed at her as if she was something wondrous to behold, when really she was only a girl who had seen something wrong and decided to do something about it.

At the front of the circle were six men who Karina assumed to be the leaders of this camp, and the oldest of them said something in Darajat that made Malik snap to attention. He quickly explained to Karina in Zirani, "Their scouts report that Farid is less than a day's ride from here, with an entire contingent of both regular soldiers and Sentinels. It doesn't seem like he knows this camp exists or that you and I are here, but he's blocked off each pass so that there's no way in or out of the valley without going through one of his checkpoints."

Gods, to think Farid had been so close behind her and Malik the entire time. If he had caught up to them when they had been vulnerable in the cave yesterday . . .

"How is the camp planning to handle this?" she asked.

"They're torn. A few of them want to stay hidden, in hopes he gives up and leaves without ever discovering this place, but they don't have enough food and water to last more than a few days. Some are suggesting we send a group of warriors to draw them away from one of the passes so the rest can escape through it. And our third option . . ." His eyes darkened. "They want to turn us over to him to try to negotiate for peace."

It was easy to tell from the hostile stares who around them

supported the latter idea. But Malik had subtly placed himself between Karina and the crowd, looking like he'd fight anyone who even tried to touch her. She placed a hand on his shoulder, imbuing the touch with her gratitude that he was willing to fight so hard for her, and his tension eased just a bit.

"What do you think we should do?" she whispered.

"I don't know. You and I might be able to make it through the blockades on our own, but if Farid finds this place, he won't hesitate to torture the people here to find out where we've gone."

Rahila clung to her son, her expression hardened with a mother's fierceness. "You are not leaving my side again," she declared. "Wherever you go, we will go."

It was a beautiful sentiment, but Karina and Malik both knew that bringing his mother and grandmother along would only slow them down, though she would never ask that he leave them behind. And Malik was right—if Farid thought for even a moment that these people had aided their escape, he would rain destruction down on what was left of these villagers. They couldn't stay, but they couldn't leave the camp undefended either.

It felt like all Karina had done since Solstasia began was run. Run first from her duties as queen when her mother had died, then away from Ziran to save herself after the coup. She was tired of running; let her face whatever was to come with her head held high. Let her die knowing she had done everything she could, even if it wasn't enough.

And there was still the matter of the Rite of Renewal and the blood oath. With or without Farid, they would still need to perform the ritual to avoid all the disasters . . .

"Malik, what were the four omens that followed the Rite of Resurrection again?" Karina asked slowly.

"The locusts, the earthquakes, the plague, and then the beast."

"We've dealt with the first three—where's the fourth?"

"Maybe the beast is off terrorizing some other unlucky bastards on the other side of Sonande?" guessed Caracal, who had come with Ife to join their impromptu meeting. Karina shook her head. So far each omen had begun around wherever she and Farid were, as if the world knew they were the ones responsible for the first ritual. If the beast was going to appear anywhere, it would be here.

As ever, Karina felt the desperate urge to take any sort of action burning within her. But taking advantage of her recklessness was how Farid had outmaneuvered her time and time again. She forced herself to imagine their current situation like a game board. There was Farid, with his Sentinels and his army and Hanane, holding the advantage on one side. She, Malik, her friends, and the Eshrans were on the other. Farid might have greater numbers, but they had an intimate knowledge of the terrain and the element of surprise.

Karina reorganized the pieces in her mind, trying to uncover a strategy that ended with them all alive. However, it was her ancestor's words that made the final piece click into place.

Remember who needs you most.

The lich's face—no, not the lich. *Hanane*'s face bloomed across her mind. Hanane, who had had both her life and her death stolen from her by this man. Hanane, who had been screaming for help for years, but Karina had been too focused on her own feelings of inferiority to see it.

The ancestors had never wanted Karina to save Sonande. They wanted her to save Hanane.

"I'm not the one destined to take down Farid. Hanane is," she said breathlessly.

Her companions shared uneasy glances. "Is Hanane strong enough to face down Farid's magic?" asked Malik.

"Hanane might not have magic, but she's never been powerless. Besides, she was brought back by the Rite of Resurrection. A spark of that power might still be inside her." That would explain the thing Karina had seen swimming in her sister's eyes back at Ksar Nirri. Any power the ritual might have given her would be something even older than zawenji or ulraji magic, something Farid's powers would never be able to nullify. "If I can get to her, I might be able to coax it out."

"Let's say your sister does have some kind of secret power just waiting to be unleashed. What about the army? Is she supposed to take them down too?" asked Caracal.

Karina's eyes slid from the scared faces surrounding her to the glittering amethyst hanging above their heads.

"I have an idea about how we could defeat the Zirani army with minimal casualties. But it'll involve revealing this camp."

Karina quickly explained the idea to Malik, who looked at her as if she'd lost her mind but dutifully translated it for those who only spoke Darajat. A flutter of unease ran through the villagers, and a particularly bold young girl called out in heavily accented Zirani, "How do we know this isn't a trap?"

"What kind of queen plots against her own army?" another voice chimed in.

Several shouts of agreement rang through the crowd. Malik tensed beside Karina, ready to jump to her defense, but she put a hand on his arm and shook her head.

"It's all right," she said, low enough for only Malik to hear. "I won't ask you to choose between your people and me."

Karina's ancestors would have told her to assert her dominance. She was a queen—she had the power to make these people do as she commanded, whether they wished to or not.

But she had more forebears than just the conquerors and the queens—ancestors from the generations before Bahia's uprising, ancestors who had known the violence of oppression and subjugation, same as the Eshrans. It was the knowledge of those ancestors that told Karina what she needed to do.

A new queen must rise, her mother had told her, and so Karina knelt, her forehead pressed against the dirt in the humblest apology she knew how to make.

"I know my words only carry so much weight because of who I am and what my people have done, but from the bottom of my heart, I am sorry for each and every wrong we have committed against you," she said to the gathered crowd. "I deserve your judgment and your disdain for the pain my family has inflicted. I know these words will not bring back all that you've lost, but I offer them all the same."

The stone bit into her palms, but Karina did not lift her head.

"And I selfishly make one request—I ask not for your forgiveness or even your respect, but for your trust. Trust that I will do everything in my power to help your people survive this threat. I swear this to you not only on my grave, but on my mother's and father's as well. Let me begin to make things right."

Alaharis didn't kneel. It was one of the few lessons Karina had taken to heart—it was the very reason Grandmother Bahia had founded Ziran to begin with. But there was a difference between kneeling because someone else had forced you to and kneeling out of respect. All Karina could do now was pray the Eshrans would see the sincerity in her words and aid her in this mad last stand.

After a minute that felt too long and like no time at all, one of the elders finally said, "Rise, Karina Alahari."

Karina did so. The Eshrans now regarded her not with warmth, but a kind of grudging respect. Malik's gaze felt heaviest of all, and she could not bring herself to look at him out of fear that his people might see her declaration as motivated solely by her feelings for him.

"Tell us more of your plan, princess," said Fatima, and Karina took in the wide space, the frightened people, the lack of exits. She grabbed a handful of gems and placed them on the ground in front of her, strategically arranging them to resemble the entrance to their hideaway and the mountain pass in front.

"Here's what I think we should do."

41

Malik

Karina's plan was wild, terrifying, and quite possibly the most reckless thing Malik had ever heard in his entire life.

It was also the only chance any of them might have to walk away from this alive.

They spent the next several hours going over the plan with the villagers and making sure each person knew where they needed to be and when. Malik stayed by Karina's side the entire time, translating for her at increasingly harried speeds and helping her understand the terrain, what skills the villagers had, and which weapons they had at their disposal. He helped Karina craft a simple letter telling Farid where to meet her come dawn, then pretended not to notice the way her hands shook as she passed it to the messenger.

Soon the preparations were complete, and the camp descended into tense silence as everyone attempted to get some rest during the longest night of their lives. Karina had returned to the diviners' tent at the insistence of that Moon-Aligned zawenji friend of hers, and Malik had joined Mama and Nana in their small corner of the cave to share a meal and stories of all that had happened since they'd last seen one another.

He told them everything. Even though his voice shook, he told them about how he'd unlocked his powers after Nadia had been taken hostage. How he had killed Driss and tortured Dedele. How he had come so close to ending it all in Talafri after Leila and Nadia had abandoned him, and how he couldn't promise he'd never feel that way again. Malik laid every dark, broken corner of his soul bare for the only family he had left.

When he was done, he lifted his head, ready to receive the reproach he deserved for becoming even worse than the monster of a father who had sired him.

He wasn't ready for his mother to gather him in her arms, her tears falling down her face onto his. "My baby," she sobbed. "My baby, my baby."

Over and over again, only those two words. Malik choked back his own tears. How could she forgive him, how could she still love him after all he'd done wrong?

He must have said those last words out loud, for Mama cupped his face in her hands. "Because you're still here. And if you're here, you can still make things right."

He could practically see Idir's smirking face in his mind's eye. *You were ready to rip those elders limb from limb, but a kind word from your mother leaves you blubbering.*

Instead of responding, Malik let his mother's warmth envelop him for what might possibly be the last time.

"Your father once told me that his grandfather claimed to see visions," said Mama when his tears finally dried. "He took out his fear of them on his children, who then took it out on their children. Up until the last day I saw him, even the slightest hint of the supernatural would send him into a violent rage."

It was the first time Malik's mother had spoken of his father since he'd left them, and Malik could tell how much the words cost her. Though he would never forgive the man for what he'd done to them, Malik mourned the way this world gave its fathers and sons no outlet for their traumas besides violence and anger. He swore to himself that the cycle of parent hurting child in his family would end with him, even if it took him the rest of his life to figure out how.

Malik sneaked a glance at the diviners' tent, which Nana did not miss. "Go, see to your princess. Leave us gossipy old hens to our whispers," she said, and though Malik knew he was giving the rumor mill fuel to last several more years—if they all survived that long—he gave his mother and grandmother one last kiss on the cheeks before going to see Karina.

He found her sorting through the food they'd be sending off with the children, the elderly, and everyone else too weak to fight tomorrow. When he offered to relieve her of the duty, she shook her head.

"I can't sleep anyway, so I may as well make myself useful," she said.

Malik joined her, and they rationed out the limited supplies of fruit, dried meat, and cassava tubers in companionable silence. From the way Karina hummed so full of life, it was hard to believe that just a day ago she had been inches from death.

"So do you carry every girl you meet up a mountain, or was that just for me?" she finally asked. Even now Malik didn't know how he'd survived that climb, and he doubted he ever would. It had also been only about a third of the mountain, but now didn't seem the time to nitpick.

"Only for you," he said softly. "I'd only ever do something like that for you."

Surprise flashed in Karina's eyes, and she looked away quickly. For once, he had flustered her instead of the other way around. So this was what that felt like. "This is the first time I ever touched a yam in my life—and hopefully the last," she said. "They're so hairy. Why are they so hairy?"

Malik picked up a yam and ran the bristles of it down her arm, eliciting a shriek from her. Karina threw a melon at his head, which he expertly dodged as he let out his first true laugh in . . . he couldn't remember the last time he'd laughed, actually.

The laughter died when he remembered just what was awaiting them come morning. As a child, Malik had wanted to be like a hero in a folktale, going on adventures and battling monsters. But now all he wanted was to share a bowl of lemon juice and orange slices with his sisters. He wanted more laughs with Karina, more kisses, more nights spent sitting side by side doing nothing at all. He wanted to live, and he wished he'd realized it before they reached the point where that was no longer possible.

"Aren't you scared?" he asked, and the smile fell from her face.

"I'm terrified," she admitted. "If I'm wrong about this, and I've put what's left of your village at risk for no reason . . ."

Malik laced his fingers through hers. "This will work," he promised. She leaned her head on his shoulder, and Malik truly considered kissing her right then and there, nosy grandmothers and judgmental elders be damned. He imagined kissing her until she forgot every worry that weighed her down, imagined feeling her hands pressing against the planes of his stomach and going lower, until they finished what they had begun that night in the dream by the river.

"I miss him," she said suddenly, smashing Malik's fantasy to bits. "It's so twisted, isn't it? I hate Farid and I miss him and I don't know how I can feel both at the same time, but I do."

Malik let out a sigh. "Farid knows how to give people exactly what they want. He reaches inside you and twists your mind with his words until you doubt everything you thought you believed about yourself. It's what he did to Hanane. It's what he did to me. You are no more at fault for falling for it than anyone else."

He looked down at his and Karina's intertwined hands. "But nobody held a knife against my neck and made me do what I did. Every awful thing I did for Farid was my choice, and no one else's. And even then, after all I'd done for him, when I was at my lowest, he was ready to throw me away."

Karina cupped Malik's face with her free hand. Malik leaned into the touch, and he wondered if there would ever come a time when he would not close his eyes and see every line of her face awash in purple gem light like it was now. "Farid is wrong," said Karina. "I'm so happy you're still here. The world is better with you in it."

This moment felt so delicate and fragile, a tiny dot in the grand scheme of the world but the culmination of something that had been brewing for centuries.

Actually, no. Perhaps their histories were intertwined by forces beyond their control, but this right now was simply him and

Karina. No one and nothing else mattered.

"Thank you," he murmured.

"Thank you for supporting this absolutely mad plan."

"There is no one I would rather rush into a foolhardy and meaningless death with than you."

For Malik, the worst part about his constant anxiety was feeling like an afterthought within his own life. All too often it felt like every voice mattered but his, and he was so exhausted trying to sort through what everyone else could possibly want or need, he had no energy left to discern what was truly for him.

But this certainty he felt as he promised to aid Karina, this rightness that for once what both his head and his heart wanted were completely in sync . . . Malik wasn't sure how long it was going to last. But as long as it did, he was going to follow it.

He looped one of her braids through his fingers, taking more than a bit of pleasure at the way her eyes darkened. "This hair is still too damn long," she said with a frustrated sigh.

"I can help you with that," Malik offered. At her incredulous look, he added, "I'm no expert, but I've cut both my sisters' hair before."

It wasn't exactly a sweeping endorsement of his skills, but Karina still turned her back toward him, her braids spilling in a river down her back. His heart blocking his throat, Malik began removing the filigree and the gems. Once her hair was completely free, he summoned the spirit blade to his hand, and paused.

"How short would you like it?" he asked, his fingers grazing the back of her neck as he gathered the first handful.

"I don't care," she said, and Malik wondered if he imagined the breathlessness in her voice, as if she too was imagining his hands pressed against her in a different context. "Whatever you feel is best."

He nodded, even though she was not looking at him, raised the blade, and made the first cut. Soft silver curls fell away around them as he worked. He was trying to get it to resemble how it had looked during Solstasia, but he overestimated how much needed to go, and by the time he was done, Karina's hair was a silver halo around her head, reaching just below her ears.

Panic pooled in Malik's gut as she reached to touch the blunt ends. "I cut it too short, didn't I? I'm so, so sorry, maybe someone can fix it—"

"It's perfect." Karina turned back to him, and the girl he saw now looked nothing like Hanane, yet everything like herself. "It's perfect," she said again.

With that they returned to work, the small light of each other's company keeping the darkness at bay for that much longer.

42

Karina

The Zirani army poured into the ruined valley that had once been Oboure right after dawn, just as Siwa's scouts had said they would. From their vantage point near the top of the mountain, Karina watched as a small party of riders, flanked by Sentinels, pulled away from the main column, veering quickly in their direction.

Her brother had answered her call.

The camp sprang into action, their own warriors rushing down the mountainside to engage the Zirani army at one of the blockades, while Ife and Siwa led the elderly, the children, and everyone else who could not fight down a path on the other side, where they should be safe from the worst of the battle.

Dressed in traditional Eshran horse rider's garb of a long slitted dress over woven pants, her hair shorter than she'd ever worn it and her knuckles tight around the algaita, Karina began to shake. Last night the idea of trying to spark the dormant power inside Hanane and turn it against Farid had seemed possible. But clearly she should have run when she'd had the chance, foolish, foolish, she was leading them all to early graves—

Someone touched her shoulder, and she looked up to see Malik, resplendent in his own black-and-gold native robe, looking down at her with an expression that made her want to pull him into one of the hidden corners of the mountain and keep him safe from whatever was about to happen. He summoned the scepter from his skin and handed it to her.

"Whatever happens, I'm with you until the end," he said. The nervous fluttering in Karina's chest calmed. Even if she couldn't believe in herself, she could believe in the fact that Malik believed in her.

They both understood at the same moment that this might be the last time they ever saw one another. As much as Malik deserved to confront Farid too for all the ways he'd hurt him, she needed him elsewhere for this plan to work.

"Karina, I—" he began, and that was all he managed to say before she kissed him, not caring that the entire camp was watching. Karina pushed into the kiss the strength of everything that had happened between them and everything that never would, and she felt from the way he melted against her that he was doing the same.

"Don't die," she ordered when they finally broke apart, and Malik kissed her brow one last time before he went to face his battle and she went to face hers.

The Rite of Resurrection had required fire for its sacrifice. The Rite of Renewal needed water.

That was why Karina had told Farid to meet her at dawn at the caldera on the very top of Mount Mirazzat. It was the coldest place in all Sonande save the Snowlands, and a layer of frost hardened the edges of the water and coated the light shrubbery dotting the rocky landscape. According to Malik, the Eshrans had a legend that this lake had been formed when the Great Mother had pressed her thumb onto the mountain and wept tears of joy for all she would create.

Farid crested over the ridge surrounding the caldera just after dawn. More than a dozen Sentinels flanked him on either side, and Hanane rode beside him, her face drawn and tight.

"You remain as punctual as ever," said Karina when he came to a stop less than ten feet away from her.

"It would not do to be late for such a momentous occasion." Farid's eyes swept across the caldera, likely checking to see if Karina was as alone as she'd promised she would be. "Where is my traitorous apprentice?"

Karina drew to mind the worst heartbreaks and betrayals of her life so that the hurt in her voice would sound genuine. "When he realized that he couldn't save me from the Rite of Renewal, he tucked his tail between his legs and ran."

As she spoke, she kept her eyes trained on Hanane. Her sister was a shadow of her former self, her shoulders slumped and her eyes unfocused. She didn't look ready to fight anyone, least of all the man who had made her this way.

Karina could practically see the wheels in Farid's mind turning, searching for the trickery in her words. But there was none, because Karina had been truthful when she had written to him that she was ready to perform the ritual.

And she was. Because if she was wrong about Hanane having the power needed to defeat Farid, then Karina was ready to die if it meant Sonande would be safe.

"If you truly mean what you wrote, then give me the scepter," he demanded. Karina obediently kicked it over to him.

. . . *the scepter to form the altar touched by gods.*

Farid took the scepter and used it to draw a series of glyphs in the rocky dirt at the edge of the caldera. Nkra crackled through the air as the scepter drew his magic from his body into the earth. The vision had shown Karina what the ritual looked like, but it had not prepared her for the absolute rush of power, like they were standing at the very edge of creation itself.

. . . *a song half-forgotten played on the flute lost to time.*

Without waiting for Farid to give the order, Karina put the algaita to her lips and played the song her father had sung to her when she'd hovered between life and death. A bright light like a small sun glowed from within the caldera, growing into crystalline pillars and arches not unlike the buildings formed of roots in Doro Lekke. Flat steps led to a circular dais at the center of the altar. Only once the last column of the crescent-shaped structure was complete did Karina lower the instrument and take in the stricken look on Hanane's face.

"Baba's lullaby," her sister whispered.

Karina nodded. "Remember how he used to sing it for us whenever we had a nightmare? And sometimes, after we were asleep, Mama would come and sing to us too. She wasn't nearly as talented as he was, but whenever she sang it I just felt so . . . loved."

Remember them, thought Karina. *Remember how they loved us. Remember the warrior they raised you to be.*

The shadows lurking behind Hanane's eyes grew bolder, and her expression shifted from distress to clarity. "That song . . . I haven't heard it in so long—"

Farid placed a claw-like hand on Hanane's shoulder, and the shadows dimmed. "No more talking. Get on with it," he snapped, and Karina wondered if the holy sanctity of this place would be besmirched if she punched him in the face.

But she wasn't here to fight Farid. She was here to save her sister.

. . . a psalm prayed near water that connects this world and the next.

Core-shaking power tore through Karina the moment her palms touched the dry earth. For a single moment, she was the mountain itself, ancient and immovable.

"I give this psalm to the ancestors who walked this land before me, carving a path so that I might follow," she said, and the words of the ritual entwined her body and spirit to this place until she could no longer tell one from the other. "I give this psalm to those who walk this land in tandem with me, learning the hard-won lessons of the past and righting the mistakes left behind. I give this psalm to those who will walk this land after me, who will look back on me as I look back on those before me and begin the cycle anew."

Even as Karina said the words, she realized how limiting it was to think in terms of ancestors and descendants when they were all one, connected by a line unbroken with no beginning and no end. Tears streamed down her face, matching the ones on Hanane's.

"I give this psalm to my sister, so that she may see the strength untold within her, and that she may cast away all who mean to dim her light."

Hanane was shaking now, but still she made no movement from Farid's side. Had Karina bet wrong? Did her sister not have what it took to stand up to Farid after all?

. . . and the soul of a queen, to bind it all together.

Stepping onto the dais felt like seeing the world for the very first time. Karina was no longer just a conduit for the magic but of it, and it was of her, the entire shining web that connected everything and everyone pulsing through this one point in time.

The water was calling to her now, sweeter than any song, and Karina knew it would embrace her as tightly as a lover, caress her as gently as a mother. Hundreds of years from now, the people would remember this queen who had made the ultimate sacrifice, and they would rejoice.

But Hanane wouldn't.

"I have one last request," Karina said, and the world seemed to still as she stared into Hanane's grief-stricken eyes.

"I want Hanane to deal the final blow. If I'm to die, let it be by my sister's hand."

43

Malik

Having spent so many years trying to avoid the Zirani army, Malik never would have dreamed that one day he would charge straight into their ranks.

But charge he did, on the back of another denzik, flanked on both sides by the fastest riders Eshra had to offer.

"Do you see Issam yet?" he called out to Caracal, who rode beside him. The former Sentinel terrified Malik, but Karina trusted the man, and that was enough for him.

Caracal, outfitted head to toe in more weapons than Malik could name, shook his head. "Not yet, but he's here. I know it."

Malik had been skeptical when Karina had first told him the enchantment that ruled the Sentinels could be broken. But Caracal was living proof. While Karina confronted Farid and Hanane at the caldera, Malik's role was to try to break Issam's enchantment so that he could call off the rest of the soldiers. If that did not work, then they would have to resort to their backup plan.

The strategy had sounded simple enough when Karina had explained it to him last night, but here, beneath the harsh light of morning, the task before him seemed impossible.

All wars are impossible until they are won, said the Faceless

King, and Malik let those words steel his fear into resolve as he and his riders continued down the mountain in search of their target.

They found Issam at the other end of the pass, overseeing the construction of a barricade that would block the Eshrans' only chance of escape. Somewhere deep inside the Sentinel commander was the Eshran boy who had been stolen from his homeland, and Malik wondered if any part of Issam was rebelling against the desecration he was ordering to his ancestral home. A glimpse of the man's true self had come through back at Ksar Nirri; Malik prayed that it remained close to the surface.

As soon as they spotted Issam, Caracal jumped from his denzik and let the wind carry him to his former teammate's side, while Malik hid with the other riders behind a boulder.

"Ready to finish what we started back at Doro Lekke, Issam?" Caracal roared. Fire flew past his head before the words were even out of his mouth.

As the mountainside grew alight with wind and flame, Malik took advantage of Issam's distraction to try to feel out the contours of the enchantment on his mind. Malik's magic surged up against it, but the enchantment was a wall of adamant. What illusion would be strong enough to unravel something embedded in this man's very soul?

But Malik had to try. For Karina, for all of them, he had to try.

"There are no chains binding you," said Malik. "Your will is your own. You are your own."

Ahead of him, Issam's flames died, and his body went completely rigid as Malik's illusion of freedom wove over him. Malik hardly dared to breathe. Had it worked?

The tether connecting him to the illusion went completely taut. It broke.

The Sentinel commander turned toward Malik, flames spilling from his mouth with every breath. Their eyes met, and Malik wheeled his denzik into a gallop just as a ball of fire exploded right where his head had been.

Time for the backup plan.

44

Karina

"Absolutely not," thundered Farid, which was exactly what Karina had expected him to say.

Karina ignored him, focusing only on Hanane. "If I have to die, I want you to be the one to do it. It's only fair, as I was the one to kill you."

She was hoping the reminder of her death might spark something in Hanane, but her sister remained frozen in place. Farid stalked toward her, any semblance of patience gone.

"No more demands. No more games. This ends now."

Hanane made no movement as Farid grabbed Karina by the front of her dress and lifted her into the air. Some primal instinct made her struggle in Farid's grasp, even though she had told herself that she would go to her death quietly.

"Hanane!" At this point, Karina wasn't even sure what she was begging her sister for. The water of the caldera churned beneath her in a flurry of brilliant colors, the power of the gods ready to swallow her whole. "Hanane, please!"

Hanane shook but didn't move.

She had been wrong. Hanane's love for her was not enough to overcome years of grooming and abuse. Tears leaked from

Karina's eyes, not for herself but for her sister, made to believe she was so weak and vulnerable when she was anything but.

But though Hanane could not free herself from Farid's influence now, one day she might still be able to. As soon as Karina hit that water, the Great Mother's anger would cease and Sonande would find a way to survive, as it always did.

Hanane. Caracal, Ife, Afua, Dedele, Aminata. Malik. She let the images of her friends, these people whom she had loved and who had loved her, fill her with calm. Hanane would be queen, as she'd always been meant to be. Caracal and Ife would go on more madcap adventures. Her sweet, gentle Malik would find a place in this world that recognized the shining, brilliant heart in him.

Tunde had once told her that he looked forward to the day she decided she was ready to fight for something instead of against everyone.

This was it. This wasn't about her dying. It was about the people she loved getting to live.

Karina stopped struggling. She closed her eyes, raised her face skyward, and prepared herself to join her mother and father at last.

She felt Farid's grip on her loosen.

Then he stopped.

Confused, Karina opened her eyes to see Farid staring over his shoulder at a wide-eyed Hanane, who had taken the scepter and pressed it into the small of his back.

"L-Let her go," Hanane warned. The palace steward dropped Karina onto the dirt as he turned his full attention to the elder princess.

"Hanane, dear heart, put that down," he said, and Hanane pushed the tip into his chest. Karina had seen her sister hold weapons hundreds of times before, but never with such fear.

"You are going to step aside." Though Hanane's hands shook, her words were clear. "You are going to allow *me* to perform the Rite of Renewal. This is what I want, Farid. This is how it should be. I need to go back to where I'm from."

"You're upset. You're not thinking straight."

"If Karina doesn't leave this mountain unharmed, I will kill you. I don't care if you resurrected me. If you lay another finger on her, I will kill you where you stand."

The nkra in the air was a living thing now, golden threads swirling brightly around them in time to the flickering behind Hanane's eyes. Farid's face twisted into a mask of pain.

"How can you say such cruel things after all I've done for you? After I moved the heavens to bring you back?"

"Who asked you to do that? Because I certainly did not!" screamed Hanane. "You didn't resurrect me for my own sake, but for yours! You claim you love me, but someone who loves me wouldn't threaten my sister! He wouldn't push his own apprentice to the brink of suicide! And he certainly wouldn't lie to me about killing my mother!"

Farid began to stammer an excuse, but Hanane was not done. "I knew from a young age that I did not feel the same way for you that you felt for me, and my guilt over not being able to give you what you wanted led me to placate you in ways I shouldn't have. I destroyed myself to make you happy! You're the reason why I look over my shoulder everywhere I go, why I feel like an invader inside my own body! Yet you claim that you love me? That everything you've done has been for me?"

Hanane stepped so close to Farid that Karina almost missed the next words out of her mouth. "You call me your salvation, but I can't save you from yourself."

Karina watched Farid's heart shatter.

She watched him try to arrange the pieces into something that could still beat.

"You're upset," he said, his words tight. "So much has happened, and you're not thinking clearly. I understand. I can fix this. I'll fix it for you."

Farid reached for Hanane, and she flinched. "Don't touch me."

But Farid wasn't listening. "We'll start over. It'll be as it was— no, this time it'll be better. I'll make it better for you. Please, I deserve another chance."

A wail rose in Karina's throat as Hanane's grip wavered. Hanane lowered the scepter until it hung limply at her side, and Farid shot Karina the most feral, possessive smile she had ever seen.

"Oh, Hanane. What would you do without me?"

Farid brushed the back of his hand down Hanane's face, and she gave a shudder of revulsion so visceral that Karina felt it in her own chest.

"I SAID, DON'T TOUCH ME!"

Before Karina could even draw a breath, Hanane punched the scepter straight through Farid's gut, her hand glistening crimson with his blood on the other side.

45

Malik

Caracal flew through the air at Issam, drawing his attention back away from Malik. But the rest of the Sentinels charged for Malik's riders, forcing the group to split off in different directions. The air was alive with magic as the Sentinels used their powers to try to cut off the Eshrans' retreat. Dazzling ribbons of light from the Sun-Aligned warriors blinded the riders, while the ground shook with the powers of the Earth-Aligned.

But the Eshrans had expected this, which was why they'd hidden their own archers at the top of the pass. Someone yelled out a command in Darajat, and a deluge of arrows rained down on Malik's pursuers.

One by one the Sentinels behind them fell, and Malik dared to believe he might make it off this mountain alive. He could not see the summit from where he was, but he could feel through their connection that Karina had not died yet. Just knowing she was still alive, that she was still fighting, gave him the strength to press forward.

One of the Sentinels pulled out a crossbow, and a yell of warning went up through the ranks as they fired it toward the archers. A young man—not a man, a boy really—took a bolt to the chest and tumbled down the cliffside directly into the path of Malik's denzik.

The beast reared back, only for a crossbow bolt to hit it in the side and another in its back leg. Malik was thrown off the dying creature, and he lay dazed on the ground as Zirani soldiers circled him. His magic flared, but Malik stifled it until he looked as small and as helpless as he had always been.

"Please! Don't hurt me, I beg of you!" he sobbed. The eyes of the soldiers around him were bright with battle lust—the win had been too easy. They hungered for blood, and right now, Malik was the best source if it.

He tried to crawl away, but the captain of these forces, recognizable by his distinct horned mask, slammed his foot onto Malik's hand. Malik screamed, pain tunneling up his arm.

"Where are the rest of you kekki rats?" called the man.

"I'll take you to them! Please, just spare me!"

The captain's lips curled into a sneer. "See how quickly they turn on their own?" he yelled, and the roar of laughter was a thunderstorm to Malik's ringing ears. The captain kicked him in the side. "On your feet, coward. Show us where the rest of you are hiding, and I'll consider sparing your miserable life."

The soldiers bound Malik's hands and forced him to walk behind the captain's horse like cattle. They jeered and prodded him with their spears, threw all sorts of insults and foul substances his way. All around Malik, the wraiths screamed their fury at their descendant being treated in such a way, but there was nothing they could do.

Two arrows quickly silenced the guards poised outside the

entrance to the camp, so there was no one to warn the Eshrans when the Zirani swarmed into their sanctuary like water bursting through a dam. Malik watched the carnage unfold from somewhere far past his own body, fighting back the wave of memories of raids just like this one. No matter where he went or how powerful he became, it always came back to seeing his people brutalized and powerless.

Another column of soldiers trickled through the entrance, and the knot of anxiety in Malik's stomach tightened. Just how many soldiers were there? Had they vastly miscalculated what they were up against?

He tried once more to replace the enchantment over the Sentinels with one of his own illusions. When the captain saw Malik's mouth moving, he backhanded him across the face.

"You are a fool," the man drawled. "Mwale Farid would have made you a prince of his new world. You could have had everything. And now your death will be meaningless, just as your life has been."

A call came up from one of the Zirani lieutenants—the last of their soldiers were finally in the cavern, with a smaller group outside as guard.

"One more thing," Malik said, his feigned frailty gone. "Farid told you I make illusions, right?"

Shouts of alarm rang through the air as, one by one, the Eshrans in the cavern vanished, leaving behind the confused Zirani soldiers. As the illusion unraveled, Malik let out a high-pitched whistle. Outside the cave, someone whistled back, and then the singing began—the same song Siwa had used when she had first opened the cavern, now used to close it forever.

Malik took advantage of the sudden confusion to summon the spirit blade between his clasped hands and stab it through a chink in the man's armor. The captain went down, and Malik sawed off his own ropes, then grabbed the man's shield as cover. He gave his would-be tormentor one last glance.

"I wanted a new world. Just not his," he said, and then Malik did what he did best.

He ran.

"Once the song begins, you'll have a minute before the doors close completely," Siwa had warned him. Malik estimated half of that minute had already passed by the time he even neared the entrance. The mountain felt like some great beast, the entrance to the cavern a jeweled throat quickly closing around him. Malik had known the risk he'd been taking when he had volunteered to be the one who lured the Zirani army into the mountain, but the terror of actually being sealed away in here for the rest of his life pumped speed into his battle-worn body.

Great spikes of amethyst jutted from the walls and ceiling, each layer of the tunnel closing like the tumblers of a lock sliding into place. Blood streamed down Malik's face as he barely made it through the first wall before it shut behind him, and then another, then another.

A bright spot in his vision grew—sunlight from the entrance. He was almost there, just a little farther . . .

He had almost made it out when someone grabbed him by the ankle.

"You damn kekki!" the captain roared. The man pulled Malik backward, ready to drag him into death with him—only for the final wall of amethyst to slam down between them. Malik stumbled back, the stump of the man's hand tight around his ankle, and the Zirani soldiers trapped deep in the belly of the mountain.

Malik stared at the severed hand in shock. Outside, the Eshran fighters had made quick work of the Zirani soldiers who hadn't entered the cave, and now everyone who was not combat capable was currently piling great heaps of rocks, wood, and anything else they could find onto the sealed entrance. And unless the Zirani had someone in their ranks who spoke Darajat, it would be a very, very long time before anyone went into or out of the cavern.

Malik could hardly believe it even as his people cheered and screamed all around him.

They had won.

Though his head understood that they had just made history, his heart was on the summit. His magic flared as he sensed something putrid permeating the air, and felt Karina's desperation surging through the connection. Heart heavy in his throat, Malik ripped the severed hand from his leg and raced toward the caldera, no thoughts in his mind except getting to Karina's side.

46

Karina

The world slowed as Hanane pulled the scepter out of Farid.

His body collapsed to the ground, and she held a shaking hand—now glistening with blood—to her face, as if staring long enough might erase what she'd done. Karina stared too, her mind unable to process what she had just seen.

Hanane let out a guttural, inhuman scream. A wave of power pulsed from her, knocking Karina off her feet. She rolled down the slope, inches away from slipping into the caldera.

Seconds ago, there had been Hanane and there had been Farid.

Now there was only a bloody corpse on the ground and a screeching hell beast where Hanane had been. Straggly, coltish limbs sprouted all along its body, bursting through layers of putrid, rotted flesh. The beast had a head like a ram but a body like a lion, flashing scales and goat-like eyes in a head so big it blocked out the sun. Karina could only watch in horror as the lich tore into what was left of Farid's body, splatters of his blood spraying across the ground as it feasted.

And when the Great Mother's displeasure grew as great as it could go, she worked the beast into a frenzy, and everywhere it went, only destruction followed.

And now she understood the warning signs that they had all missed: the last omen would never arrive, because Hanane herself *was* the last omen—a monster to rain destruction from the skies with no force of humankind powerful enough to stop it.

"N-No, Hanane," Karina whispered, crawling toward the thing that had been her sister even though her instincts told her to run. "Stop this."

When nothing remained of Farid but a smear of blood staining the lich's snout, it turned its great horned head Karina's way. Searching its filmy yellow eyes for even a single trace of Hanane, Karina crawled closer.

"I-It's all right, Hanane." She extended a single hand toward the monster like she'd seen animal trainers do to rabid beasts. "It's just me."

With a scream like a million souls dying at once, the lich charged for her.

Someone tackled Karina to the ground, and they both went rolling out of the way of the lich's iron fangs. "Karina!" Malik cried as he helped her back to her feet, and she was so grateful to see him that she could have wept. "What happened? Where's Hanane?"

The horror on her face was all the answer he needed. The Sentinels Farid had brought with him had finally regrouped after the death of their master, and they formed a ring around the lich, their weapons little more than toys compared to its gargantuan size.

"Fire!" yelled their leader.

"No!" cried Karina as a wave of arrows embedded in the monster's flesh.

The beast's roar of pain shook the entire mountain. A pair of broken, bat-like wings unfurled from its body, and it used them to launch itself into the air. The ground where it had stood had been reduced to rot; the once-clear water of the caldera now foamed black with decay. The lich's very existence was the antithesis of life, expelling destruction everywhere it touched.

"How do we stop this?" Karina cried as the lich landed on one of the crystal towers and screamed again.

"I don't know," said Malik. "The Faceless King says every time the Rite of Resurrection was done before this, the Rite of Renewal was performed before the lich spiraled out of control. He doesn't know what can stop it now."

The Sentinels continued their assault, only serving to anger the creature further. It grabbed one by the shoulder and tossed him over the mountainside, the man's screams cutting through the air. The sky had turned crimson and black, a storm not even Karina could control brewing in tandem with this dying world. The lich smashed its tail into one of the towers, and Malik rolled protectively over Karina, blocking a slab of debris from hitting her with his arm.

"Maybe if we finish the Rite of Renewal, she'll turn back?" Karina cried, but she knew in her heart the time for that had already passed. Now that the final omen was here, the ritual was useless.

The realization dawned on them both at the same time: the only way to save Sonande from this creature was to kill it.

But how did you kill something that was already dead?

The Sentinels were now using their magic against the lich,

only adding to the destruction around them. One Water-Aligned Sentinel sent a wave of the black caldera water flying across the summit, almost drowning Malik and Karina where they stood. At this rate, if the lich didn't kill them, the Sentinels' frantic attempts to subdue it would.

Karina felt each lash against the creature as if it dug into her own skin. Everyone else might see death incarnate, but that monster had been her *sister*. Letting it live was an insult to everything Hanane had stood for.

"If Hanane is still in there, maybe I can reach her," said Karina. "But I need someone to distract the Sentinels."

Fear flooded Malik's dark eyes, but he nodded. "I can do that."

She threw her arms around him, and let herself be engulfed by the feeling of him one last time before she took a running leap into the sky on a rush of swirling wind.

Karina allowed herself a single laugh as she dipped and rode on the wind, swooping through the currents as gracefully as any bird. From this high up, the mountain's peak was in perfect focus. Just like in the vision she'd seen so long ago, the ritual had turned the lake into a churning mass of power. But without the soul of a queen to bind the magic, it continued to intensify, pulling everything toward it in a vacuum of shifting energy.

Down below, the last of the Sentinels were a mass of white and Malik was a tiny blur rushing to meet them. She wanted more than anything to face this enemy by his side, but her focus right now was the lich.

"Hanane!" Karina found herself screaming. What if she was wrong, and there truly was nothing left of her sister inside that thing? Hanane would never make those sounds; Hanane couldn't toss soldiers in the air as if they weighed no more than dolls. What if there was nothing left but to kill this monster?

Karina sang the sky awake the same way the Eshrans had sung the mountain, and it awoke with a righteous fury. Rain poured down on the lich in a deluge that would have drowned a lesser creature, but the monster remained unfazed. It screeched in her direction, sending a wave of power toward her that had Karina rolling through the sky.

"Come on, you can do this," Karina muttered to herself as she stabilized her freefall with an updraft, just like Caracal had taught her to do. The lich snapped open its wings and leaped into the air, racing toward her with the precision of a bird of prey. Karina dove low over the heads of the Sentinels locked in combat with shadow warriors Malik had woven to fight at his side.

"Malik, I need help!" she screamed, and his magic rolled over the world, pulling the mountainside somewhere entirely new. Where before there had been lush meadows and soaring cliff-sides, now there were golden sands and red crags. They were in the Odjubai Desert, and the Sentinels scrambled in confusion at the change. Even Karina, who knew this was all an illusion, was thrown for a second by how real it felt to be flying through her homeland.

She threw another slice of wind at the lich, which it dodged. It landed on top of a flat plateau, and the rock immediately burst, the illusion dying beneath the monster's touch.

Malik's magic scrambled to fix the world even as the lich destroyed it, a force that could only create versus a force that could only consume. A line of knife-sharp hail soared past Karina's face, burrowing into the lich's side. Someone pressed against Karina's back as the creature screamed in pain.

"This is why I don't spend time with royalty!" Caracal yelled. Back-to-back, the two Wind-Aligned zawenji created a bubble of hardened air that the lich could not penetrate. The creature tore at their shield, blood-soaked claws gouging through their protection.

"Go help Malik!" Karina screamed when the shield broke. The former Sentinel nodded before diving into the battle below, leaving Karina alone with the monster again.

The illusion shifted again. Now they were in the jungles of Arkwasi, and she and the lich wove in and out of the trees in their wild cat-and-mouse chase. Karina threw a gust of wind backward, but instead of hitting the lich, it picked up one of the trees and slammed it into the creature. Malik had somehow given this illusion solid weight, and Karina couldn't help but grin at this new weapon in her arsenal.

She weaponized the jungle, using her powers to rip the forest from its roots and skewer the lich with a barrage of wood and earth. Down below, each of Malik's illusion warriors fought with the fury of ten men, using weapons made of stone and fire and light to push the Sentinels away from Karina and the lich. In the middle of it all was Malik himself, dodging blows from behind his shield even as he wove the battlefield into being. Karina lingered on him for a heartbeat too long, and in her distraction she was too slow to avoid the lich slashing for her face.

Pain like her body was splitting open tore through her as she plummeted to the earth. The battlefield shifted again; no more

trees now, just an endless savanna of swaying grassland. Low cries
trumpeted all around them as a stampede of wildebeests and other
bush creatures thundered past. The lich was caught in the chaos,
giving Karina time to climb back into the air. She wiped the blood
from her face, not sure how much longer she or Malik could keep
this up.

It was time to end this.

All her life, Karina had found increasingly self-destructive
ways to channel the near-limitless energy inside her, often to the
detriment of herself and her loved ones. But here at the end of the
world, she had found the one creature in existence who could possibly bear the full force of what she could do. Here, she no longer
had to hold back.

This time, the lightning was an old friend to her, one Karina
wielded as deftly as any instrument. She threw bolt after bolt, relishing the pure energy that was no one's but hers to command, her
power and her fury given life.

But despite its size, the lich was fast, and it zipped between the
lightning bolts with a leopard's speed. Karina flew past the cloud
layer, up so high that the air was too thin for anyone but a Wind-
Aligned zawenji to bear. The lich followed her through the heart
of the storm, and once they were high enough, Karina summoned
all the magic she possessed into a lightning bolt larger and more
fearsome than the monster before her.

As her lightning illuminated the sky in brilliant white light, the
lich cowered, and Karina saw then what she had missed in the
frenzy of battle—her sister's eyes, scared and alone, staring back
at her from the face of a monster.

The rain froze, a thousand pearly drops suspending in midair as Karina stopped the lightning an inch from the lich's face. Her mind flooded with memories of the last night of Hanane's first life. On that day too, Karina had thrown lightning just like this. On that day too, her powers had ended her sister's life before it had really begun.

She refused to kill Hanane a second time.

Karina twisted the bolt away from the lich. It slammed to the ground far below them.

All at once, the spell was broken, and the rain fell once more. The lich lunged, but now that Karina had seen her sister's heart hidden in its skin, she could not bear to keep fighting.

"Hanane!" she cried, and the lich screamed in response. It was so large that a single one of its talons could have ripped Karina in two, but she knew what she had seen. Her sister was somewhere inside this gargantuan beast, which meant there had to be some way to reach her.

"Hanane!" she cried again, twisting and diving between the lich's attacks. "Can you hear me? Hanane!"

The lich grabbed her by the torso. Stars danced in Karina's eyes as all the air left her lungs.

"I'm sorry," she wheezed out. "You tried to tell me what Farid did to you, and I didn't listen! You have every right to be upset!"

Karina wriggled out of the lich's grasp and rode the wind to a stop in front of its face. "I know what it's like to lash out because you're hurt and you're scared, but this isn't you."

The lich stilled, leaving its soft underbelly completely exposed. Now would have been the perfect time to strike, to slay an enemy the likes of which no Alahari queen had ever faced before. Surely if she did so, the people of Sonande would sing her song for generations to come, and no one would ever doubt again if she deserved to call herself queen.

But Karina did not strike. Instead, she gathered the lich's bloody snout in her hands.

"You are the eldest daughter of Sarahel Alahari and Jibrail Belhouari. You love to walk barefoot, you hate figs more than any other food in the world, and you can't stand to lose any wager, no matter how small. And you've been hurt so badly by me and by others who should have known better. You deserve to be as angry as you need to be to heal from what happened to you." Karina pressed a kiss to the monster's nose. "I'm sorry. I love you. Come back to me."

A growl vibrated through the lich's body, but what came out was a cry as human as any Karina had ever heard. She ran her hand up and down its nose in the same calming motion Malik had done to her when she'd been dying of the plague.

"I'm sorry," she sobbed. "I'm sorry, I'm sorry, I'm sorry."

There was another rush of power, this one moving inward to the lich instead of outward from it. Karina covered her hands from the piercing flash of light. Seconds later she was tumbling through the air.

And Hanane was tumbling beside her.

"Karina!" sobbed her sister, her tears rushing upward as they plummeted to the earth. "Karina!"

Karina let out a cry that was more joy than words, flipping herself over so that she was falling face-to-face with Hanane. She clasped her sister's hands and her tears fell upward too, along with a fair amount of snot. She slowed their descent, until they were gently spiraling toward the ground.

"I'm here, I'm here," promised Karina as her sister repeated her name again and again, half a prayer, half a plea. "I'm always going to be right here."

Somewhere far below, Malik still battled the Sentinels, and the Great Mother's anger still needed to be dealt with. Sonande itself was broken in ways that were going to take decades, maybe centuries, to fix. But right then, somewhere between the heavens and the earth but far from either, Karina had her sister in her arms, and everything was the way it was meant to be.

47

Malik

Trickle stream river trickle stream river trickle stream river flood in flood out every day fish seaweed reef shore trickle stream river trickle stream river flood in flood out trickle stream river again and again and again and again motion and tides in and out never changing never breaking never ending.

Malik was the Gonyama River roaring to life in an endless cycle of motion and tides and shores and his thoughts were not thoughts because thoughts were for simple creatures like humans, what need did he have for thoughts when he was eons of existence swelling and breaking like the tide, he was endless, he was infinite, he was power itself.

For the first time, the Faceless King's magic entwined itself with Malik's instead of fighting against it, the two working in perfect harmony against the onslaught of Sentinels facing them down. With the obosom's power amplifying his own, Malik spoke into being warriors to fight beside him, whose weapons tore through flesh and bone as if they were real. He commanded the battlefield, changing it at a whim to disorient their enemies as Karina and Hanane battled overhead like twin stars locked in combat.

It felt like Malik had been asleep his entire life, and now he was truly awake as his magic bent the world to his whims. Now he understood why his pharaoh ancestors had conquered Sonande as they had, for once you'd tasted absolute power, how could you give even an inch of it up? In the heart of a frenzy of battle and blood, Malik had never felt more *alive*.

The wraiths were ecstatic, all their centuries of unbridled rage funneling into him. The lich's emergence had weakened the barrier between realms, and now there was nothing stopping them from twisting Malik into the weapon for their vengeance.

And then Karina unmade the lich.

Malik felt the moment it happened. It was like an unraveling, the very fabric of the universe tearing apart in the wake of this thing that should not have been possible.

He watched as Karina and her sister fell to the mountain peak, right at the edge of the caldera. Both were so stunned from what had just happened that neither noticed Issam limping up the mountain, fire in his hands and desperation in his eyes, the enchantment that commanded him compelling him forward even though neither Karina nor the lich was a threat any longer.

Malik, no! screamed Idir when he sensed what he was about to do, but the Faceless King could not stop Malik from reaching for the upper limit of both of their powers. In that instant, the entire web of nkra was Malik's to control, and he grasped tight onto the enchantment that bound every single Sentinel all across Sonande together. He'd meant to command Issam away from Karina, but now that he had the warriors completely at his mercy, he realized that nothing and no one could stop him from ending this threat to his people for good.

After all, he wasn't attacking innocents—the Sentinels were murderers and torturers with countless generations of Eshran blood on their hands. He could force them all to fall on their own weapons. He could force them to throw themselves off the nearest ledge. He would feel absolutely no remorse, for any one of them would have killed him given the chance.

Not by choice, whispered a small voice in Malik's head, fighting to be heard beneath the weight of his power. *The Sentinels have never had a choice. You do.*

But that didn't matter. Malik tightened his control, relishing the pain he felt searing through Issam's and every other Sentinel's body.

But—

But—

Malik did not know many things. He did not know why the sun rose in the east and sank in the west. He did not know why, out of the millions of people in Sonande, he had fallen for the one person history was determined to pit him against, nor why his own mind felt like a battlefield when it should have been a sanctuary.

But he knew in his heart, for all its broken, scarred pieces, that this wasn't justice, no matter how good it felt. He did not know who he wanted to be, but it was not the kind of person who would do this.

But his powers and Idir's had never been meant to mix, and now their combined power was too vast for Malik to stop. This was bigger than fighting for control of his own mind; this was a tsunami of magic with no dam big enough to hold it back.

Malik couldn't stop the rush of power pouring out of him. But he could redirect it from a force of destruction to something new, something better.

And so, once he was certain he had the attention of every Sentinel across Sonande, he told them a story.

He told the Sentinels a story of freedom, of chains both physical and mental breaking free. He told them a story of a world that did not fear or enslave magic but lived beside it, same as they lived beside the ocean and the skies and all the other unknowable forces around them.

The enchantment that kept the Sentinels dull and obedient broke beneath the weight of Malik's magic. For many, their minds were now their own for the first time since birth, and the feeling of it was so wonderful and so new that a few of the warriors broke down in huge, heaving sobs. Issam fell to his knees, his fire sputtering out as he stared at his hands in horror.

The wraiths howled and screamed at Malik's decision, their anger ripping through him like a thousand daggers to the heart. But he did not care, channeling their toxicity into freeing every last Sentinel. He offered his own psalm to the gods, a prayer for a better world.

When the last warrior was free, Malik's ancestors' anger was so strong he could almost taste it on his tongue. *Blood traitor,* they called him. *Unworthy,* they called him. However, he swore he saw for a moment Khenu smiling down at him before her wraith became indistinguishable from the rest.

But the only person Malik truly saw was Karina, running toward him with her arms outstretched. He reached for her, wishing that when they'd been alone at the camp he'd had the courage to tell her the truth that had been building inside him for far longer than he'd realized it had.

The truth was that he loved her, in any and all ways she wanted to be loved, and that it wasn't much, yet it was everything he had to give. He loved her anger and he loved her fierceness and he loved the way she called his name as she ran to him as if no one else in the world existed.

Malik needed to tell her that, but he did not get the chance, for then the last of his magic fizzled into nothing. His legs buckled, sending him tumbling down the side of the caldera and beneath the surface of the water.

48

Karina and Malik

Three things happened in rapid succession after that.

The first was that Malik's body sank fast, as if the water had known he was coming and had been waiting to pull him under all along.

The second was that as soon as Malik slipped beneath the waves, Karina dove in after him. She felt no fear or hesitation, did not stop to wonder if perhaps the world would be better off with one less ulraji. The only thing on Karina's mind as she dove beneath the surface was a single burning determination to save the boy she loved. The water devoured her just as eagerly as it did him.

The third was that a being that should not have been on the mountain sauntered to the edge of the caldera and peered into the inky water. Her arrival was odd, for hyenas were rarely seen this far west, but nobody commented on it, for nobody on the peak saw her.

But though no one saw Hyena, they heard it when she threw her head back and laughed a laugh that reverberated through the sky as Malik and Karina sank together into the heart of the world.

They fell together, sinking deeper and deeper into a place few had seen and fewer would ever know. For Malik, who believed in the

Great Mother and the gods, it felt not unlike the divinity he had prayed to his entire life. For Karina, who believed in none of these things, it felt like slipping under a blanket after a long day, warm and exhausted and content.

It felt a lot like love, and all the wonderfully unknowable things that came with it.

The heart of the world embraced them with both welcome and confusion, for the time for the Rite of Renewal had passed, and even if it had not, there were far too many souls here.

The third being disentangled itself from its host and slowed the descent for the other two, until they hung suspended in a world being made and unmade all at once.

"Not yet," said Idir, and the heart of the world hummed in agreement, satisfied that the true sacrifice had made himself clear. "Not you two, not yet."

And as both Malik and Karina were neither alive nor dead, they could not stop the Faceless King from pushing them up through the water and back to the realm of the living, just as they could not stop the magic from claiming what was left of the spirit's soul to form a new covenant, not of resurrection or renewal but something completely new.

49

Karina

When Karina came to, the sky above her was a cheerful blue. Her memories of what had happened after she and Hanane had hit the ground felt like the back of a vast tapestry, impossible to comprehend without seeing the other side.

She remembered unleashing the fury of the sky upon the lich, only to reach Hanane with nothing but the bond only sisters could share. She remembered Issam stalking toward them with fire in his hands and desperation in his eyes, until he and all the other Sentinels had suddenly frozen.

And she remembered the ice that had gripped her heart when she'd watched Malik fall into the caldera. Going after him hadn't even been a choice—after all they'd been through, she knew now that she would always save him, just as he would always save her.

Everything after that was . . . fuzzy. Karina suspected that she could spend every moment of the rest of her life trying to recall what she had experienced in the heart of the world only to come up blank. This was probably for the best; there were some truths that had been born in the dark and that were meant to remain there.

But all that mattered right now was that she was still here and the world was too, the lich's destruction having been contained to the mountaintop. And Malik—her brilliant, compassionate, shy Malik—was there too, curled up on the dark rock beside her.

But he was still. Far too still.

Karina's heartbeat flooded her ears as she turned him onto his side. "Malik?" She shook him. "No, no, you can't—Malik! No!"

She called his name again and again, pushed hard on his chest and kissed his face, but Malik did not wake. Tears blurred Karina's vision, but she didn't stop shaking his body because this couldn't be happening, they hadn't survived the end of the world for him to die like this.

But then she felt it—the exact moment his heart beat its last, unable to bear the weight of using the Faceless King's full power. The connection between them snapped.

And Karina felt him die.

Sorrow and grief poured into the place where Malik had once been, enveloping her even more completely than the magic of the caldera had. She was coming apart—she was coming undone— Hanane was trying to pull her away from the corpse but Karina pushed her away because she wasn't leaving him like this, she *couldn't* leave him like this—

With a primal scream, Karina slammed her hands onto Malik's chest.

Pure power radiated from her palms, her lightning racing through every inch of Malik's body. She withdrew in horror, visions of other charred bodies flashing through her mind, when Malik's body convulsed once, twice, three times. His eyes flew open, and he gasped.

"I . . . wha—Karina?" he mumbled, and he gazed up at her with those too-big, too-wide eyes that were now . . . brown. Instead of the night-dark eyes she had come to love, Malik's eyes were now a rich, warm brown like the bark of a freshly planted tree.

Karina threw herself over him with a strangled sob. He winced in pain but wrapped his free arm around her, burying his face in the crook of her neck. He whispered something against her skin, and she reluctantly pulled away, tears streaking down her cheeks.

"What?" she sniffed.

"Your hair . . . it's black."

He stretched out one of her coils for her to see. Karina's hair had lost the silvery sheen all Alaharis were known for and was now a very common, very lustrous midnight black. Perhaps once Karina would have despaired at this, but she did not care. She disentangled Malik's fingers from her hair and pressed them to her lips, flushing with pleasure at his flustered expression. It took all her restraint not to kiss every part of his body that she could reach, not caring if all of Sonande saw them.

A surprised cry broke Karina from her thoughts of kisses and all the places they could go.

Everyone on the mountaintop stared at a stream of creatures floating far above their heads. They ranged in shapes and sizes, tiny bonsam and chuckling ghouls, ifrits and shetani and creatures from stories Karina had never even heard. Malik's eyes filled with tears as they landed on the spirits cautiously floating out of the cracks the lich had torn in the sky.

"You can see the grim folk?" he whispered. Too awed to speak, Karina nodded. "But . . . ?"

"The rip in the veil between worlds caused by the Rite of Resurrection has been fixed," whispered Hanane. She was looking far into the distance, the power that connected her to the lich still coursing through her. "No, it's more like—the veil is removed. There is no separation between our world and the spirit realm anymore."

Grim folk and humans on the same plane of existence once more, as they'd been when the Great Mother had first created the world. All three of them looked at one another, and Malik asked the question racing through everyone's mind.

"What do we do now?"

Karina had no idea, but she was fairly certain they were about to find out.

As it turned out, unleashing spirits onto the world was one of those things that tended to frighten the common person. The next week was the most chaotic of Karina's life as she attempted to stop her people from falling into complete anarchy. The merging of the human and spirit realms had shifted everyone's understanding of the world, and Karina and Hanane felt it their duty to soften the blow as much as they could.

They made their base of operations right in Oboure, and from there they wrangled the Zirani community in Eshra into some semblance of order. There was territory to be redrawn, and there new alliances to be negotiated. Orders had to be made to remove the Zirani soldiers from the region posthaste.

Many of the Zirani were just as panicked, even more so, than the Eshrans, which was truly a sight to see—for all her people's unwarranted sense of superiority over Malik's, it seemed that they were all painfully, predictably human in the end.

The sisters threw themselves into the work with a gusto, Hanane the fearless leader and Karina her loyal second-in-command, just as she'd been born to be. Malik helped them investigate which grim folk were mostly benevolent and which were too mischievous to be left on their own. He was even called to testify during an emergency meeting between the warring clan leaders, where they agreed to a temporary ceasefire so everyone could take stock of their new situation. It wasn't a full peace, not yet, and it would be a long time before the region would return to true stability, but it was a start.

Despite the general chaos and confusion, those days were some of the happiest of Karina's life.

But they could not stay in Eshra forever, and soon the time came for Karina and Hanane to return to Ziran. One evening they were stretched out on a large pile of cushions, Karina's legs in Hanane's lap as they both ignored a stack of scrolls and papers beside them in favor of tossing orange slices into each other's mouths.

"All right, how about the baker's son, Rashid?" asked Hanane.

"Joined the army," replied Karina. "You wouldn't even recognize him."

"Wow, little Rashid, a soldier! Who knew?" Hanane threw another orange slice at Karina, who caught it effortlessly. "All right, what about our old math tutor, what was her name—"

"Chaimae? She got married a few years ago, but then her wife left her for a traveling actress and took the children too. It was the scandal of the court for months."

Hanane shook her head. "So much changes in ten years . . ."

"We'll be home soon, and then you can start making your own changes too."

For the first time, the thought of returning to Ziran filled Karina with something other than dread. Issam, Ife, and Caracal had all agreed to join their court, and the thought of Ksar Alahari filled once again with laughter and joy brought tears to her eyes. She was so enamored of the idea, she pretended not to notice the hesitation in Hanane's eyes when she softly replied, "Right. We'll be home soon."

The elder princess placed a hand against her own chest, a far-off look in her eye. "Tell me about him," she said, her voice hardly above a whisper. "Tell me about Tunde."

Even though Karina's throat still closed up at his memory, she told her sister all about the wonderful person whose heart she now carried, until they curled together on their shared pallet just as they'd used to do as children.

It was well past midnight when Hanane gently shook Karina awake. "Let's go for a walk," her older sister said, and Karina blearily agreed.

The grim folk preferred night to any other time of day, so they watched from their dark corners as the sisters walked from their tent and through the beginnings of the slowly rebuilding Oboure. Through Hanane's legs were so much longer, her pace was agonizingly slow, and Karina had to walk at half her normal speed so her sister could keep up.

"Can you do something for me?" Hanane murmured as they rounded a bend, and oh, how small her voice sounded.

"Anything."

"I've never seen snow before. Can you make it snow?"

Karina did so, crafting a swirling cloud of flurries all around them. Hanane laughed as they kissed her lashes. One clung to her eyebrow, and there was something about that solitary flake holding on so desperately to the only place it could land that made Karina want to weep.

"There'll be more snow when we go home," she promised. She was ready to promise anything in the world if it would make that wistful look on Hanane's face go away. "I don't care if it's the desert, I'll make it snow every day for you. And the ocean! We've never seen the ocean! There's still so many places we haven't visited and things we haven't seen!"

Hanane's eyes fluttered closed. She forced them open again. "The ocean . . . maybe later . . ."

Karina was sobbing now. "Don't leave me. Please. I can't be all alone again."

"Oh, baby bird, the dead are the dead are the dead," said Hanane. "There's no place in this world for me, not anymore."

"If this is about the lich, we'll find a way to keep it contained—"

"You're going home, Karina. Let me go home too." Hanane looked far down the path at something Karina could not see. "But not yet. Come, let's keep walking."

Karina wiped her face with one hand and laced the other through Hanane's. Hand in hand, she walked with her sister through a flurry of snow and magic and tears, and they were walking, and they were walking, until she saw up ahead a great river sparkling like liquid starlight. Their parents stood on the banks of it, dressed in robes of the brightest white, and they beckoned for Hanane to come with them.

Hanane kissed Karina on the forehead. "I'll see you soon," she promised.

"I'll see you soon."

And Karina stayed behind as her family walked off into the star-flecked night.

50

Malik

Malik did not have to ask what had happened to Hanane. He took one look at Karina's face when she came to the small hut he shared with his mother and grandmother the next morning, and he knew.

For more than a week, Karina did not eat. She did not speak. They slept in the same bed, no longer caring what rumors might spread about them being together. Truly all they did was sleep— well, Malik slept. Karina simply stared off into the distance. Malik told her stories each night, and when he ran out of those, he just held her. Her friends came by every day, but nothing eased her ache.

And then one night Malik was coming to join her when he found Karina hanging halfway through a window, fighting with something that had gotten stuck in the hibiscus bush outside. It was a kestrel, one of the bird's gray wings trapped between two branches. After minutes of struggling, Karina finally got the bird free, and she was rewarded with a peck in the face for her efforts. She watched as the bird flew off with two more in tow before letting out a sound somewhere between a laugh and a cry.

"Fine, you win!" she screamed, and burst into sobs for the first time since Hanane had returned to the Place with Many Stars.

From there, Karina improved day by day. She returned to her

work of fixing the relations between the Zirani and the Eshrans, Malik at her side. It seemed these blissful days might continue on forever until—

"Tomorrow, a caravan of merchants will be leaving for Ziran, and I intend to go with them," she declared over a bowl of steamed rice they were sharing. "There's a spot for you too, if you'd like it."

Karina said the words nonchalantly, but Malik knew her well enough now to see the vulnerability hiding behind her aloof tone. To allow him to become a member of her household, of her family—it was a risk of the highest magnitude, and Malik was moved that she would make it for him. He imagined them in another world and another life, one where he was a simple farm boy and she was a simple musician, and they both had all the time in the world to care about nothing except each other.

But no matter how complicated and painful their histories had been, they had brought them to this moment. The imagined Karina and Malik would only ever be just that, which made them inferior to their broken yet fully real selves.

"My old home is about an hour's walk from here," he replied. "Would you like to see it?"

She said yes.

Karina's hand was warm in Malik's the entire walk through what had once been Oboure. Despite the days he'd spent helping his people adjust to their new lives, he hadn't felt strong enough to return here. But with Karina beside him, he finally did.

She bore silent witness as he picked through the wreckage, pointing out the details of his life that poked through the rubble.

The moon bathed the world in a silver glow bright enough that they needed no light to guide their way along a path higher up the mountain. They followed the well-worn trail until they reached Malik's house.

Or what had once been his house. Most of the walls were still standing, but the interior had been completely destroyed. This was no natural destruction like the rest of Oboure; human beings had torn this place apart, and it had been quiet as a graveyard ever since.

"It honestly looks better than I remember," mused Malik. "The clan wars were at their height, and our house sits right at the heart of a disputed territory, which left us vulnerable. Maybe we could have rebuilt but . . . it made more sense to leave."

Karina squeezed his hand. "I'm sorry," she whispered.

He squeezed hers back. "There's one more thing I want to show you."

He led her around the back to the lemon grove. A few of the trees had survived the omens, and now, at the height of harvest season, the fruits were bright and heavy. Malik stopped beside a tree with several horizontal notches up the trunk, the highest stopping right below the top of his head. "In Eshra, whenever a baby is born, the family plants them a tree so their soul will have a place to come back to if they ever feel like visiting the human realm after they pass. This one is mine."

It was the real-life version of the exact tree Malik had once kept the Faceless King tethered to in his mind. He did not exactly miss Idir's presence, but he wasn't quite used to having his mind back to himself yet. His thoughts kept prodding the hole where the spirit had been, the same way a child would keep agitating the gap in their mouth after losing a tooth.

Karina pressed her palm flat against the trunk, her face awash with awe. "So each one of these trees—"

"—is a member of my family." There were easily hundreds of trees in this grove, some as young as Malik's, others centuries older. "We've been here a long time, even before Khenu's child arrived. I don't care what happened in the past or what Farid wanted me to believe. This is the family and the legacy I claim, not the pharaohs."

It was dizzying to imagine all the small twists and turns of the world that had conspired to bring him and Karina together in this place at this time. They were a thousand bloodlines weaving together, a product of both Bahia's and Khenu's treachery and loyalty to one another, yet they were also just one girl and one boy standing beneath a lemon tree.

Malik sat down at the base of his tree, and Karina joined him. "I owe you an apology, by the way. And an explanation for . . . everything."

What followed was the tale of all that had happened since he'd first arrived in Ziran. He left nothing out, not even what he had done to Dedele. The air felt heavier once he was done. Karina's fingers found the scar on her chest from when he had stabbed her all those months ago, then touched the matching scar above his own heart from when he'd tried to kill Idir in his body.

The old anxiety crawled into Malik's gut. Now the truth was finally out in all its ugly glory. Whatever Karina would do with it was up to her.

She cupped his face, filling his nose with that rainwater scent once more. When she kissed him, a small sob escaped Malik's lips at having someone truly see him and not turn away. The aching desire he'd felt back in the dreamscape flared up deep in his core once more, but there was one last thing he had to say before he could allow himself to follow where it might lead.

"I wish more than anything that I could go with you," he whispered when they finally pulled apart. He looked at the two trees clustered closest to his—Leila's, slightly taller than his own, and Nadia's, smaller but sure to catch up to theirs soon. "But I can't. Not yet."

Karina's face fell. "Your sisters."

He nodded. "I let them down. I violated their trust, and now I have no idea where they are. Which is why I have to go find them and try to make things right."

He had made a promise to Mama and Nana that their family would be whole again. He would not return to Oboure unless it was with his sisters.

And Malik knew himself well enough to know that if he went with Karina now, he'd retread the same pattern he'd fallen into with Farid—wrapping his identity so tightly around another person that he lost sight of himself. He had come so far from the panic-stricken boy who had used to climb these trees and pray to the gods to free him from his own mind. But he still had farther to go before he was ready to stand at her side.

But Malik did not have to say what he and Karina both knew—that there were a million and one places to hide in Sonande for two girls who did not want to be found. It was at best months and most likely years before the siblings would be reunited again.

But just as Idir had once told him, Malik would walk forward one step at a time, and the journey would fall into place however it was meant to.

"You asked me once what I wanted out of life. I didn't have an answer then, but I do now. What I endured at the hands of Farid helped me realize it." Malik hadn't voiced these thoughts aloud yet, not even to himself. Yet he couldn't think of anyone better to share this tiny dream with than her. "After I find my sisters, I want to build a school here in Eshra that rivals even your university in Ziran. That way children like Nadia and those after her can have every opportunity the previous generations were denied. And I'd want to teach there. I know that sounds ridiculous, given my background but—"

"It's not ridiculous. That's amazing," said Karina, her eyes sparking with wonder as she imagined his vision coming to life. "Whatever you need from me to make it happen, I'll provide. But even without my help, I know you'll succeed."

Something brighter than all the magic Malik had wielded bloomed within him: a purpose, one chosen under no one's influence but his own, pointing his life in a direction that finally felt right. He squeezed Karina's hand, and she squeezed back.

He watched the full understanding that he wouldn't be coming with her flood her eyes. He watched her nod, giving him a small smile even as she fought back tears. A leaf had fallen in her now-black hair, and as Malik removed it, his thumb brushed against Karina's temple. She shuddered, and even though the connection had severed when he'd died, he felt the movement deep in his core.

Slowly, oh so slowly, he ran his thumb down her face, pressing gently against her bottom lip. The mountain air that evening had been wonderfully cool, but now Malik's skin was blooming with heat. He cupped her face with his other hand, and they were so close he could feel her breath ghosting over his cheek.

Just before their lips brushed together, Malik stretched her cheeks wide apart, crossed his eyes, and stuck out his tongue. The surprise of it sent Karina into a bout of laughter, and it was while she was laughing that Malik kissed her.

It was not their first kiss, but it was the first one without any lies hanging between them. Just Malik and Karina and a kiss that started sweet but quickly devolved into anything but. She pulled him forward so that he was kneeling over her, her back nestled comfortably against the base of his soul tree, her fingers gripping his hair.

Malik's inhibitions melted away as his hands became surer, as he kissed down the line of her jaw, dipped his fingers beneath her waist beads and heard a groan escape her lips that sent a line of heat trailing down his spine.

And then she pushed a little too hard on his left arm and Malik flinched, letting out a hiss of pain. Karina pulled back in alarm.

"Did I hurt you?" she asked breathlessly, and he shook his head. Several conflicting emotions ran through his mind before he rolled up his sleeve, revealing the multitude of scars marking his flesh, most old and faded but a few still puffy and new.

"It looks worse than it feels," Malik tried to reassure her, but that didn't stop Karina from lightly running her fingers over the scars, taking extra care with the newer ones. She cradled his arm to her chest and placed a gentle kiss on the inside of his wrist.

"I told you, you never have to downplay your pain when you're with me," she said, and when Malik kissed her again it was slower, unhurried, and there was nothing else but this, nowhere worth being but here. The fear he had felt the last time they had approached this line reared up once more, but this time, Malik felt ready to cross it.

"I don't have much experience with physical intimacy," Malik admitted when they broke apart. Karina grinned up at him with a smile that made him wonder why he ever did anything besides kiss her.

"Luckily for you, I have more than enough for both of us. Just talk to me. Tell me what you need, and I'll tell you what I need. And tell me if—or when—you want to stop."

Malik nodded. When she touched him again, her hands dipping lower than anyone had ever touched him before, and she asked once more against his skin if she should keep going, he told her yes.

Karina had never been rejected by a boy before. Gods, she'd never been rejected by *anyone* before, at least not in a romantic capacity. Then again, she wasn't sure if rejection was exactly what she should call what had happened between her and Malik, especially considering how they had spent the night in the lemon grove.

"Do you think your ancestors mind us doing this here?" she'd asked hours later, with the mountain air cooling the sweat on her body and the rough-spun fabric of Malik's tunic scratching against her still-pulsing skin.

"Probably."

"Do you care?"

He thought about it for all of three seconds before pulling a leaf from her hair and flicking her nose with it. "Absolutely not."

So yes, not quite a rejection, but not enough to change the fact that it was morning and she was packing up the wagon that would be taking her, Aminata, and the rest of the caravan back to Ziran, and Malik was nowhere to be found.

Karina was holding herself together far better than she expected, but the knowing glances Aminata kept sending her pierced through her mask of calm. That morning when Karina had returned smelling of both lemons and Malik, her maid had held her as she'd cried, and had gotten her a contraceptive mash that Karina herself had been too distraught to remember to take.

But that was the beautiful thing about a friendship that had survived as much as theirs had. They always seemed to know what the other needed before she herself did.

Though Karina hadn't expected Malik to come send her off, she couldn't ignore the way her heart leaped when he arrived at her tent, both his mother and grandmother in tow.

"I'm sorry I'm late, I slept later than I meant to," he gasped out. She raised an eyebrow, fighting back the delirious grin that wanted to spread across her face.

"Something must have kept you up last night, huh?"

Malik grew flustered, rubbing at the back of his neck with a nervous laugh. "Um, yeah, something like that."

Rahila and Fatima shared a knowing glance, and Karina was completely certain that they knew exactly where Malik had been all night, just as she was certain they were pretending they didn't in order to keep the boy from melting into a puddle of mortification. Before he could sputter his way into incriminating them both further, Karina pulled a piece of parchment from the pack at her waist.

"Before we go, I wanted to show you this."

Malik only read the first line of the scroll before his eyes grew wide. "Is this—"

"A declaration of my intent to renounce Eshra's status as a Zirani Territory and give the region back its sovereignty," she replied. "It's only a draft, and I still have to run it by your clan leaders to make sure these are terms they agree to, but I hope to have the negotiations finished within the year."

Karina was no fool; she knew it was going to take more than a piece of parchment to undo the centuries of oppression and bigotry that had tainted their peoples' shared history. But this was the first step in that process, and there were no words to express the emotion that shined in Malik's and his family's eyes.

A free Eshra. For the first time in hundreds of years, Malik's people were going to see a free Eshra.

"Thank you," Malik whispered, and Karina shook her head.

"I don't deserve thanks for returning something that never should have been taken in the first place," she said. "Ziran will never be perfect, but it can always be better—I'm going to *make* it better."

Malik handed the document back to her before gathering her face in his hands and kissing her deeply. When they broke apart, he held her to his chest, her chin atop his head.

"I'm not sure if I mentioned it yet, but I think I might be in love with you," he said, and she laughed because if she didn't laugh she would cry, and if she cried her reputation as the fierce warrior queen who had saved all of Sonande would be shattered.

"I still can't believe I saved you from certain death, and all I get as thanks is you running off into the wilderness. Know that I reserve the right to offer up your position in my court at any time to this extremely cute healer girl I met back in Balotho."

He grinned and kissed her again until Aminata shouted, "I swear to all the gods, Karina, if you are sticking your tongue down that boy's throat instead of helping me pack these crates, I will come over there and I will beat you!"

Karina pulled away from him with a huff. "The promotion to grand vizier is really going to her head." She gestured for Aminata to come over, and when she did, she grabbed each of their hands. "I care about you both very much, so it would mean a lot to me if you could make peace before we leave."

Malik and Aminata eyed each other warily. "I'm sorry I almost slit your throat," Malik offered.

"I'm sorry your face looks like the bottom of a foot," Aminata snapped back. Karina squeezed their hands, knowing that for all her former maid's blustering, she was going to miss Malik too.

She turned to Rahila and Fatima, bowing deeply before doing the Zirani gesture of respect. "I hope we meet again one day under brighter skies than this."

Rahila's eyes danced with amusement before she jabbed Karina in the gut and said something in rapid Darajat. Karina winced while Malik looked on, mortified. "What did she say?"

"She, um, likes you," Malik sputtered, and his mother kissed her teeth.

"I said you have a good pair of birthing hips," she snickered, and before Karina could react, both women were gathering her in their arms. "Swift travels, Your Majesty. We left an entire pack of pies and sweetmeats with your servants. Remember to eat three times a day, and to never beat a drum after sunset lest it draw the spirits right to you."

Karina wanted to point out that technically the spirits were everywhere now, but she chose not to ruin the moment. She'd always wondered what it might have been like to grow up with aunties and grandmothers, and with a pang she realized it probably felt exactly like this—being mocked and treasured in equal measure, and understanding on a visceral level that she was more loved than she could ever know.

Suddenly all Karina wanted to do was stay in this bubble of warmth she had found in the most unexpected of places, but it was time for her to go, just as soon Malik would go on his own journey, with no telling when they would ever see each other again. She gave one more look at the boy she had been destined to hate.

"You can speak my language, but I can't speak yours," she said suddenly, and maybe she was just delaying the inevitable, but she didn't care. "Teach me something in Darajat."

"Anything?"

"Yes."

Malik leaned down to whisper something into her ear, and it took all her self-control not to hold on to him and refuse to let him go. "What does it mean?" she asked, and he gave her that sun-after-the-storm smile she'd seen for the first time on the last day of Solstasia.

"I'll tell you the next time we see each other."

And then the last of the luggage was packed, the last of the camels were watered, and Karina was climbing into the wagon with Aminata and the rest of their entourage climbing in after her. They were off, Malik and his family waving and waving until the wagon crested over the little hill with its crossroads guardian and there was nothing behind them except open road. It was long after she couldn't see them anymore that Karina pulled her hand back into the wagon, and longer still until she regained her composure enough to speak.

Aminata nudged her gently. "Remember that old saying about how if you love something, you should let it go?"

Karina sniffed. "And that if it truly loves you, it'll come back?"

Her newest vizier let out a scoff before pulling out a bottle of palm wine from the pack at her feet. "Actually, I'm pretty sure the second part goes 'and then you should wallow in misery and drown your sorrows until the pain goes away.'"

Even though her heart felt like it had ripped into so many pieces it might never be whole again, Karina laughed, thinking back to all the nights she and Aminata had spent sneaking out of the palace and sharing a bottle just like this one. So much had changed, and yet this hadn't.

"Thank you," she whispered. She lifted her head to gaze into the faces of her friends both old and new. "For going on this journey with me."

Ife bounced excitedly in their seat, having finally recovered from days spent healing soldiers and villagers alike in the wake of the lich. "It's not every day you get to embark on a new character arc," they said, and Caracal—Tabansi, she was still getting used to calling him by his old name now that he'd chosen to reclaim it—rolled his eyes but gave them an affectionate grin.

"Well said as always, my friend."

Only Issam remained silent, staring down at his hands with the haunted look all the Sentinels Malik's magic had freed often wore. Some of the ex-Sentinels had chosen to remain in Eshra, while others had chosen to return to Ziran, while others still had gone to seek new fortunes in the various corners of Sonande. But what mattered most was that they had all chosen their new paths for themselves, unencumbered by any magic besides their own.

The Fire-Aligned zawenji swallowed thickly. "I don't know how much use I'll be to you, Haissa Karina," he whispered, and Karina wondered if she'd ever get used to hearing the sultana's title beside her name. "After what I almost did to you on the mountain . . . after all I've done . . . I don't know if I know how to be anything other than a Sentinel."

Karina gently squeezed the man's knee. "The past devours those naive enough to forget it," she said softly. "You shouldn't forget the Sentinel you once were, nor would I ask you to. But your past doesn't have to dictate your future."

Tabansi pulled an arm around Issam and kissed his temple. The former mercenary did this often, touching the latter in the smallest of ways every moment he could, as if he still couldn't believe that they were no longer enemies. He'd been holding Issam's hand too when they had both accepted Karina's offer to become the new captains of her royal guard, and when he had informed her that he'd be going by Tabansi once more, though he reserved the right to return to the Caracal moniker if any roguish needs came to light.

"Luckily for you, I have much experience not being a Sentinel that I'd be more than happy to share." He shot Karina a grin, looking once more like the wildcat he had named his persona for. "And as it turns out, I'm actually a pretty good teacher."

Karina grinned back before lifting her hand and letting a spark of lightning dance around her fingers with perfect control. She thought once more of her final moments with Malik, and asked Issam, "By the way, do you know what this means?"

She repeated the Darajat phrase Malik had said to her, and the former Sentinel's eyebrows shot up. "It's the phrase said during a traditional Eshran wedding ceremony. The closest translation would be, *I feel you in my pulse.* I certainly hope whoever said that to you offered to pay your bride price as well."

I feel you in my pulse.

Even without the connection, Karina felt Malik there, echoing through all that she was and all that she was becoming. He'd be there in her pulse when she finally stepped into her role as queen, the spirits of all who had come before her guiding her forward.

As full as her heart felt, she couldn't help but mourn for the two friends who should have been here but were not.

For Dedele, who was no doubt still recovering from the horrors she'd survived in the dungeons of Ksar Alahari.

For Afua, tied for the rest of her now-immortal life to Doro Lekke. Somewhere deep in her soul Karina knew all three of their paths would cross again, but when that might be, only the gods knew.

The lightning died, but the wind song rose louder than ever in Karina's ears, calling her forward.

Calling her home.

Karina let out a breath, resolve rising in her where just a few minutes before tears had been.

"All right, that's enough sentimentality for one trek across the desert. Now it's time to get to work. According to Malik, Ziran is a city divided, its people torn between those who remain loyal to me, those who remain loyal to Farid, and those who remain loyal to Driss and Tunde's families, who apparently staged a counter-coup while we were gone."

Tabansi let out a whistle. "So we're basically leaving one war zone for another?"

Karina grimaced. "More or less. But seeing as I killed my own sister twice, dealing with this feels like child's play in comparison."

The air grew heavy—it was the first time Karina had mentioned Hanane since the mountaintop, and the first time she had joked about it. All her companions knew she had been near catatonic after her sister's second death. However, no one but Malik knew about the bird she'd rescued, and how it attacking her had been the catalyst she'd needed to rise from her stupor and wash her face, to take her first tentative steps back into the world and find it hadn't left her behind after all. Even after all she'd experienced, Karina wasn't sure if she believed in ghosts, but the thought of her departed loved ones gently pushing her forward gave her one more reason to face each day.

The silence stretched on until Tabansi barked out a laugh and slapped his knee.

"There's the fire I remember from the girl foolish enough to try to fight a tornado with another tornado!" He leaned forward, as did all the others in the wagon. "Tell us the plan, Your Majesty."

Emotion rose in Karina's throat. She hoped that wherever her family was, they were watching this, the moment she truly began to feel like the sultana of Ziran.

"All right, so here is what we're going to do."

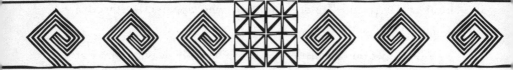

. . . Why are you looking at me like that? That's it. If you want more, go bother some other griot about it, for that's all you're getting from me.

Ah, you're upset. What kind of ending is that, your eyes are asking. This was supposed to be a story of triumph, of love conquering all. How can it end with our lovers parted?

That is the end of my tale, yes, but that is not the end of the story. No, the story began long before the first line, and will continue far beyond it. Let us imagine, just for a moment, what happened next.

Perhaps the young queen returned to her homeland and spent her reign fighting an uphill battle to help her people unlearn the prejudices that had built their society. Perhaps she faced obstacles on all sides, but with time and work, Ziran slowly began to resemble more of the ideals on which it had been built. Perhaps she reconnected with the friends she could reconnect with and made peace with the ones with whom she never could.

Perhaps the boy searched far and wide for his sisters. Perhaps he found them on a sun-kissed beach somewhere, or deep in the heart of the jungle, where the earth breathes and the trees know your name. Perhaps the road to reconciliation was long and halting, but forgiveness waited at its end.

Perhaps both the boy and the girl spent every night dreaming of a person who was never there when they woke.

Yes, perhaps all those things happened. Or none of them did. Who knows?

Certainly not I.

But one more perhaps, for you have been so faithful to this tale.

Perhaps on one warm afternoon—oh, let's say today, why not—the queen looks out her window and sees a bird—not just any bird, a kestrel—fly by. The sight of that bird would tug on some old whim deep inside her. It would cause her to abandon her duties for the day, much to the chagrin of her friends and advisers, so she could slip into the city as she often used to do.

And perhaps the boy—man now, really—would let his family convince him to take a break from the school he ran and see the world beyond their mountain range once more. Perhaps their travels would bring them back to Ziran, as news of the small but thriving Eshran community there would pique their curiosity enough to see what had become of this place that had once shunned their kind. He and his sisters would walk down these streets marveling at how much had changed over the years, and how much had not. The boy would see the alabaster palace shining on the horizon and think about how he had once been able to stride in and out of it as he wished, but surely that was no longer the case, surely too much time had passed for the girl to remember him.

The boy would get lost, as he was wont to do, and wander the streets with his head full of dreams. The girl would not be lost, as the twists of the streets echoed in her blood, and she would wander through the crowds half drunk from the energy of her people.

Perhaps she'd see his back from a distance, or he'd see the sudden flash of amber eyes. They'd step toward the other, then turn away, chiding themselves for their own foolishness. No way that was her. No way that was him. It had been years, after all, and even though neither ever forgot their time together, the letters they'd sent so frequently at first had eventually stopped completely, each busy with separate lives and separate loves that had nothing to do with the other. What if the other had changed? What if she had forgotten him in favor of a more advantageous match to the throne, or he had forgotten those words he'd whispered to her the last time she'd seen him?

And then perhaps they'd both stop at opposite ends of a street, both enraptured by the very tale I just told you now. Perhaps the story would crack open something deep inside them and let all the light in. They'd both wander in a daze after, neither of them seeing the figure in front of them until they'd already collided.

They'd likely stare.

He'd smile.

She'd smile back.

The years would have changed everything and nothing, and just like that, the page would turn to a new story, one waiting to be told to a pair of inquisitive ears just like yours.

And that's the beautiful thing about endings, for even them coming back together again would not be the end. What seems like the end is simply another beginning, another place where an old dog like me can jump in and start spinning words into magic.

So don't be saddened, my friend. Come closer, warm yourself by the fire.

Abraa! Abraa! Come gather, one and all, for a story is about to begin!

ACKNOWLEDGMENTS

They say you never truly learn how to write a book, only how to write the book you're currently working on. This could not be truer for me and A *Psalm of Storms and Silence*. This book challenged everything I thought I knew about myself, writing, and what it means to be an author.

Given the fact that it was written during the height of the COVID-19 pandemic and during a series of intense personal changes for me, the story in your hands is my bit of light born from when all the world felt dark. It's not the story I thought it would be when I began the A Song of Wraiths and Ruin series, but it's the one I believe these characters and world deserve. And it would not exist were it not for the efforts of a number of amazing people that I am honored every day to know.

To my agent, Quressa Robinson: I still don't know how I ended up with the best agent in the game, but you know what, I'm not complaining. Thank you for always pushing me to dream bigger, and for never letting me settle for less than what I deserve. Thank you to my film agent, Alice Lawson, and entertainment lawyer, Wayne Alexander, for shepherding this series through the labyrinth that is Hollywood.

To Kristin Rens, editor extraordinaire: thank you for never

giving up on me or this book even when I had long given up on both, and for bringing the clarity, warmth, and sharp-eyed analysis that elevated this tale from a bunch of tears in a Word doc to a cohesive story. Also, I will make no apologies for what I did to your favorite character. You're welcome.

Thank you to the entire team at HarperCollins for all you've done to bring this series to readers around the world—thank you to Shona McCarthy, Jessie Gang, Jenna Stempel-Lobell, Alison Donalty, Sabrina Abballe, Anna Bernard, Kadeen Griffiths, Vanessa Nuttry, Patty Rosati, Mimi Rankin, and Katie Dutton (I will write that hot bodyguard story one day, I promise, Katie!!!). Thank you to any other publicity, sales, marketing, design and Harper-affiliated people, past and present, who have worked so hard on these books.

Thank you to artist Tawny Chatmon for these covers that still take my breath away every time I look at them. Thank you to models Tania Toussaint and Aidan Wheeler for bringing Malik and Karina to life for little Black kids everywhere.

To the Wildcats—Swati Teerdhala, Tanvi Berwah, Chelsea Beam, Crystal Seitz, and Lena Jeong. Thank you for always welcoming me back with open arms no matter how often I drop off the face of the earth. Also, for posting the most hilariously strange memes.

Thank you to my writer friends, old and new, in no particular order—June CL Tan, Deeba Zargarpur, Leah Johnson, Tracy Deonn, Namina Forna, Hannah Whitten, and so many, many more for all the DMs, feedback, and general laughing/crying sessions. Thank you to the established authors who took a newbie author under their wing and answered all my questions, no matter how odd. We have the weirdest job, for real. I love it.

Thank you to Deborah Falaye for being there through it all. From the start to the end, you are stuck with me!

Thank you to Brittney Morris for being one of the most compassionate people I have ever known. Every day I'm in awe of your passion and your drive. You are still wrong about Christmas decorations.

Thank you to Kyra Kevin, Hanna Greenblott, Jackie Dubin, Theresa Soonyoung Park, Meredith Guerinot, Lucy Hall, and Jenny Park for being the most amazing friends a girl could have. Check your DMs; there's probably an anime meme from me waiting for you as we speak.

Thank you to my family—to Mom and Dad for obliging me when I wanted to sit inside and read all day as a child; to Rachel, Mariah, and Emma for showing me some bonds can never break and for always being down for an adventure; to every other family member on both sides. There's too many of you to list. You know who you are!

And to you, dearest readers, for all your memes, jokes, fan art, and hilarious headcanons. Your love for Malik, Karina, and their world has changed my life. Thank you for coming on this journey with me, and I hope to see you on the next one!

MAGICAL TWISTS, DEADLY ROMANCE, AND THE POWER TO TRANSFORM THE WORLD.

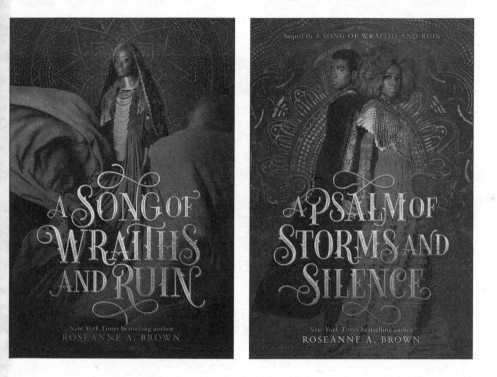

Malik and Karina's journey comes
to an explosive end.

JOIN THE

Epic Reads
COMMUNITY

THE ULTIMATE YA DESTINATION

◀ **DISCOVER** ▶
your next favorite read

◀ **MEET** ▶
new authors to love

◀ **WIN** ▶
free books

◀ **SHARE** ▶
infographics, playlists, quizzes, and more

◀ **WATCH** ▶
the latest videos